VICIOUS LITTLE PRINCESS

COVETED KINGDOM, BOOK TWO

LEIA KING

VICIOUS LITTLE PRINCESS
Blurb

They're trying to break us.
What we've built.
What we've found with each other.
It's all on the line.

They're demons disguised as gods.
Their depths of depravity know no bounds.
Only the most ruthless will survive.

No more working in the shadows.
It's time to bring this battle out into the open.
Watch us rise, watch your fall.

Author's Note

This is a Dark Mafia Reverse Harem Romance with scenes of M/M.

A list of TWs can be found at leiaking.com.

There are *spoilers* for the VICIOUS THINGS series in this book.

I'm always watching.
Watching and waiting in the shadows.

The monster you never see coming.

~Nico~

"You just walked into a kill zone, mafia prince."

Carlo's words ran through my mind.

I was sure he intended them to be received in a haunting way.

But the bold statement with a healthy dose of a threat thrown in had actually given him away.

Not to mention this entire setup he'd arranged.

The heavy-handed nature of it wasn't doing him any favors in concealing his true intent, either.

He didn't need three dozen men to take us out.

It wasn't just overkill or a demonstration of his power, because Carlo Benzino didn't operate like that. He wasn't insecure in his standing, with his position in our world. Even with this recent fucked-up shift with the alliances and the complete shattering of the three families treaty. He didn't feel the need to prove himself. He knew how damned good he was, how accomplished, and how impressively adaptable he was.

This display was all for show.

What's more was that you didn't tend to announce

your plan to murder someone. You just fucking did it. There was no preamble. You got a shot to take out your enemies; you took it. Immediately. It was an unspoken reality in our world. Unless torture was involved, but that would have been arranged a whole lot differently to this. Not with a face-off or a perceived ambush of this particular nature. It would be more a case of grabbing somebody off the street, tossing them into an unmarked vehicle, then transporting them to a dark hole somewhere, or a warehouse, to be brutalized. A place that would also make it easy to dispose of the body—or what was left of it—inconspicuously.

Carlo wanted something from me.

Or he wanted me *for* something.

He'd arranged all of this to gain my undivided attention.

Away from the Marchettis and Leones.

"Lay down your weapons," I told Milo quietly.

"What? You're serious?"

"Would I really be anything else in this sort of situation?"

He sighed, but did as I'd instructed, lowering his gun, securing it, then slowly laying it down on the ground before kicking it away. As he did the same with his backup gun, I divested myself of both of mine too, kicking them out of my reach.

My assessment of the situation was proven correct in the next moment as all of Carlo's soldiers lowered their weapons in quick succession.

Carlo's lip curled with appreciation. "You're a great deal more intelligent than your uncle." He shook his head to himself. "Fucking hothead, beyond all sense of reason."

He was right on the money there.

I strode toward him, Milo tense and in his ready-for-anything state beside me.

"Where are my men?"

"Your men… hmm. Your first concern is them, rather than the rather lucrative coke shipment you need to deliver tonight to Harlow."

I felt my eye twitch. He shouldn't know about her.

"That bodes well," he went on. "As does all my research on you."

I played along—for the moment, unless he delayed on revealing where my soldiers were—and asked, "Research, to what end?"

"To determine the most optimal way to acquire your cooperation, of course."

I scoffed. "And you truly believe that attacking my soldiers and commandeering my shipment was the way to do that?"

"You wouldn't have come willingly. You would have believed it to be a trap anyway if I'd asked for a meet. It also had to be tonight. While the Marchettis and Leones are stretched thin due to some poor decisions on their part—seeking vengeance when they should be reinforcing their territories and business partnerships."

Our thinking on such matters—and certain people—was very similar.

"I see you share my assessment. Not just on that, either. Isn't that right?"

He knew something.

Obviously, I needed to know what that was in order to protect myself and my loved ones.

And he damn well knew that, the self-satisfied smirk spreading over his face making that clear.

He was good, I'd give him that.

But he also needed something from me.

That gave me leverage.

"This conversation goes nowhere unless you take me to my men."

"As you wish," he said, gesturing toward the diner. "Come with me."

Two of his men joined him, sticking close to him for his protection, while Milo did the same with me as we made our way over there.

The curtains were drawn, even one over the door, so I couldn't see a thing within.

One of his men opened the door and Carlo stepped inside.

Bracing myself, I followed, with Milo being sure to stay close, especially as the two guards followed in after us.

Red vinyl booths filled my vision as we strode along the beige linoleum floor. There were a couple of his soldiers sitting on stools up at the counter, their sharp gazes focused on the rear of the diner.

As we veered around the corner, I realized exactly why they had their eagle-eyes focused in that direction.

Carlo came to a stop just before the swinging doors leading into a storage area.

And there were my soldiers, sprawled out before the doors and some visible even inside the storage area itself. They were unmoving, laid out across the space.

Surprising me, there was no blood pooling around them, and only a few scratches and bruises between all ten of them.

"Milo," I said, snapping my fingers.

We'd worked together so long and so closely that he knew instantly what I was getting at, and he went to them, crouching down beside each of them and checking them over.

He moved swiftly and efficiently and within moments,

he'd checked them all and came back to my side, reporting, "All alive. Virtually unharmed. Looks like tranqs, judging by the marks and bruising I saw on some of them."

"They'll wake up in a couple of hours." Carlo told me. "With one hell of a headache and hangover, but unharmed, nonetheless. The automatic fire you heard from Rocco's call was just for effect, to lay down the law and hold them off until we could get them all tranqed and nullify the threat they became to my plans to lure you here tonight when they fought so intensely to defend for you. The shipment also hasn't been harmed. In fact, that truck outside is now empty, and the product has been delivered to Harlow in one of mine. On your behalf. You should be receiving confirmation from her at any moment."

What the hell?

Milo and I exchanged a look.

"You're not my enemy," Carlo insisted. "And I apologize about the lengths I had to go to in order to bring you to me tonight. Unfortunately, extreme measures were required and made necessary by the complicated circumstances we are all immersed in with this foolish decision made by Marco and Santino to shift the balance of power and spit all over our treaty."

Before I could respond, my phone buzzed in my pocket.

I pulled it out to see a text he'd predicted.

Harlow: Shipment received ahead of schedule. I'm impressed, Nico. Look forward to doing continuous business with you.

"Is that her?" he asked.

"Yes."

He looked far too pleased with himself.

I didn't want him believing in his twisted mind that he'd done me a favor. Because he fucking hadn't.

And owing anyone in our world was a bad way to be in.

"So you've undone something that you caused in the first place. Am I supposed to be grateful?"

"You're supposed to see it as the peace offering that it is."

Enough bantering and circumventing the real issue.

"What do you want from me? Why go to all this trouble to get me here to you?" I demanded.

"Phones off, then we'll talk." He gestured at his men and Milo. "Alone."

I nodded at Milo and we both shut our phones off, then pocketed them.

"I need eyes on him the entire time," I told Carlo.

"Fine," he said, gesturing at one of his men who then opened a couple of the curtains so there was a view outside.

Satisfied, I gave Milo the signal to leave my side.

We didn't have secrets. And that wouldn't change now.

I hadn't just demanded that I have him in full view for his safety, it was also because he could read lips exceptionally well, so he'd be kept abreast of everything as I spoke with Carlo Benzino.

As he and the guards took their leave and went outside, Carlo slid into the nearest booth and settled himself.

I joined him, sliding in on the other side.

He finally got right down to business, telling me, "This new situation isn't sustainable. Your father is flailing and Santino's unhinged megalomania is now completely unchecked without the balance and the boundaries that our truce enforced."

Interesting.

"And why are you coming to me about this?"

"I understand. You don't want to give anything away

for fear of betrayal. You're protecting yourself and your own."

"I'm doing what anybody would do in my position when being approached by somebody who is now considered an enemy to my Family and the new alliance that has been formed with the Leones."

"I'm not talking about you protecting the Family. I mean Emilio out there and Julian Carver."

"My guard and my college acquaintance, who serves Marchetti interests?"

"The true brotherhood that you serve."

Our gazes clashed.

He tried to push me further to get to what he wanted from me, commenting, "Of course, that also now includes that exceedingly impressive new wife of yours."

"Obviously she's under my protection, it's my duty as her husband and to the Marchetti-Leone alliance to safeguard the property given to me." It took a lot to not cringe as I uttered those words. "And, yes, her business acumen is impressive. That's been well-noted and documented throughout the city."

"I'm not talking about her business acumen." His lip curled. "And we both know she doesn't need your protection." He leaned forward, clasping his hands on the tabletop. "Furthermore, I don't believe for one moment that she's being *owned* by you."

"Whatever you *think* you know—"

"Everyone else's preconceived notions and a healthy dose of misogyny and fear led them to misinterpreting your playful war with her into an act of domination on your part, painting her as a weak link in the process, a submissive party, and giving those Leone bastards a sick thrill at believing that was what was happening to the woman who walked away from them and thrived from doing so. It was the only way they could allow themselves to look at it and still save face and not acknowledge their own failings." A smug smile spread over his face. "When in actual fact it was you and Caterina sparring, conducting some sort of complicated and rather twisted mating ritual. She thrived from it and you experienced the closest thing you ever had to freedom, to having something that your family couldn't touch." He leaned back, shaking his head. "Although, now they've touched it and they have their hands all over it, wanting you to fulfill their sick intentions. That can't be sitting well with you in the least."

Fuck.

"I'm doing my duty for the Family."

"You don't trust me, so you're denying everything. You're skilled at wearing that mask of yours, I'll give you that. However, it's not conducive to what I'm trying to do here."

"That's too bad."

He scrubbed his hand over his face at getting nothing from me. "Nico, I'm not trying to catch you out. I'm not trying to play you. I'm trying to help you. To help both of us. I know you're not on board with the way things are progressing—or regressing, as it truly is. Keep in mind also that now the chaos of the wedding reception attack is waning, it will no longer be so easy to keep the true reality of your marriage to Caterina Leone off their radar. They want her hurt and controlled, broken. And they want you on a leash, expending a great deal of your time working on *training* her. They'll come knocking asking for proof soon enough. The situation isn't sustainable. None of this is. You're smart and astute, so I'm sure you're well aware of that. As such, it stands to reason to infer that you're doing a whole lot more than merely resisting their despicable orders when it comes to your new wife, more than putting on a well-crafted façade."

"You're actually accusing me of working against the Family, against this new alliance? That would be an act of treason, punishable by severe torture and death."

"I'm well aware of what the stakes are. It's why I understand your continued denial *and* why I'm being incredibly patient with you, despite me knowing much better."

"Beyond these baseless accusations and *guesses* on your part, what exactly is it that you want from me?"

He sat forward again. "Theoretically speaking, if you were intending to do something about the current situation —undermine it, possibly even destroy the new insane reality created by this foolish Marchetti-Leone alliance—it won't be enough. It would leave a mammoth and very dangerous power vacuum. The three families alliance served to keep everyone in check, to ensure that not one single family possessed—and therefore abused—too much power. Between us, we also have differing areas of exper-tise that, when combined, form a whole of sorts, enabling our business ventures to be extremely diversified, which is needed in the world we operate within to stay ahead of competition, our enemies, and the law." His eyes burned into mine as he said, "*You* need to take power over the Marchetti Syndicate, Nico. And Caterina needs to do the same where the Leones are concerned."

I started at his suggestion.

"And *that's* why I lured you here tonight. To make it clear that destroying what exists now and then running and disappearing into the ozone as the ruins settle won't achieve what you want to. It will just open the way for worse forces to take the power you would have ripped from Marco and Santino. You need to step up and take what's rightfully yours. You and Caterina. The three of us will work together well." He shifted his weight, urgency spilling from him. "To do that, you'll need my help. My resources, for one. Not to mention my insights and experience."

"What you're suggesting—"

"I know it's a great deal, especially when trust hasn't yet been established between us. Although, keep in mind that I didn't strike directly against you and only you, Nico. We both know that me sending the Red Vipers to your warehouse was merely for show." He screwed up his face. "Until Leo made it a great deal more with his ridiculously overwrought retaliatory response." He blew out a breath. "However, you need more. I understand that, especially given the stakes. You need confirmation of my sincerity. That will require endorsement from a reliable and already supremely trusted third party. Fortunately, for us, that individual does exist."

"Who are you referring to?"

"Look into Joseph Stover."

"Never heard of him."

"I'm not surprised. She's trying to protect him. He already warned me she'd do as much and be reluctant to bring him into this situation, despite him being more than willing to participate. Of course, given that he's like the father figure she never truly had in that disgusting Santino, it's to be expected."

"You're saying that this person is connected to Caterina?"

"Very much so. To the both of us now. All of us, in fact. So, look into him. She would be the best source, at least to start with. Do so carefully. Then contact me."

He rose to his feet. "Those vehicles belonging to your men that were damaged during my surprise *attack* will be taken care of. I have my team of mechanics prepared to receive them and several tow trucks will be here within moments, so all of this will be covered up nicely, leaving the Marchettis and Leones none the wiser. My soldiers will also be transporting yours back to their respective homes within the next few moments, so you're not left with that headache either. It'll be as though this meeting never happened as far as they're concerned." As he rounded the booth toward me, he leaned down until he was eye level with me. "But it did, as far as you and I are concerned. I *can* help you. We can help each other. You are Marco's true successor, and you should never have been passed over. We'll remedy that. We'll remedy it all." With that, he rose back to his full height, adjusted his suit jacket, then told me, "It's been nice having this sit down with you, Nico. I look forward to working with you and yours."

I rose as he made his way to the door.

He paused as he reached for the doorknob and turned back to me. "Oh, while you're looking into Stover, you'll also be receiving a gesture of good faith from me." He gestured at Milo, who was watching closely, frowning when he saw Carlo bring him into the conversation. He turned as though knowing that he'd been reading our lips this entire time, his back to him as he told me, "I understand that his parents' murderer was never identified, that you suspected one of my soldiers as being the culprit. With us slated to work together, that lie can no longer be upheld, especially not for the good of the alliance that has now fallen apart, as I'd initially agreed to. I can confirm that they weren't Benzino kills. In fact, Enzo Bardi was never my target. Like you, he possessed a temperament and decision-making that I favored. Him dying was detrimental to me. I'll send you proof of the true culprit."

"Why not just tell me here and now?"

"Because you won't believe me without incontrovertible

proof. Especially given who is truly responsible. You'll suspect it as my intent to sway you." He smiled. "Have a good night, Nico."

With that, he strode on out, giving Milo a polite chin lift, then swept away through the parking lot, two of his men leading him to his town car in the distance, while his other soldiers headed inside the diner and began hauling up my men to ready them for transport back to safety.

I stood there, my gaze clashing with Milo's, trying to absorb what the fuck had just transpired.

EVERYONE WAS FINE.

My soldiers, many of whom had woken up during transport, had been debriefed about the situation, told a version of the story that hadn't involved the reality of Carlo Benzino organizing it all just to lure me to that meeting.

I'd told them that Milo and I had run them off and managed to save the shipment and also liberate my men from their clutches. I'd had to come up with a complicated explanation to make it believable that two of us had won out against thirty-odd supposed enemy soldiers. I mean, as their Capo, they'd accept my word and what I said, but I also didn't want quiet suspicion right now, or any sort of dissent, albeit something they wouldn't dare to act on. Soon, I would be testing their loyalty to the max as it was, when it was time to call on them to follow me through fucking hellfire with this war. To do that, I couldn't afford anything impacting their faith and trust in me.

As I walked to my Ferrari, finally able to head home after one hell of a night, I turned on my phone, fortunately only finding one text message.

Julian: Out riding with Cat. Let the fun reign! Text me as soon as you're clear, need to know you're safe.

I winced when I determined that the message had come in nearly two hours ago, just after I'd had to turn my phone off for that meeting, and then been swamped afterward.

"Nico!" Milo whisper-yelled, rushing toward me down the steps of Rocco's house after I'd just finished up filling him in. Milo had needed to take a piss, hence him trailing behind a little.

"I know we need to talk," I said, as he reached me and my car. "About everything that was said tonight. Including what Carlo wouldn't let you read." How he'd known Milo was capable of that was concerning. How he knew half the things he did was.

"Yeah, we will, but there's another priority." Urgency was basically spilling off him like crazy as he held up his phone and spun the screen toward me. "Right now, there's this."

Adrenaline flooded my system yet again tonight when I took in the red flashing alert on his screen that indicated Caterina's panic button beneath her engagement ring had been activated.

"Two fucking hours ago!" he cried.

"Have Julian or Caterina contacted you in any way since then?"

"No. I just got this text from him, the last one he sent."

He basically shoved it at me in his worry and haste.

Julian: Out taking Cat riding. When we all get back to the house, I'm gonna be riding you, big boy. And while Cat swallows your cock and Nico takes her sweet ass.

"I thought him not sending any more was him not wanting to bother us or distract us while we were in the middle of what we believed to be a dangerous situation at the time, but clearly not." He starting spinning around, then gnawing at his knuckles.

Usually Milo didn't panic in the face of such circumstances, but when it came to Julian—and now Caterina—all bets were off.

I sucked in a breath, working on keeping myself calm.

The only thing that would help him, though, was to give him a task.

"Track the location she was at when she pressed the panic button."

"Okay," he murmured, getting to work, rapidly typing and swiping on his phone. "Yeah, I can do that… last known location… all right."

I eyed Rocco's house, considering bringing him in on this. But he was still reeling from the effects of the tranquilizers, as were the rest of my soldiers available to help, the others with Tony escorting another shipment tonight or safeguarding our territory.

"Got it," he said. "Here." I took in the specified location, then threw open the driver's door of my Ferrari. "All right, let's go."

Fuck. What the shit had happened? Caterina wouldn't activate the panic button unless the situation had been really fucking dire.

2

~Emilio~

It had taken close to a half hour to get all the way from the other side of the city to back near Charon Manor where Julian and Caterina had been riding and where the signal from Caterina's panic button had been activated from. If it hadn't been for Nico's Ferrari and him driving like a man possessed, it would have even been a whole lot longer than that.

As it was, it had already been too long.

They were clearly in danger. I needed to be there instantly.

Not only had Caterina activated the panic button, but I'd also been calling them constantly since we'd gotten into the car and neither of them had picked up.

"Almost there," Nico assured me, looking between me and the road as he finagled the dangerously winding back roads in the dead of night, just his headlights illuminating the way.

I knew we were. I was watching the map on my phone every second. But it helped to hear him utter that out loud, and he'd known that it would.

"Neither of them are helpless," he reminded me. "Far from it, in fact. Keep that in mind with whatever we find here."

Judging by the iron grip he had on the steering wheel and him grinding his jaw, he was trying to remind himself of that fact as much as me.

We were almost upon the designated location when his headlights caught on something in the brush.

"Pull over," I told him.

"What are you—" he caught sight of what I had, chrome in amongst the heavy brush.

He came to a jarring stop; the tires screeching and burning rubber and giving both of us one hell of a jolt.

And then the both of us were rushing out of the car and heading toward the sight.

I barreled into the brush, removing torn branches here and there that had clearly been used to hide what was beneath. Whoever had been responsible hadn't done a very thorough job, though, which was why I'd been able to catch sight of something.

As I threw more and more out of the way, Nico helping me, I was finally able to make out the twisted chrome monstrosity of what had once been a Harley.

"Julian's," Nico choked, recognizing it as I had, even in this state, with all the work Julian had had done on it to make it unique—just like my Sunshine.

The state of it… they'd had one hell of a crash.

"Goddammit," I rasped, staring at it in horror.

Nico was gone from my side then, inspecting the immediate area and even rushing up the last few feet to the actual location where the panic button signal had come from.

As I was caught there frozen with my hands trembling at the awful implications, I zeroed in on the camera Julian had fitted onto the bike because he liked to record his stunts for posterity. Footage that automatically uploaded to the Cloud. *Yes!*

"Nico!" I called out. "The camera footage from the bike!"

I spun around just as he was already coming back to me.

My gut twisted when I saw him carrying two smashed phones in his hands, the cobalt-blue glittering case of Julian's taking my attention.

His haunting gaze met mine as he reported, "There's blood along the road. Scuff marks too."

"They were dragged," I ground out. "Somebody did this. Caused the crash, then took them."

"Yes. The evidence is speaking for itself."

"Who the fuck would do this? The Lone Gunners have gone to ground. The Benzinos made it clear they're with us. And the Marchettis and Leones have no reason to do anything like this, seeing as though they believe you and Caterina are following their orders. I don't… I don't understand," I said, shoving my hand through my hair.

I saw Nico's sapphire eyes flicking back and forth, the sign that his mind was going a million miles a minute, trying to sort through the data available, to figure out all possibilities.

"Someone who has an unhinged hatred for both Julian and Caterina in equal measure," he finally spoke. "Only one person comes to mind."

Our gazes clashed.

"Angelo," I breathed. "Do you really think he'd stoop to this and risk *this?* He'd be going against Santino to carry this out."

"Would he? Santino wants Caterina punished."

"Which he believes is already happening by her

marrying you. You're being paranoid because of what happened earlier with Carlo."

"Perhaps. Either way, even if he's acting alone, that makes this worse."

"Because there are no boundaries or restrictions involved," I realized.

"Exactly."

"Goddammit."

Nico had his lighter out, flicking it on and off wildly. "All right, this is what we're gonna do. I'm gonna access Julian's footage of the ride from the Cloud, confirm what we suspect, and see if there's anything to go off from there. License plates, other players involved, anything. Meanwhile, you try to track Caterina's panic button."

"Yeah, okay," I uttered, fighting to move from freaking out about their wellbeing to action-mode and doing something to remedy it, to bring them the fuck back to us.

As we rushed back to the car, I said to Nico, "If this was Angelo, if he did this—"

"He can't survive it."

"No, he fucking can't," I growled. "But how are we gonna put him to ground, given that he's Santino's second? That's an act of war. Big time, Nico."

"Let me worry about that," he said, as he slid into the driver's seat.

I joined him on the passenger side, watching that dangerously dark look take him over.

"Focus on finding them, then we'll handle the rest."

The fucking disturbing thing was that if it was Angelo like we suspected, he was a true psychopath, a sick motherfucker through and through.

The things he could subject Julian and Caterina to in the meantime… it had me sick to my stomach.

What if we didn't get there fast enough, and he'd already… started in on them?

What if—

"Milo."

I jolted from my thoughts to see Nico shaking his head at me as we sped toward the manor.

"Focus on the task at hand. Nothing beyond that will help or enable us to get to them faster." He laid his hand on mine. "All right, brother?"

"Yeah," I said, squeezing it back. "I hear you. They need us and we'll come through."

"There's no question."

"We'll bring them back to us ASAP."

"I have no doubt whatsoever."

I smiled out at him. He was a steadfast and levelheaded leader—outside of the *feral* state thing, which only happened once in a while—and he knew how those close to him thought and operated, which he used to their advantage, wellbeing, and peace of mind. It was a great comfort, even in situations where finding comfort shouldn't be possible.

It made him a step above the rest.

"You are Marco's true successor, and you should never have been passed over. We'll remedy that. We'll remedy it all."

That was what Carlo Benzino had told him earlier.

And as much as I didn't trust the bastard yet and as much as I hated them for what they'd done to my parents, he'd been right on the money there.

Nico Marchetti was the leader that we'd all been denied, the leader we all needed more than ever.

He caught me staring out at him intensely and smiled. "I've got you, Milo."

"I know. You always do."

And I knew he always would.

3

~Caterina~

An irritating beeping blasted through my subconscious and jolted me awake.

My eyes snapped open, and it took me a few moments to clear my blurry vision.

That wasn't helped by the pounding in my head, which worsened as I raised it from its lolled forward position.

It took me a moment to discern that infuriating sound that had woken me to be that of a large truck backing up.

Backing up where?

Where the hell was I?

The last thing I remembered was being with Julian on the back of his bike, having the time of my life, and then... then Angelo had been there with his goons and... he'd caused that crash.

Shit! Julian!

I went to bolt up from my seated position only to find resistance, realizing I was bound to a fucking metal chair. I moved my fingers around behind me, determining that my hands were restrained by a pair of cuffs.

I was still in the black leather pants that Julian had

gifted me, although my boots were gone and I was barefoot. I was down just to my white strappy tank too, and I could make out the bloodied scrapes all down my arms, likely from the crash. Or, for all I knew, being dragged in here to this chair by Angelo or his muscle.

I strained to take in the room, a bland concrete monstrosity. I noted the track twenty feet ahead of me and the closed double garage doors.

So I'd been left in a garage somewhere.

There was a truck that I'd heard just outside.

That didn't really narrow it down location-wise.

A grating scrape jarred me from investigating my surroundings further and I looked out toward the direction of the sound, just as a light was turned on and a metal door was pushed open, someone stepping inside.

I blinked rapidly to adjust my vision to the sudden influx of light.

And that was when I took in that all-too-familiar Ivy League haircut and the goatee, followed by the gray leather jacket that he always wore, come winter or the height of summer.

Angelo Simone.

"Ah, you're finally awake. Good. I need to head out elsewhere, but I didn't want to leave without explaining what's about to happen. Or seeing your face when I did. I was about to have one of the guys I've got with me fetch a hose to wake you up that way if you hadn't come around naturally soon." He grinned at me nastily. "That would have been fun to see, but no matter, they can still use it for other purposes if they like."

"What the hell is the meaning of this?" I demanded. "Where's Julian?"

"Two birds with one stone."

"What?"

"Julian is due punishment for what he did to me. When I saw the two of you were together, I decided to exact said punishment on you as well. Besides, it really didn't seem like you were suffering as you should be, riding on his bike and yelling excitedly and happily. Guess Nico isn't getting the job done. Change of plans then."

"What plans?"

Stroking his goatee, he told me, "These friends of mine work for a buyer I've been busting my ass to acquire for your father, since our previous ones for the whores we'd procured fell through when they betrayed us. So as a test and proof that we can work together, I'll be handing you over to him."

"You… what?" I choked, unable to stop a shudder from taking me over at his sick plan. "Does my father know about this?"

"Not yet. But I'm sure once he comes around to the idea, he'll be grateful when it both gets you out of the picture once and for all and earns him one hell of a lucrative partnership for his flesh trade aspirations."

"What about the alliance that my marriage to Nico solidified?"

"As far as Nico and the Marchettis will know, you were kidnapped by one of their numerous enemies." He smiled sadistically. "They'll never find you, of course. It will just be an unfortunate tragedy with the alliance still intact. In fact, they'll have to fall in line, or Santino will blame Nico for letting you get taken on his watch."

"That's beyond convoluted. It won't fly. Not with any of them."

"Ah, but I can be very persuasive." He strode right up to me, looking me over and clearly relishing the sight of me bound and seemingly helpless. "Don't worry your pretty little head about it. I'll sort it just fine." He grasped

22

my jaw, making me hiss at his harsh grip. "Now, the reason you're not already on the truck outside headed to my buyer is because they want you broken in first. They can't accept a hellcat like you currently are." He released me roughly. "We're gonna take care of that right now."

He whistled and in the next moment four men in black tracksuits wearing balaclavas walked in and made themselves known. Yeah, they definitely weren't my father's soldiers. They never hid their identities. They were proud to be associated with the Leone Family. Or they had been. As my research on Leone and Marchetti soldiers had begun to build a picture, I'd managed to discover that many of them weren't as on board with things as they were portraying to the families. Something Nico and I would be working on shortly.

"You're really going to go this far? Have me set upon by these guys of yours? All because I rejected you years ago?"

He came close again, making me tense, especially when that sick smile spread over his face again. Then he had me cringing as he drew his fingers across the tops of my breasts. "It will give me immense personal satisfaction, yes. To know that you're being owned and utterly destroyed by my new friends here." He had me gagging as he licked the side of my cheek. "Mmm, I would get in on the fun myself, but I have Carver to tend to. *He* gets my worst tonight. Maybe tomorrow and even the day after that. His surrender will be much more satisfying than that of a weak little bitch like you."

"No. Leave him the fuck alone, you fucking psychopath!"

He slapped me across the face, making my head snap to the side painfully, and I tasted blood on my lips from the vicious force of it.

Dumbass.

Bloodlust activated.

In a way it hadn't been for a long time.

In a way it hadn't been allowed to be.

Him striking me, touching me, the adrenaline tearing through my system from the four guys waiting in the wings to assault me in horrific ways, and then Angelo's intent to have me taken to some sick bastard to have that continue forevermore, had the monster in me awakening. Knowing his intentions for Julian just took that to a whole other level.

He sneered at me, then stepped back and told his guys, "Make her your trashy little sex slave. And be fucking rough with it. She needs to hurt, to scream, to fucking bleed. And when she's begging you for a shred of mercy, just turn up the brutality even more." He blew me a sarcastic kiss. "Enjoy, Caterina."

He walked out then, leaving the door wide open behind him, and the four guys drew closer to me.

As they started talking amongst themselves and eye-fucking me in the process, I heard a car starting up, then driving off.

One of the guys, whose blond hair was sticking out of his balaclava, drew a flip knife from his pocket and opened it, then approached me. "I'm Trent. I'm telling you, because I want you screaming out my name for the next few hours. Helps get me off."

Urgh.

As he made a show of the knife for me, I finagled my fingers in the cuffs, so I had enough leverage to do what I needed to.

I was ready and in position, but I needed something to cover up what would happen the moment I went ahead with it.

The idiot gave me just that when he stepped up to me and cut through one of the straps of my white tank.

I gritted my teeth as I dislocated my right thumb at the exact same time, and he grinned, thinking that reaction was for him and what he was doing.

I did the same thing with my left thumb as he cut through the other strap.

And as the other three cheered when he shred the rest of my tank from my body, I slid my hands discreetly from the cuffs behind my back.

Instead of moving to cut through my white lace bra that was now visible and on display for them all, the sickos salivating over the sight, the guy went to reach beneath one of the cups.

"Touch me and I'll break your fucking jaw," I ground out.

He stilled, caught off guard by a threat coming from what seemed to them like a sure thing, a victim who was theirs for the absolute taking.

His buddies snickered, and he took a step back and cocked his head to the side. "Yeah?" he questioned, amusement dancing in his eyes. "Is that right, pretty girl?"

"That's right," I answered with an eerie calm that had *Trent* looking confused and his buddies eyeing one another, unsure.

Perfect.

"Angelo didn't mention you were a tough talker, sugar," Trent said, jolting toward me in a pathetic effort to scare me, trying to reinforce his dominance after me undercutting it so easily. "Tell us, how tough are you gonna be talking when we're ripping into your fuck holes, huh?" He grabbed my throat. "We were gonna start with your mouth, but now I'm thinking we'll skip right to your ass."

He squeezed, making me choke. "Ever had two big cocks ramming into that tight hole before?"

"Yeah, that's it," I heard one of the guys behind him uttering. Then the three of them shucked off their pants, their hard dicks coming into view.

Trent released my throat, then grabbed me between my legs, squeezing my pussy.

At the same time, I snapped my thumbs back into place, letting out a scream that they all believed was because of his hand grabbing me obscenely.

His eyes gave away his grin that was hidden beneath the balaclava. "Well, you're gonna. And while you've got two stuffed in here at the same time. Ready for that, sugar? Hmm? Where's the tough talk now?"

He released me, him and his buddies laughing, turning and looking at one another.

Distracted.

"I warned you," I spoke, a moment before I burst off the chair now I was free of the cuffs, snatched up the heavy metal thing and swung it—right at the bastard's jaw.

He shrieked like the true bitch men like him doing things like this were, and reeled back, cupping his jaw, dropping his knife in the process. I'd heard the delicious crack as I'd struck him there head-on. It was definitely broken.

They'd wanted pain, they were going to get just that. Only *I* would be the one inflicting it.

The other three guys came at me, slow in getting to it from their obvious shock.

Well, predators weren't used to becoming the prey.

I shoved the chair at the closest one, knocking him back, then dove for the blade, snatching it up, dodging a punch aimed at my throat from another, then snagged his arm, wrenched it down, then drove the knife straight into his dick. He squealed, and that got ever louder when I ripped the blade out, then spun into another asshole attempting to grab hold of me, and stabbed it deep into his throat. Blood sprayed all over my hand and splattered my face. He slumped to the ground, bleeding out right before my eyes, essentially drowning in his own blood.

That left the fourth guy and the one whose jaw I'd broken, who I noticed in my peripheral vision was finally pushing off the wall where he'd been reeling.

I didn't get the chance to retrieve the blade from the fallen guy's throat because the fourth guy lunged at me. He swung his fist, intending to put me down with a hefty punch to the face, but I reacted quickly, dodging out of the way, then sweeping my leg at his ankles. He landed hard on his knees. Then I was there, wrapping my arm around his throat and working on choking him out. He dug his nails into my arm in an attempt to weaken my grip, but the pain just spurred me on, skyrocketing the adrenaline surging through me.

More than that, calling to the monster in a deeper way.

I'd finally let it out after so long, there was no stopping it now.

I tugged ever harder, making the shit gag and splutter.

Movement behind me reached me, and I thrust my foot out, kicking back the attempted attack.

The guy I was holding weakened in my hold enough for me to fist my hand in his hair, then drive my knee into his face. Over and over. Bloodying him, breaking his nose, and hell knew what else as I just kept slamming into him wildly, giving no quarter, absolutely fucking mercilessly.

I only stopped because I was set upon again.

I released the guy just in time to deflect a punch coming from Trent. Then I spun into a kick that plunged into his ribs and sent him staggering back.

Before he could recover, I executed a round house that sent him stumbling and tripping on one of his fallen buddies. I snatched up the chair and rammed it down onto him; the legs grinding into his flesh and making him curse out into the garage as I put all my weight into it. "Now we've gotten started, let's move onto the meat of it," I spat, as I held Trent hostage on the concrete, while savoring the whimpers and pained grunts from those remaining conscious.

Down but conscious.

That wasn't enough for me.

Especially not for the monster.

It needed blood.

It needed agony.

It needed screams.

It *needed* their fucking lives.

"You're not… done?" Trent gasped.

"Not even close, *sugar.*"

I pushed off the chair and smashed my foot into his balls, making him scream.

Then I looked around at all those I'd felled.

"Mmm. Time to really get started, you sick pieces of shit."

4

~Nico~

My tires screeched as I made a sharp turn off the back road onto the dirt driveway that led to our target location, the place where Milo had managed to track Caterina's ring to.

Mud sprayed my windows as I tore down the way toward the dilapidated shithole house in the distance.

I was coming in hot, despite not knowing what we were hurtling into.

I didn't give a fuck.

We didn't have time to approach carefully.

From what I'd been able to ascertain from Julian's bike cam footage, we'd confirmed it had been Angelo who'd stopped them on the road *right* by my place and caused the crash. I'd also watched him sedate Julian, who'd been conscious afterward. Caterina hadn't been, but the bastard had shot her up with a needle, too. She'd been unmoving as she'd hit the ground really fucking brutally. I was hoping that the tough gear Julian had insisted she wear would have absorbed some of the damage, at least. But I didn't know that for a fact.

What I did know was that Angelo and his men who'd been concealed behind oversized sweats and balaclavas, had stripped both of them down on the road, tossing their jackets and phones, then hauled them into one of the unmarked vans, fucking kidnapping them.

With Angelo's intentions for Caterina through her father, the suggestion of what she could be enduring was god-awful enough. And with Julian crossing Angelo, he would be considered fair game in that respect, too.

As much as I'd tried to stay calm, now I'd seen the footage of them being set upon, then dragged away like that, I couldn't stop the hellish thoughts of what they could be suffering through right fucking now with every additional moment it took us to reach them.

I was halfway to the house when Milo roared by on his Harley, gun drawn and at the ready, riding one-handed as he tore ahead of me. That wasn't just his urgency, it was him always in the headspace of defending me. No matter what.

I caught up and pulled up just as he basically dropped his Harley, then started scanning the area while moving his gun back and forth, on high alert, prepared to fire in a split second.

Beside the two-story log cabin type house, there was a free-standing two-car garage. A white transport truck was parked next to it, the back open and facing us. I growled low in my throat as I took in the benches there fitted out with restraints. The thing was running, its lights on.

I signaled to Milo, and we approached it, splitting up, him taking the right side, heading to the front passenger door, me taking the left and going for the driver's door.

As I came to it, I started when I saw a bloodied hand-print on the white paintwork. I didn't see anyone sitting up there. I grasped the handle and threw open the door, and darted back as a body crumpled out, falling with a hard thud in a heap on the ground at my feet. No wonder I hadn't seen him. He'd been hunched over. I kicked him over, noting the stab wound in his throat, blood completely dousing him. Each one of his fingers was broken too.

"Shit," Milo exclaimed as he rounded the hood and came to me. "Nothing in the passenger side, but look what you've got there."

"He was tortured before he was killed."

"Sure looks like it." His eyes lit up. "This bodes really fucking well. Julian and Caterina must have—"

A shriek tore through the quiet area, jolting us both, and we swung our heads toward the sound coming from the garage, just a second before a guy decked out in black sweats stumbled out from a side door, slapping his bloodied hand to the wall, only to be suddenly wrenched back inside, and I saw a flash of that beautifully familiar brown, wavy hair.

We were bolting over there in the next second.

I burst through the door with Milo right at my back.

And then I pulled up short, my breath catching in my throat as his face was being smashed into the wall over and over by none other than Caterina, who was half fucking naked, her hair matted with sweat and a whole lot of blood. Her whole body was actually doused in it.

"Hell fucking no," Milo choked.

She swung her head at the sound of his voice, eyes flaming wildly and... inhumanly.

A snarl escaped her, before she turned her attention back to the guy, spun a knife in her hand, then drove it deep into his throat, right through his carotid artery.

He spluttered and gagged as blood sprayed all fucking over her, then she released him roughly and even gave him a kick in the junk as he slumped to the floor, bleeding out.

As if that hadn't been enough, there was the scene taking up the rest of the space inside the garage.

Blood.

So much fucking blood.

Splattering the walls, drenching a metal chair, *and* soaking five bodies, and now this one we'd just seen her take out too, littering the floor like a macabre carpet.

Bodies that weren't even fully… intact anymore.

Dismembered.

Sliced into.

Shot apart.

Beaten beyond recognition.

There was a butcher's knife, several handguns, and even pocketknives strewn all over the place.

"He had two more guards waiting when I was done with the four assigned rapists," she uttered. Her clouded emerald eyes fell on Milo, who couldn't hide his shock, then she screamed, while waving the knife wildly, "They deserved it! They deserved all of this!"

Rapists. "What did they—"

"They didn't get to do anything!" she yelled before I could finish my sentence.

Milo held up his hands. "All right, let's just calm down now. It's done. They're all down. Take a breath, Caterina." His eyes darted all around. "Where's Julian? Is he finishing off another one of these assholes? You and him worked together to—"

"He didn't do anything!" she yelled, growing more irate. I realized why in the next moment, when she screamed, "He's not here! He was never here! Angelo took him somewhere else and I don't… I don't know where! He's gone! He's being hurt right now, like Angelo ordered these bastards to do to me—to… to tear into me… to break me! But they didn't! I stopped them!"

32

Fuck me.

When we went to ask more, she ran at me and slammed me into the wall of the garage, choking the shit out of me from the shock of it. "*I.* Broke. *Them!*"

She wrenched me off the wall only to slam me back against it over and over, snarling and roaring like the animal she clearly was right now.

Completely unhinged.

Utterly irate.

And beyond reason.

I knew how that felt.

I understood that rage, that bloodlust, all of it.

But I'd never had it directed at me before like this.

I'd been the one dealing it out.

It had me fucking stunned to shit, and she clawed at me and screamed.

It was Milo who managed to snatch her knife before she brought that into play. He wrenched it from her grip, making her cry out at the force he'd had to use to accomplish it fast enough. He tossed it away across the room.

And then he was wrenching her off me, trapping her in a chokehold in the process.

"Don't hurt her," I managed to eke out as I pushed off the wall.

"Trying not to," he grunted, as she fought him and shrieked.

He used his powerhouse strength to maintain his hold, and I watched as it started to take effect, her body slowing, her eyelids starting to droop, until she finally stopped fighting entirely and went limp in his all-encompassing hold, losing consciousness.

"Damn," he uttered, scooping her up in his arms. He looked around, then eyes filled with a shitload of pain met mine. "He's not here. Julian's not fucking here, Nico."

"I know, brother. I know. We'll find him. I swear to you, we'll find him."

"We both know the person best equipped to do that is her," he said, nuzzling against her, not caring that blood was smearing all over his cheek in the process.

I hadn't fucking cared, either. Even as she'd been wailing on me and digging into the hard leather of my jacket and even penetrating through my skin all over my neck and chest, I hadn't fucking cared about the pain. Just that she was here with us. Just that we'd found her, that she was safe. *Fuck.*

Rapists... I couldn't get that word out of my head. What she'd alluded to, what Angelo had ordered them to do to her. It was a struggle and a half not to give into my own animalistic side right now and lose my shit all fucking over the place *and* tear into the assholes who were already mere corpses.

That wouldn't help anything.

Julian needed us. And to help him, to find him, level heads and rationality needed to prevail.

But once we did locate him, all bets would be off.

There would be absolutely no mercy.

Humanity would take a backseat.

And the worst of me would reign.

"I'll see to her and get her back to the house," I told Milo. "I need you to see to *this.*"

"So many dead bodies, the mess... it's a lot to sanitize. I can't do it alone. Not fast enough to be able to help with tracking Julian. Want me to call in Rocco? Tony, maybe?"

I shook my head. "Carlo."

"What? You're serious?"

"Consider it the test of his loyalty to us."

"Nico, I don't know if—"

"He has the resources that we don't currently have

until we're sure which of my soldiers are loyal to me, independent of the Family." I pulled out my phone and fired off a text to him.

Nico: Need your assistance. Milo will contact you with the details.

He responded right away, surprising both of us.

Carlo: My resources are yours, Nico.

I sighed and stowed my phone back in my pocket, confirming to Milo, "He's on board."

"Why doesn't that fill me with a whole lot of relief—or any?"

"Desperate times make for deals with devils, Milo. It is what it is right now."

"Being restricted, backed into corners… I hate this shit."

"As do I. But the situation is fluid. This is just where we are at now. It won't remain as such. I fucking promise you that."

"And I trust you. I just… Julian is… fuck, Nico."

I laid my hand on his shoulder. "We'll bring him back to us."

"What if it's too late by the time we manage that? What if Angelo… what if his *punishment* shatters him? After what happened with his father, Julian is susceptible to certain—"

"He won't succeed in breaking him. You know how devious and resourceful Julian is when it's called for. He can hold out until we get to him." I gave his shoulder a squeeze. "You know that too. You're just panicking, getting emotional."

He frowned at me. "And you're not… how? Us being threatened, it's a major trigger to you and your *feral* side."

"Believe me, I'm feeling it, but you all need me to be above it right now. It's the only way we'll win out here."

"Thank you."

I smiled. "You know that I would never do anything less for the three of you."

Sentiment threatened to get the best of me as he stared back at me with so much intensity, so I released him and looked away, telling him in my commanding tone, "Pass me Caterina. I'll get her back to the Manor and see to her. Sort this shitshow with Carlo's help."

"Yeah," he murmured. "Yeah."

He handed her off to me and I swept her up in my arms as he pulled out his phone and started snapping into action and communicating with Carlo.

As I carried Caterina outside and toward my car, I breathed her in, hating that I couldn't smell her usual Chanel scent and only other people's blood. "We've got you. You're going to be just fine. *Everything* is going to be fine."

They were more than hollow words of comfort.

They were a fucking promise.

And a brutal warning to all of our enemies.

5

~Nico~

"This isn't her."

"Did you really think there wouldn't be a massive emotional toll to enduring all that shit at your wedding? Or even all the shit before then? Santino and Angelo's abuse? Getting stabbed? Being pulled back into this world she worked so hard to escape from? Having to now go to war?"

When I'd expressed my concerns about Caterina's state of mind and the toll everything of late had taken on her, I hadn't wanted things to go *this* way, with her going to the extreme that she had tonight.

Sure, in a way she was back on track, no longer reeling like she had been, but in the most dangerous way imaginable.

Not to mention, a highly unpredictable way with the complete loss of control that letting the monstrous side of her loose involved.

I had enough unpredictable elements to deal with as it was without this becoming another.

Hell, *she* couldn't afford to be that way with what we were up against.

Carlo's words to me kept playing on my mind.

"You need to take power over the Marchetti Syndicate, Nico. And Caterina needs to do the same where the Leones are concerned."

I knew a great deal about Caterina, but even *I* couldn't predict how she was going to react to his intention there.

I watched the last of the dirt and blood swirling away down the drain as a whole lot of special soap and the warm water cleansed it from her skin, while I held her tightly against me in the shower of her ensuite at the Manor as I cleaned her up.

"Nico."

I pulled from my thoughts at the soft sound of Caterina uttering my name.

It was the first time she'd said anything since she'd woken up on the drive back to when we'd been six minutes out. She'd just looked at me, a mixture of guilt and shame flitting across her features before she'd then held up her hand to me in order to discourage me from getting into what had happened, and she'd spent the rest of the drive just staring aimlessly out of the window while slumped in the passenger seat exhaustedly.

I'd had to carry her into the house and also help her out of her soiled clothes when we'd reached her bedroom, because she'd been shaking so much, barely able to walk straight. From my own familiarity with entering my *feral* states, I recognized it as a mixture of high-level adrenaline and a massive expulsion of energy, as well as the struggle of her regular, rational mindset trying to reconcile what that monstrous mindset had done.

With her not all there in the moment, I hadn't left her alone for even one nano second. Not even to shower. Especially not to shower.

"Yeah?" I responded carefully, trying to keep my voice

soft. Well, as *soft* as a brutal bastard like me could actually manage to pull off.

It seemed to be good enough because she didn't flinch or react negatively to my one-word response.

In fact, she raised her head and met my eye line, even loosening her death grip on my biceps, wherein she'd been clinging to me in a very uncharacteristic way since I'd brought her in here to wash up. Like I was her lifeline.

While, sure, it did feel good on the one hand to be needed that way, especially by her, the woman I'd spent years being immersed in deep obsession with and who I'd developed a whole lot more than mere obsession with in the recent weeks, it also didn't feel right. It didn't feel like us. It wasn't our usual dynamic. And I also didn't like the shift in the power dynamic either. I didn't like it with her when things weren't even between us, when she was more… submissive like this. Her being strong and domineering in her own right and being able to match me on every fucking level was the woman I knew, the woman I respected, the woman I… cared for a great deal.

Anything else just felt… wrong.

Unsettling.

And, yeah, fucking upsetting at seeing her like that.

Not herself.

Fucking lost to me.

I hated that all this shit was doing this to her, hurting her so much.

And I felt like it was doing more than that—as if that wasn't already bad enough—that it was taking her from me, pulling her away.

It had taken *so* long for me to bring her close and to earn her trust, to be with her in a way that wasn't just my one-sided fixation on display for her to see, beyond our war, that the idea of anything impacting that, risking that… it made me sick to my stomach. Hell, it threatened to make me rage in a way that the world and I, myself, had never seen the likes of before.

"How long have I been… out? Spacing out, I guess?"

"Almost an hour."

She frowned, looked down at herself standing there naked, pressed up against me while I was clad in my pants and white shirt, the latter now see through from being utterly soaked. The only things I'd taken off were my socks and shoes, and my leather jacket. Well, and also my holsters.

"You're in here fully clothed?" she questioned.

"I figured you might need that barrier right now." *After what happened to you tonight, after those fucking rapists set upon you while I wasn't there to stop them, while you were taken under my fucking watch, while I was failing all over the place to safeguard the people I love.*

"Thank you. But I'm fine." She grimaced as she looked me over, her eyes darting all over the scratches she'd inflicted when she'd lost control on me earlier. "I'm so sorry, Nico. I wasn't in my right mind, but that's not even an excuse. I hurt you."

"It's nothing."

"Of course it is and—"

"Come on, we both know you were holding back when you came at me. Majorly. In that state, the damage you could have really done is far beyond these mere slight grazes."

"I'm still sorry."

"No, *I'm* sorry," I said, reaching out and stroking her face carefully. "Because you're actually hurt," I said, gesturing at the nasty scrapes along both of her arms, a red-raw handprint around her throat, bruising along her jawline, *and* nail marks… between her thighs.

40

"It's not a big deal," she insisted, even as she winced when she shifted her weight.

I saw her look down and realize what had caused the discomfort. She caught my eye and started shaking her head vehemently. "It's not what you think. It was just a brutal grab."

Just?

A growl escaped me before I could swallow it down.

"I mean, they didn't get any further than that." Her eyes darkened briefly as she uttered, "I made sure of it."

"It shouldn't have happened in the first place," I gritted out. "I'm sorry that——"

She pressed her fingers to my lips. "Shh. It did happen, and the fault is Angelo's. But I handled it. I stopped them from doing what they'd planned."

"You most definitely did."

She flinched and pulled her fingers away. "You think I went too far, don't you?"

I turned the shower water off and stepped out, grabbing a towel, then handing it to her.

I went to take her hand to help her out, but she batted it away and got out on her own, much steadier on her feet now. "Don't avoid the question," she said, taking the towel and securing it around her.

Normally, I'd be hard-pressed to keep my hands off her with her just being right in front of me, let alone wet and naked. But with her like this, not fully herself, even though I could see her getting there bit by bit, and after what she'd been through tonight, all I could see was the clinical side of things.

"I'm the last person to judge any of that," I told her. "You know what I've done. Well, some of the things. You've even borne witness to some particularly brutal instances." I shrugged my soaking wet shirt off, then opened my pants. "Furthermore, *I* wasn't the one bound to that chair and facing off with four sexual predators intent on *breaking me in* for when I was shipped off to some sick sex slave buyer."

She gasped at my words and stilled. "How did you know that part?"

"The guys were ID'd by a source of ours and Milo put the pieces together from there."

"Source? What source?"

I shoved my pants and boxers down, then kicked them off, thankful to be free from the uncomfortable feeling of wet clothes sticking to me. I snatched another towel off a rail, then wrapped it across my hips. "We'll get into that later. When you're… better."

"Better? I'm fine now."

I scrubbed my hand over my face. "Caterina, stop."

"Stop what?"

"Acting like *this* can just roll off your back."

"Isn't that what you want from me?"

"What?"

"You think I didn't hear you talking to the guys when you sent me upstairs to get dressed for our sparring session that never actually ended up happening because of other dire circumstances? You thought I'd gone soft, lost my edge, that I was reeling from everything. *Weak.*"

"That's not—I was airing my worries out loud in a burst. They weren't all perfectly—"

"You need me this way. *I* need me this way. Able to take the hits and keep on moving. Not absorbing the trauma, not letting it touch me."

"Not *processing* it is really what's happening with you. And it's an issue. You bury it down deep, hit after hit, but it can't all be contained, and then it threatens to break you apart. You *need* to process it, acknowledge it. What happened in that garage is proof enough of that, of what can happen if you don't."

"I destroyed them, Nico."

"There's a difference between putting down an enemy and what *you* did."

"So you do condemn it? After wanting to see that side of me, to bring it out in me, *this* is how you respond when I actually do unleash it? Is it because it wasn't sexually? Is that why you're condemning it? Because you didn't get anything out of it? Because you and your dick didn't benefit?"

Well, she'd certainly come fully out of her withdrawn state now.

But there was a whole lot of lashing out going on.

"You feel guilty."

"What?" she bit at me.

"This is remorse kicking in. It's why you're lashing out, getting angry. It's creeping up, and it feels like shit." Or, so I'd heard from Milo and Julian whenever they'd crossed lines like this before over the years.

"No, this is about you con—"

"Condemning you, right. Except I'm not and I never actually said that."

"Then what? What exactly *is* your point?" She smashed her fist into the wall, making a dent in the process. "Just fucking say it!"

Yeah, this was guilt, for sure. And the rage that came along with trying not to feel it and shove it back down quickly to avoid the hurt of it. Again, as I'd heard from Milo and Julian when it came to this sort of thing.

I strode to her and grasped her wrist, eyeing her now bloodied knuckles. "Stop. You're already hurt. No more. No fucking more tonight." She went to pull free, but I held fast. "*Listen.* Just fucking listen."

She stopped resisting and blew out a breath. "Fine."

"I don't condemn what you did. I'm just concerned. You *unleashing* and being your true self is absolutely magnificent. There's nothing else like seeing you free and uninhibited, not bound by yourself, anyone, or anything. And I love every moment of it." I glared at her. "Even the parts not related to servicing my dick, for the record." I sucked in a breath to calm myself after the sting of that insulting accusation, and went on, "*But* what you did earlier to those guys *wasn't* that. It was *pain*."

"Wh-what?"

"Not pain from their intentions, because that would have been dealt with by simply putting them down, hurting them enough to nullify the threat. But you went much further than that. *Because* of everything else that's been building up." Still holding her wrist, I pushed into her so she could feel me against her, and hopefully use it to ground herself to the moment with me, *and* for some comfort at the same time. "What I hate, what I *condemn*, is you getting to the point of needing to unload that much fucking agony."

"It is what it is right now."

"Caterina—"

"No. Why do you think I left the family, cut all those connections, even basically to my mom, too? Why do you think I was so intent on going out into the world alone with nothing to my name, starting from scratch, clawing my way up from the fucking dirt all alone? To escape that. To escape what they made me feel, what they did to me, what all that misogyny and control and abuse that zapped my power did to me." She pushed me away, and I let her, because at least she was talking about it and not just trying to shut it all down again right away.

At least she was letting me in.

"Tonight, Angelo tried to take my power in one of the most heinous ways imaginable. I've put up with a lot of their shit since I was pulled back into all of this. Their verbal abuse, the threats, being hurt by my own father, having to stand back and not respond with a massive show of force when my mom was under threat and having to send her away instead, having to be demeaned as a forced mafia princess bride, being kept from what actually gives me purpose and a sense of control and power in my work, then having to move in here under the guise that I'm being *trained* by you to be a submissive, broken wife with no agency of her own. But tonight… that went beyond all of that. Even just putting those assholes down wasn't enough. I needed to rage, I needed to take back the power that's been stolen from me, that I essentially even had to fucking give up to carry out this mission with the three of you."

"I hear you. I hear every fucking word. And I'm glad you're admitting that it *has* impacted you."

"It's more than that. And I guess I was trying to pretend it wasn't true, to shove it down. But it is true. There's no more denying it now."

"What's that?"

"This is who I am when I'm embroiled in this, when I'm immersed in my family again."

"No," I said, shaking my head vehemently. "You're wrong."

"Nico—"

"You accept that and you're letting them win. This is what they want, remember? To break you? To make you inconsequential?"

"Even so—"

"Santino isn't afraid of what you might know, what you might do, he's afraid of *you.*"

She stilled. "What?"

"Your mom told me everything. He's afraid you'll oust him. He knows what you're worth, and it scares the living shit out of him. Short of killing his own daughter, he's trying to wipe you off the board in this way. And that fear, Caterina, that's everything to us, something we can absolutely use to our advantage." I went to her and took her hands in mine. "More to the point of *our* conversation, it demonstrates that he's actually well aware of your true worth, your capabilities, and skills. And you're such a force to be reckoned with that he's going to these insane lengths as a result."

It took her several moments to take in the heaviness of my revelations.

Then she stared up at me. "You're in a similar situation with them trying to leash you."

I nodded. "And all this leads to something else that we need to discuss. But not yet. First, there's Julian. It's why I wanted us to talk this out, to make sure you were—"

"Mentally stable after what I just did?"

"Stable confidence-wise too, that your rationality had returned as well, yes. And that you still had hope, that all this shit that's happened hasn't undercut that. Because when it comes to finding someone who's being hidden by the likes of Angelo, it can take nothing short of a fucking miracle and a whole lot of steadfast determination."

"Not a miracle, just some impressive ingenuity." Her lip curled. "Fortunately, thinking outside the box is kind of my thing."

With that, she stalked to the bathroom door, threw it open, then strode on out back into the bedroom.

I followed her as she headed for her chest of drawers and started pulling some clothes out and tossing them on the bed. "I need coffee and lots of it. I can still feel that fucking sedative in my system. I'll meet you in the living room—the main one—in ten minutes, and we'll get started."

Relief rolled through me at seeing her like this and I smiled at her issuing orders.

"What?" she asked distractedly as she shoved on her panties and a pair of black yoga pants beneath her towel, jumping on the spot to pull them on quickly.

"Nothing. I'll get that coffee going."

"When will Milo be back? And come to think of it, how the hell is he going to clean up the mess I made all by himself?"

"I'll answer the first question. The second we'll get to once we find Julian. Milo texted me before we headed into the shower. Another twenty minutes and he'll be here."

I could see her urge to ask more about the second part. Fortunately, she obviously recognized the need to prioritize right now, and she merely nodded and said, "Okay, good."

"I'll need to dress your injuries while you're doing your thing."

"I'm fine."

"Your arms are scraped up to shit. From the crash, no doubt."

It was fucking lucky that it hadn't been worse than that.

Julian had protected her with that special riding gear he'd acquired for her.

Of course he had. He was always going above and beyond for those he loved.

And I'd make damn sure we did the same for him now.

"Then there's the fact that you had open wounds while covered in other people's blood. Infection is a very real concern. We'll get you on a course of antibiotics right away."

"Twice in a few weeks. That's not the best."

No, it really wasn't.

Her getting hurt *again* wasn't something easy for me to digest. Hell, I couldn't swallow it. I never would. I just had to hold off my true feelings concerning it until we located Julian.

Just until then.

I walked to her and kissed the top of her head. "It will all be okay. You're back here, safe with us now." I breathed her in. "Where you belong."

Her eyes widened at my words. My confession, in a sense.

It had just… come out.

The words had slipped out so easily.

And they'd felt so fucking right when I'd voiced them.

I smirked and walked out, leaving her to absorb it.

6

~Emilio~

Carlo's guys had been swift, efficient, and strategic.

A well-oiled machine.

Professionals, even.

Not just thugs with guns and raging tempers, which was pretty much what the Marchetti Syndicate and the Leone Family had become lately.

No, the Benzino soldiers that Carlo had shown up with at Angelo's hideaway tonight had been streamlined, strategic, and detail-oriented. Really fucking on the ball.

I'd been impressed.

If only that hadn't been tainted by the past.

Something I'd thought I'd made peace with.

As much as anybody could actually make peace with their parents being murdered in an all-out brutal mob war that had taken over the city a few years back.

It had been a tossup between the Benzinos and the Leones as to who had invaded my parents' home the night they'd lost their lives. Everyone across the three families in a position of power had been a target during that tumultuous time. Fair game, basically. As Underboss at the time, that had obviously included my dad. The Leones had blamed the Benzinos for it, but the Benzinos had never actually denied it, so they'd been seen as the more likely culprits. Marco had struck back with one hell of a bloodied attack against both families for it, and the matter had then been considered settled. Brutal justice had been achieved. Shortly after that, the war had run its course and the three families alliance had been formed, so any further reprisals had been outlawed all around.

So I'd just had to accept it. To let it go. To take comfort in the fact that justice had been done, that my parents' murderers had been ripped from this world.

Over time, I'd buried it down deep, the fact that we'd never identified who exactly had been responsible. Not the precise individual, nor who'd pulled the trigger on both my dad and my mom. We weren't supposed to go after the families of our enemies, especially not women and children, yet the culprit had.

But burying it all… that had taken a hit lately.

First with having to step into the Leone Estate for the fake wedding, and with Caterina being thrust into my life who was Leone by blood, although nothing else, fortunately. And then tonight, first facing off with the Benzinos, then having to work with them on the cleanup.

Normally, I'd be able to keep a handle on it, but with Julian missing, it made me more emotionally vulnerable than I normally ever would be. As if it hadn't already been bad enough with what Caterina had been through, or the fact of having them both taken in the first place. Now he was still being held captive somewhere by that fucking slimy psychopath.

"I want you on your knees kissing the ring with a heartfelt apology."

Angelo Simone's words to Julian the day of the

wedding had been swirling through my mind, torturing me with the implications of what could be happening to my Sunshine in relation to that.

Worse, though, had been Julian's observations of him, that which he'd called Angelo on that day.

"If anyone is gonna be on their knees, it's you. For me. And that's what this is really about, isn't it? Your closeted need for just that."

He'd read that sleazy bastard and determined that he had a hard-on for him. He wanted him. And from what I'd heard about Angelo *and* how he'd been with Caterina— someone he'd taken a liking to a while back—he didn't react *normally* when attraction was in play. Nico's obsession with Caterina looked completely wholesome in comparison to how Angelo was.

Yes, obviously, in a fight, Julian could hold his own.

But this situation was different.

He'd taken a hit from the crash, he'd been sedated too, so he was starting off in this battle from a major disadvantage.

And there was also the fact that he was susceptible to certain things. Susceptible to being *triggered* in a way that could make it very difficult for him to see straight or even hold on, let alone actually fight back. Because of what had happened with his father, a lot about Angelo when he was on one of his tears would... *affect* Julian.

He'd recognized that himself when Angelo had tried to come at him and I knew it was why he'd put him down so quickly and ended the confrontation right there and then, before it had been able to get its claws into him, before it had thrown open the door for him to be haunted by the ghosts of his past.

That door might be flying wide open right now, though.

And it really fucking worried me.

I rushed down the corridor carrying two more laptops and a bunch of cables for Caterina.

As I burst back into the living room where she was on the edge of the couch typing rapidly on her hardcore military-grade laptop like a machine, my gaze shot to Nico, who was pacing back and forth on the phone. It was the content of his conversation that caught me off guard.

"Your Capo dragged my wife from the outskirts of my property line, kidnapped her, then set up four men to rape her with the intent to then transport her to a buyer of fucking sex slaves! *My* wife! My charge, my property!" he was yelling heatedly.

Caterina lifted her head at the last part and growled at him, but then let it go immediately, knowing he was just playing up the role, before then returning her hyper-focused attention to her task at hand of filtering through a wealth of information in a bid to track down our boy.

When I'd returned home following the cleanup, I'd found her showered and back in clean clothes, her emerald eyes bright and focused. Back to herself and out of that monstrous state she had been in earlier. Her arms had been wrapped in gauze, Nico telling me that he'd treated her while I'd been gone. I'd double-checked that he'd done it properly and hadn't forgotten anything like a whole lot of antiseptic or feeding her antibiotics. Nico was more for causing damage, rather than healing it. But he'd actually done a good job, and she'd heal well.

"You're close, I know that," I heard Nico continuing down the line. "You treat him like your lieutenant more so than your actual Underboss in Dante, but we had an agreement, an ironclad fucking agreement. This marriage is the cornerstone of our new alliance, Santino. The implications of this in relation to that are dire, to say the least. Especially when my father hears of it. If action isn't taken here, I will mobilize my—what? Yes. Acting alone on this? How can I trust in that, given what you want to befall your own daughter? No, I'm gonna need more than that. Words aren't enough or—yes. Exactly. Good, then I want to see it. Leash him and punish him. He came onto *my* fucking territory, took what belongs to *me*. Contacting you instead of pursuing action myself is to honor the alliance, but if you don't reel him in and do what needs to be done, I'll forgo all sense of courtesy. This won't stand. Cut out the rot in Angelo before it infects us all."

He hung up, then all that rage instantly disappeared, and he smirked out at Caterina, who lifted her head and grinned. "Nicely done."

"What's going on?" I asked, making my presence known as I strode over to Caterina and put the additional laptops down on the coffee table for her.

As she snapped into action, sorting them the way she wanted, setting up what she needed to, Nico explained, "While you were searching out supplies for Caterina, the two of us determined a way to get more boots on the ground with our search for Julian. Manipulate the Leones into searching for his captor in Angelo. Make him their target. Santino won't give two shits about Julian being taken, but making it about Caterina being kidnapped violates a whole lot of shit, including the new alliance. It puts Santino in the position of being forced to act against Angelo and scour the fucking city for him, which will, in turn, cross off various possible locations that Caterina has identified so far."

"That's ingenuous. Risky, though. You basically challenged Santino."

"With the alliance at my back. The risk was mitigated due to that."

Not taken out of the equation altogether. But it would

have to do as it was, because Julian needed us, and he needed us fucking quickly at that.

"What if they get to the correct location first?"

"It's a possibility. The fact is, the three of us can't head out to check all of them. The priority is finding Julian. Seeing to Angelo is second. But he *will* be seen to."

"You don't think Santino will bury him?"

"No. He's his pet Capo. He'll punish him to save face, but that will be the extent of it."

"And how are we then going to get in there to murder the fucker when he's back under Leone protection?"

"Off the top of my head," Caterina spoke. "Long range sniper shot taken the moment he's away from the mansion, which we then manipulate to look like the work of that buyer he was intending to send me to. You know, for him failing to follow through?"

"Damn, that's vicious," I said. "And fucking perfect."

She lifted a shoulder, then went back to work.

"Any progress since I've been gone?" I asked her.

"You mean, in the three minutes it took you to grab those laptops for me?"

I pinched the bridge of my nose. "Sorry, I just—"

She grasped my hand. "It's all right, I get it." She gave it a squeeze, then patted the cushion next to her. "Come, sit for a few moments. I'll explain exactly where we're at and what I'm doing. Information *is* power, but it can also be comfort."

I smiled. "Thank you."

"I'm gonna reach out to my father, take the chaotic energy up several notches," Nico told us, before heading out of the room, dialing on the way. I heard that dangerous tone of his echoing down the corridor as he went.

Good. He was piling on the pressure on that end of things.

I sat down beside Caterina and the first thing I noticed as I stared at the laptop she was currently on, while two more were now churning and cycling through a ton of data, was the insane facial recognition software she had up and running. It was analyzing gait and body language, not just facial features. "Where the hell did you get that?" I asked her. She had some mad skills, but I wasn't aware that they included software development.

She shot a look out the door, clearly making sure Nico wasn't near. Then, satisfied that he wasn't, she revealed, "It was a gift from Levi."

Good call not bringing that up right now while things were tense as hell. While Nico might have come around on it more than any of us had thought possible for him, all for Caterina's benefit, it was still sore subject matter and something that could come to the surface for him when a whole lot of intensity was in play.

"It's a hell of a gift."

She merely nodded, then got down to business, pointing at the laptop she was currently working on right next to me, "I'm tapped into surveillance around the city—news outlets, police, government, and even those of security companies that cover individual homes too so we can have eyes through locations not in built-up areas. The facial recognition software is running on all facets of that surveillance, searching for both Angelo and Julian. I've also written a program that's scouring social media posts. Julian's a public and very beloved figure. Any sightings of him are a big deal, even in passing. And even a glimpse of him could help us."

"Okay, what about Angelo's car? That Audi of his? He brought it to the crash site where he took you both."

"I found it, but it was abandoned on the outskirts of the city. And not by him. One of those guys he was using tonight."

"One you killed?"

"No. This one is still alive. I'm working on tracking him." She pulled up another tab, showing me a photo she'd captured of a guy wearing a balaclava, his eyes highlighted by the facial recognition software.

"And Angelo's phone? Can't you ping it to a cell tower near him? At least we'd have something to go on then to mobilize and search out an area."

"His phone is completely offline."

I cursed under my breath.

"We'll find him. There's just a lot of ground to cover, so it'll take some time."

"Too much time," I muttered.

"This isn't all that I'm doing, Milo."

I cocked an eyebrow.

She moved down to her next laptop and pulled up a map of the city, turquoise dots marking several locations. "As you know, I was watching Angelo for several days when I was trying to locate the house where the Leones were holding those human trafficking hostages. During that time, I identified these areas as those that he frequented when off-duty. I've managed to rule a bunch of these out from tapping into the surveillance at bars, strip clubs, even his home surveillance. Now Nico has basically activated the Leones, they'll check the rest for us." She moved to the third laptop, and I took in everything on there too, as she told me, "Meanwhile, I'm also following the money. I've accessed all of Angelo's accounts—yes, again. It's just a matter of untangling things."

"A whole lot of money laundering going on?"

"Pretty much. As much as it pains me to say it, he's smart. Where this is concerned, anyway."

"Coming after you and Julian definitely is the exception. Then again, when he sets his sights on someone in a twisted affectionate way, all bets are off."

She grimaced. "They are, yes."

I tugged at my hair, trying not to go down a dark path with my thoughts again of what that could mean for Julian. "We know he wouldn't take him to any venue connected with the Leone Family. Nor would he risk taking him to anywhere belonging to their allies or places under their protection. So, it's gotta be somewhere *he* owns."

"Hence me looking into his accounts, trying to determine any purchases he's made over the last few years with siphoned Leone funds that he's taken as his own."

"All right," I murmured, taking it all in. "You've got a whole lot covered here, but I need to do something as well. I can't just sit here and—"

"Milo, I know, and I can't cover everything. I'm aware of your skills, so I need you to use those and access both Leone and Marchetti mansion security so we can keep an eye on how they're handling this situation, exactly where they're sending their soldiers at any given time, so we can check those off as they go. I'm also going to get you into Santino's phone, so we can monitor him directly. He can't be trusted with this. He may just do the minimal to appease Nico."

I rose to my feet. "My laptop's in Nico's office. I'll be right back. Then we can do this and coordinate together."

"Milo," she called out to me as I reached the door.

"Yeah?"

"We'll bring him back to us."

"I know we will."

We had to, because the truth was, I couldn't live with it any other way.

The problem wasn't *if* we'd bring him back; it was *when*.

And what fucking damage he would have sustained in that time from that demented psychopath.

Please hold on, Sunshine.

7

~Julian~

Five Years Ago

I COLLAPSED ONTO MY BED, *fighting to catch my breath.*

"Fuck, the way you take me, darlin'. Perfection."

Suddenly Milo was lunging from his sprawled out position on his stomach, enjoying the hot-as-fuck sensation of my cum trickling from his ass, and pouncing on top of me.

I groaned at the feel of his big, hard body and all that delicious muscle and ink surrounding me.

Those groans turned to growls when he licked the drops of sweat off my chest, making his way down my body before slicking that talented tongue of his all over my cock, eating up every drop of cum left remaining.

He suckled at my crown, then tugged at my piercings with his teeth in that way he loved to do and the way I fucking loved him doing, sending shocks of pleasure through me that had my hips lifting off the bed.

"Jesus Christ, I need a few minutes before another round."

"We're already at three rounds. Gonna make it four."

"And we will, just after some hydration and coming up for air."

He licked me from my balls, all the way to my crown, making me buck wildly.

And then he abruptly sat up. "All right."

"Damn you."

He grinned. "Right back at you, Sunshine."

And then he was climbing off the bed and pulling on his boxers and jeans.

"You're leaving?"

"Gonna get us some snacks and some water from the cafeteria. Don't leave the bed. I'll be right back."

"You know I can't just lie still for seconds, let alone minutes."

"Do your IG bullshit, then. But just stay on the bed for me."

"And then what?"

"And then when I get back, I'm gonna sit on your cock and let you fuck up into me like a goddamn jackhammer."

A hot thrill ran through me. "Jesus Christ, yes. But you don't get to move at all. You'll take it all as I see fit, even as I clamp my hand down around your cock and fuck it with my hand like a beast."

His whole face lit up, and a sly smile spread over his face.

Yeah, he loved that kind of dominant shit.

It was a time when he didn't have to think and worry for once, where he could finally let go and give into the pleasure and wildness of it all in a safe space with me leading him through it.

"Goddamn," he uttered, before snatching up my boxers from the floor and tossing them to me. "Put these back on. If I walk back in here and you're still naked on the bed, it's gonna be impossible to eat and hydrate first before getting right back to a fourth round."

I chuckled. "You're so easy."

"When it comes to you, yes. The shit you do to me… damn, there's nothing else like it. No one else like you."

"Don't I know it."

"Arrogant dick," he jested.

"Hmm, yes, my dick is highly arrogant." I wiggled my eyebrows. "Rightfully so, wouldn't you say?"

He rolled his eyes.

"Well?"

"Fine. Yes."

I laughed. "That's right."

"Happy now?"

"Oh, very."

He shook his head to himself, but amusement danced in his pretty espresso eyes. "Put those on now," he reiterated, gesturing at my boxers that he'd tossed onto my abs.

I grumbled, but pushed up to a sitting position, then pulled them on. "Get me something chocolaty."

"For dessert only. Just a small chocolate bar."

"What? No."

"You need to eat properly. Vitamins, iron, protein and—"

"Protein? Well, why didn't you say? We've got that covered."

"We're not subsisting on cum."

"But just the suggestion spilling from your pretty lips is getting me hard."

"Even the protein of—" He stilled as he saw me grinning at him. "You're screwing around."

"That I am. Go forth to the cafeteria like you want. I am actually hungry."

He walked to me, kissed my cheek, then headed on out of the room.

I slumped back on my pillows and tried to relax while he was gone and use the time to take a beat.

But my mind wouldn't allow for that.

That usual eeriness once I was alone started creeping up on me.

It was the step that came before the bad thoughts, just moments away from that dark door swinging wide open and all the fucked-up memories blasting free and inundating me all at once.

I blinked hard and snatched my phone off the bedside table.

I opened my IG.

There wasn't much happening there to keep my attention, so I took a selfie shirtless with my nipple hoops on display, my hair all wild and looking just-fucked. I uploaded it with the caption:

Those nights where you just can't get enough. Here legends are made. #sexmarathon #bringithard

It wasn't long before the likes and comments started rolling in, thankfully taking my attention.

Then a text came in while I was responding and enjoying the interaction.

Nico: *So that's where Milo is. Am I right?*

Julian: *Right you are, N.*

Nico: *Put him on.*

Julian: *Call him yourself. Kind of busy with my IG right now.*

Nico: *I can't. His phone is on your pillow along with his wallet. You know, the brown suede one I got him for his birthday a couple of weeks ago?*

Frowning, I swung my head and sure enough, there was Milo's stuff on the pillow. I guess he'd grabbed it off the other bedside table right there intending to pocket it once he'd gotten dressed, but then dropped it in the process of pulling on his clothes and forgotten to pick them back up when we'd been talking.

Julian: *Oops. He's not here in my dorm room, anyway. Went to the cafeteria to get us some food.*

Nico: *I see.*

Julian: *Is this urgent?*

Nico: *Was expecting his company on a hunt.*

Julian: *Targeting Ray Simmons? The guy who threatened you and disrespected you?*

Nico: *Yeah.*

Julian: *Worst person he could have crossed, huh, mafia prince?*

Nico: *He'll learn that lesson soon enough.*

Julian: *I told you I can help you with that, N.*

Nico: *No. You're not getting involved in any of this.*

Julian: *Mafia justice?*

Nico: *If you really need to call it that.*

Julian: *I do. But you don't need to keep me out of it.*

Nico: *Yes, I do.*

Julian: *Nico.*

Nico: *Once you cross that line, there's no way back. This is us protecting you, J.*

A knock sounded at the door.

Julian: *Gotta go. Someone's here. Probably Milo realizing he forgot his wallet.*

Nico: *Can't be. He just walked into the cafeteria. Don't open it.*

I rolled my eyes at his paranoia.

Life as the son of a mob boss in our home city would do that.

But we weren't there now. We were hundreds of miles away at college together, away from all of that and the nightmare that went along with it for him and Milo. And for me—just not the mafia angle. That wasn't what gave me nightmares. Unfortunately, I had my own shit where that was concerned.

See where my thoughts went when I was left alone without enough distractions? I mean, it was probably nothing to do with any of that. Nico likely didn't want me to open the door because it could be one of my fuck buddies knocking. That happened quite a bit. We were in college and I was living my best life, so, yeah; I had a lot of fun and even more sex. But I wouldn't invite somebody else in while I was with Milo. And Nico should know better than that by now. I was aware that it bothered Milo seeing my horde of sex buddies, *as he called it, up close, so I kept it separate and away from him. When he was with me, it was just the two of us.*

I rolled off the bed and crossed to the door, noting that it was locked. I hadn't even seen Milo do that. Sweet fucker, always protecting us. He'd forgotten his own damn wallet, but he'd remembered to do this for me in a bid to keep me safe.

I was just a couple of feet out from the door when another few knocks came, these much more aggressive and exhibiting an urgency too.

It had me hesitating on opening it.

"Who is it?" I called out.

I really wasn't worried about security as a rule. Not while we were here living on the college campus. I mean, really? But I guess Nico had gotten under my skin where that was concerned.

There was a weird delay before a familiar breathy female voice responded, that breathiness turning me on when I'd first heard it. It was one of the main reasons I'd taken its owner to my bed.

"It's me, Jules."

And calling me Jules was the reason I'd only taken her to my bed once. She'd kept screaming that out while we'd been fucking.

"Lindsay?"

"Yeah!" she cried, excited that I'd remembered her name.

Of course, I had. I remembered everybody I'd been with. I wasn't an asshole, and I didn't like it when disrespect was present just because it was casual sex. Why couldn't both parties—or more, in my case— be treated well and enjoyed at the same time? I didn't get that shit.

I unlocked the door and opened it to find her on my doorstep.

She smiled out at me nervously, her long blonde hair cascading down her bare shoulders, a pink sundress doing her a hell of a lot of justice.

Wait. Nervously?

"What's up?"

"Nothing, I mean—"

"Sweetheart, I'm already booked for the night. Got a friend over. He's just getting us some food and he'll be back any minute."

"I'm sorry," she said. "He just... this guy... he offered me a lot of money and I... I really needed it and—"

She was suddenly wrenched away as a hand shot out from around the corner.

"You're done. Get gone."

I froze at the sound of that awful voice.

He rounded the corner and then stood there right before me. "I knew you wouldn't open the door if you knew it was me."

I choked as adrenaline tore through my body like live wires as I stood staring at the last person I ever wanted to have in my vicinity, any-fucking-where near me.

Dirty-blond hair that was like mine was wilder than I remembered it, grown out and unkempt like he hadn't had a haircut in so long and like he'd been shoving his hand through it repeatedly. Normally clean-shaven, his jaw was now plagued by thick facial hair, verging on beard territory. He stood there in a rumpled black suit with a white dress shirt beneath that had a coffee stain on it right near the loose, plain black tie. Even his shoes were all scuffed up, adding to the down-and-out look.

But it was his eyes that were the main concern to me.

There was that look in them that I remembered all too well.

They were shining with malicious intent.

And an interest that made me sick.

Gabriel Carver.

My father.

"What are you doing here?" I somehow managed to get out.

"Can't a father miss his son?"

"Not when that father is you."

His lips twisted. "I see you've grown bolder since you've been away. I arrived just in time to beat that defiance out of you."

He thrust his hands into my chest, knocking me back into the room.

It all happened so fast then with him forcing his way in, then locking the door behind him, then swinging his fist.

The first hit plowed into my gut, making me choke and double over.

He followed that through with a nasty punch to my face that had my head snapping to the side, blood spraying from my mouth from the brutality of his fucking hit. I had to slap my hands down on the foot of the bed to steady myself.

That was a big mistake as I realized in the next moment when he came up behind me, wrapped one arm around my throat and wrenched my head back, while his other grasped my dick through my boxers.

I shuddered and almost retched, but his grip around my throat prevented it from happening.

It got worse when I felt his breath at my ear as he spoke. "You belong to me, boy. You exist because of me and you'll follow orders without complaint. You may think you're free out here in college, but you'll be back home soon enough and controlled again. It makes me sick that you're fornicating with all sorts here, especially the Bardi boy. Is it not just an experiment anymore? Is that what you're really into? It won't stand. Do you hear me?"

"Why... are you... here?" I rasped against his constricting grip.

"My hedge fund is in trouble."

"Need... money?"

"Yes."

"How... much?"

"A couple hundred thousand."

I frowned. That sounded like much more than mere trouble. It sounded like he was going under.

"Somebody ratted me out to the SEC. They turned over evidence about illegal deals, trading, bull about extortion going on."

It wasn't bullshit. I knew that for a fact.

He'd hurt a lot of people.

And I might have done something about that.

It had taken a long while for it to reach fruition, though. Then again, it had triggered a massive, in-depth investigation and that was a lengthy process.

Finally, it was happening.

Although, it was really biting me in the ass right about now.

"Let... go."

"You need some convincing first. Isn't that right?"

"No," I ground out.

"The way you spoke to me at the door would indicate otherwise."

He started stroking my cock then.

"Give me one, then I'll let you go."

"Stop... no." I bucked against him, but he just tightened his chokehold making me fight for breath, my body weakening from the significant lack of air.

He stroked faster, his fingers all over me.

And then he shoved them inside my boxers.

I could no longer speak or make a sound as he choked me with his awful grip.

Twisting away and bucking didn't help either. He just followed where my body turned.

A violent thud sounded and then a ferocious roar tore through the room a moment before my father's arm was forcibly wrenched away from my throat. He screamed as a crack sounded, before he was ripped off me entirely.

Trembling, it took me some time to turn around, and when I did, I saw Milo on him, beating on him brutally, his hits coming hard and fast and absolutely mercilessly, while my father couldn't defend himself at all.

A sick satisfaction betook me at the sight of him being dominated like that and utterly destroyed by a force more powerful than him.

"Milo!" Nico's voice came a moment before he burst into my room also, then ran to him. "Not here. It can't be here. Pull back. Just for now, I promise."

With another roar, Milo smashed my father's face into the carpet and knocked him out cold.

Then he turned to me, so much pain in his eyes as he looked me over. "Sunshine," he uttered on a broken whisper.

I slumped onto the bed and hunched over, hanging my head. "Jesus Christ," I choked, burying my face in my hands.

The trembling just wouldn't stop.

I felt angry, sick, and ashamed all at the same time.

67

Arms wrapped around me and I heard Milo and Nico's voices like lifelines in the face of the storm that was threatening to drag me into the undertow and away into its black abyss.

━━

"ARE you sure you want to be a part of this?" Milo asked me as we stood outside the abandoned warehouse that Nico had driven us to in his Ferrari. "It's gonna happen either way. Your participation doesn't need to occur for this to end, all right? There's no pressure at all."

He didn't want me to be a part of it. That much was clear.

Before I could answer, Nico strode out from the warehouse.

The blood staining his hands was the first thing I noticed. As he drew closer under the lights beaming down over the parking lot, I saw his face was splattered with it.

He was dressed all in black, but not in his usual stylish way. Just a pair of baggy black jeans and a hoodie on. Milo was also similarly dressed, just wearing black tactical pants instead of jeans. And he'd advised me to come in all black as well. I had my riding leathers on.

"All right, he's ready," Nico told us. He looked at me. "To be clear, you do this and you become complicit, J. It will also bind us together in an irrevocable way. I know you want to be closer to us and you've asked to be part of this side of our lives before, the dark and dirty of it, but you need to know that there's no going back after this. Not just with us, but for you in a very personal way. To Milo and I, you're already joined with us, no matter what. So don't do this for that reason. Honestly, I don't want you doing it at all. But I also understand if you feel like you need to. If that's what you believe you need to purge those demons that the sick bastard in there created in you."

"A compromise would be if you just watched," Milo offered. "Let Nico and I take it."

"I need to see him." It was all I knew right now as the weight of their words took time to be absorbed as I struggled with it.

"Yeah," Nico said. "Follow me."

And I did, with Milo at my side, as we trailed after him into the warehouse.

The place was completely empty of whatever it had been used for before, so I saw my father right away in the center of the large space. He was bound to a chair, the legs which were screwed into the concrete.

Blood stained the path all around him.

His head was bowed, and he was shaking.

I took in his hands that looked... wrong.

"All his fingers are broken," Nico informed me when he saw me looking.

"He used those hands to touch, torment, and hurt you," Milo spat.

As we drew closer, I heard my father wheezing.

"A couple of ribs too," Nico told me.

There was a baseball bat in the corner and Milo strode to it and snatched it up.

Then, as Nico and I stood before my father, Milo swung the bat and clocked my father across the jaw. He let out an ear-splitting scream.

"Broken jaw now too," Milo said, spinning the bat in his hand.

"Son," my dad croaked, barely able to speak. "Help... help me."

"Help you?" Milo scoffed. "Are you fucking kidding me? He's the one who needs help from you. And that's exactly what we're gonna give him. I just walked in on you feeling up your son and choking him out at the same time, fucking threatening him. And all for what? Money? To force his hand there? Or to force yourself and your rule onto him? All of the above, you sick motherfucking demon!"

Nico laid his hand on Milo's shoulder, well aware that Milo didn't lose his temper like this. He was as calm and as collected as they came.

Yet here and now he was barely holding his rage in check, now he'd come face-to-face with my father again.

My heart broke that it was for me. That he was hurting for me.

It wasn't the first time either.

And it had taken a twisted turn and become... sexual... since my eighteenth birthday. Since that very night, actually. Something else he'd ruined for me.

Although I'd tried my best to hide all of it from him and Nico, my father had hurt me too many times to count, and the two of them had seen through my upbeat façade and beneath to the awful truth of it all once or twice.

I knew, I just fucking knew that it would continue on like this for years and years if something wasn't done about it.

If I didn't do something about it.

Moving away and being here at college clearly wasn't enough.

Distance wasn't.

Nothing was.

I was bound to the bastard by blood.

And only one thing could break that link.

Death.

It was the only way I'd ever be free.

He'd brought it here.

I stepped up to him, rage coursing through my veins.

Rage and conviction.

It drowned out all the rest.

It buried the pain, the shame, the grief of the innocent boy that he'd taken from me years ago.

"You're worse than a monster. Everything you've done to me has brought us to this moment. You kept coming, you kept hurting me, kept trying to degrade and humiliate me. You were so desperate to control me and tear me down, so fearful of what I could become, of my potential to completely eclipse you and your success." I shot forward and fisted my hand in his greasy hair. And this time when those eyes connected with mine, I didn't feel fear. For the first time in so long, I saw him for what he was. An abuser. A weak man who got off on victimizing others, on hurting his own son. On using and assaulting his own blood. "It ends here tonight. But before it does, before you go

to your grave, I want you to know that I did beat you. In fact, I destroyed you. It was me who tipped off the SEC when I found out what you'd been up to. You cost dozens of innocents their fucking homes because of your greed, something that the money you wanted from me is rectifying as we speak. And the rest? The rest is building an empire of my own that will transcend yours utterly. So as you perish here tonight, know that the name Carver will rise and belong only to me, will be known only as mine. The mark you think you've made on the world will disappear as though it never was."

"You... fucking..."

I jerked on his hair, growling, "You'll die as nothing."

"Scared... little... boy. That's all... you'll ever... be."

I released him roughly. "You're wrong. Just like you were about so many other things."

He sneered. "No. I've made my... mark on you. It'll remain."

A shudder rolled through me.

Nico snarled.

Milo growled and pulled his gun, taking aim at my father's skull. "Shut the fuck up, you sick piece of shit!"

A twisted smile played on my father's lips as he glared at me. "Broken... boy."

Nico snatched up the baseball bat.

And then it just happened.

Like a switch flipped all of a sudden.

I fucking snapped.

The next thing I knew, I was grabbing the bat from Nico, then sweeping it at my father.

Groans and grunts filled my ears, and it served to egg me on.

I needed more of those sounds of pain, of suffering, of fucking misery.

It called to the same that he'd inflicted on me. Over and over.

I kept swinging, losing myself to it, as his awful words played like a haunted soundtrack.

Until his groans turned to screams, drowning it out, burying it deeper and deeper as blood spewed, bones cracked, and punishment was delivered in its most brutal form.

Mercilessly.

Relentlessly.

Another scream cut through the space and it took me time to realize it was mine as I kept swinging and connecting, even as sweat poured off my body and I started to weaken from the insane level of exertion.

I just kept going and going.

"Sunshine."

That one word reached me through all the rest, the noise from me and swirling around my head.

The care in it, the love, what it truly meant.

That somebody could see who I wanted to be, irrespective of the agony and darkness that threatened to get the best of me day in and day out.

That somebody could see the light that still existed in me.

That light that hadn't yet been snuffed out by Gabriel fucking Carver.

I stilled and looked out at Milo.

An eerie silence filled the space.

Nico had a dark look in his eyes and a sadistic smile spread across his face as he looked at my father hunched over in the chair.

"He's... is he... did I?"

"The motherfucker is dead," Nico confirmed.

"You're... you're sure?"

Nico lifted his chin at Milo, who took the cue and stepped up to my father and pressed his fingers to his throat. He looked out at me. "He's dead, Sunshine."

"It's... it's really over?"

It didn't compute.

A world without my awful father in it? I'd never imagined it possible.

I couldn't believe it.

And it was because of them, the two friends I'd had by my side since high school.

"Thank you," I breathed, as I tried to wrap my head around it all.

Milo came to me and wrapped me up tight. "He'll never hurt you again. No one ever fucking will."

Nico was there then, stroking my hair. "This stays between the three of us."

"It dies with us," Milo said vehemently.

"Absolutely," Nico confirmed. "We've got you, J. Always."

"Always," Milo echoed.

8

~Julian~

I was startled awake, my head snapping to the side, my cheek stinging.

"Finally," a disgruntled voice spoke.

I blinked, trying to clear my vision.

My head was swimming.

I felt... light. And groggy too.

It was a real struggle to wake up properly, to even focus.

I was so fucking tired.

And my body was aching, especially my ribs.

I looked down, seeing a bloodied and bruised display all over them.

My shins were also scraped up pretty badly.

I went to move to get a look at my arms, only to find that I couldn't move them.

I jolted in panic as I took in the sight of my arms pulled high above my head by cuffs fed into chains that were screwed into the ceiling. In my panic, I looked down to see that my ankles were also cuffed to the floor, my legs spread wide.

Hell, I was spread-eagled hanging in the middle of some room, dark red walls surrounding me, a concrete floor beneath my feet.

And I was stark naked.

No. No. No.

The crash... Angelo... had he actually—

I jolted again as he suddenly appeared in front of me.

He grasped my jaw and stared at me, searching my eyes for something.

"Maybe I gave you too many painkillers. I didn't want your injuries being a detriment to what I planned to do with you." He slapped my cheek, making me grunt. "Do you see me, Carver?"

"Yes," I rasped, choking from uttering that one word with an extremely dry throat.

A bottle was shoved into my mouth in the next moment and then I was drinking down a lot of water, swallowing it desperately and choking at the same time, until it poured down my chin and over my bare chest.

It was dragged away, then put down on a black cabinet against a wall just a few feet from me.

I frowned as I was able to take in more of the space as I became a bit more lucid.

There was another set of chains against the wall to my left, a St. Andrew's Cross to my right. A few feet from that was a spanking bench, along with some stocks. I craned my neck to see a round, spongy black bed in the corner.

"What's going on? The crash? Bringing me here? What the fuck are you playing at?" I stared up at the chains, realizing that they were more than that. They were set up as some sort of pulley system, adjustable, fucking heavy-duty bondage restraints. *Jesus.*

"I told you before. Punishment, *tesoro.*"

"I'm not your treasure."

"Hmm. So, you've picked up some Italian from your boys. Then in answer to your question: *ai mali estremi, estremi rimedi.*"

"These are more than drastic measures. You're crossing so many lines here. Have you stopped and thought about that? The ramifications of you causing that crash, then kidnapping us? *Us?* Where is she, where's Cat?"

"Let's just say she's being dealt with."

"No!" I yelled, pulling at my binds. "Let her the fuck go! Don't fucking touch her!"

"I barely laid a hand on her." He smirked nastily. "I'm saving all of that for you." As I continued yelling and pulling at the chains, the clanging echoing painfully through the space, he wrapped his hand around my throat, squeezing hard enough to almost completely cut off my airflow. "Caterina isn't here, so there's nothing you can do. If you don't calm down, I'll sedate you again and you'll be out for hours more. And how will that help anyone? *Or,* you focus on me and I'll release you once I've gotten what I need."

He was telling the truth about letting me go.

And he was also right about the sedation. If I calmed down and remained conscious, I could figure out a way to break from this insanity and track down Cat and break her free, too.

I stopped struggling.

"Good bitch," he said, trailing his fingers over my cheek.

I jerked my head away.

"If you're reacting negatively to that slight touch, what's coming is going to be unbearable for you."

"What are you talking about? Why did you bring me to this room?"

"Why do you think? To make you my little bitch, of

course. Do you remember me telling you that on the road before I had you sedated?"

"Yes. Do you remember me telling you that you're making a big mistake?"

He waved it off, literally, and gestured around the space. "This is part of my new sex club."

"Sex club? This isn't just your own personal BDSM dungeon?"

"No, it's the real deal. Or it will be. This is the only room that's been partially furnished so far. I don't get a lot of time off from my work with Santino, so I do what I can."

"Where is it? Inside the city?"

"The more undeveloped end of the entertainment district."

"So this is your way of exploring all that closeted desire of yours," I mused aloud. "Through intending to provide that outlet for others without actually indulging in it yourself and thereby outing yourself as bi? Santino won't care, you do realize that? There are others in the Family who are—"

He slapped me across the face again.

"That's my business."

"Yet you're clearly intending to make it mine by bringing me here to this room of yours and stringing me up naked."

"I brought you here because you need to be punished. You tried to own me, dominate me. It's your turn to suffer through that now."

"I put you down because you came at me planning to do much worse."

"I did, yeah." He laughed. "Secret's out, huh? You caught my eye the moment you started up *Nocturne*. I've been following you closely on social media for ages. Then you finally put yourself in my path at that business gala. Offered to top me and everything. Mmm, I couldn't stop thinking about it, wanting to get you alone. Then when you hurt me, it all became so clear. What I'd do to you, what we'd explore together, how I'd dominate the fuck out of you."

"You're a Submissive."

"The fuck I am."

"There's nothing wrong with—"

Another fucking slap stung my cheek. "Shut the fuck up with that."

"There's a big difference between being a Dominant and a bully," I warned him.

"Yeah?"

"Yes. It's an exchange of power, not a fucking power grab. You guide and protect your Sub. It requires trust and *consent*. None of that is present here."

"Hmm, you won't give me your consent?"

"No. Now stop this and release me."

He smirked at me. "You look nervous. Can't say I've ever seen that from you before. It can't be the naked thing, you're very comfortable with your body—your social media says it all where that's concerned. Can't be the chains because, again, you're comfortable with that."

"I'm here under duress! What the hell else would it be?" *Jesus Christ Almighty.*

"It's more than that." He pressed his hand to my chest. "Wow, your pulse is racing. You're scared all right. Actually, terrified is more accurate. Because of him, isn't it? Gabriel Carver?"

I froze at his words.

"Yeah, there it is. Right on, huh? I told you, I've been into you for a while. It means I looked into you. Deeply. I know a shitload about it and what happened to you. It's gonna make this so much easier."

"Make what? What exactly is your plan?" I forced out, trying to think of anything except for my father and everything that came along with venturing down that path.

"To break you, of course. *That's* your punishment."

I swallowed hard.

He flicked my nipple hoops in turn, sending unwelcome jolts of sensation through me. "Like I've said, I'm gonna make you my little bitch, Carver." His creepy gaze roamed over me. "Dripping with sex, aren't you?" He ran his hands over my pecs, down to my abs, making me squirm. "This body was made for fucking." His eyes flicked to mine. "Let's say we see just how much it can take."

Wow, all the clichéd dirty shit was coming out now as he was very worryingly getting more turned on by the second. "Let's not."

"No?"

"No," I ground out. "Get your hands off me."

"You're being so rash about this. Are you certain that it wouldn't actually be consensual on your part?"

"Like I said, get your fucking hands off me."

"My hands, huh?" He pushed into me, making me feel his very hard dick through his pants. "How's this instead?" he said, grinding against mine, sending shocks through me that I didn't want to be feeling, especially not in response to something this psychopath was doing to me.

"Get off me."

"Why? I can feel you responding to me."

"It's just a physical reaction."

"Soon that won't be the case." He jerked down his pants and pulled his dick out, then he wrapped his hand around both our lengths, forcing them together, and making me hiss as I felt him skin-to-skin. Then he started jerking us both. "You have such a pretty cock. And all this jewelry… feels fucking amazing," he said, using my piercings for his own pleasure as he ground against them.

I tried to squirm away, but he grabbed my ass with his free hand, dug his nails into my right ass cheek, and used the hold to keep me steady to him.

He picked up his pace, and I squeezed my eyes shut, trying to block it out, trying to block him out.

"No, you don't," he said, his hand leaving my ass and fisting in my hair instead, making my eyes snap back open with the harshness of his grip as he pulled painfully. He held my head steady, forcing me to look into his eyes as he continued jerking our cocks, becoming rougher and harsher with every moment that went by. "No denying it. I want you to know it's me who did this to you. I want you to feel every moment of it and have it ingrained deep down, so you'll never be able to fucking forget that I made you my little bitch."

"Stop this insanity."

"Just getting started… ungh… yeah… that's it… just a little more. Look at you getting so hard for me. That's hot as fuck. Oh, shit… *shit.*"

He yelled out his release, removing his hand and stepping back just in time so he could spray his fucking cum on my cock, coating it all over.

He patted my jaw. Hard. "Good little bitch."

"You'll never survive this. I promise you that."

He fisted my hair again and licked the length of my cheek, sending a shudder through me. "Aww, don't worry, you'll enjoy it. I want you to," he said, as he started stroking my jaw slowly. "I want you to hate that you enjoy it. Given that you're a sex addict, should be easy enough for me to pull that from you. I'm actually surprised you didn't already come, but I guess you just need a whole lot more first." He released me abruptly, then slapped my balls brutally, earning a yell from me. "It will prove impossible for you to resist soon enough. Mmm, yes, you'll break for me so beautifully."

I bucked in the restraints, roaring out into the room.

His laugh rang out. "Excellent start. Fucking perfect."

"Don't fucking do this! Don't!" I found myself screaming.

He ignored it and walked around me, pulling something from his pocket. I heard it rip when he was right behind me, and then something slick touched my asshole. "Did your Daddy play with you here? Is it off the table now? Some Dominants take it up the ass and—"

"Stop! You're taking this way too far. This is beyond settling a score or some fucking punishment. There's no honor in this. None!"

"Honor?" he scoffed. "You've been spending far too much time with Nico Marchetti. That's a useless, idealistic notion. It has no place today or in our world. And, believe me, it will be the death of him if he doesn't get a clue soon."

I grunted as he slid two lubed fingers into my ass. I fisted my hands and squeezed my eyes shut as he twisted, pulled out, then drove deeper, working me open bit by bit.

"Such a hot little ass. Can't wait to fuck it until you scream for me and come all over yourself."

"I'll kill you."

"You won't be saying that soon. You'll be begging me, *tesoro*. Fucking begging and desperate for more of the intense pleasure I can give you."

He curled his fingers right on my sweet spot and I lurched, an involuntary cry escaping me.

"Mmm, right there, huh? How's this?" He zeroed in there, stabbing and curling over and over until my thighs were shaking as the unwanted sensations tore through me.

He reached around and grasped my dick. "Getting there. You're growing harder. You like my stickiness all over you, huh?"

"No," I gritted out.

"Lies. You're about to lose the fight where that's concerned."

He wrenched his fingers out, and I jerked in my binds.

Then he spread my ass cheeks wide and dove in, lashing my hole with his tongue, then eating my ass with his lips, teeth, and wild tongue like a fucking madman, while he started fisting my cock roughly, the sick feel of his cum sliding back and forth along my shaft.

"Fuck," I grunted. "*Fuck.*"

He was pushing me further and further.

He suddenly stabbed his fingers deep and pounded rough and hard and fucking rapid-fire.

And that was it. I came, cursing and spurting all over his hand.

I couldn't swallow down the whimper of shame that bubbled up.

He made it worse when he pulled his fingers free, then came around to my front and gathered all my cum up and started licking his fingers and palm clean in full view of me, making a show of it.

"Yeah, pretty little bitch, that's the stuff. More."

"No more," I groaned.

"*Yes* more. Lots more."

He strode over to the cabinet and took out several vibrators, all different kinds and shapes and sizes.

Smiling at me with disturbing glee, he walked back to me, clipped one to either nipple hoop and turned them on full blast.

The intensity had me gritting my teeth.

He held another vibe up in front of me, one that looked like a cross between that and a cock ring, then he slipped it on over my cock, driving it right down to the base, before then adding another near my crown.

As if that wasn't enough, he finagled one onto my balls, pulling and pinching them in the process, eliciting groans of discomfort from me.

He turned all of them on and I jolted, panting at the torment all over.

It got worse when he showed me the final one he'd grabbed. It looked a lot like anal beads, but there was a hook at one end and the beads weren't really separate, more like one continuous, connected shape. He pointed at the hook. "This will prevent you from being able to push it out." He fired it up, and it buzzed fucking violently.

And then he walked around behind me, spread open one of my ass cheeks, then started pushing it inside. I twisted, but he remained ever creepily patient and kept driving it deeper and deeper until I was jolting as it pushed against my sweet spot while buzzing wildly.

"Fuck!" I cried. "*Fuck!*"

It was one step too far with everything else he'd attached to me, tormenting the hell out of me, so that I was straining, panting and crying out in my binds as his toys ravaged me and sent a flurry of wild pulses of pleasure through me.

He twisted the hook, making me roar as it jostled the whole toy inside me and bore down on my prostate in an overstimulating way I could barely breathe through.

And then he rounded me again, walked to the door and opened it, then carried a metal chair into the room, wherein he slumped down, pulled his cock from his pants and watched me as I endured his crafted torture.

"You're gonna come fucking hard and you'll keep coming over and over. The only way I'll stop it is if you beg me to. But keep in mind that you'll also be begging me to fuck you." He licked his lips, enjoying the sight of me shuddering and trying to fight it. "Until then, come apart for me. I'm gonna relish every moment of this sexy fucking show you're gonna give me."

"Stop, stop this madness."

"Not the right words."

My body twisted almost of its own accord to escape the erotic torture, but Angelo just watched in elation, growing harder by the moment as he got off on my suffering, while the binds held me steady, forcing me to endure it.

Before long, cries and whines were spilling from my lips and my whole body trembled from the overstimulation.

"Yeah, pump those hips. There's my pretty little bitch."

"Argh!" I roared, tugging wildly at the restraints as desperation and too much fear gave way to absolute fury. "Argh! *Argh!*"

9

~Caterina~

I wasn't calm.

That fury I'd unleashed in that garage was just temporarily dormant.

I hadn't let it go.

And I wouldn't.

I needed to be ready to go there again at a moment's notice.

I couldn't bury that monstrous part of me like I had been used to doing. I'd seen it last night, just how much power it had given me.

Not being afraid of it.

Not just accepting it, but relishing it.

The big issue was maintaining control to some extent during it so I didn't hurt the boys like I had Nico earlier. I mean, *shit*, that could have been so much worse that it had been.

There was also the mass amount of energy that it expended *and* me spacing out for a long time afterward. There wouldn't always be the option to do that, or to entertain that kind of exhaustion.

As I was finding out now when it came to the latter aspect.

I staggered into my room, having to stop at the bed and slap my hand down on the mattress as a surge of light-headedness took me over, making me waver on my feet because it was so fucking intense.

That was nothing compared to the nausea that was taking me over.

It became unbearable all too quickly, and impossible to hold back, and then I was staggering into the bathroom, throwing up the toilet seat, and collapsing to my knees a moment before I vomited into the bowl.

Seeing as though I'd barely eaten anything in the last forty-eight hours, it was mostly bile and some nasty dry heaving before I was able to draw in a steady breath without retching again.

Panting, I lifted my head and flushed the toilet, then pushed back to my feet.

Thankfully, the lightheadedness had dissipated, and I was able to make it over to the sink easily enough and then start brushing my teeth.

"Caterina?"

"Milo?"

I stilled just as I was spitting out some toothpaste, which unfortunately set me off again, and then I was rushing to the toilet again and throwing up a whole lot of nothing, just retching violently.

"Goddammit," I heard Milo utter again, as he took over holding my hair back for me, enabling me to brace both hands on the toilet.

When it finally stopped, I lifted my head, but Milo didn't ease back that much and he was actually crouching down in front of me. He stroked my hair gently, worry all over him as he looked me over.

"What's up?" I croaked. "Did one of my alerts go off?"

"Not yet."

My heart sank. "Oh."

"I came in here to tell you I'm making some food and to ask you what you were in the mood for. But given what I just walked in on, that seems to be moot now."

"Food?" I asked, frowning. "I've been snacking on those protein bars and stuff that you've been bringing me while I worked."

"No. You opened one, and that was it. You didn't even take a bite. You've been downing a hell of a lot of cups of coffee, and even a couple of energy drinks that Nico had left in the cupboard from months ago."

"Huh. I guess I wasn't paying attention."

"You were laser-focused. You have been for the last thirty-six hours since we started the search for Julian. You've only left the living room couch to pee. And, worryingly, that was only twice. Not including this time."

"Right," I said, flushing the toilet, then pushing back to my feet. "And I need to get back to it."

He rose with me, shaking his head. "You just hurled. You need to take a beat, rest."

"I can't. Not until we find him."

"You've put everything in place possible. Your system is searching. We've got the Leones and the Marchettis hunting down Angelo as we speak too."

"Yeah, they've been searching for ages, but turned up nothing at any of the locations. I need to do more. I need to—"

The pain all over his face pulled me up short. *Shit.* I reached out and stroked his arm. "I'm sorry."

"No, it's okay."

"I know how much you're hurting. And the longer this goes on—"

"Shh," he said, stroking my hair again with one hand, the other grasping my fingers on his bicep. "You're doing everything you can. We all are. We're closing in around that motherfucker, ruled out a ton of locations now. Nico is going through his wealth of financial transactions, back-tracking the money Angelo has laundered the shit out of through several financial institutions."

"It's a fucking web. Worse, a maze."

"And Nico's great at this sort of thing. He'll crack it. We're just looking at five years' worth of data and move-ment, so it's a lot to go through." He dropped his hands to my hips. "While he does that, everything else is set up with your many alerts should we find anything of substance. Until then, you need to get some sleep. And you need to see a doctor."

"We have other priorities right now, rather than me throwing up."

"I also saw you stagger in here. You were dizzy."

"Yeah, probably a side effect from that shit Angelo shot me up with to knock me out."

"A doctor will be able to determine that. And maybe it's not just physical either."

I cocked an eyebrow.

"Nico mentioned that you might be feeling some guilt over putting those guys down in that garage?"

I pulled away. "I… this isn't the time to get into that."

"I get like that too."

"You do?"

He nodded. "After a brutal takedown, some of the nastier aspects of my work with the Marchetti Syndicate, yeah. I'm not actually a huge fan of the violence of it all. I can bring it when necessary, of course. To protect you, Nico and Julian. And, before things got so bad, also as part of my duty to the Family. But I don't relish it like Nico and Julian."

"Julian? The night we worked together on that take-down, I saw him enjoying the adrenaline rush, but I didn't think he was getting off on the actual brutality of it."

"It's a long story. And it's partly my fault. And Nico's."

"What are you talking about?"

He held up his hand. "Let's just focus on what's going on *here*," he said, gesturing the length of me. "Whenever things have gone further than a beat down and I've actually had to take a life, it's stayed with me. Even when they've deserved it, when it's been justice, or necessary. Even a kill or be killed situation. Even then, it's still had me feeling that way, being haunted by it for a while, by the guilt of it all, remorse creeping up."

"And you think this vomiting could be a reaction to that?"

"It's a possibility. Especially when you haven't had time to process it."

"Nico told you this because he wanted you to come to me about it?"

"Yeah, although not at this particular moment. When we'd found Julian and all hell wasn't breaking loose among the two families with the search for Angelo. But witnessing this, I couldn't hold it off."

I frowned as I took his words in. "Why didn't he just come to me himself?"

"Because Nico doesn't feel that sort of thing… in a conventional way."

"You're saying he doesn't feel guilt and remorse?"

"He compartmentalizes it."

That was an intriguing notion, albeit more than just a little disturbing.

"No, that's not the right way to go about it for you,"

Milo spoke, obviously realizing where my mind was headed.

"How do you—"

"It hurts him, Caterina. It fucking hurts him."

"I—"

"Look, we'll continue this later, once we get you to a doctor. We can rule out the physical and deal with this weight of the rest, the emotional and mental toll that what happened in the garage has taken on you."

"It's not a big deal," I said, walking to the sink and starting to brush my teeth. Again.

"Yeah?" he said. "Is that right?"

I murmured an affirmative response as I continued brushing, getting that nasty taste out of my mouth.

I'd just finished up and turned back around when I watched Milo storming out of the bathroom and back into my bedroom.

Then he bellowed in that deep voice of his that carried through a hell of a lot, "Nico!"

I shook my head in disbelief as I walked into the bedroom. "Seriously? Calling in the big guns?"

"His obsession may have caused me and Julian a lot of worry over the years, but it does have its upsides. And this is one of them. His neurotic need to ensure your wellbeing won't allow you to just blow this off. He won't stand for this."

"Jeez, it's not—"

Nico blew into the room in the next moment, his eyes darting around every which way, on high alert. "What is it? What's happened?"

I shoved my hand through my hair as Milo relayed what had happened, what he'd walked in on.

And then Nico was pointing at my bed. "Get into that bed right now and sleep."

"What? No. I can't. We need to focus on finding Julian."

"That's your final answer?"

I started as that dangerous tone of his came to the surface. "What are you—"

"Is. That. Your. Final. Answer?"

"Yes!" I yelled back at his infuriating question.

"Fine," he muttered.

And then he strode out of the room.

"Where is he going?" I asked Milo.

"No idea." Milo started for the door. "Nico! Nico, what are—"

They collided as Nico returned quickly.

He rounded Milo and then I saw some cuffs in his hands.

"I'm claustrophobic," I reminded him.

"Nice try. Small, confined spaces bother you, but not actually bondage or restraints."

Crap.

I stepped back. "You can't be serious. You are *not* going to—"

He was on me in the next second, gathering me in his arms, then tossing me onto the bed.

I'd barely got my bearings from the shock of it all when he snapped a cuff to my right wrist, then attached it to the headboard.

"Nico, stop!" I yelled, twisting and trying to free myself.

But I didn't get far as his full weight bore down on me and in my current state, I couldn't do much to stop any of it before he'd snapped one to my left wrist too, essentially binding me to the headboard.

He pulled something from his jacket pocket and I found myself looking at what appeared to be a belt from a bathrobe. In the next second, he was tying my ankles to the foot of the bed too.

"Are you fucking kidding me?" I yelled, bucking on the bed.

"Nico," Milo protested. "There's doing what's necessary, then there's blowing right past that into extreme territory."

Nico pushed off me with a growl. "Really? So you think she'll rest without venturing into *extreme territory?*"

"I... maybe not, but—"

"But nothing. She's exhausted, she's sick, she's suffering. And she's in obsessive mode, trying to find Julian, so she can't see anything else. Believe me, I recognize the signs." He eyed me. "You haven't slept for over forty-eight hours. You haven't eaten either. You haven't stopped for a fucking second."

"This is what it's like when you're down to the wire trying to—"

"You were shot up with a heavy-duty sedative. You were nearly gang raped. You were in a motorcycle accident. You took down several big motherfuckers all on your own." He leaned over me. "You. Are. Resting."

"How the hell am I supposed to sleep like this, anyway?"

"You'll be able to. *I* could."

"What?"

"A few times, his *feral* states necessitated it," Milo told me.

Jeez, that was brutal.

It almost had me softening toward Nico.

Almost.

"I swear to fuck, if you leave me like this—"

"You'll what?" he demanded with a snarl, his eyes flashing.

"I'll break your dick off," I snarled right back.

He started, obviously not expecting the challenge, or the animalistic nature of it to rival his.

The corner of his mouth turned up, indicating that he actually liked it.

That was the last thing I wanted. "Let me go, you fucking maniac!"

"We both know how much you worship my dick. You'd never risk that." He stroked my cheek. "Nice try, though."

I jerked my head away. "You're being absolutely insane. This is an extreme overreaction!"

He ignored that and eyed Milo. "Turn the TV on. Not too loud. Just enough where she can focus on that and fall asleep to it. Put that *Merlin* show on that you downloaded for her."

They'd downloaded a show for me?

As Milo set that up, Nico walked into the bathroom, then came back with the small garbage can. He put it down on one of the nightstands. Then he took the chair from the desk and pulled it up to the bed. He gestured at the bucket and told me, "If you feel like you're going to throw up again, let me know. That's what this is for."

"Fuck, Nico. I need to be downstairs working the leads, following the many trails we've identified regarding Angelo."

"You've set everything up. We'll take it from here. I'm almost done untangling the financials. Milo will handle your side of things."

"I can't just sit this out, I can't... I can't... fail."

"Fail?" Milo uttered, after getting the TV show on, and coming to the bed.

"I'm good at what I do. Excellent, in fact. I should've been able to find him and Julian by now."

"He's off the grid, away from any tech, cameras, the

whole nine," Milo reminded me. "You've done everything you can. More than anybody else would actually be capable of."

"We're close," Nico told me. "Because of *you*, Caterina. We'll find him."

But what state would Julian be in by then?

I knew how fucked-up Angelo could be and what he'd done, coming at us in the way he had, setting up the despicable things that he had… it indicated that he'd taken that to another level, that he'd completely lost his fucking mind.

And because of that, the things he could be subjecting Julian to… I could barely even imagine. But what I *could* imagine was bad enough.

I looked out at Milo, seeing his need to focus on the mission of finding Julian and not the other stuff, not what could be happening to him right now.

I doubted he could even bear to hear it.

So, I didn't speak to it.

I sank down in the bed and blew out a breath, murmuring, "Okay."

As ridiculous and overwrought as Nico tying me to the bed to get me to rest was, if I continued to fight it right now, it would only cause more stress and take the two of them away from focusing on the search for Julian.

That was what mattered right now.

It was all that could be allowed to matter.

Besides, maybe I *could* use a little bit of sleep.

I would awake with my mind sharper and maybe that would make the difference in our search.

"I'll call the doctor," Nico told Milo. "Bring me the laptop with the financials on it, then get some rest, too. I'll take the first shift."

When Milo went to argue, Nico held up his hand. "If

anything happens, if any of the alerts Caterina's set up go off, I'll wake you both up. You have my word."

"Okay," Milo agreed, albeit clearly reluctantly. He came to me and planted a soft kiss on my forehead. "Please rest up, *bellezza*. We need you with us. With Julian gone, I can't also worry about—"

"You won't have to. I'll get some sleep, I promise."

"Good. Thank you." He looked out at Nico. "Wake me up, all right?"

"I will."

With that, he took off out of the room.

I turned my head toward Nico, who'd pulled his phone out and was scrolling on it. "Yes?" he asked, feeling my eyes on him.

"I didn't want to upset Milo, but know that you and I are not done with this. Tying me up... we *will* settle up where that's concerned."

He eyed me over his phone. "I wouldn't expect anything less from you." He smirked. "*Wife.*"

"You little fucking—"

He leaned forward and grasped my thigh, startling me. "It was already too close, *principessa.*"

"With Angelo taking me?"

"Yes. His intentions for you too. I can hardly fucking stomach that as it is, and you're home safe now. But you being in danger and almost taken from us entirely... I can't fucking reconcile it, okay? Now hearing that you're unwell... I can't fucking lose you. Do you understand me?"

Before I could get a word out, he squeezed my thigh, but not hard enough to cause me any pain, just to making it clear he was there holding me. His sapphire eyes burned into mine. "These are the extremes I go to for the people I love." Off my stunned look, he said, "That's right, I fucking *love* you, Caterina. I'm undeniably, obsessively, and dangerously in love with you."

"Nico, I—"

He held up his hand. "I don't expect you to say it back or reciprocate. At least, not at this juncture. I mean, I just tied you to a fucking bed after all." He rose to his feet. "But that's where it's at on my end." He gestured at the door. "I'm gonna get a coffee and I'll be right back. Just… please get some sleep, all right?"

I cleared my throat from the emotion that his words had wrought. "Okay," was all I could manage.

And then I watched him walk out.

Holy shit.

10

~Julian~

"I can't lose you. Do you understand me?"

"Julian, it's—"

"I can't. You're my family. The only family I have left."

"I know. It's the same for me."

I opened my eyes, feeling groggy, my head fuzzy and my body as exhausted as it always was every time I woke up here in this place.

Every time I woke up to find myself restrained in some way with Angelo hovering nearby. Sometimes right over me.

Like the last time when I'd awoken to being bound over a spanking bench with a fucking machine pounding into my ass, wherein Angelo had then rubbed his cock all over my face throughout the ordeal until I'd lost control and started licking him. He'd been so elated that I'd finally responded in some way to him that he'd shoved his cock down my throat. That elation had turned even more dangerous when he'd quickly realized that I didn't have a gag reflex, and he'd fucked my throat like a machine, outdoing the actual machine that had been pounding into my ass. He'd come all over my face. And as soon as he'd recovered, he'd done it again. And again. I'd lost count.

I'd actually lost track of a lot, including how long I'd even been here.

This time as I woke up again, I was bound to the circular bed, my arms restrained above my head. My knees were bent to my chest and bound with ropes to either side of the bed, leaving me in a worrying spread open position. Of course, I was naked as usual. All for his sick viewing pleasure.

My throat was sore from all the brutal face-fucking and as I tried to swallow, I ended up coughing. Pain radiated from my ribs at the strain of it and I looked down to see how bad the bruising had become. When I stopped coughing, I realized how straining it was to draw in a full breath, how much it hurt. The damage from the crash was taking its toll. Given that I hadn't been allowed any time to recover, that wasn't too surprising.

I winced as I took in the deep grazes on my shins and thighs bleeding all over the place.

A groan of pain escaped me.

"I'm here," that awful voice rang out, a moment before a hand was thrust in my face with two pills on it.

When I resisted, that familiar slap assaulted my cheek. "Swallow them. Painkillers. I let you sleep longer this time because I had business to attend to. That's why you're feeling those injuries now. The previous doses wore off."

I opened my mouth, and he pushed them along my tongue, then I swallowed them down with some difficulty.

As he stepped back, I watched him shrug off his gray leather jacket, then pull his t-shirt over his head, so he was just down to his jeans. He shoved a hand through his light blond hair as he muttered, "Nico and his accomplices are causing me a load of shit. Keeping off their radar hasn't been easy. Even with me throwing up roadblocks all over the fucking place."

"They won't stop," I rasped. "They'll find me... find you."

"Don't worry your pretty little head about all that. I'm taking care of it."

"How long... how long... have I... been here?"

"A few days."

What?

"Does that surprise you?" he asked, coming right up to the bed and perching on the edge. "Does it feel shorter? Longer?"

"Not sure," I murmured. "But I need... need... hospital."

"You'll feel fine once the painkillers kick in."

"Still be... hurt." I coughed again and grimaced as it put strain on my ribs.

"I'll let you go once I'm sure you'll be drawn back to me. And until you surrender and give me what I want, that can't happen."

"What do... you want?"

He frowned. "You don't remember?"

I shook my head.

The moment I did, I regretted it, the thing swimming, a wave of dizziness taking me over.

I jolted as he pressed his palm to my forehead. "You're burning up."

"Hospital," I pushed.

"Don't overreact. You'll be fine. Just relax."

"No... I—"

He slapped my dick, making me cry out at both the shock and the pain of it.

"Enough." He grasped my shaft hard and my eyes flew to his. "Good. Keep those gorgeous eyes on me. As a reminder, what I want from you is to break you, *tesoro*. I want you begging me, becoming my little bitch through and through. I want you to recognize who owns you and I want you to rejoice in that fact."

I squirmed as he started pulling and pinching my piercings. "Stop."

"Shh. I have a story to tell you. Focus on that while those meds take some time to kick in." He released my shaft then, but it was barely a reprieve as he started trailing his fingers around my asshole. "It wasn't until a couple of years ago that I realized I had a thing for pretty dicks. One night, Santino was on a tear. The rages the guy can get caught up in… I've never seen anything else like it. Anyway, that night, I was in his sights. I was waiting in his office expecting to be given orders on how to fix a certain situation that had been brought to our attention, one that had cost him a lot of coin. Instead, he caught me off guard, pinned me to his desk, then basically shoved his dick down my throat. He held me down too, making damn sure I took it all until he filled me with his cum."

Jesus.

"He hurt… you. Rap—"

"No," he spat. "He helped me, ignited something in me."

"That's not—"

He shoved a finger deep inside my ass, making me grunt.

It turned into a coughing fit, but he didn't pay it any mind, even adding a second finger and pounding into me fiercely.

"Don't tell me how it was. That night changed everything for me. He kept me close to him after that, gave me more power, fucking made me. *And* it ended up bringing you and me together."

That was an extremely worrying and convoluted way of looking at things.

It hit me then, and it all collided. Everything he'd done, everything he'd said. "You wanted.. my… guidance?"

Was that really why he'd been fixated on me? Why he'd really done all of this? In his twisted way, had he actually wanted my help? To teach him how to progress in this area, to help him understand it and this new part of himself that had been awakened?

"Maybe," he admitted, starting to curl his fingers.

It had my abs clenching, my hips rolling of their own accord, which all made me cry out as pain radiated through my side, right where the worst of the bruising was.

"What's the story behind your angel wings tattoo on your back?" he asked, catching me off guard. An obvious attempt to redirect if I'd ever heard one.

"Covering… scars."

"From a belt, right? Being used like a whip?"

I nodded.

"Your old man?"

Another nod.

"You're not over it. That was clear from the way you freaked out when I brought him up on your first night here. You should take a leaf out of my book."

"*You're* not… over it. It tortures you. All this… the abuse… to Cat… to me… it's you… inflicting pain and… sexual domination over others… to purge what happened… to you."

He pulled his fingers free with a growl, his face twisted. "Shut the fuck up. You don't know."

"You wanted… my guidance. This is—"

He pounced on the bed on either side of my bound legs, looming over me, glaring down at me fiercely. "Beg me, Julian. Fucking beg me already. Your ass was clenching down around my fingers, desperate for more, desperate for me."

I was sweating all over. I could literally feel it dripping all over me. And with him on me, my breathing became even more labored. I couldn't even see him clearly despite his face being just inches from mine.

He jostled the bed as he lifted up a little and jerked his jeans off, baring his hard cock.

The rough movements had nausea rising up.

I closed my eyes against it, trying to block it out, to block everything out.

Sleep threatened to take me over really fucking quickly.

That lightheadedness… it surged like crazy.

I was gonna pass out. I was gonna—

Something pushing at my ass had my eyes snapping open.

Through blurry vision, I looked to see Angelo prodding my hole with his dick.

He made me whine as he dragged his fingers through the blood dripping from my legs, then lubed his cock with it.

"All this time and I haven't taken this tight ass yet. Can you fucking believe it?" He kept pushing against my hole, only to pull away.

Every time my eyelids drooped, and I started to fade away, he slapped my cock.

Over and over while teasing my hole mercilessly.

He took it further when he grabbed hold of my shaft and jerked me fiercely, spitting on my crown until his saliva fucking coated me all over.

He drove me to the edge like I had a fuzzy recollection of him doing since I'd been here, ways that kept slamming into me the more he played with me.

Again and again he brought me right to the brink of coming before he'd abruptly stop.

It just wouldn't end.

He wouldn't fucking tire of pushing and pushing me.

My body was reeling, pain radiating through me. I felt sick and like I was on fucking fire with how overheated I was.

"Please."

That one word hung there in the air between us.

It took me a few moments to realize it had come from me.

Angelo fisted my hair and jerked my head at an uncomfortable angle that almost had me retching right then. "Say it. Say it again."

"Please... do it... fuck me... fuck me now."

An animalistic rumble came from him as he released my hair, then slammed his hands down on my pecs a second before he slammed into my ass, his cock tearing into me and making me choke from the force of it.

"Fucking shit, yeah!" he yelled in rapture. "Way better than I even fantasized! Fuck *me!*"

I couldn't take it.

His cock reaming me so fucking maniacally, igniting pleasure so intense I couldn't handle it in my current state.

The heat setting my body on fire in the worst ways.

And that fucking nausea and lightheadedness.

I choked, fighting for breath.

And then it all disappeared.

Blackness took me.

~Nico~

"I've got something."

Milo spat out his mouthful of eggs and literally vaulted across the kitchen island and landed right beside me where I was standing working on the laptop while we'd been eating lunch.

"What is it?" he asked, his urgency not contained in the least.

He wasn't the only one.

Since this had started, I'd been in a perpetual state of stress, my body coursing with so much adrenaline that my fucking limbs were shaking with it. That had only worsened when Caterina had thrown up and shown signs of sickness caused by it all.

And the fact that the Manor was now surrounded by security personnel. Marchetti soldiers of my father's. He'd put that in place last night with Angelo still not being located, in a bid to protect Caterina from being taken again.

Or so he'd said.

Really, I believed it to be his attempt to appease me, so

I didn't lose my shit all over the place and fuck up his stupidly valued alliance with Santino. The fact that neither he nor Leo had shown up at my door bolstered my theory even more. They hadn't wanted me antagonized, so he'd sent his soldiers without interfering in my *marriage* or my household in any other way. It also wasn't really about protecting my wife. It was to make it difficult for me to make any moves on my own to hunt down Angelo directly, moves he definitely didn't want me making.

I felt like all of it was boxing me in, like I couldn't fucking breathe through it.

Something had to give.

And the worst part for all of us was that I already knew exactly what that needed to be.

"These three payments you've highlighted? Is that what you're getting at?" Milo asked me.

"Yes. After not finding anything recent, I went back further. Two years further."

"You went through two years' worth of data in a matter of hours?" he asked, incredulous.

"I did."

"Damn, you've outdone yourself this time."

"Anyway, that was when I found these. In one month, Angelo made three large payments, each exceeding one hundred grand."

"To three different entities, though, according to this," he said, eyeing the data.

"So it seemed initially. These are shell corporations. They all belong to one individual."

"He made a mistake. He should have funneled it through more, gone through another level."

"He obviously got impatient."

"And who is this individual?"

"Victoria Munsen."

"That slumlord?"

I nodded. "The slumlord that Caterina hates with a vengeance."

"She had a couple of run-ins with her, right?"

"Victoria crossed a handful of the women who frequent Caterina's lounges, trying to intimidate them and tear them down so she didn't have to entertain competition in the real estate sector. Caterina put a stop to it and even built a case against her that put her behind bars for eighteen months."

"This sounds promising. Somebody who hates Caterina, just like Angelo. Victoria has a whole network of contacts through the underbelly of the city that even the three families haven't been able to ID. She could be helping Angelo to stay hidden. And judging by these payments, he may have even bought property from her that he's now using to hold Julian in."

"That house where Angelo took Caterina was one of hers. I just confirmed it before bringing this to you."

"Fuck, this is it then! Let's go!" he pushed away from me, but I grasped his arm, yanking him back.

"Get a grip. Focus. There are a dozen soldiers outside. Also, we don't know where Victoria is, nor where the property is."

"I can help with that."

We both looked to see Caterina now walking into the kitchen. "When did you untie me?"

"Five minutes after you fell asleep."

"So it was just for show?"

"Just to get you to rest, yeah."

"And the doctor? Did she come and check me out and find everything was fine, that I just needed some sleep like I said?"

"I decided to wait until you were awake before I

brought her in. I didn't want you to feel violated from being examined while you were unconscious."

"Really? As insane as you were being about it?"

"Yes, really."

She smiled.

And then she stared at me rather intensely.

Likely because of what I'd said earlier.

Or, more accurately, confessed.

Fuck, it had been the worst time for it.

While all of this was going on.

It had just… I'd put it out there in a bid to make her understand why I was doing the things I was, why I was being so *extreme.* I'd fucking weaponized it and I hated that I'd done that. I hated that nothing was sacred, that I couldn't give her anything that wasn't tainted by the world around us, by our mission, by all of it.

Even that.

I broke eye contact.

She looked a little dejected, but instead of speaking to it, thankfully, she snapped into action and came to us, moving in front of the laptop and getting to work.

In moments, she was inside Victoria's phone. Actually, phones, plural.

Off our looks, she told us, "I've tapped into her shit before."

She started bringing up more data, accessing files, deeds, legal documents. I watched her cross-referencing it with what I'd put together from Angelo's accounts, the amounts, the dates, all of it.

While she was working on that, all of our phones buzzed.

I pulled mine out quickly to see that it was one of the alerts that she'd set up.

"Damn, you did it," Milo told her.

She sure had. Her search had just picked up the one guy who'd survived her massacre, the guy who'd been involved in Angelo's kidnapping.

"We've got the location of one of Angelo's accomplices," I told her.

"Where?" she asked distractedly as she focused on what she was doing.

"Tolhurst General," I informed her.

She started, then told us, "Hold on."

I watched as she hacked into the security system at the hospital within moments.

"Damn," Milo exclaimed.

"Got him," she said. "There."

We both looked to see the guy still wearing that fucking balaclava and baggy clothing bursting into a supply area deep down the corridors of the hospital, grabbing medication and supplies.

"What's he taking?" I asked Milo, who was much more familiar with that sort of thing.

"It's hard to see. The footage isn't exactly high-res."

"I can try to scan the barcodes, but it will take time," Caterina offered. "Especially if I just get pieces of them from the grainy footage."

"It doesn't matter. It's got to be for Julian. He would've been hurt coming off his bike like that," I said.

"If Angelo's risking sending his guy into a fucking hospital, it must be really fucking bad. He must be getting worse," Milo choked.

"And Angelo cares about that?" Caterina questioned, and rightly so.

"It's Julian. Charismatic and majorly popular. Angelo must have taken a real liking to him," Milo said.

Caterina and I exchanged a look. That wasn't actually a good thing. Not where Angelo Simone was concerned.

"He'll want to keep him, won't he?" Milo asked, unfortunately realizing what we were. "He could be planning to move him out of the city. This guy he's got doing his bidding works for that sex slave buyer, a son of a bitch who knows how to hide and how to make others disappear into the ozone. Fuck, if we don't get him now, it's gonna be too late. We'll never get Julian back."

Caterina brought up the Victoria-related data again, frantically working to determine the location we needed.

After a few moments, she was cursing. "I've got two properties. Bought at the same time. Both hers. Both are outside the city at either end. We need to cover both. We don't know how much time we have. Interrogating Victoria might be fruitless. She won't be easy to break *and* she might not even know which one Angelo is at currently, anyway. It could just waste away time that we don't have."

"Simple. We tail the guy back to Angelo," Milo said.

"What if they aren't slated to meet at the location where Angelo is holding Julian?" I pointed out.

"Torturing the true location out of Angelo will be impossible, believe me," Caterina informed us.

"Goddammit!" Milo roared, slamming his fist into the counter and making one hell of a dent in the process.

"What about using your father here?" Caterina asked me.

"I can't trust his intentions."

"Agreed," Milo grunted. "We can't trust anyone with this but the three of us. Everyone else has their own agendas." He eyed me. "Yes, including Carlo."

"Carlo? What does he have to do with it?" Caterina asked.

I glared at Milo. But I left it at that, knowing what a state he was in and that it couldn't be helped currently.

"Once we bring Julian back, I'll explain it," I told Caterina.

Fortunately, she accepted that, recognized that we needed to prioritize. *Fuck*, she was amazing. Truly fucking amazing. I knew how much she hated being kept in the dark, but here she was willing to suck that up so we could focus on this.

It was why, as much as it was against my protective instincts when it came to her, I asked her, "How are you feeling? Are you combat-ready now you've had some much-needed rest?"

"Yes."

"Swear it to me."

"I swear it," she said, slapping her hand to her heart. "I feel wide awake and much better. There's no nausea or even dizziness." She looked out at both of us. "I wouldn't risk Julian by going into this situation if I didn't feel up to it."

"Fine," I said. I pushed back from the laptop. "Milo, you tail Angelo's guy. Caterina and I will split between the two locations. We'll go in with COMMs under continuous contact. *No* one break from that, am I clear?"

"Rules of engagement?" Milo asked.

I stared out at them both.

I was done with this.

I was fucking done playing the game, toeing the line.

Hiding what we were truly capable of.

Toning everything down to the max.

Look what it had cost us.

Look what we'd almost lost—and still stood to lose all the while Julian was being held captive.

I sucked in a breath, then uttered a command that I knew would shift everything. "Decimate."

12

~Caterina~

I tapped my earpiece as another transmission came through.

A moment later, Milo's voice sounded in my ear, while I drove like a crazy person through the city streets in my Lambo.

"Hostile's not meeting with Angelo. At the strip mall on West-wood and Garde. A transport truck just pulled up. Two guys got out and greeted him. They're now loading the supplies the hostile stole."

Nico's voice was next. *"Sounds like they are planning on moving Julian tonight."*

"I'm gonna move in and beat some answers out of them."

"Authorized."

Even if he didn't get anything out of them, which was very likely, it would at least give Milo a much-needed release.

He was really on edge. To be expected given what was at stake here. But it could be problematic if he wasn't given an outlet—which he now had in those guys. When we'd been strategizing how to sneak out of the Manor without Marco's security realizing, Milo's only plan had been to run right through them and put them all down. Fortunately, Nico and I had managed to talk him down, but the fact that it had been a plan of his at all was the worrying thing. He was usually the cautious and careful one all about protecting and safeguarding, not going on the offensive and pulling some insane shit like that.

We'd get Julian back tonight, and it would put an end to that for him.

It would calm him. Hell, it would calm all of us.

"Arriving at Site B now," I reported down the line.

No response came from Milo, obviously because he was busy laying into those assholes at the strip mall.

But I heard Nico's voice a moment later.

"Proceed with caution. But if you come across our target, let loose, principessa."

"Believe me, I will."

"There's our woman."

I smiled to myself.

As much as he'd been worried about me unleashing in that garage, he also knew that it was the best way for me to protect myself. The fact that we'd all split up to do this wasn't sitting well with him, especially after how worried he'd been about the garage situation and then me getting sick. But there hadn't been much of a choice. We were all needed to cover different areas if we stood any chance of being able to stop Angelo from stealing Julian away.

It was a desperate situation.

I pulled my car over on the dirt road just a few blocks from the designated location.

I hurried out, pulling my gun as I went, then approached the lone three-story house with the red roof. It was down by Brimbank Waterfront, of all places, right on the edge. No one and nothing else around for several blocks, fortunately. I didn't have to worry about having my gun out in plain sight.

I headed for the rear, vaulting over a dilapidated fence and landing in a backyard with overgrown grass and dead plants. A floodlight guided the way through the dark night just enough for me to locate the backdoor. There was no basement, just a crawl space. But that still left me with three floors to cover. Yeah, this situation really wasn't ideal.

I tried the door carefully, finding it locked as pretty much expected.

Pulling out my lock pick set, I made quick work of it, then opened it slowly, readying my gun.

No sign of any hostiles.

I stepped inside, finding myself in a large open space with a scuffed hardwood floor that had seen better days, along with two walls that had been torn down, revealing big gaps through the rest of the area. I walked through a makeshift arch and found myself in a wide corridor with closed doors on either side, listening carefully as I went.

Muffled sounds reached me, sending a surge of adrenaline flooding through my system.

I followed them to the first closed door on the left.

Taking a centering breath, I kicked it open and burst in, ready to clear the room, only to find it empty.

Well, of people.

I'd walked into a surveillance area.

The equipment looked brand new and as I peered closer; I saw that it was actually state-of-the-art and it really stood out from the rest of the place that I'd observed so far.

Hmm. The place was being renovated, not just in the process of being torn down, as the state of those walls had suggested.

This was one of the first rooms to get the renovation treatment.

I walked to the monitors, finding them observing different rooms inside the house. Most were empty.

But then I saw one decked out like a BDSM dungeon, somewhat similar to a few of the rooms at *Nocturne.*

My breath caught in my throat as I took in Angelo stalking around a black bed where somebody was bound naked.

I peered closer and nearly vomited when I identified the person as Julian.

"Oh my God," I breathed.

He was shaking his head from side-to-side and writhing in clear pain on the bed.

I found the volume button and turned it up enough to hear what was actually going on.

"Please, just stop. I can't... I can't take another second."

"You begged me to fuck that sweet ass. And, hell, did I make you come. I'm still wearing it all over me."

"To end... this. It's done... just... stop."

Angelo lunged forward and wrapped his hand around Julian's throat. *"You were playing me? After all we've done together? After how you melted for me? I'm getting you medication and treatment tonight and this is how you repay me? You are fucking mine. That isn't changing. Just for that, you're gonna take me raw. I'll show you how much you belong to me, tear through all this denial bullshit."*

I cursed, then stepped back.

I couldn't tell which room they were in. It could be any of them.

A creak sounded, and I just managed to activate the panic button beneath my ring and spin around in time as one of Angelo's masked men lunged at me.

I kicked him back and as he fell into the control panel, an idea occurred to me.

So, when he came at me, I pretended to lose my grip on my gun, and I let him drive me into the wall. He snatched the gun up and shoved it against my temple.

"I know who you are," he told me. "The boss is gonna want to deal with you personally."

Excellent. Plan progressing nicely.

I let him drag me out of the room and down the hallway, shoving me every few steps, then jamming the gun into my back to make it clear it was still there and very much a threat.

He grabbed my arm and hauled me up a set of dirtied carpeted stairs to the second floor, down another corridor, until we came to the room at the far end straight ahead.

There was a keypad door lock and I took in the code as he typed it in all too slowly.

The door chirped open, a hefty steel thing, before the guy threw me inside, and I landed on my knees, before he then shoved the gun to my temple again.

I rapidly took in the room, the same space I'd seen on the monitor.

"What the fuck is this?" Angelo yelled, pushing off the bed and storming toward me, glaring at his guy. "Why—what—how is she here?"

"I told you I got word that she escaped the others and now I just caught her trying to sneak in. No idea how she knew to come here, but I figured you'd want to deal with her."

I saw Julian register me. Although, only just. His eyes were glazed, and he seemed barely lucid as he frowned out at me, like he wasn't sure I was actually real. *Shit.*

Angelo came to me and yanked on my hair, forcing my gaze to his.

"Came to play too, did you, Caterina?"

When I didn't answer, he slapped me across the face—one of his signature moves. I grunted as my head snapped to the side and I tasted blood on my lips.

"No!" Julian cried weakly. "Leave… leave her."

"She just broke into my place!" Angelo called over his shoulder. He yanked on my hair harder, ripping out strands in the process. "And how did you? How did you know I was here? *Tell me*, whore!"

"I know a lot more than you think."

Worry flitted across his features, and he looked wonderfully creeped out by my eerie response. *Good. Fucking good.*

He stared at me in black tactical gear, the empty holster at my right hip. "Is that hers?" he asked his guy regarding the gun he had trained on me.

"Yeah. Bitch couldn't keep hold of it for long, though."

Angelo frowned.

"Hmm. Are you bait, Caterina? Did your husband send you in here as a sacrificial lamb to get his longtime best buddy out of here?" He laughed. "Wow, I guess he is doing his job of punishing you, then, after all. Let's take that up a notch, shall we?"

In the next second, he used his hold in my hair to yank me to my feet.

He gestured around the room. "What would you like to start with? I'm partial to watching that fucking machine tear your cunt apart. Or maybe I'll tie you to that spanking bench and beat your little ass until it's bloody as you cry and beg for the punishment to end? Hmm, so many amazing choices." He grabbed himself through his jeans obscenely. "Just the thought of it is getting me hard, and that's really saying something, seeing as though I only just finished up fucking my little bitch over there not ten minutes ago." He gestured at Julian. "You see him wearing my cum so nicely? All over his pretty cock? Dripping from his well-used ass?"

I shuddered and had to look away so I didn't lose focus. So emotion didn't get the best of me.

"You're a monster," I hissed.

"Don't worry, he enjoyed it." He lifted his shirt and gestured at the cum stains all over his abs. "See? He was pleasured a hell of a lot during his time here." He eyed Julian over his shoulder. "And that's what you'll remember, isn't it, my pretty cock slut? Just how much everything I did to you got you off. How much you really relished it while merely playing the unwilling one. You fucking wanted it, wanted *me*."

Rage burned through me at his poisonous words, his clear attempt to recondition Julian into actually buying that disturbing bullshit.

A growl reverberated low in my throat, building and building as my fists clenched white-hot.

Angelo's eyes widened.

The guy with the gun trained on me shifted his weight, unsure.

And that was all I needed.

I spun to the side, snagged his wrist, and dislodged the weapon with two rapid-fire moves. As he fell back, I pistol-whipped him across the side of the head, then fired off a shot right through his throat.

"Fuck!" Angelo yelled in a mixture of shock and indignation.

He was there in the next second, jumping on my back as I watched his accomplice slide down the wall, dying right there as blood spewed from his destroyed artery.

I forced his weight back against the wall, slamming him in the process, and he grunted as his back jarred painfully into the drywall. He had hold of my gun, preventing me from firing or moving my arm at all. His other was wrapped around my throat trying to choke me out.

Julian was tugging frantically at his restraints, freaking out and in severe distress.

"Fucking cunt!" Angelo roared.

I dug my nails into his arm that was wrapped around my throat and he hissed, loosening his grip a little. But not enough.

"The only *cunt* here is you!" I wrenched at his knee with my boot and it destabilized him enough for me to take advantage of it, rip his arm from around my neck, and then spin into him.

He yanked my gun from my grip at the last second, but I managed to kick it out of his hand before he could turn it against me. It ended up sailing right across the room.

It didn't matter.

I didn't need a weapon to take the fucker down.

I *was* the weapon.

Something he was about to discover for the first time.

In a very painful way.

"You're not going to ruin this for me like you ruined things before by turning down my marriage proposal!" he yelled, before lunging at me.

I spun into a kick that clocked him across the jaw and sent him reeling back, crashing into a set of stocks. As he grabbed at the apparatus to maintain his balance, I came up behind him, fisted his hair, and smashed his face into the wood. He spluttered as blood sprayed from a clearly broken nose.

He thrust his elbow back, clocking me underneath my jaw, making my head snap back and causing me to stagger a little.

It was all he needed to grab hold of me and toss me into a black cabinet over by the door.

I caught sight of a set of keys there. Likely to Julian's binds.

I swallowed down the pain, adrenaline, and that monstrous blood-lusting side of me helped me out with that in a big way. And, as he came at me, I snatched up a whip, spun and cracked it across his fucking face with all my strength.

He screamed as it tore into his cheek, blood spewing.

I was there in the next second, ripping his legs out from under him and taking him down to the floor. I slammed his head against the floor over and over, disorien-tating him.

As he tried to snag hold of me, I drew a knife from my ankle holster, spun, and drove it into his right hand, stab-bing all the way through it and into the floor below.

He shrieked like the little bitch that *he* was and writhed beneath me in utter agony.

It called to my bloodlust like nothing else.

But before I could satiate it, footsteps rushing down the corridor outside caught my attention.

Shit.

I kicked Angelo in the face, knocking him out cold, then I ran to the cabinet and snatched up the keys.

I bolted over to Julian and rapidly undid the cuffs binding him to the bed, doing everything I could not to look directly at him while he was in such an awful state.

"It's okay. It's over now. I'm gonna get you out of here."

"Cat," he uttered weakly, reaching out for me and touching my cheek. "Go. Run."

"No, I'm not leaving you."

Sobs sounded from him and I lost the battle with trying not to make direct eye contact or take in the state of him.

There he was lying there in so much pain, bruised and

cut, covered in Angelo's... fluids, and he was crying, tears streaming down his cheeks.

The door flew open, making me swing my head around to see four guys with balaclavas barreling in. I rapidly calculated my chance of making it to my gun in time.

It didn't bode well.

The sight of Angelo sprawled out unconscious on the floor pulled them up short for a few seconds.

I pushed away from Julian and strode to them, ready to let myself go completely and utterly decimate them.

But then a ferocious roar rang out, drawing their attention as well as mine.

In the next second, Milo hurtled into the room.

His gaze darted to Julian briefly, and then his eyes turned utterly black.

"Motherfuckers!" he bellowed, before running at the guys and tearing into them viciously.

Within moments, screams, bones cracking, and even begging filled the space as he went apeshit all over them.

Another three burst into the room and I ran back into the fight, beating them back and keeping them away from descending on Milo.

It all became a blur of undiluted violence and brutality as each hostile melded into the other, everything coming hard and fast, and my reactions coming faster than that as I was in the throes of my monstrous state.

I slammed one of them up against a wall, then literally ripped them apart with my blade, tearing them open and savoring their shrieks as it called to the power I had over them, over their fucking disgusting lives.

I sensed another coming at me and I spun, snagged the guy's arm, then wrenched it, dislocating his shoulder and making him scream for me.

I used the hold to swing him around and haul him into the black cabinet.

As he crashed into it, I was there, wrapping both hands around his throat and choking the life out of him, the monster in me desperate to see the light drain from his eyes as I stole it away like a fucking dark god.

But a shot rang out before I could accomplish it, blowing the guy's skull apart.

I jolted and looked out to see Julian standing there, grabbing onto the wall to steady himself. He fired a bullet off to the side of me and I saw it kill the guy I'd shredded open in an instant, too.

"It's over," he rasped. His gaze darted to Milo, who was literally tossing an already dead guy across the room. The guy crashed into the St. Andrew's cross and decimated the thing at the impact. "Milo... stop. *Stop.*"

Milo jolted at the sound of Julian's voice and swung toward him.

Julian wavered, dropping the gun, and collapsing onto the ground.

"Fuck!" Milo cried, rushing to him just as I did.

He ran his hands over the stark bruising around Julian's ribs, particularly on one side. "Internal bleeding," he told me. "It looks like internal bleeding."

"Oh my God."

"Contact Nico. Tell him I'm taking Julian to the hospital right fucking now."

"All right, yeah," I said, reaching up to tap my earpiece to do just that, until I noticed something missing from the mess we'd made of the hostiles.

"Angelo's not here," I told Milo.

"What?" he grunted as he lifted Julian into his arms carefully and rose to his feet with his unconscious form cradled against him.

"He's gone. He must have escaped during the chaos of the battle." I gestured at Julian. "Get him to the ER immediately. I'll go after Angelo."

"No," Milo rumbled. "We tend to Julian. The rest comes after."

I stared out at him there in Milo's arms.

So pained.

So beaten down.

So gaunt and near lifeless.

I swallowed hard, trying to choke back the emotion that threatened to get the best of me now.

"We've got him," Milo told me, seeing my distress, even as he tried to hide his own.

I reached out and stroked Julian's hair. "He's coming home."

That was what mattered.

Milo was right, the rest would come later.

13

~Emilio~

He'd almost fucking died.

That psychopath had been so fucking focused on breaking Julian that he hadn't noticed the symptoms. He should have at least registered the progression of them.

The doctor had said that any longer and the damage would have been fatal.

Julian had been suffering from internal bleeding caused by a ruptured spleen. Trauma he'd sustained from the crash. The deep scrapes on his legs had been infected as well. He'd even suffered damage from Angelo's repeated sexual assault.

The good news was it would all heal.

He *would* be okay.

At least physically.

Caterina had hacked into the surveillance system she'd found there and shown Nico and me the footage of what precisely had happened, what that sick fucker had done to Julian, and to say it had been horrific didn't cover it.

It had made me sick to my stomach.

He'd already survived that sort of thing in his life

before. For so many years. And now it had happened all over again. He'd been subjected to that disgusting torment yet again.

The urge to put every ounce of my focus and strength into hunting down that motherfucker and ripping him to shreds was a living, breathing thing inside me.

But I couldn't… I couldn't leave my Sunshine's side.

He needed me more than *I* needed to avenge him right now.

That wasn't to say that nothing was being done about it.

Caterina and Nico were using their specific skills to hunt the fuck.

They'd find him.

And then we'd destroy him.

The fact he'd slipped from our fingers had been nagging at me since the moment I'd watched the hospital staff rush Julian away into emergency surgery.

He'd been right fucking there! Right there!

I'd lost control. It was how he'd been able to escape. I'd been caught up in the violence, dealing out punishment on those who'd been complicit *and* about to hurt Caterina when I'd walked into that dungeon.

I'd expected Caterina to lose it. Nico had basically sanctioned it, because he believed that was when she was her strongest and the best combatant she could be.

But I was different. I wasn't supposed to lose control. I *was* control.

Steadfast.

Rational.

Dependable.

But the moment I'd seen Julian lying there like that… *dammit*, I'd snapped.

My phone buzzed in my pocket and I looked away

from staring at Julian unconscious in the hospital bed as I pulled it out and took in a text message from Nico.

He and Caterina had stayed until Julian had been brought in here after surgery, and then Nico had led her off to get her seen to by a doctor as well.

Nico: She's being seen right now.

Milo: Good. It will give us all peace of mind there.

Nico: She kicked me out, making me wait outside the exam room. Should I go in any way?

The corner of my mouth turned up. The fact that he was asking me and being so unusually vulnerable about it really showed how much he wanted to do what was right for her now, not just what felt right to him from his obsession standpoint when it came to her.

Her and Julian being taken had shifted something in him.

Hell, it had shifted something in all of us.

Milo: Give her the space she's asking for. But you can text her after another few minutes just to check in.

Nico: Sounds good. Is J awake yet?

I was about to text back a *no*, but then I saw his fingers twitch.

Milo: Waking up now.

I pocketed my phone and watched carefully as Julian's striking hazel eyes locked onto me, a little glazed, as he tiredly tried to make sense of what was going on.

"You're okay. You're at the hospital and you're going to be absolutely fine," I told him quickly.

I grasped his hand in a gesture of comfort, but he flinched and an awful cry escaped him.

I released him instantly. "Fuck, I'm sorry."

Tears welled in his eyes and he squeezed them shut, pain blanketing his features.

It was absolutely brutal to witness.

His agony was so acute, so distressing.

What he'd been through… I couldn't… I just *couldn't*.

But I *had* to.

I had to handle it.

For his sake.

"You're safe here with us now, Sunshine," I told him softly. "It's over. It's all over."

He trembled as he brought his hand to his face, trying to get a handle on his emotion.

"You don't need to hide it. I'm here."

"I… I don't want to… feel it," he told me through his sobs.

"I know. I know you don't."

Several moments passed where he held his hand to his face, crying, his whole body trembling with it.

The urge to reach out to comfort him was overwhelming and so ingrained in me that I had to dig my nails into the seat of the chair to prevent myself from doing it. He'd already shown that he couldn't stand to be touched right now. I wouldn't fuck up again where that was concerned.

He brought his hand down onto the covers, revealing his blotchy face and red eyes from crying. "Is—I mean—am I… damaged? Physically?"

"No. No, you'll be sore for a while, but you'll heal perfectly well there," I told him, knowing what he was getting at.

"Everywhere?"

"Yes, I promise. Is it causing you pain right now?"

"A little."

"If you let me, I can shift you so you're not pressing down where it hurts. But we need to be careful because you just had surgery for a ruptured spleen."

"Jesus." He looked out at me and swallowed hard. "Okay," he murmured. "Can you... move me?"

"Of course." I rose to my feet and his eyes widened. *Dammit.* Before I reached out, I told him, "Look at me. Keep focusing on my face, don't look away."

"Okay," he murmured again.

I carefully grabbed hold of him, feeling him shuddering as I did, and I managed to shift him into what would be a more comfortable position. As soon as I was done, I released him immediately and sat back down. "How's that?"

"Better. Thanks."

"No worries."

His eyes darted around for a bit as he took everything in. And then he asked me, "Is Cat okay? I thought I saw him hurt her? Strangling her?"

"That was part of what happened, but she overpowered him afterward. Then I showed up. You actually helped and took out some of his guys."

He stared at me blankly. "Really? I don't remember doing that."

"To be expected, it was right before you passed out."

"So, he's... he's dead?"

"He will be."

"He got away?"

I nodded. "I'm sorry. But you don't need to worry. You're safe with us now. We'll find him. You can count on that."

As I reassured him, he didn't actually seem that concerned about it, nor scared that the man who'd hurt him so much was still alive and out there somewhere.

What was happening?

Maybe it was because *he* wanted to be the one to end Angelo? Was he relieved that he wasn't dead so that *he* could exact vengeance on him? Like he had with his father all those years ago?

I knew one thing. Now really wasn't the time to ask any of that.

I heard a commotion outside in the corridor, and Nico's deep voice carried to me.

I smiled at Julian, not wanting to alarm him or bring any negativity to him. "I'll be right back. Just a couple of seconds, okay?"

"Okay," he murmured in a very worn down way again.

I grimaced internally, then opened the door and stepped out.

It didn't take me more than a few seconds to locate the source of the commotion just a little way down the corridor.

There Nico and Caterina were arguing back and forth.

She slammed her fist into the wall as she yelled at him, "Will you just let it the fuck go? For *once*, you stubborn, over-the-top, suffocating bastard!"

Whoa.

"Suffocating?" he bit back at her.

"Is that the only thing you heard?"

"I heard it all. That was the concerning aspect."

"What?" she asked exasperatedly.

"Is that how you really feel? That I'm suffocating you?"

"Right now, yes. Obviously."

"What's going on?" I asked, cutting into their argument. "I could hear you from inside Julian's room."

"Sorry," Caterina offered right away. "Nico just set me off."

"Me? You were the one who burst out of the exam room before the doctor even took your blood and finished your exam."

"You texted me that Julian is awake. I wanted to see him."

"You could have waited a little longer. Milo was with him, he wasn't alone, and he never will be again."

"You say such heart-melting things like that, yet you can also be such an infuriating fucker," she told him. "Talk about a walking contradiction."

Nico fisted his hands down at his sides. "Fuck, *wife*, you're really pushing my buttons." His eyes flashed at her. "But you already know that, don't you?"

"I just want you to back off. The doctor said I was dehydrated, that I needed to eat, and that I needed some more sleep. Simple as that. I'm fine. So, please, for the love of crap, let it go now." She flashed her eyes right back at him. "*Husband.*"

Oh fuck.

He stepped into her and pushed her against the wall with his hips. Looming over her, he growled, "Careful, I'm seconds away from fucking you into submission right against this corridor in full view of everybody. Do you want them all to see you spread open at my mercy as I fill your glorious cunt with my big dick and punish the fuck out of you?"

She stared up at him, meeting his challenge head on. "Please, you won't allow anybody outside of our foursome to see me in that sexual state. And you also don't like my submission." She grinned at him. "Not one little bit."

He snarled, then kissed her forehead and drew back. "Well played."

She smirked. "I thought so."

"Go see Julian. But once he's settled back at the house, you *will* let my doctor come to see you at home and run the tests you missed here. Make me that deal and I'll let it go."

"That's not exactly letting it go."

"It's the best you're gonna get," I warned her.

She rolled her eyes, but told him, "Deal."

"Now that's sorted, I need you both to tone it down majorly before you go in there. And do not, under any circumstances, touch him. Not even holding his hand," I told them.

"Okay," Caterina murmured, pain playing on her features.

Nico scrubbed his hand over his face, then gave a nod.

We headed back into the room, Nico and Caterina following after me to find Julian scanning the room intensely.

"What's wrong?" I asked.

"My phone. I need my phone."

"It was crushed during the crash," Nico told him. "We'll get you another one by tomorrow morning."

"No. I need—I can't be without it. Lying here in this bed, in this room, nothing to focus on except—I can't... I fucking *can't!*" He grabbed the IV about to pull it out, but Caterina called out, "Stop, it's okay! Here, sweetheart." She walked to him then and pulled a phone out of the inner pocket of her turquoise leather jacket, telling him, "I cloned your old one. Everything is on here as you like it. It's not the same snazzy cobalt-blue glittering case, but that can easily be remedied." Off our startled looks, she explained, "He told me how it is with him and his social media stuff, so I figured once we found him, he'd need it."

Julian beamed out at her. "Thank you, Cat. Thank you so much."

She smiled at him. "This is what it means to be mine."

Nico and I exchanged a look at her uttering a version of our words to her. Our promise, in essence, to be good to her and take care of her as one of us.

She put the phone down on the covers within his reach,

keeping well to the no-touching rule I'd laid down outside. She also pulled out a charger and plugged it in, then draped the cable carefully over the small cupboard beside his bed.

Julian turned on the phone, then looked up at her. "What's the password?"

"Carver Babes."

He chuckled.

Actually laughed in spite of everything.

Because of her.

Last time he'd suffered through something like this, we hadn't had Caterina with us. But now that we did, it had me realizing that it could be different, that it could be easier to pull him through it. She added a different energy to our dynamic and that could be exactly what was needed to help him.

He scrolled on his phone for a few moments, before telling her, "This is perfect, everything just how I remember it." He held it to him protectively as he looked out at us and said, "Thank you to all of you for getting me out of there. I know it can't have been easy. Was there a price I need to be aware of?"

His gaze went to Nico as he asked that last part, who was leaning against the wall with his arms folded across his chest. "Not to worry. Everything is as it should be."

"N, when you get cryptic, it's rarely a good thing."

"There was opportunity to be found in the challenge that the takedown tonight posed."

"Yeah, that's not really veering away from the whole ominous nature of it all."

"How about if I told you that I made lemonade from lemons?"

Julian shook his head. "Not at all. Nico, if there's—"

"It's fine. Everything will be fine. What I need is for

you to concentrate on getting better. Physically first, then the rest afterward. Okay? I really need that from you."

"Nico," I spoke, not liking him pushing Julian. It was too early for that.

It had me tensing majorly when Julian squeezed his eyes shut again and tried to bite back emotion that was rising up once again.

But then some of that was alleviated when he uttered on a pained rasp, "I know. Can you reach out to Roslynn for me?"

"Doctor Williams? Yeah, of course."

As much as it killed me that it had come to that, it was actually a really good sign.

"You'll need to stay here in the hospital tonight," Nico informed him. "But tomorrow I can move you. This room will be well guarded, so you don't need to concern yourself with that."

"*I'm* also not going anywhere," I spoke up.

"Yeah," he said, taking everything in. "Thank you." He shifted his weight in the bed. "If you get a lead on Angelo, you'll tell me, yes?"

"Are you sure that's what you want, what you need, J?" Nico asked worriedly.

"Yes. I'm sure," Julian answered.

So he could obsess about it and be stuck in the nightmare of it all? I went to protest, but Caterina pulled a Nico Marchetti and held up her hand. Then she said, "Information is also comfort, right?"

Dammit. Her words to me the other night.

They sure packed an emotional punch.

Especially given the subject matter in question.

"Yeah, okay."

Julian smiled out at her.

Then he placed his new phone down on the covers and sank back against the pillows, clearly tiring.

"We're gonna head out," Nico said, noticing. "Let you get some rest, all right?"

"You need anything, you text us, or let Milo know, okay?" Caterina told him.

He smiled weakly. "Yes, and yes. Thanks."

Nico gave my shoulder a squeeze as he passed on by, and told me quietly, "Rocco will be arriving in moments. He'll supervise security on Julian throughout the night."

"Got it. I'll liaise with him."

"No need. I'll take care of it. You just worry about Julian. And try to get some sleep when he sleeps."

I nodded, and he walked to the door, holding it open for Caterina.

She threw her arms around me and held me tightly to her. "Do you want us to bring you anything? We'll be bringing a change of clothes for Julian by tomorrow, but anything else?"

"Nah, all good," I said, stroking her back. "And now he's got his phone, he's good to go on his end. I want *you* to get some rest and eat properly, though. Do you hear me? Don't make me pull a Nico."

She chuckled. "You don't need to."

"Good. I'll text you and keep you posted on Julian."

Satisfied with that, the two of them headed out, closing the door quietly behind them.

"I'm sorry," Julian uttered, sleepily.

"Sorry?" I asked as I walked to the chair beside his bed and sat down. "You have absolutely nothing to be sorry for, Sunshine."

"That I couldn't… that when you grabbed my hand, I reacted… the way I did."

"It's all okay. I didn't take it personally and I won't.

There's no need to rush it, to rush yourself, and certainly don't feel bad about it."

"I love you, you know that?" he uttered, his eyes drooping.

"As I love you, brother. Fucking always."

A smile graced his lips before he then closed his eyes and fell back to sleep.

Good. He needed rest. And a lot of it.

But it would be a miracle if he actually managed to sleep through the night.

If last time was anything to go by, he'd be waking up screaming every couple of hours.

Pained and tormented.

Exhausted and wrecked.

I wished I could take it all away for him.

I wished there were words or a gesture I could make that would do that.

Hell, I wished I could undo it entirely.

But wishful thinking wouldn't accomplish anything.

All we could do right now was to be here for him, listen to his needs, and keep a close eye on him in every way until we were certain that he was back on stable ground again.

He was surrounded by love, understanding, and safety in each of us.

He'd be okay.

He'd get through this.

We'd get him through this.

Angelo hadn't broken him, he'd just shaken him.

That was all.

That was fucking all.

14

~Nico~

Rocco was right on time as usual.

As Caterina and I stepped out into the hospital parking lot on the southeast side of the building, there he was striding along with two more of my soldiers at his back, the two of them blending well into the night in their black leather jackets and jeans.

Rocco stood out a little more and not just because he was a decade older than Vin and Mike who were in their early twenties, but also with his light gray jeans, the flashy motocross jacket, and mostly, the numerous piercings in his face and ears that glinted in the dark from the hospital lights and those of the lot. Hell, his ears were more metal than flesh, really.

He shoved a hand through his overgrown dark crew cut as he caught sight of me and jogged the rest of the way to us.

"How's he doing?" he asked me right away.

"Stabilized. He'll make a full recovery."

"Good. Really good." He shook his head in disbelief. "That shit, Angelo, we all knew he had some screws loose, but this is another thing altogether. I'm sorry this happened to Julian." He eyed Caterina. "To you too, Caterina." His gaze darted to our joined hands, her fingers currently stroking the back of my hand because she was well-attuned to just how on edge I was. After seeing Julian like that, viewing that disgusting footage of what had been done to him, having the location she'd been headed to turning out to be *the* location where he'd been held wherein she'd then been set upon by Angelo and his men... *fuck.*

He looked back at me and the moment our gazes met I saw him register the truth I was giving him concerning Caterina.

Mine.

He smiled as he looked between the two of us. "Understood, Boss." He shoved his hands into his pockets. "And just so you know, I'll be here running protective detail on Julian until *you* tell me the job is done. No one else." His eyes flashed. "Do *you* understand *me* where that's concerned?"

I smiled. "Absolutely."

"I'm glad, because that's where my loyalty lies." He thumbed Vin and Mike and they each gave me a respectful chin lift. "Them too. Many of us, actually. With *you*, Nico. Nobody else."

I nodded. "We'll talk. *Soon.*"

"We look forward to it."

With that, he gave me a chin lift, smiled at Caterina, then led the guys into the hospital.

"Let's go," I told Caterina, giving her hand a squeeze, then leading her back to my car that I'd left at the far end of the lot.

"Do you trust him? Rocco?"

"There are different levels of trust. Especially in our world."

"There are, yes."

"We've been working together for years."

"I'm well aware."

"Of course." I eyed her. "My obsession wasn't one-sided, hmm?"

"Know your enemies."

I slapped my hand to my heart. "Ouch. You're really going to leave me hanging like this?"

"Maybe it wasn't just an enemies thing. Although, it was easier to make myself believe that." She pressed her hand to mine over my chest and smiled up at me. "Or so I thought." She stroked my hand, then stepped back, moving into her business mode, as she told me, "I said I'd look into your soldiers so we could try to determine where they stood with you versus the Marchetti Syndicate as a whole, and I have been. With what happened with the kidnappings and then focusing all our energy on searching for Julian, I haven't completed that research or obtained all the intel that we need, but I have turned up some interesting things on Rocco Barone. All pointing toward a positive outcome and his claim that his loyalty lies with you only being solid."

"Such as?"

"He's looking into a backup for his family. Searching out schools for his two toddler-aged kids miles outside the city, having his wife send out resumes in and around these areas for another Executive Assistant job. And he's also altered his life insurance, signed the house over to her alone, and he's had a will drawn up." She grimaced. "He thinks he's going to die."

"Because he's intending to go against the Marchetti Syndicate."

"For you."

"If you already knew all of this, why did you ask me if I trusted him?"

"I wanted to make sure you were trusting your instincts. That you weren't second-guessing them because the stakes are so high."

"I see."

When I fell quiet as we reached my Ferrari, she rounded on me. "We can get into that in more detail later, but right now, we need to do damage control to manage the fallout of what happened tonight. You had to call in your father's men to clean up the bloodied mess, the massacre, really, in that house that we extracted Julian from. Doing that also alerted the Marchetti Syndicate to the fact that we snuck out around the security watching the Manor and carried out that op unsanctioned. A lot of lines were crossed. I have some ideas of how we can spin it to—"

"There won't be any *spinning* it."

"What?"

"What happened over the last few days, what you were subjected to even before that... the people I love are suffering *because* I've been treading so carefully, because we're still capitulating to the Marchettis and Leones. Doing so hasn't protected any of us." I blew out a breath. "As despicable as it was that Angelo did what he did, it has provided an opportunity."

"You're framing it as a show of force, as a demonstration of what you're capable of. A warning to Marco *and* Santino."

"Yes."

"You want them to fear you."

"To fear us."

"If they challenge that, if they come at us while we're lacking resources—"

"We won't be."

"You're talking about Rocco and your soldiers? Well, I can certainly get back to investigating all of them now that Julian is safe, and—"

"I do need you to do that, yes. I need a list as soon as possible. Verified beyond a shadow of a doubt. But I was referring to other resources as well."

She cocked an eyebrow.

I leaned against the hood of my Ferrari and told her quietly, "The attack that Milo and I were called to the night you and Julian were taken wasn't really an attack. It was Carlo Benzino's way of luring me to him for a meet."

"What? Why didn't you tell me this sooner?"

"Because we had our hands full with trying to locate Julian. This requires full focus."

"What was the content of this strange meet?"

"Before I tell you, I need you to do some hard thinking on the drive home."

"About what?"

"Whether you're really all in. Especially now things are about to heat up. Majorly so."

"Of course I am. How can you even ask me that?"

"Because of Joseph Stover."

She started.

"He's not a part of this."

"He needs to be, Caterina. Like I said, hard thinking. You told us you weren't ready beforehand to reveal all your secrets. It's time to open up more where that's concerned. Where he's concerned."

I opened the passenger door for her, but before she could sink inside, the screeching of tires caught our attention, and I looked to see an irritatingly familiar gray BMW speeding into the area. It shot down a couple of rows of the parking lot before zeroing in on my Ferrari, then coming to a rough stop just a few feet from it, wherein Leo then bolted out.

His ponytail swung from side to side as he stormed toward us.

That seemed about right.

"What the fuck are you playing at?" he demanded, stopping just shy of my personal space.

I instinctively pushed Caterina away at the clear aggressive threat coming off Leo.

His gaze darted to her and to the gesture itself. "I see that was all bullshit, too. You're not doing your duty where she's concerned. Not *training* her like Santino wanted."

"The fact you all thought that was possible where she's concerned is laughable. And fucking pathetic."

He got up in my face, growling, "You need to get back in line. *Now.* Calling in Marco to clean up that fucking massacre at Angelo's place for one of your friends because you knew it left us with no choice or the Leones would find out what you'd done, which would have been considered a show of force against them, something that wasn't sanctioned, was fucking unacceptable. Despite what he's done, Angelo Simone is one of *his* own, not ours. It falls under Leone jurisdiction, not ours. You damn well knew that, and you used it to force our hands. All for that fucking playboy."

"That *playboy* is a Marchetti Syndicate asset. My earnings reports prove that beyond a shadow of a doubt."

"Don't give me a fucking party line."

"That attack was also justice for a Leone Family member kidnapping my wife and intending to do a whole lot worse than even that."

"You were ordered to stand down. It was being handled."

"It wasn't. You were trying to manage me."

"You're so far off your leash, you think you're damn near free. Let me tell you something, you aren't. You're fucking lucky your father chalked this insanity tonight up to your reaction to the kidnapping, to the insult of somebody taking your property." He looked at Caterina. "Her."

I growled low in my throat. "She's not my property. She's fucking *mine.*"

He scoffed. "So you're pussy whipped now?"

"Nothing but a neanderthal, are you?" Caterina said.

He sneered at her. "You're fucking lucky too, lucky that Marco's got his eye on you for lucrative business purposes."

"Luck has nothing to do with it. I'm just that good."

I smiled, then told Leo, "If you'd all recognized that sooner, none of us would be in this position right now."

"And what position is that?"

"Being Santino's bitches," Caterina answered. "My father is using you."

"You're misinformed. This alliance is beneficial to both parties. It's going to bring back the glory days and put the Marchetti Syndicate on the map in a way that's never been seen before."

"I'm never misinformed," Caterina told him.

"She really isn't."

Leo stared between us for several moments, trying to understand what we were alluding to, looking unsure. *Good.* Doubt had been planted.

But then he did what he always did when he felt ill-equipped—he fell back on extreme reactions and aggression. He fisted his hand in my leather jacket and hissed in my face, "Fall back in line. Stay in your fucking lane, boy. You come off your leash again and you won't like the consequences. I will—"

I dislodged his grip, snagged his arm, then used it to haul him around and slam him down over the hood of my car. He grunted, then struggled, until I shoved his arm up his back, forcing his submission. "We're done with that. There's no more leash. So come at me. I fucking dare you. Because you strike at me and mine in any way and I will destroy you. You've been pushing me over and over. Big fucking mistake. Because this is the result of that. You brought it here, now you'll face what you fear in me."

I released him roughly, and he pushed off the hood and scrambled back, trying but failing to hide his very real fear at what I was really capable of. "And while we're at it, I want Marco's security off my territory by the time I get home in twenty minutes. If it's not done, I'll see to it myself. Believe me, you won't like that."

"Do you realize what you're doing here? Challenging the Family?"

"I'm well aware."

"This won't end well for you."

"We'll see."

He hissed at me, then turned and strode back to his car.

I kept watching, kept staring after him, until he drove out of the area and disappeared into the city streets.

"Well, that certainly put him in his place. He was scared. It was all over him."

I turned back to her. "I'm what he's always feared."

"What they all have."

"Alongside *you.*"

"And now?"

"No more holding back. Now we really go to war, *principessa.*"

15

~Caterina~

I eyed Nico across the kitchen table as I munched on the sandwiches he'd ordered in when we'd arrived back at Charon Manor.

To none of Marco Marchetti's security. They'd pulled them off the property before we'd made it back, just like Nico had basically ordered.

Clearly, it was the calm before the storm.

Nico had started something tonight that was going to come back on us all, something that couldn't be undone.

But he'd needed to.

Angelo's insane actions had highlighted a lot of things, namely, that we couldn't continue on as we had been, that intending to systematically and covertly take down our enemies wouldn't be enough. Not without us all enduring a whole lot more suffering. He'd told me that during his messaging with my father, the bastard had mentioned that he'd be sending some of his soldiers around in a couple of days to get a *progress report* on my condition, that being that I was suffering and being destroyed by Nico, that my *husband* was fulfilling his duties as laid out in that despicable contract.

Nico was sick of it, sick of playing the game, just like I was.

It was more than even that, though.

I could see it all over him.

Making that stand tonight, shifting the tide the way he had, he'd done it to protect the three of us. He'd done it *for* us.

Out of love.

Love.

That was really what it had been.

And not only that, all of his actions lately.

"I fucking love you, Caterina. I'm undeniably, obsessively, and dangerously in love with you."

I hadn't had time to absorb his confession with everything that had been going on.

But now we had a moment, I was trying to do just that.

To figure out how it had landed for me, where I stood in relation to it. To him. And to Milo and Julian as well. To the whole thing that had developed between us.

"You're back here, safe with us now. Where you belong."

Those other startling words of his hung heavy for me too, because it meant that he didn't just see me moving in here under the guise of doing what the families had demanded as being a temporary thing.

He wanted me here with him. They all did.

Permanently.

"You're staring."

I blinked out of my thoughts to see Nico's brow furrowed as he looked up from my laptop that I'd set in front of him with all the intel concerning Joe that he needed in order to understand who he was to me.

"Can't I stare at my husband, the apple of my eye?" I

teased, looking him over in the black lounge pants and V-neck tee that he'd changed into when we'd arrived back, his sexy tattoos on display in all their glory. The sword down the length of his left inner forearm with the words, *Si vis pacem, para bellum*, certainly hit deep right now. *If you want peace, prepare for war.*

"Hilarious." He shifted his weight. "But I know you. That's the look you get when you're trying to figure something out, something that's got you stumped. Something about me."

"Well, you do play things close to the vest."

"Pot. Kettle."

"You mean Joe? I told you when we got back here that it wasn't something I was actively and intentionally keeping from you. It wasn't my secret to tell, to expose him. And I certainly didn't see him being pulled into what we're doing."

"Otherwise you *would* have mentioned him?"

"Yes."

"Really?"

I reached out and took his hand, tracing my fingers over his dragon's head ink. "We're in this together. We're a team. I have your back, just like the three of you have mine."

"What if this mission wasn't a factor?"

"What?"

"What if you essentially weren't forced into being here at my place, forced into this marriage?"

"It doesn't feel *forced* when I'm here. Especially with everything the three of you have done to make me feel comfortable here, all the special items you brought in for me, the things you set up in my room. It's meant a lot to me."

"That's something." He murmured. "I guess."

"Nico, what—"

He spun the laptop around, a photo of Joe in full dress uniform on the screen. "This guy is ex-military, a decorated vet, in fact, and a distinguished sniper. Following that, he went on to work for a private security firm, then disappeared for several years. Your research cites that he spent that time working for a black ops team."

"All correct. Your point?"

"Why did he suddenly drop off the grid? Why is he registered as dead, in fact?"

"Because of my father. Joe was with my mom beforehand. They were high school sweethearts. Then they went off to college together and to medical school. They were engaged at one point. And then he enlisted."

"Enlisted? Just like that? With him on a medical school track alongside your mom?"

"His best friend was murdered. It impacted him in a major way. It set him on a different path. And it drove him and my mom apart. She ended up meeting Santino. Apparently, Joe came back for her at one point, but she was already too entangled in my father's world. The only way for them to be together was for Joe to pull her out. She would have had to give up the career she loved and had worked so hard for. So she stayed with my father. Little did she know he would become the monster that he is now. He wasn't always like that with her. He cherished her in the beginning. But I guess all that power and fighting to hold on to it, playing god over people's lives… it corrupted him. And it just got worse and worse."

"And how did *you* meet this guy?"

"When I left the Family and went off to college, my mom reached out to Joe for the first time in years. She knew that what I was doing would endanger me, but she also understood that I couldn't stand being suffocated any longer, that I needed to be free. So, he discreetly trained me. Intensely. For months and months on end. Hence, my combat know-how."

"He protected you."

"He taught me how to channel all that rage and pain inside me."

"He made you into a killer."

"That's one way of looking at it. Either way, it was necessary. And that training has saved me several times over." I sank back against the chair. "How he's connected with Carlo Benzino, I really don't know. The more pertinent question there, though, is *why.*"

"I need you to reach out to him."

"I will."

He eyed me across the table, curiosity sparking. "You said Santino cherished your mom in the beginning, that he wasn't initially the twisted psychopath that he ended up becoming with her."

"Yeah. And?"

"*And* is that something you worry about?"

"In relation to what?"

"Me, Caterina. Us."

"The three of you are nothing like him."

"Not how he is now, no. But—"

"Can we not do this right now? Let's just keep our focus on the major news you told me before these delicious sandwiches arrived. That being that Carlo Benzino approached you wanting you not only to form an alliance with him but also for me and you to take control of the families. I mean, that's not an easy pill to swallow. Would you want that? To take power over the Marchetti Syndicate? Of course you've thought about it before with being Marco's heir, but then you were passed over for Underboss in favor of Leo, so I'd imagine you ruled it out after that."

"Our goal is our freedom."

"That can be brought about by taking power."

"Only to an extent."

"No. If the families are destroyed—"

"There would be a power vacuum created, as Carlo pointed out."

"But we wouldn't be impacted by it like we are now."

"We would be the ones who took down the Marchettis and Leones. That would make us a target of anyone else who tried to take power in their stead."

"Then we leave. Embrace the Reincourt Construction thing that you had Julian set up as a backup to start over."

"That was an extreme last resort. We'd lose everything. Especially you and Julian. Everything you've built here would be ripped away. And what about your expansion plans? Brimbank Waterfront? That wouldn't be able to happen. You'd have to give it all up, Caterina."

"Yet, if we take power, we'd be trapped in this life forever. In this fucked-up world."

"The nature of it would be different with us at the helm."

I took him in, his answers, all of it. "You don't think you could live without the brutality, do you?"

"Growing up as Marco Marchetti's son, living this life, it made me a certain way, shaped me. I guess..." He scrubbed his hand over his face. "I don't know."

"Just so you know, we can definitely find other outlets for your *feral* side beyond this nightmare we live in here with the three families."

The corner of his mouth turned up. "Well, I've already found one. In you."

"Right back at you."

He rose from his chair all of a sudden. "We'll lay all this out with Julian and Milo, see where we're all at in regards to Carlo. Meanwhile, reach out to Stover." He gestured at my plate. "I'm glad you've gotten your appetite back."

Yeah, I'd eaten four sandwiches, a bowl of fries, and half a vegetable plate. "I guess the physicality of the mission tonight made me extra hungry." At least, that was what I was telling myself. What I *had* to tell myself right now.

His gaze roamed over me in just my silk robe, which I'd changed into once we'd arrived back, before I'd handed all my intel on Joe over to him like he'd asked.

I hadn't wanted him to think that I was purposely keeping that from him. I hadn't wanted him to think that I wasn't with him, Milo, and Julian. It was really important to me that they knew I was all in when it came to them.

But the fact that he'd had to question it bothered me.

Was I not putting it out there properly? How much they'd come to mean to me? That it had stopped being about the mission long ago? That what hurt them, hurt me? That what made them happy, made me happy?

That we'd become inextricably and irreparably linked forevermore?

He looked away quickly again.

And then he moved away too, telling me, "Now you've eaten well, it's time to focus on the sleeping aspect. Okay? Rest up, Caterina."

With that, he headed for the door to the kitchen.

"I don't want to sleep alone. And I don't want you to either."

He stilled, his back to me. "You've gone through a lot. You need your rest."

"Then help me rest, *bello.*"

He turned around slowly. "Caterina—"

"I can feel it from you, see it all over you. All the stress and upset that's weighing on you. Seeing Julian like that. Knowing we were all in danger. Challenging Leo. It's all putting a strain on you. It's building up and hurting you. You need to let loose. So do it." I rose from my chair. "All. Over. Me."

Because he wasn't alone there, *I* really needed to let some things out too.

In the next second, he was on me, shoving me against the wall with jarring force, his hands grasping my arms and essentially pinning me there before him.

"*Principessa,*" he groaned at my ear, his warm breath on my neck sending delicious tingles through me.

I turned my head and nipped at his jaw and a hot thrill infused me when it drew a sexy growl from him. One of those dangerous ones that promised a whole lot of destruction. Or, in this case, sexual devastation.

Fuck, yes.

I slicked my tongue along the grazes I'd made, and then he had me squealing as he jerked my robe open, then ripped me off the wall, spun me around, and slammed me down on the counter.

Before I could catch my breath, he was there, grabbing my thighs, wrenching them apart, then diving in with that merciless tongue of his.

"Ah, shit!" I cried as he devoured me like a fucking savage, pleasure sparking everywhere and overwhelming me in seconds. *God,* he was on another level when he was in this state. Fucking feral to the max. "Yes!" I screamed as he thrust his tongue deep inside me, then stabbed violently and at crazy speed.

I yanked at his hair and it just spurred him on, more so, and he dug his fingers into my ass, then forced me closer, his tongue thrusting deeper.

I shrieked as he then slathered my juices all over my clit, before then grazing it with his teeth.

And that was it. I went off violently, drenching his face.

He smirked devilishly as he made a show of lapping up every drop of me and savoring it.

He released my ass, then dug his fingers into the soft flesh of my right breast, making me hiss from the sting of it.

"Spread those sexy thighs wide and put your feet flat on the counter," he ordered. "Open to me. All the fucking way."

As I did as he asked, his dark eyes flamed while he opened his pants and shucked them off, then stroked his cock a couple of times, before he reached over me and snatched something up.

I wasn't able to take it in until he already had it sliding through my folds.

I jolted when I saw him holding a cucumber, one he hadn't needed to use earlier.

His hand left my breast and then he grabbed something else and I looked to see him holding a spatula.

In the next second, he brought it down on my breast with stinging force that had me gasping. He picked up the pace and then concentrated directly on my nipples, making me cry out from the biting intensity.

I dug my nails into the sides of the counter, trying to take it.

And then he pushed the cucumber into my pussy, making me choke from the shock of it.

"Mmm, fuck, yeah. Take it, dirty girl," he groaned as he kept striking my now burning breasts with the spatula while driving the cucumber deeper inside me, stretching me open.

I was bucking on the counter in moments, my thighs

shaking as I struggled to keep them spread wide in such a vulnerable and wanton position.

"Look at your wet cunt swallowing it so desperately."

He tossed the spatula, then leaned down and bit one of my nipples so hard that he drew blood.

"Oh shit," I choked as it took me to another place altogether. "Yes, more," I found myself begging as I rolled my hips rougher and rougher, basically fucking against the cucumber, as I lost myself to it all, the pain, pleasure, and insanity of it all crashing into me.

When he pulled back, his darkened sapphire eyes meeting mine, blood dripped from his lips.

He twisted the cucumber inside me, then abruptly yanked it out.

Then he was slapping my pussy, earning a shriek from me.

And still I begged for more.

"Fuck, woman," he groaned. "On your knees. Rub those sore breasts all over the counter. I want them to burn for me."

Shakily, I got on my knees and then he was there shoving down on my back and forcing my breasts against the hard surface, making me press them onto it and feel the ache from his delicious abuse.

He stepped up behind me and spread my ass cheeks wide a moment before he spat into my ass. I mewled at the sensation of it oozing inside.

He did it again, his finger following and sinking inside, stirring it, as he spat inside more.

"Fuck, Nico," I moaned.

"Filthy little princess," he grunted.

He had me jarring as something a lot larger pushed inside alongside his finger.

I turned my head to see him driving the cucumber into my ass. "Oh my God."

"Your cunt is dripping all over the counter. It's getting you off being fucked in the ass by a vegetable, baby."

"Ungh," I choked as he twisted it, then drove deeper, burying it further and further, grazing my walls, opening me up for his demented pleasure.

And I fucking loved it.

Every crazed moment.

Everything he did to me.

The way we fed off each other in the most glorious ways.

"Reach back and hold your ass open," he commanded.

The moment I did, he yanked the cucumber out, then stuffed it back in deep in the next second, the intense sensations making me scream.

He didn't stop then, pounding inside at a fearsome pace that stole my breath away, reaming my ass mercilessly.

"Hot little ass," he uttered.

Through it, he flicked my clit.

Once.

Twice.

And then I came apart, my orgasm slamming into me, and I shuddered on the counter, losing my grip on my ass cheeks.

Before I could even recover, Nico dragged me halfway off the counter so my feet were touching the floor, but I was still folded half over it. He kept the cucumber buried in my ass and then he slammed into my pussy, driving so deep in one brutal go that it had me choking.

He power-fucked into me right away and smacked the end of the cucumber, making me buck beneath him with every hard hit that became like a vibrating force of motion. That intense sensation tearing through me combined with his cock driving into me like a merciless beast had ecstasy crashing into me, spreading all fucking over as I clenched down around his cock and the cucumber and came all over the place.

A snarl escaped me as it went on and on, taking me higher and higher.

Nico pulled out of me, then went to rip me off the counter, but I reacted faster and took him down to the ground.

I pounced on him, straddling his lap, then slammed myself down onto his cock.

"Fuck!" he roared.

Digging my nails into his shoulders, I rode him like a wild thing, lost to it all, just completely fucking consumed.

He patted my cheek and I opened instinctively, wherein he then shoved the cucumber in, pounding it down my throat, essentially fucking my face with it.

So fucking dirty.

So completely fucked-up.

And it only made me ride him harder.

I slapped and pinched his nipples, dug my nails deep into his pecs, then raked them down his abs, and through it all, his snarls and growls infused me, that and him brutalizing my mouth with the cucumber just urging me on, dragging me deeper into the dementedness of it all.

He suddenly pulled the cucumber from my mouth, then dragged it over my breasts.

And then he was lifting me off him and getting to his feet.

When he held his hand out to me, I batted it away, then shrieked and lunged at him, driving him into the wall.

He snagged me around the hips and hauled me up, and I fought him, kicking and biting and scratching like the wild thing he'd brought out in me—that we'd brought out in each other.

The next thing I knew, we were stumbling out down the corridor and slamming each other back and forth into the walls near the stairs.

He shoved me up against one wall by the back of my head, then thrust inside me, taking me deep, and I fucked back against him as he roughly grabbed my pussy in a burning grip.

I broke his hold, and he grunted as his dick was forced out of me, only to grab me and basically toss me up the stairs. I'd barely landed on my back when he was there, pouncing on me, his body covering mine. He dragged his cock through my dripping folds, his dangerous gaze burning into mine.

"No," he snarled. "Need to fuck you like an animal."

In the next second, he pushed off me and as I went to adjust my position, he had me squealing as he snagged my ankle and pulled me back down the stairs a moment before he pounced on me, covering my back.

He thrust back inside me and I clawed at the stairs for purchase as his thrusts became animalistic in mere seconds.

"Fuck!" I cried through the delicious brutality, both of his cock slamming inside me and the stairs bruising my skin with his every thrust.

"Too much?" he challenged, all breathy at my ear.

He pulled out, flipped me around so I was on my back, then grabbed my thigh and slammed back in deep, making me scream.

"Never," I gasped.

Our eyes locked, all that intensity flaming between us.

"So fucking perfect," he rumbled. "Not giving you up. Fucking ever."

He kept saying that over and over as he fucked me,

wrapping his hand around my throat to hold me steady to him, to connect with me on a primal, inescapable level.

Pleasure crashed into me, taking me over again and again until I couldn't see straight.

And we still kept going.

━━

"WHAT ARE YOU DOING?"

I looked up from my phone as Nico walked in carrying two glasses of water.

"Texting Milo. Julian's awake, so him too. I've sent a covert message out to Joe, I'm looking into some more of your soldiers, and I just checked out a possible Angelo sighting which turned out to be nothing."

"I've been gone barely fifteen minutes, making those calls to get the place outfitted for Julian's discharge from the hospital tomorrow and setting up sessions with his therapist."

I lifted a shoulder. "I don't mess around."

He put a glass down on the nightstand closest to the opposite side of his bed, then passed the other to me before climbing back onto the bed. As I took some big gulps because I was so thirsty after all that fucking and to also soothe my throat from all the screaming, he stared at me in surprise.

"What?" I asked.

"I lost count of the number of times you came. You should be passed out cold, but it seems to have somehow energized you instead."

"Worried I'm in my animalistic state and gonna maul you at any second?" I jested.

"Worried about it? Never. Worried about you? Always."

I sighed and finished up a text to Milo, who'd just reported that Julian had fallen asleep again after being up for about ten minutes. I put my phone down, then turned on my side toward Nico, who settled with his hand propping up his head on the pillow. "I just… leaving Julian and Milo there, not having them here with us… it's upsetting."

"I told you he wouldn't have been able to handle all of us being in that tiny room with him. He can barely handle Milo being there right now, but there's no way Milo would take no for an answer where that's concerned. Plus, even with my security, Milo believes he's the only one able to protect Julian if Angelo came for him there."

"And you needed to get things ready for him and also have me get the ball rolling where Joe is concerned."

"And do damage control. I knew the ramifications of what went down tonight would be severe. I suspected that Leo would come at me too and I didn't want that to happen around Julian while he's… like this. Male aggression right now will be one of the worst things for him. That's how it was last time."

"Shit, Nico, what he suffered through… I can't… it was beyond brutal. It was worse than I'd already worried about it being."

He wrapped his arm around me and tucked me against him. "I know. But Julian is strong. He's full of life too. And he has the tools to work through it. He'll be back here with us tomorrow and I'm gonna make sure that's where he stays while he's recovering. So all three of us can be there for him, so he's looked after."

"So he's loved."

"Yeah. So he's loved." He looked out at me, a whole lot of confusion coming at me.

"What's with the look?"

"Just a little surprised that the word came spilling from your pretty lips so easily."

"*Loved?*"

"Yes," he answered tightly. "That's the word. While we're on this, you haven't even commented on our marriage."

"Why would I? It's not real."

"Legally, it is very real."

"You know what I mean. It's just for show." I sat up, smoothing down my black negligee. "And you may have also noticed that the boys haven't commented on it either. Not really. With the four of us being together, I'm sure they're not over the moon about the fact that you and me have been bound by this supposed marriage with the two of them left out. But they get that it's fake too, that's why the issue hasn't been raised. Although, I'm sure the reminders from our families about it don't help."

"There have been more *reminders* than you're aware of."

"What?"

"I get messages about it nearly every day from my family and your father."

"Why didn't you tell me?"

"There's enough going on without you having to be subjected to that, or hearing the lies I've told to tide them over."

"Lies about what you were doing to me?"

"Yeah."

"How you were breaking me down, forcing the fight and *attitude* out of me, making me nothing but a submissive, weak mess of a person?"

He scowled, showing me how much he hated even the thought of it.

I knew he did.

It absolutely repulsed him, not just that I could be

subjected to that, but the idea that they all thought it was possible at all. That he would do that. That I would endure that.

"I was in a position to spare you from hearing about that day in and day out, so I kept it off your radar. I know you don't actually need my protection and I know you don't like people thinking you do, or actions being taken to protect you, but—"

"No."

He raised an eyebrow. "No?"

"I don't like the suggestion that I need protecting or that I can't protect myself, because of course that's demeaning. But I *do* like the idea of us protecting *each other*. I like that a lot. This team element I wasn't familiar with before the three of you burst into my life... I can't imagine not being a part of that camaraderie now. That together-ness. The unconditional support. The understanding." I eyed him pointedly. "That *love.*"

I shifted on the bed until I was sitting cross-legged facing him, urgency radiating off me as I told him, "For so long, you were the only one in our fucked-up world who didn't discount me. Even as twisted as our little war was, I saw what you were really doing—beyond the obsession of it all, anyway. You challenged me, you always saw me as an equal and you wanted that from me. You pushed me, you wanted me to dominate, you wanted me to come into my true power in a way I'd been struggling with." I took his hand in mine, stroking his fingers softly. "You saw the real me before I did. And you fucking worshipped me for it. You went out of your way to safeguard that when I was pulled back into the Leone bullshit. And you put your trust in me even when it came to your brotherhood. You've believed in me at every turn."

"Caterina—"

I pressed my finger to his lips as I rose up onto my knees and sank my fingers into his soft black hair. "How could I not *love* that? How could I not love *you* for that?"

His eyes widened, his disbelief blatantly apparent, so much so that it had my gut twisting. "That's right. You heard me correctly. I love you, Nico Marchetti."

He eased my hand from his mouth and stared up at me, that disbelief giving way to reverence. "Why did it seem like you were so very far away from being able to admit that, or entertaining the notion of it at all?"

"Because of the circumstances. Being surrounded by this nightmare. I didn't want something so special tainted by all of this. Something so pure being poisoned by it. I guess I wanted to wait until it was all over, until we were free so that it would just be about that and not burdened by anything else. By this war, or this fake marriage, or all the pain the four of us have been through and are still likely to face with what's coming."

"I worried about the same thing. I even weaponized it when I confessed as much to you when I was trying to get you to take some time, to rest. I just couldn't hold it in any longer. I needed you to know. But I'm sorry for it coming out like that and—"

"I get it."

"Yeah?"

I nodded. "After what happened in that hellhole, getting Julian out and walking into that kind of danger, knowing it will be far from the last time... it hit me so brutally just how uncertain things are for the four of us. Whether we'll come out of this, whether we'll survive it. And even if we do, will it be in pieces? And with that, I just... I couldn't stand holding onto this a moment longer either, to you not knowing just how deeply I feel for you, how much I adore you. That I do, in fact, love you, Nico."

"And you don't like being vulnerable."

I smiled. "That too. *But* you have been for me, so here it is, me reciprocating."

His eyes lit up, basically shining at me, and that sweet, boyish grin spread over his face. He looked so happy, so unburdened, if only for this moment in time, that it sent a beautiful thrill through me.

I wrapped my arms around him and he did the same, pulling me down with him. "Thank you, Caterina. Thank you for giving this to me."

"I'm not leaving you. I'm not leaving any of you. When this is done or whatever happens, I'll still be here with you as yours. The time for walking away has long passed for me. I promise."

His hold tightened around me, and he nuzzled against me. "Good, because we're never letting you go."

I chuckled as he held me to him, both arms encircling me and his leg even draped over me, essentially trapping me to him.

But it was the good kind of trapped, not the claustro-phobia-triggering kind. It was the right kind, the comforting kind.

The belonging kind.

Unfortunately, the sweet intimacy of it was cut all too short by the sound of my phone ringing.

Nico grunted at the disruption, but admitted, "It could be urgent."

"Given everything going on, yeah."

He very reluctantly lifted his leg off me, then loosened his hold on me too, enough for me to reach my phone, but not enough to actually let me go. It had me laughing as I snatched my phone off the nightstand.

I was tensing in the next moment as I sank back into his embrace and saw the name flashing on the call display.

Levi Knight.

Talk about awkward timing.

"Take it," Nico said, when I hesitated.

I went to push from his hold to do so away from him, but he tightened his grip on me. "No. Here."

"Ramping up the awkwardness," I muttered.

"It'll be fine."

I swiped it open. "Levi."

"Put it on speakerphone," Nico spoke, loud enough that I was sure Levi heard.

I did as he'd asked, but before I could get another word out, Levi's voice sounded through the room.

"Are you two a package deal now? Or does Rina have no choice in the matter where that's concerned, mafia prince?"

"You know her better than to believe she'd ever let that be the case," Nico responded, strangely civilly despite the opposite coming from Levi.

"I'm fine, Levi," I assured him, knowing he was just concerned.

"If that stops being the case, just say the word."

Now *that* got Nico going, and he rumbled, "And you'll do what exactly?"

"What will I do? I'll lay it out in excruciatingly painful detail and—"

There was a commotion in the background, and then we heard a female voice.

"Levi, stop. You're seriously laying down a threat against Nico Marchetti?"

"I don't like him with her. He's a dangerous—"

"We're all dangerous. Besides, she's told you that she's fine. Several times. Play nice."

"I can't just—"

"Lovely, come on. Just take a breath."

"Screw the breath, your hands on me are doing the job, Wildflower."

I grinned at Nico and whispered, "Told you he's completely and utterly in love with his girlfriend."

Nico actually cracked a smile. "She has the ability to reel him in too, it seems."

"That's an overexaggeration," Levi said, coming back on the line again. "So watch yourself."

I blew out a breath. "Levi, why did you call? Is something wrong?"

"Right," he said, clearing his throat. "I actually dialed you because your phone is secure, but the message is for your *husband,* too."

"Seriously, Levi?"

"Fuck, fine."

We heard movement in the background again; him grunting, then the woman with him, who was obviously Brianna, giggling.

"You're lucky you're so fucking irresistible and I'm in a fantastic mood."

"Then don't let this call sour it. Or sour it for Caterina who you haven't spoken to in a while."

I heard Levi clear his throat, then he told us, "Malcolm Lynch is buried. *Osiris* is gone. Wiped out would be a more accurate way of putting it. Obviously, that means the deal your father was trying to make is dead in the water. You're good to go there, free of that insanity. It's over."

"Good work," Nico told him.

"This is amazing," I spoke to Levi. "It must be surreal for you."

"It is, yeah."

"I'm really happy for you, Levi. I know what this takedown means for you, how much it was needed." And how long he'd been fighting for it.

"Thanks, sweetheart."

"You must be celebrating like crazy."

"We're about to, yeah. I just wanted to relay the news to Nico—and you—first."

"We appreciate it," Nico said, surprising me.

Surprising Levi too, it seemed, because there was a delay before he responded, unsure, "Right… okay, thanks."

"I'm impressed," Nico continued. "Taking that psychopath out of play was no small feat."

"Well, I'm a relentless bastard. Takes one to know one, right, Nico?"

"Point made," Nico said, amusement in his tone.

"I also had a great team with me, something I understand you do, too. Especially with Rina now a part of it."

Hmm. The way he was talking, he knew it for a fact. He'd clearly been looking into things here. Even while being swamped with his own mission.

"That's going to be the key to what you're up against there. It's power. Use it well. But guard it well too. And if you need an assist, you know I'm always here too, all right?"

"Thanks, Levi."

"It's appreciated," Nico told him.

"I make a much better ally than an enemy, Nico. As so long as you treat Rina well, I'll remain as the former."

"Understood."

"Good. Well, I'll let you get back to… whatever it is that you're doing, and I need to get back to my loves."

"Talk to you soon, Levi," I said.

"Definitely. You hear that, Nico?"

"Fine," Nico grunted. "Yes, don't be a stranger to Caterina."

"Wow, good then. Until next time."

With that, he hung up, and I stared at Nico, stunned.

"Yes?" he asked, grinning at me.

"What was that?"

"He's important to you. It was clear from his tone with you that it's purely platonic on his end. He's a great support for you. You were also all lit up as we spoke with him—he obviously brings out a lighter side of you, and I want that for you, especially while we're caught up in all this madness." He reached out and tucked some strands of hair behind my ears, the tender and reverent gesture sending a surge of warmth through me. "Again, I'm sorry that I ever tried to interfere with that. You make your own choices and it's not for me to get in the way of that. He's your only friend and you need that in your life, somebody you've given your trust to who's safeguarded it well."

"Wow," I breathed.

He eased my phone from my hand and put it down on his nightstand. "Plus, I'm not at all worried." That self-satisfied smirk with a hint of deviousness was out in full force. "You just told me that you love me."

I chuckled and wrapped myself around him, then pulled the covers up over us. "Come here." His arms encircled me again, and I rested my head on his chest. "Stay here holding me all night. Don't let me go."

"Never," he said, tightening his hold. He kissed the top of my head and nuzzled against me. "Sleep now, *amore mio.*"

16

~Julian~

They were walking on eggshells.

And they were trying to act like they weren't actually doing so.

It was all very… complicated. And awkward as shit.

Jesus.

I'd thought it might have lessened a little over the last several days since I'd been discharged from the hospital and staying at Charon Manor again, that they'd calm down and ease into it where I was concerned.

But they hadn't.

The three of them were tense too, outside of what had happened to me being factored in.

Something had gone down.

Some shit had hit the fan in a major way.

I suspected it was related to whatever the three of them had needed to do in order to get me out of that hellhole. There *had* been a price. Nico had dismissed it when I'd asked him at the hospital, obviously not wanting to stress me out. But the fact that he still hadn't brought it up, that none of them had, was now doing the opposite and stressing me out in a big way.

Because they were cutting me out.

I knew they were just trying to do what they thought was best for me, to keep everything light and fluffy, but that wasn't the life we led, and it wasn't *us*. There was a powerful undertone of darkness and danger present for us.

As fucked-up as it was, without that, it wasn't... real. It felt fake.

Worse, it didn't feel normal.

And feeling like that was one of the worst things for me right now.

I didn't want to feel... wrong.

Not like me.

Like I was damaged.

Like *he'd* managed to damage me, like he'd actually won out.

"Please."

"Say it. Say it again."

I shuddered as the memory of uttering that one word played on my mind, coming to the fucking forefront once again.

It had been so much more than a word.

It had been me giving Angelo want he'd wanted.

Giving in.

Cracking.

"Mmm, yes, you'll break for me so beautifully."

Was that what had happened?

Had he actually succeeded?

Had *I* actually failed to hold out?

I thought I'd been delirious at the time, but I still remembered saying that word, begging him like that. According to my doctor and Milo, I'd been really sick, really fucked-up. But did that matter? I'd still given in, hadn't I?

I'd only uttered those words to get him to stop.

He'd tried to skew it into making me believe I'd actually been begging him to fuck me, when I'd really been desperate for him to stop torturing me, to end the whole twisted thing.

"I want you to know it's me who did this to you. I want you to feel every moment of it and have it ingrained deep down, so you'll never be able to fucking forget that I made you my little bitch."

Gritting my teeth, I closed the lid of my laptop after getting up at the crack of dawn to deal with Carver Group business. My mind hadn't been as clear as I would have liked, so it had taken longer than it normally would have to see to things. It had been a struggle, actually.

I'd been telling myself that it was the painkillers and my body needing longer to heal. And maybe it was partially, but there was also definitely an element to it that wasn't just physical.

An element I was having trouble acknowledging.

Just like I didn't want to acknowledge *him* in those flashes.

That was what he wanted. What he'd even said repeatedly that he'd wanted to do to me. To have what he'd subjected me to *ingrained in me deep down* so I wouldn't be able to forget it.

Worse, so he could control, taunt, and torture me even though I was no longer there in that hellhole with him.

I grabbed my cane and pushed to my feet.

It was a flashy thing—just my style—that Cat had got for me. My favorite cobalt-blue covered in a whole lot of glitz and glitter and even boasting a gold handle that was jeweled. She'd gone all out with it and it made me smile whenever I looked at it or walked around with it.

Milo had also gone all out by working his ass off to get me a replica of my pimped out Harley made after it had been totaled in that crash. He'd been on the phone to parts suppliers and mechanics for days on end.

And Nico had also pulled out all the stops by basically converting one of his living rooms—his favorite one at that —into a suite for me. He'd brought in a ton of things. A bed, a portable closet, a freaking gaming system, mountains of books and DVDs, an epic flatscreen TV. This room was even right next door to the big ground floor bathroom that had the Jacuzzi tub inside it, along with a waterfall shower. It meant I didn't have to walk up any stairs while I still wasn't the best on my feet.

Like I said, all of them walking on eggshells.

It was sweet; I knew that.

Loving and beyond caring. So thoughtful.

But I couldn't take another moment of it, of being treated like I was a victim, like I needed the special treatment, like I was fragile.

I didn't want this to impact me like it had before when my father had... done what he had.

I couldn't go through that again.

I couldn't allow it to infect me the way it had last time around.

It had taken *so* long to even begin to move past it.

It felt like I'd be back to square one in a sense if I registered what had been done to me by Angelo on the same level as that.

That was what had become brutally apparent to me during my back-to-back sessions with Doctor Roslynn Williams, the same therapist I'd seen regarding my past... issues.

When I'd asked Nico to bring her in, I'd thought dealing with it head on with no waiting had been the best way to go, because I'd just wanted it over. I'd wanted to hurry through it, I guess, move beyond it as quickly as possible, and get back to me.

But it was just dredging up everything. Even the stuff with my father. As if I hadn't worked so fucking hard to bury that over the years, now it was rising back up. It had caused me to have flashes of the things Angelo had done to me, some things that I hadn't even remembered at first because I'd been in a delirious state or something from the sickness I'd suffered as a result of the crash injuries I'd sustained.

Just as I was heading for the living room door, Cat burst in.

Or back in.

The three of them had been taking shifts with me, making sure I wasn't left alone for even a moment.

But then Nico's doctor had shown up to check her out, so she'd had to step out for the last little while. She'd accepted that I'd be fine when I'd told her I'd needed to finish up dealing with Carver Group business.

Milo or Nico hadn't been able to take over because they weren't home right now. They'd headed out on *Marchetti business*. Whatever that meant these days. And they hadn't told me either.

More of them keeping things from me.

Maybe I was reading too much into it because I'd noticed the tension coming off them. Maybe it was just par for the course, general day-to-day business that Nico, as Capo, was dealing with, running his territory and all of that. I mean, things had calmed down since the Lone Gunners had attacked the wedding, so maybe things were going back to normal. Or whatever normal meant with them now allied with the Leones.

"Hey, do you need something?" Cat asked me, taking

in the fact that I was standing with my cane and about to head on out of the room. "What can I do?"

"You can tell me how it went with the doctor."

"Oh, it's all fine, just as I insisted to Nico."

"Well, you did manage to push it off for quite a while," I said, grinning at her. She definitely had an impact on him, even able to get him to change his mind on certain things and to reconsider things he normally would have been entrenched in doing his way.

"Yeah," she murmured.

"So you're really okay?" Milo had at least told me about her dizzy spells and the vomiting.

"Right. Fine," she murmured again, this time with a faraway look in her emerald eyes.

Something was off.

Or was I misreading her because I was off my game, maybe?

"You don't like doctors? Was that why you resisted being checked out?"

"No, it's not that. There was just a lot going on, so it wasn't really a priority."

"It's about looking weak, huh? And even feeling weak, too?"

"Something like that, yeah."

I smiled. "You've come a long way, you know that?"

"I have?" she asked, raising an eyebrow.

"Admitting to that. You wouldn't have a few months back. You would have completely denied it and anything you were feeling. I'm happy you feel safe to do that now. I'm glad you've found that in us. You were alone for so long. I mean, you were doing your thing amazingly well, but not having anyone in your corner... that was brutal."

"Yeah, despite how insane things are, in some ways, they are better. Definitely where the three of you are concerned. I didn't think I'd be able to function well as a part of a team, but it's really grown on me." She smiled. "In fact, I can't imagine it being any other way now."

I reached out and took her hand. "We can't imagine it being any other way either, darlin'."

I saw her try to conceal her surprise that I was making physical contact.

It was the first time I'd touched any one of them since that hellhole.

The urge to pull back was there.

But I didn't let it rule me.

I kept hold of her hand, even stroking her fingers, my gaze focused on her to ram it home to my brain that it was *her* I was connecting with.

"You know, the night we went out riding, before the crash, I was actually planning on telling you something. The guys as well once they'd come back from that attack on Nico's shipment."

"What's that?"

"It's well-established that I'm a thrill seeker."

"Definitely," she said, looking nervous.

Probably because I didn't look like I was in any state to see to that right about now.

That nervousness escalated as I went on, "And that included sex. Some may call me a sex addict. Whether I am or I'm not, the fact is I've always needed a lot of it and a whole lot of intensity along with it. I hadn't been able to get that from just one person before. Something that was always hard for Milo. But on his end, he couldn't live up to that because he was focused on his work for the Marchettis, always too distracted to commit to being that person for me. And I'm also a lot to take. *But* with the four of us coming together, it's changed things. Having you as a part of it has also brought that intensity I've needed. You've brought out the wilder and dirtier side of Milo. Jesus, before this, he barely ever got the urge as it was. And when we come together, all four of us, it's better and more satisfying than anything I've ever felt before, even with my activities at *Nocturne*. As such, I haven't felt the urge to seek out my Subs, to seek out anyone or anything else for sexual gratification." I shifted my weight with my cane. "What I'm trying to say is, that night, I was going to tell you that I don't want that to be an option anymore. I want to be exclusive. I want it to just be about our foursome. It feels fucked-up thinking about going outside of the four of us now, anyway."

That sentiment obviously had made what had happened with Angelo even worse, that he'd torn into that, tried to take that away from me, from us. He'd inserted himself where I didn't want anybody else inserting themselves, just wanting it to be the four of us from here on out.

"That's lovely," Cat said, beaming out at me. "It's going to mean a lot to everyone. And I understand what a big deal it is for you, too." She eased from my grip on her hand. "Do you think it's the best idea to be talking about this sort of thing right now, though?"

"Our foursome?"

"The sexual aspect of it."

There was that walking-on-eggshells thing again.

"Yeah," I said, stepping closer, right up to her. "I do."

"Julian—"

"You look sexy as fuck in this," I said, running my fingers along the bust of her strapless black Layered jumpsuit that was adorned with a crystal belt. Her hair was flowing down in soft waves. She was wearing a pair of her favored Vivier pumps.

She was dressed up again how she always used to be for work to run her Camlann Corporation empire. Before all of this shit had gone down, including everything that had come along with her forced marriage to Nico.

It made me happy to see her as the powerhouse business tycoon that she truly was.

Before the doctor had shown up, she'd been working remotely too, opposite me.

She sucked in an unsteady breath as I trailed my fingers along the tops of her breasts. I saw her swallow hard and force her focus, telling me, "As I was heading back in here, I was hoping you'd be done with Carver Group business for the day so we could get into discussing our partnership plans for expansion." She wrapped her fingers around my wrist and eased it from her. A gentle smile graced her lips as she said all too carefully, "Let's see to that, shall we?"

"We can. After."

"After?"

I pushed into her and brushed my lips over the side of her throat, tracing the fading marks there. "You and Nico certainly like to mark your territory."

He'd come down the stairs this morning in a rush still buttoning up his shirt, and I'd seen fading scratch marks all over his torso. From a few days ago, something that had clearly happened before I'd been discharged from the hospital. Nothing had happened since, not with Milo included, either. And I knew it was because of me. They didn't want anything sexual occurring near me or even upstairs, but still in the same house as me. The three of them abstaining wasn't exactly the best idea right now with how tense they all were.

None of it was the best for any of us.

So I needed to put an end to it.

Fortunately, Cat was here with me.

And as I was touching her, maybe it was the fact that

there was no male aggression present, but I didn't feel unsettled by making contact.

More than that, my cock was reacting very favorably to the teasing touches I was dealing out to her and the way I could feel her responding and wanting to sink into it.

"I need you," I breathed in her ear.

She moaned and slid her fingers into my hair as I licked her throat, then teased her lips too.

"Julian," she uttered in the sexiest rasp I'd ever heard, a moment before she opened for me and I slid my tongue into her mouth.

Her nails dug into my scalp as she rose to it, the kiss becoming a burst of passionate fury within moments, a lot of the intensity being driven by my desperation to have her, to have this, to wipe out all the rest.

She suddenly pulled her mouth from mine. "No," she breathed.

I took that word more seriously than anyone and stepped back immediately.

"I meant, not like this," she said. "Not that I don't want to. Of course I do. I'm just concerned."

"And that's what I can't stand," I ground out with enough edge that it had her tensing, digging my fingers into the handle of my cane. She wasn't used to aggression coming off me. It wasn't really my thing. Unless I was provoked.

"You think doing this will numb what happened?"

"Not *numb* it, per se, But I do think doing this will mean that *he* wasn't the last one to touch me, Cat," I bit back.

She stared at me for several moments, a struggle taking place.

"I want to know I can be with you, be with those I love. I need to be. I need to be *me.*"

"This… your sexuality… it's only a part of you. There's so much more."

"I know that, but—"

"All right," she said, suddenly coming to me, then dropping to her knees right in front of me.

"Jesus Christ," I breathed.

Our gazes clashed as she slowly pulled down my blue satin pajama pants until my cock sprung free.

I was hard as fucking granite under her gaze, and her eyes hooded at the sight. She even licked her pouty lips a little.

I sucked in a breath from the sweet warmth of her hands starting to stroke my thighs.

I kept one hand tightened on my cane and the other I slid into her soft hair. "Yes. Show me that tongue, darlin'."

She rose to it, her eyes sparking, as she opened her mouth and stuck out her tongue, holding it steady, keeping her mouth wide open.

I pulled my hand from her hair and grasped the base of my cock, then slid it along that wet warmth, stroking her tongue, giving her a taste.

She was submitting to me.

She was actually giving this to me, knowing I needed it this way, reading me so well. It was nice for that to be reversed for once.

And it made me feel… safe.

After she'd gotten me nice and slick, I pulled out, then drove back in deep, making her swallow me whole.

Pleasure shot through me like a beast and my cane shook in my grip as I tried to absorb the intensity of it.

That got a whole lot harder as she started to suck and swallow around my shaft, then swirl her tongue around my crown. "That fucking tongue should be outlawed," I choked. "Jesus Christ."

She grinned around her mouthful of cock, her eyes hooded, and she grasped my balls, kneading and even scratching the way I liked.

I plunged in and out of her mouth and she took me so well.

It should've been right up there as the best head of my life.

But the pleasure wasn't building like it should have been. It was just in some sort of stasis.

Frustration set in and I growled.

She drew back, my cock slipping from her mouth. "Fuck my throat."

"What?"

"Take full control the way I think you need."

Yeah, that had to be it.

With Caterina, I didn't do that. We didn't usually do this outside of a group setting. I wasn't used to entering that Dom headspace with her, nowhere close to fully anyway. Only when I was feeding off Nico and Milo in the moment.

I was holding back.

And obviously not just because of that.

There was a lot fucking with my mind.

I didn't want that.

I didn't want what had happened to take *this* from me.

I grasped her hair with my free hand, then thrust my cock back into her sweet mouth.

And then I used it as a handle to drive brutally in and out, hitting the back of her throat each time and making her gag.

I felt everything build as I used her and dominated her like a fucking animal, pounding into her mouth, thrusting my hips wildly, and chasing that skyrocketing bliss coursing through me.

"Ungh… Christ, darlin'. Yeah, that's it. Swallow me."

Her eyes were shining with moisture, saliva dripping down her chin.

I pulled out roughly, and she choked, gasping for breath.

And then I slammed in deep again, stealing it away in the next second.

Through it all, she took me, took everything I dealt out and there was a spark in her eyes as she did.

Her fingers went wild on my balls, while she dug her nails of her free hand into my thigh.

Everything slammed together and then it happened, ecstasy tore through me, and I came, spurting down her throat and roaring out into the room as it took me over completely, in the best fucking way.

When I pulled out, staggering back a step with my cane, she was there, licking the length of my shaft, then sucking at my crown, her teeth even grazing my piercings as she cleaned off every drop of my cum that still remained.

The moment she rose to her feet grinning at me, I slammed my lips to hers, taking her in an utterly devouring kiss.

When I finally pulled back, raw emotion threatened to take me over as I uttered unsteadily, "Thank you." I pulled up my pants. "Thank you for giving that to me."

"Of course."

"Let me reciprocate," I said, sliding my hand up her thigh.

She snagged it, stopping me from getting to my target.

"What's wrong?"

"I don't need you to reciprocate."

"You do know that I can now, yes? It's been several days, the surgical incision is healed up, STI Panel all clear, and I'm getting stronger every day. I might not be able to bring my full power and stamina to the table, but there's certainly still a lot that I *can* do."

"You shouldn't, though."

"What?"

"This... the blowjob was a good start. But anything else—"

"I can handle it," I snapped.

She jolted at my harshness.

I wasn't surprised, people weren't used to that from me.

It wasn't who I was.

And yet.

Christ, it was him threatening to impact me again.

Clearly, the ways in which that was happening weren't all obvious.

Being touch-averse for the first couple of days, that made instant sense.

But something like this... it wasn't as... direct, I guess.

I scrubbed my hand over my face. "I can't stand this, okay? This from you guys, tiptoeing around me *and* keeping me out of everything. It makes me feel—"

"Like a victim?"

"Yeah. And like I'm so far from being myself. It's making it harder for me to reach out and snatch that back."

She nodded, her eyes shining with understanding. "I'll talk to the boys."

"You will? Just like that?"

"Yeah, I hear what you're saying. It's not working for you. It actually sounds like it might be hurting you too. None of us wants that. But it's just... it's not you, okay? The reason why I didn't want you to *reciprocate*, as you so sweetly put it."

"I don't understand." She'd most definitely been fired

up after that incredible head. I was very good at gauging that to begin with, but I'd also learned her specific cues over the time that the four of us had been together.

She eased back and sat down on the couch, patting the cushion beside her.

I took a seat and laid my cane beside me.

"What's wrong, darlin'?" I asked, my concern mounting at the unsettled and withdrawn demeanor coming off her. "Does it involve what that psychopath did to *you*? Is that why you're hesitant to tell me? Because I meant what I said about it not being necessary to treat me with kid gloves anymore, that I can't stand it being this way either. I'll be fine, I promise."

I'll make sure of it.

"We can talk about it, Cat. If you need to get it off your chest, I hope you know that you can do that with me, with all of us."

"I've been quietly enraged this whole time since all of it started, a simmering rage, if you will. But the kidnapping brought that to a head. I unleashed all over those men that Angelo sent in to attack me. I lost control in a demented, animalistic way, a hugely destructive way. And that happened again the night we extracted you. And I can't let go of that now. It's like it's burning through me, calling out to me, warning me *not* to let it go because of the power it holds, the power it gives me. And that's coming out in other ways, not just violence."

"You mean, sexually?"

"Pretty much. So that's one of the reasons I didn't want to risk letting anything else happen. Not until you're back to full strength and able to handle the aggression. Because I don't know if I can control it when I'm in this state of not wanting to tamper down the other part of it, the battle born part."

I frowned as I took her words in, her pained confession.

What this world *and* this mission were doing to her.

What she thought she needed to be in order to survive it all.

"You've been in combat before and gone all out, but you've then pulled it back. So something must have triggered this. Not being able to let go of it, I mean. And being so determined not to as well. Feeling that initial helplessness of being kidnapped and scrambling to find me after that?"

"Those were definitely factors for why it went down like that. But it remaining this way, it's something else. And I know exactly what."

I stared at her expectantly, waiting with bated breath.

But she got that faraway look in her eyes again and then slumped back against the couch.

"Cat?" I pressed carefully.

She blew out a breath and then burst out in a disjointed rush, "I thought I might be, but I'd pushed it into the background with everything else happening... but I was late... I convinced myself that it was stress, the nightmare going on around us." She shoved both hands through her hair. "What I told you about everything being fine with the doctor's checkup was true, but there was something else. I wanted to keep it to myself. One, so I'd have some time to sort out my thoughts. And two, because now is absolutely not the fucking time for this. But... us talking like this... you being so brave earlier... I just... I had to tell you."

Christ. "You're actually saying that you're—"

"I'm pregnant."

17

~Caterina~

Julian stared at me, openmouthed.

The shock of what I'd just confessed was like the wheels had suddenly stopped turning for him and he needed a few moments to get them moving again.

I pushed off the couch and started pacing, something that I'd clearly picked up from Nico.

Julian cleared his throat and then finally spoke for the first time in what had seemed like minutes. "Well, that's... unexpected."

"*Unexpected?*" I scoffed. "Really? That's toning it down in a huge way, don't you think?"

"You're on birth control, but you've also been on a couple of courses of antibiotics, so it must have interfered and—"

"Yeah, I get it. I've already done the math as to the *how-the-hell* of it all."

"Okay, well, the most important thing is, how do you feel about it?"

"The most important thing? We're at war and I'm pregnant, Julian!"

He grabbed his cane and rose to his feet, coming to me and taking my hand. "Take a deep breath. Or several."

He gave my hand a squeeze, then stroked my fingers in a clear attempt to ease my skyrocketing panic.

Putting it out there, actually telling someone, had made it undeniably real all of a sudden. It'd had all the implications slamming into me all at once.

"You need to take all the rest out of the equation for now. The timing, the circumstances surrounding us. We can deal with that. We can always find a way. But, first and foremost, when it comes to this, you need to determine how *you* feel about it. Nothing else matters beyond that at this juncture."

"Thank you," I said, at him being so sweet and thoughtful.

"Of course, darlin'."

I eased my hand from his, then we sat back down on the couch and I turned to face him as I told him, "This wasn't in my plans. At least not this early on. But, I did one day envision making my own family. One built with support and unconditional love—well, as close to that as it's actually possible to get. One surrounded by love."

"Something you don't have with your own."

"Something none of the four of us have. And, yeah, it would be nice to have a little heir too. Someone I can pass my empire onto. But whenever I envisioned that, there was always something stopping me."

"Let me guess, your father?"

"Him and the entire Leone Family organization. I would never want my child to be born into what I was, to have to hurt through that, to have to suffer and fight so hard for their independence and just to live their life as they saw fit. I never wanted a child of mine to be brought into all this darkness and danger."

"That's what we're doing here, changing all of that, upending the system, taking back our freedom, Cat."

I scrubbed my hand over my face. "Things have… heated up recently. And with this… development, this is the worst time for it."

"So there was a price for extracting me that night?"

"Yes," I admitted.

"I need you to tell me what that is. But, keeping to the current subject at hand, regardless of what it was, like I said, we'll find a way through. If you want this baby and—"

"Do you?"

"What?"

"You haven't said how you feel about it."

"Because I want you to decide where you stand first."

I laid my hand on his thigh. "I appreciate it. I really do. But I want to know."

A broad smile spread over his face as he spoke about it with a light in his eyes that I hadn't seen from him since before the kidnapping nightmare. "I think that this is a beacon, darlin'."

"A beacon?"

"Through all the dark and pain we've been caught up in for way too long. I think it will change a lot in the best ways. Expanding the family the four of us have been forming together? That love and care? What could possibly be bad about that, huh?"

I smiled. How could I not from his beautiful words? "Yeah, I can see that."

"Yeah?" he asked, tipping my chin up with his index finger to guide my gaze to his. "This is our chance, Cat. To have something innocent, something pure and positive in our lives. A bright spark through all of this. If that's what you want, I'm on board all the way. But obviously you need to be sure. Just don't let what's going on around us impact that decision for you. Don't let them take more than they've already taken from us."

A knock sounded on the door, startling the both of us.

"Yes?" I answered.

"Security," a familiar voice spoke. "Need a word."

"Come in."

A moment later, the door opened and Tony Amato walked on in.

I saw Julian's surprise.

He'd thought that Rocco and his unit had still been watching the house because Nico had initially told him that when he'd been trying to reassure him that he was safe from that psychopath, bringing in some of his own soldiers to guard Charon Manor.

But with what Nico and Milo were immersed in today, Nico had switched that out to Tony for the time being.

Tony was a year younger than the boys, but he'd proven himself to be one of Nico's top soldiers. Not as good as Rocco, but he was definitely getting up there and proving himself.

He gave Julian a polite chin lift, then shoved a hand through his short, curly blond hair as his gaze went to me. "Sorry to bother you, but we've got two surprise visitors at the gates wanting passage to meet with you. Leones. Dante Rivera and Matteo Ricca. Nico's unreachable right now and he ordered us to defer command on security issues to you anyway while he's not here."

He shifted his weight in his navy denim jacket and black sweatpants as he awaited my response.

"They want a meet concerning what exactly?" I asked.

"They wouldn't say. They insisted that they'd only relay that to you. But Dante told me to pass on a single word. *Wharton?*"

185

I jolted, and I saw Julian register the recognition in my eyes.

"Send them in."

He gave a nod. "Nico's office?"

"No. Here," Julian cut in.

I swung my head toward him. "It'll be better if I receive them in Nico's office. Alone."

"Why?"

I shifted my weight uncomfortably. "Because this partially pertains to a certain someone I don't want to bring up in front of you."

"You said you'd keep me updated on your search for Angelo," he said, shuddering with it. "And, yes, I can actually hear his name uttered."

"You just shuddered as you spoke it."

"And yet I'm still standing here just fine, aren't I?"

"Shit, all right." I signaled Tony. "Send them in here. Thanks."

Tony looked at Julian, zoning in on his gauze pad and the cane he was clutching like a lifeline. When his gaze snapped back to mine, he spoke worriedly, "These are Leones, though. Allowing them in is one thing, but leaving them alone with you, especially while Julian is injured, concerns me."

"I'll handle them."

Tony, although clearly being respectful of me at Nico's behest, looked skeptical. He shifted his weight, obviously feeling awkward, as he went to push it.

Before he could, I stepped up to him and held out my hand. "Pass me your knife."

"What's that?"

"The tactical blade you have nestled in that ankle holster beneath your right pant leg."

Tony's eyes widened. "How did you know?"

"Just hand it over for a second."

Perplexed and looking more than a little wary, he did just that, retrieving the blade and handing it over to me.

I spun it in the next second and lobbed it through the air.

It cut through it rapid-fire and plunged right through the center of the clock above the door, driving into the joined hands.

Tony whistled. "Message received. *You* can handle it all on your own."

"That I can."

He walked to the clock and pulled the knife out. "Got it," he said, before giving me an impressed smile, then heading on out.

Julian chuckled. "Little does he know that you were actually holding back."

"What?"

"Last time you needed to prove you had what it took, you put me down in that storage room."

"Oh, right. Yes, fond memories." I winked at him. "Kidding."

"The hell you are."

I laughed, and it had him joining me.

It felt good.

Really fucking good.

⸻

I WATCHED Dante scrutinizing the room that was currently being used like Julian's own personal suite. The Underboss of the Leone Family turned this way and that, his leather jacket pulling taut across his broad, muscular form, the same with his dark jeans tucked into a pair of steel-toe boots. He was a hell of a big guy, almost close to

Milo's size, actually. That intimidation factor had served him well as my guard. He frowned and brushed his shaggy salt-and-pepper hair off the back of his neck as he continued looking around, just like he had been since he'd stepped into the mansion.

Matteo had been the opposite, just rolling with everything and focused on whatever it was they were here for. As usual, nothing seemed to impact him. He was as unemotional as ever. The only sign that he had any personality at all were the bold blazers that he always wore with his dress pants. This time it was a deep maroon with gold buttons. It kind of clashed with his long, gray hair falling down past his shoulders. He was almost two decades older than Dante's forty-five years and, with him, age really did mean wisdom. He'd seen a lot and been a part of a great deal during his tenure as Consigliere for my father over the last thirty years. And he'd been able to adapt to it all.

Until recent events had come to pass.

He'd been barred from attending my wedding because he'd shown his displeasure toward some of the business partners that my father and Marco had decided to get into bed with through their new alliance. He'd always been on my father's side before, utterly loyal.

But the bough was breaking where that was concerned.

Dante's eyes kept darting back and forth to me as well, taking in the healing scrapes on my arms from the crash, the marks on me from mine and Nico's wild fucking on the stairs.

He was trying to figure things out, to understand what sort of environment this really was.

For *me*.

Just like he used to do when he was my guard.

"Why do you care?" I burst out with before I could reel it in.

Julian eyed me in surprise.

Yeah, usually I was much better at keeping my feelings locked down and focusing on the task at hand when this sort of business was involved. But I guess there were some unresolved issues with Dante that I hadn't dealt with, or allowed myself to process, because too much had been going on.

Like the fact that he'd been there in the Leone Estate when my father had assaulted me and he hadn't stepped in until Nico and the boys had manipulated the situation to force it.

Or the fact that the only time he'd contacted me in any way since I'd left the Family had been to warn me off going after a piece of land that my father had also had his eye on. That had been too little too late, considering I'd already bought it and it was now the land that *Luster* sat on.

"What do you mean?" Dante asked.

"You're scanning the place like you're actually concerned for me."

"I am."

I sneered. "Sure."

"I didn't attend your forced wedding out of protest," he pointed out.

"Your heroics clearly know no bounds," I responded, sarcasm dripping.

"I also tried to get to Bianca before the unit of soldiers that Santino sent after her. Unfortunately, having to be so careful so that I wasn't spotted slowed me down too much. She managed to get away during the chaos of the motorcycle club attack and somehow stay hidden even in these weeks after it, so thank Christ for that."

"She's more resourceful than Santino gave her credit for," I told him.

"No. *You're* more resourceful," Matteo cut in.

"Excuse me?"

"We went over everything that happened that night." He gestured at Dante. "The two of us examined it all, especially who was evacuated, who left when and where."

"What? How? You weren't even there," Julian spoke.

"We weren't supposed to be there. But we were watching."

"Impossible. The surveillance system was cut really early on," I told them.

"Human intelligence," Matteo rebutted.

"You had control over some Leone security personnel," I realized.

"Yes, but not just them."

I frowned.

Dante stepped forward. "We'd developed a *friendship* with the Lone Gunners."

Matteo actually smiled for once in his life. Although it was a sly smile. "Me and Dante have been working together for a while discreetly to counteract the damage that Santino has taken to doing to the Family—our reputation, our allies, our stability, and our operations in general. When the Lone Gunners received mysterious intel warning of an impending attack, we took advantage of it, Dante and I working with the president of the club. We gave them intel on the holes in security and the best approach to take the Leone Estate, while he agreed to try to take out Angelo and that maniac, Leo Marchetti, while keeping eyes on for us the entire time."

"Jesus Christ," Julian breathed. "That's a hell of a thing."

"It *would* have been if they'd actually managed to assassinate either of their targets," I groused.

Matteo ignored that and went on, "A couple of the club members who retreated and received safe passage to do so thanks to us giving them a viable exit strategy, witnessed the two of you spiriting Bianca Leone away."

"Human intelligence is fallible," I pointed out.

"You don't need to make excuses or cover it up. We're glad she's free, glad she's safe and away from him," Dante said.

"And we just admitted to orchestrating the attempted assassination of Angelo Simone and Leo Marchetti," Matteo added.

Dante winced. "And Santino too actually."

Matteo swung his head toward him. "I thought we agreed not to admit to that? At least not yet, until we're certain about where *she* stands. And the Marchetti heir for that matter."

"The time for pussyfooting around is past, Matteo. You know that as well as I do. We need to go all in here. No more holding things back. It hasn't helped anything and it certainly won't help us now," Dante told him.

"Show her then. Show her what Santino did to you when you went against him, even in just the small way he actually knows about of refusing to attend the wedding."

Dante pinched the bridge of his nose, his distress clear.

"Dante," Matteo pushed.

"Okay," he acquiesced.

He turned his back toward me and lifted up his leather jacket and the back of his shirt.

Julian cursed, and I choked as I found myself looking at deep and very severe lashes from what looked to be caused by a whip all over the expanse of his back.

As Dante fixed his shirt and jacket back into place, Julian asked Matteo, "And you? Did he punish you also? We understand that you were banned from the wedding."

"I was. I didn't outright challenge him, though. I laid out my concerns for certain business partnerships he was intending to enter into. He humiliated me by banning me from the wedding and making me look like I couldn't do my job, painting me as an ill-equipped old man who'd lost the plot. And he also had one of his tech-savvy security personnel wipe out my life savings and funnel it into one of *his* hidden accounts."

"So that's why you've both come to me today? You know I've been abused by him too and you want to use that to join forces? To team-up? Is that it? And you're offering me this Wharton lead on Angelo as an incentive to do that, to trust you with this?"

"This lead is more than just about Angelo," Matteo informed me.

"What is *Wharton?*" Julian asked.

"Wharton Transportation Services," I told Julian. "They fly under the radar using unmarked trucks and various other vehicles to move illicit goods for their clients."

"Black market goods," Dante added in. He eyed me pointedly as he said, "Including people."

Always one to get down to the meat of business and push things along, Matteo said as bluntly as ever, "We know they're the company that Angelo used the night he kidnapped the two of you. We're also aware that you know."

"That's the intel you came to pass onto me? I've already tracked them to a specific owner. However, the guy is a ghost." For now, at least.

"*You* have?" Matteo questioned.

"What?"

"Well, we assumed it was a team effort and that Julian and Nico were combining their resources."

Dante grinned at him. "We were right. Good. This is really good."

I exchanged a discreet look with Julian.

"Good? How?" I asked, trying to hide my concern.

"Those around you here pulling on their resources was the only other explanation outside of the one we'd hoped for," Dante said. "That *you* were behind it."

"That you'd actually been behind more than that," Matteo continued.

"Dodging Angelo's surveillance on you over the years, even somehow reworking that tracking device he planted on you to send him on a wild goose chase. The same with his car's GPS that time. Surveillance he'd been about to show your father on you being mysteriously wiped out. Even him trailing you once and the bridge over the river on the east side of the city being raised out of the blue and cutting him off in his tracks."

Yeah, that bridge thing had been no small feat.

Ensuring there'd been no collateral damage with the timing had been the hardest part.

"Why is any of this important to you?" Julian asked them. "Why would you like it to be the truth so badly?"

"Because," Matteo said, stepping up to me. "It's known that Caterina possesses the business acumen, and she's respected throughout the city for that, established now. But that wouldn't have been enough. A harder edge is also required."

"Required for what?" Julian demanded, getting to his feet with his cane.

"To take power."

I stared between the two of them.

I couldn't believe it.

That fucking suggestion was coming up again.

First from Carlo Benzino, of all people.

Then Nico seeming like he was actually getting on board with it.

Now this.

"If we take power, we'd be trapped in this life forever. In this fucked-up world."

"The nature of it would be different with us at the helm."

"What's the full extent of the Wharton lead you came here today to discuss?" I asked them.

Matteo frowned. "You're not going to even consider it?"

"How about you allow her to absorb the shock of it first?" Julian bit back. "And, as if she's going to agree to this insanity without the two of you throwing some major trustworthiness her way." He eyed Matteo. "You've barely shown her any care in her entire life." He pointed at Dante accusingly. "And *you* basically abandoned her when she left the Family, even though she's told us how close you were with her as her guard, almost like a second father." He moved closer, the aggression from him ramping up in a very uncharacteristic way. "She was out on her own, fighting on her own, dealing with abuse from the Family recently too—a fuckload of abuse—and you did nothing to—"

I laid my hand on his arm, cutting into his tirade. His well-deserved tirade, of course. But one that wasn't doing the situation any favors. "It's all right. Thank you, though."

Dante scrubbed his hand over his face as the emotion of having all of that thrown at him without any sort of filter clearly impacted him. "I couldn't maintain contact once you left. The way Santino was about it… if I'd stayed close with you, Caterina, he would have used that against the both of us, it would have compromised us, and done nothing but brought a whole lot of hurt with it. But I did follow your accomplishments, your career. I still cared and that will never change."

"Those are just words," Julian rebutted, before I could absorb the weight of it all.

"Shawn Price," Matteo spoke suddenly, cutting through all the rest.

"What?" Julian snapped. "Is that the guy who owns those trucks Angelo was using?"

"It is. But like we said, this isn't just about Angelo. It's bigger than that. It's Santino's third attempt at getting his human trafficking dream off the ground. Angelo had been searching out another partner for the last few weeks and he found Price. Me and Dante have been following them very closely, and we discovered that the three of them are working together, a lucrative partnership already in the works. They're even mapping out transport routes in and around the city. Santino wants to use Marchetti Holdings to funnel a great deal of it through. Angelo isn't on his own or ostracized from the Family after what he did to the two of you. Santino is protecting him. He was the one who got him out of that house that night. He sent him to Price to further the partnership and put things in place."

"Even after everything he's done, Santino is safeguarding him. And Angelo should be running, scared for his very life, but he can't let go of his position in the Leone Family either. He's refusing to go quietly, and he's using his influence over this lucrative business partnership with Price to hold on to his place."

"It's not just about that. Not just about his place in the Family," Julian told us. "Santino raped him. From the sounds of it, more than once. I'd be confident in saying it was a regular thing. And Angelo seems to have established some sort of trauma bond with him."

I remembered hearing Angelo confess that to Julian on the surveillance footage we'd reviewed of what had been done to him. "Did you know?" I asked Matteo and Dante.

Matteo shook his head.

"No," Dante said. "But Julian's theory on the trauma bonding makes a lot of sense with the way things have played out, especially lately."

"Regardless of why it's happening, it is. And it can't continue. That's why we're here. You need to take your place as the true heir to the Leone Family," Matteo told me. "And, yes, we did come with intel as a gesture of trust, or good faith, or whatever you want to call it. Because we don't want any doubts from you that we're on your side. We'll help you to take power. It's not just us, there are a few Leone soldiers working with us covertly, hence why we were able to come here without Santino knowing, without implicating ourselves and risking our very lives. Well, any more than we already are risking our lives just by being in that unhinged megalomaniac's orbit." He stepped up to me, his urgency building, and it had Julian gluing himself right to my side in response. "Using our human intelligence routes, we've found the location of Price and his associates. And Angelo, by extension." He stared at me intently. "So? Do you think we can work together now?"

Holy hell.

18

~Nico~

"That went well," Milo commented as we stood in front of Warehouse MH14 watching yet another unit of my soldiers filter out in their vehicles and return to their respective tasks on my territory.

We'd been at it all day, meeting different units at differing locations throughout the city in order not to draw attention from either the Marchettis or the Leones.

It couldn't look like I'd called a full meeting with every single soldier of mine.

It would be interpreted as a call to war, one that hadn't been sanctioned by Leo or my father.

"Caterina's intel had been dead-on where your loyal supporters were concerned. She really did her research well."

She certainly had.

"It almost matched your instincts exactly."

"I did doubt a dozen of them, but they turned out to be solid and on board with what needs to be done."

"That was you playing devil's advocate and treading carefully."

"Something you're usually all for, but judging by how tense you were in these meetings, barely even checking your aggression, it's clear that's changed. Since the kidnappings."

He nodded. "The call you made to make the rescue of Julian about a show of force to the Marchettis and Leones has my full support, you know that. But I'm even all in for going beyond that now."

I pulled out a smoke and fired it up with my Zippo. "Then it's good timing and maybe that new attitude of yours toward these fucked-up circumstances will make what I'm about to tell you easier to absorb."

He folded his arms across his chest and leaned against the side of my Ferrari while I took a couple of harsh drags as I started to pace in front of it.

"Fuck, smoking *and* that pacing of yours all at once is never a good thing."

"I'm considering taking power over the Marchetti Syndicate."

"I thought you might be."

I took another drag of my smoke. "We were so focused on undoing the damage that my father caused through his poor decision-making regarding that deal and restoring our own power that was being compromised by the unhinged moves from both the Marchetti and Leone side of things. But getting that power back only meant not being controlled by them, by anyone. It meant our freedom by destroying the three families and the entire system. *Not* by actually taking the Bosses' places."

"What Carlo suggested got into your head. Him claiming there would be a power vacuum and that it would result in us being in danger all over again."

"Because he was right. I had tunnel vision, in a sense. All four of us did. And with the Reincourt backup in place, there was always that option to disappear, to start over. It wouldn't be starting over, though, if things played out the way Carlo is predicting. It would mean us running, *being* on the fucking run and always looking over our shoulders. It would be no small thing to be known as those who took down the three families. It would put a target on our back. With all these new players that have been brought in with the Marchetti-Leone alliance, it's served to complicate everything."

"You think the only way to be safe *and* remain free is to be at the top of the food chain?"

"It's looking more and more like it."

"Not to mention, you don't want Caterina and Julian losing everything they've built here."

"And with my soldiers on our side, showing their loyalty the way they have been today, making it clear they're willing to follow me into the tunnels of hell... to walk away afterward, to leave them floundering essentially... it doesn't sit well with me."

"I hear you. But what of Caterina? I mean, if she doesn't want to take control of the Leone Family too?"

"Then we run with Dante Rivera."

"If he even wants it after the shit he's been facing with the disrespect and insanity that Santino has been throwing his way. It could leave us with just that useless Capo of theirs, Elia Volpe. He's basically a carbon copy of Santino."

"That can't happen. It would be a Santino 2.0 situation before we know it."

"It should be Caterina, Nico. We both know it."

"We can't force that on her."

"Of course not. But I do think we need to put it to her again, not just walk on eggshells where that's concerned." He reached into his pocket and pulled his phone out.

"Speaking of that, I got this text from her about Julian while we were in that last meeting."

He held it out to me, and I took it in.

Caterina: Julian needs to be brought back in on everything. He's frustrated and pained with the way we've been treading so carefully with him. Work on Nico.

Work on Nico. As if she didn't already have the power to do that these days. Really, she knew that it was Milo who needed to be worked on where this was concerned. She was just reframing it so it didn't look like it to him, so it wouldn't put him on the defensive.

"It's only been a few days."

"I know," Milo said as he pocketed his phone. "This isn't following the same pattern as last time with him."

"If Caterina is insisting, though—you know what? Text her back, tell her to fill him in on everything."

He arched an eyebrow. "You're sure?"

"Yeah. We can't shield him any longer. We've got him past the worst of the physical healing process, at least."

"All right," he said, firing off the necessary message to Caterina.

I butted out my smoke and walked to the driver's door. "Let's head back."

Before I'd even opened the door, my phone started ringing.

I held up my hand to Milo as I pulled it from my pocket to see Cassio Quinto calling.

Frowning, I took the call, "Cassio, what can I do for you?"

"It's what *I* can do for you, Nico."

I tensed. "What's happened?"

"I just got out of an emergency meeting with Giovanni, Leo, and your father. One that you were purposely excluded from. Marco got word that his partner regarding the military arms deal has been murdered, along with the entire organization. A real good thing that it's not going ahead as far as I'm concerned. But not in their eyes. To say Marco's furious would be an understatement. He's ordered Gio and I to coordinate attacks on Benzino business interests. For my part, I'm to take their main meth lab. Gio's gonna hit several businesses under their protection, firebomb them, the whole nine. Marco also talked about how he wants to use Caterina's Camlann Corporation as a front for his illegal activities, to expand through her and use her reputation as a sign of stability to those that he and Santino are partnering with now, including a massive heroin deal that they informed us in this meeting has just been closed. It seems like that disgusting flesh trade idea that Santino is determined to follow through on will also be a part of what they intend to use Caterina Leone's businesses for. They're going to force expansion under their terms. Santino is spearheading it too. No other specifics were given on that, such as how and when they planned to put this to her."

"How about the proposed attacks?" I asked, as I rapidly absorbed all the intel he'd just given me.

"Three nights from now. Now, I can't refuse to take the Benzino lab, as I'm sure you understand. But this isn't going to land well. It will put us at war, Nico. At a time when both the Marchettis and Leones are unstable and high-level decisions are being made by unhinged individuals. I'm not in a position to stop any of this. If anybody *was* in a position to head off these attacks, though, the coincidental timing wouldn't be outed by me."

"Why are you coming to me with this? Why warn me about Caterina too?"

"You saved my life. And as I've alluded to, you're not the only one disillusioned with things. But as Marco's heir and arguably the most respected member of the entire outfit, there is something to be done about it, hope to be had, through *you.*"

"You're pledging your loyalty to me?"

"Yes, I am. Do with that as you will."

"Thank you. And thank you for bringing this to me."

"Be careful, Nico. You're definitely out of favor with Leo and Marco at the moment. Santino included. Leo has leaked the truth about your care for Caterina. They know you're not doing as was outlined in that disturbing contract."

"Punishment is coming."

"I believe so, yes. I just don't know how that will come about."

"All right, thanks for letting me know."

"No problem. Just be careful, Nico."

"Will do."

With that, I hung up and turned to Milo, who was looking on with a whole lot of worry.

"We need to get home now."

"What's going on?"

I hauled my car door open. "I'll fill you in on the way."

19

~Emilio~

Today had proven to be the day for people coming out of the woodwork and pledging their loyalty to us.

Honestly, it was about damned time. Nico had long deserved this deference.

And he wasn't the only one anymore.

The moment we'd stepped back inside the Manor, Julian had been there getting us up to speed on an impromptu meeting that had taken place here involving Dante and Matteo from the Leone Family. Basically, the two of them had pledged *their* loyalty to Caterina. They wanted her to take Santino's mantle. They'd also given her intel on Angelo's supposed location.

"Where's Caterina?" Nico asked Julian as the three of us made our way from the entrance way toward the kitchen. I hadn't eaten all day with these meetings and my stomach was fucking rumbling fiercely.

"She's up in her room working on verifying the intel that Dante and Matteo gave us about the owner of Wharton—and a whole lot more than that."

"And concerning Angelo's location," I spoke, wanting to see his reaction.

No. Needing to.

"Yeah, him too," he answered without even flinching. And saying it strangely casually.

I shot a look at Nico, seeing the same worry from him that I was trying to conceal, given that text Caterina had sent us earlier.

I honestly didn't want to bring that fucker's name up in front of Julian at all. I didn't want him to have to hear it, nor deal with any of this involved in tracking the asshole down and then eliminating him.

But Nico and I had discussed it on the way home and agreed that it was proving more detrimental to Julian all the while he was being kept out of things. He felt like he was isolated on the periphery. And that was a very dangerous thing after what he'd been through. Unfortunately, keeping him informed of what was going on meant discussing Angelo Simone, because he was one of our targets, an ongoing mission in effect. Not to mention, he was tangled up in all this, even irrespective of the kidnappings. Especially now that we knew from the intel that Dante and Matteo had given Caterina, that Santino hadn't renounced him after all and instead had him working on a big time business partnership with Shawn Price.

The sick fuck was protecting the asshole who'd kidnapped his own daughter and tried to sell her into the flesh trade, who'd tortured and assaulted Julian—from their perspective, a valuable business asset—who'd clearly lost whatever shred of his sanity had been left remaining.

Nico walked beside me as we followed Julian into the kitchen as he moved along with his cane clacking on the floor.

The sight that greeted us had me taken aback and judging by Nico's curse of surprise, he was right there with me on that too.

There, on the island and even covering the kitchen table, was a massive spread of food.

A feast, really.

"What's all this?" Nico asked, inspecting the island, then zeroing in on the table too, taking everything in.

"I had my penthouse staff come by and put this together while you guys were gone. I figured you could use it after the back-to-back meetings you were embroiled in all day long."

"I bet Tony wasn't happy about allowing all that insanity on through."

"Nah, he was fine. Well, once Cat worked her magic and convinced him."

Nico chuckled. "I can only imagine."

"Sunshine, this is fucking perfect. Thank you," I said, walking to Julian.

But, as usual, since he'd woken up in the hospital that night, I pulled up short just in time, fighting against my instinct to touch him, to embrace him. It always left me with a sickening feeling, both because of the reason I had to keep my distance from him and because I fucking missed touching him, showing affection, and just being our normal selves together. I missed that there was a hole of sorts now between all four of us.

This time, though, something different happened.

He didn't take a step back to enforce that distance and lack of physicality.

And he even went further than that, shocking the shit out of me when he looped his free arm around me and pulled me in close.

He stroked my back and even nuzzled against me.

"It's okay now," he breathed. "I'm okay."

When he eased back, I stood there staring at him.

He merely grinned at me, then turned to Nico and slap-shook with him.

"Did you have a breakthrough with Doctor Williams today?" Nico asked him.

"I actually canceled the session for today."

He lifted a shoulder like it was no big deal.

"You did *what?*" I asked.

Actually, it came out more like a harsh demand. That was how concerned it had me.

"We need to focus on the here and now. Priorities, right?"

"So, your recovery shouldn't be a goddamn priority?" I shot back.

"Cat filled me in on everything. Where you guys were today, the whole deal with Carlo Benzino. I know exactly what we're up against and exactly how things have shifted —or escalated—because of the price that Nico paid to get me out of that hellhole. So, yeah, I think all of that takes priority over me having a fucking therapy session."

"It's more than that and you know it, Julian."

"J, he's right. Last time—"

"This isn't like last time. I have the tools now to handle this. And, yeah, when I first woke up in the aftermath at the hospital, I might have doubted that, and it's why I had you call in Roslynn immediately, but I'm more settled now. I've managed to get a handle on it. In fact, Cat and I—"

"We know you skull-fucked her," I cut in. "She told us. And it was dangerous. Too early by far."

"If it had been too early, I wouldn't have been able to handle it. I certainly wouldn't have been able to get off."

"This is like piling on the pressure and weight upon already unstable foundations," Nico warned him.

"The truth is, neither of you really knows that. You're not me. You're not inside my head." He shoved his free hand through his thick blond hair. "So let me do this my way. You questioning it and treating my like glass really isn't helping."

"Because you're trying to retreat into denial," I pointed out.

"No. I'm moving forward." He gestured between the two of us wildly, anger sparking. "Do the two of you want me curled up in the corner, rocking back and forth and crying about it like a little bitch? Or do you want me up and about and living my life again, being *me* like I always have been?"

"I just want you to feel better, Sunshine." I closed the distance between us and stroked his arm, noting that he didn't flinch, not even a little bit.

I wanted to believe that it was because he was actually feeling better, but given the limited time that had gone by and the brutal extent of what he'd endured, it was much more likely a case of him delving deep into denial. *Goddammit.* "That's all any of us want."

"I get that and obviously I want that, too. So, please, let me do this my way, all right? That's what I need from you."

No, it was what he wanted.

For us to back off, to let it be for now.

For now was all I could do.

"Okay," I murmured, stepping back. "If that's what you truly think you need."

"It is, yeah. Thank you," he said, smiling out at me, so close to the way my Sunshine was known for—bright and charismatic and full of hope and vigor.

"You can't stop your therapy sessions altogether," Nico said. "Less often, yes. At least for now, and we'll see how it goes from there."

"Fine," Julian reluctantly agreed.

"Are you hurt?" Nico asked him.

"Hurt?"

"After what happened between you and Caterina? She loses control, and that's become a lot more pronounced lately, that vicious edge of hers." He smirked. "*Sexy* vicious edge," he mused to himself. "Our vicious little princess. She's bringing that out a great deal more."

"Uh, no. She didn't hurt me at all. Not even a scratch or any nail marks."

"What?" Nico questioned. "That doesn't seem feasible."

"She submitted to me. That's how it happened that way."

Both Nico and I did a double take, exclaiming in unison, "What?"

Julian lifted a shoulder. "She just wanted something different, and she was still in the zone of treading on eggshells with me."

"Sounds like more than that," Nico uttered, worriedly.

Before anything more could be said on the topic, the formidable woman herself burst into the kitchen, her phone in her hand.

She brightened as she took in the three of us standing there, all of us in one place again. That only intensified when she saw the feast that Julian had made his staff prepare for us.

Instead of focusing on that for long, though, she gestured at her phone, and reported in that business tone of hers, "I just received confirmation on the Carlo Benzino situation." She declared, "He can be trusted."

"As confirmed by Joseph Stover?" Nico asked.

"He finally got back to you then," Julian spoke.

"He did."

"And what did he say that has you sure Carlo is to be trusted with this alliance?" Nico pushed.

"*Excalibur.*"

"One word and that confirms everything for us?" I questioned, skeptical, while Nico looked on intently and Julian raised an eyebrow.

"We established several code words before we parted ways, in case we needed to transmit covert messages to one another," Caterina told us. "He's deep cover. It's been necessary. Each word carries a specific and often deep meaning. In this case, *Excalibur* was more than a mere sword in Arthurian legend. It was a symbol of hope and justice. It was about upholding a moral code, possessing honor and living up to those ideals, especially for Arthur, via his leadership."

"I get it," Julian said.

"Yeah," I confirmed.

"If you're willing to put your trust in this guy over something as vital as this, then I'll accept that as gospel," Nico announced.

I'd normally play devil's advocate, but this time I didn't find it necessary. I'd come to trust her implicitly now, and there was also the fact that the stakes had been raised substantially, so we could no longer operate so cautiously.

Caterina stepped up to Nico and pressed her hands to his chest. "You trust me that much now, huh?"

"I do."

"We all do," I told her.

She smiled at us as she stepped back from Nico, then scrolled on her phone for a few moments, before telling us, "As much as I appreciate that, I *do* actually have more than just that one word. It's something Joe sent along with it."

"Wow, you really tested us with that, huh?" Julian jested.

Some sort of strange look passed between them that I couldn't decipher, before the focus went to Caterina holding out her phone to us and playing a video.

"It's body cam footage that Joe had rolling during a meeting with Carlo," she told us, just a moment before all of us gathered around to see Carlo, himself, stepping into a clearing in a forest somewhere and looking at the camera —Joseph Stover, really, and uttering, *"You'll send this footage to her when the time is right?"*

"I will," the guy who we couldn't see, but was obviously Stover, answered.

Before it went on further, Caterina told us, "I've also run the voices and the footage through my security to verify its authenticity, just as an extra precaution.

Of course she had. She was amazing when it came to all of this.

We focused on the video as Carlo stepped right up to Joe, coming into full focus, that distinctive, trendy ash gray hair in that Pompadour style and one of his designer pinstripe suits filling the screen.

"You took a risk reaching out to me, let alone revealing yourself in this way, Joseph."

"Unfortunately, it was necessary."

"How so from your perspective?"

"You're gauging my true intentions. Smart."

"Ensuring that our agendas align. A safe alliance cannot be formed without that being the case."

"I agree. As you've said, this is a risk to me too. However, the tide is turning. It's putting those I care about in danger."

"Bianca and Caterina?"

"Correct."

"And how does that concern me? You want me to step in, get them out?"

"If that was my goal, I would simply do it myself. No, if I go that route, it will destroy everything they've both worked for, their careers. It's time to deal with the threat directly."

"You want us to work together to wipe Santino off the board?"

"You have your ear to the ground more than most, just like me. You must know what he's planning."

"I'm aware, yes. He wishes to dissolve the three-families alliance and push me out. He wants unchecked power and his rule to become completely unrestricted. With the Benzinos being the voice of reason, that cannot come to pass for him with us still involved, and him still bound by the alliance. Furthermore, Marco Marchetti is also taking rash actions that risk us all."

"Yes, the two of them are becoming unhinged. They'll come for you. And as part of that, they'll come for Caterina too, use her as a bargaining chip and pull her back into that which she worked so hard to escape. I also have intel on Nico Marchetti's disillusionment with his father's rule. You'll be able to use that to assist you, bring him to your side, take him under your wing. But you need to hurry."

"You believe he'll cut and run?"

"I believe he has the means to do so, yes, but he doesn't want to leave Caterina."

"Ah, you're referring to their little war? More like a mating dance, really."

"Indeed. There's interest there on both sides. Things point to him allying with her. That would be your window to do the same."

"I'd need to see where things fall first."

"Understood. But don't drag your feet. It's hard to see the forest through the trees where their true allies among Marchetti and Leone soldiers are concerned, so their resources will be limited. If you join

forces, though, that will all shift. Your resources, them in key positions within the families to deliver damage."

"When I'm ready to approach them, they'll need proof that I can be trusted. You'll be ready to forward this video you're making at that time? It won't work without it. Taking the risk of allying with an opposing family, which is what it will be viewed as when Santino and Marco carry out this plan to cut me out, would be a death sentence to them if I was proven untrustworthy. They'll most definitely need verification."

"As I've already said, yes, I'll provide it when they're ready to reach out. I would also advise you to give them a gesture of good faith."

"Suggestion noted." Carlo shoved his hands in the pockets of his suit jacket, then gave a chin lift to the camera— Joseph Stover. *"That concludes our business, then."*

"For now."

The corner of Carlo's mouth turned up. *"Indeed. Until then, Joseph."*

"Be well, Carlo."

With that, Carlo turned and walked away through the forest, fading from view.

And then the video ended.

"Shit, that was a hell of a thing," Julian commented.

"Particularly the fact that Stover is as plugged into things as you are," Nico told Caterina.

"Even with that video being made for our benefit, it's clear he cares about you. His words, his tone, the vehemence… that wasn't faked in the least," I said. "Plus, the fact that he risked himself to do this in the first place."

Nico nodded along, taking in everything in that usual shrewd way of his. "I'll set a meet with Carlo." He eyed Caterina. "I'll need you there with me."

"From this video and seeing what was going on with the two of them, how they've obviously being working close together, it's clear now how Carlo knew so much about Cat's skills," Julian pointed out.

"Yeah," Caterina said. "That's how much Joe believes Carlo can be trusted."

"It's more than trust," Nico countered. "It's something much more stable than that. *Need.* Carlo needs us to work with him in order to do this. He might have the resources, but he's currently on the outside. He needs us to bridge the gap there."

"Basically, we can't do it without him and vice versa," Julian noted.

Nico fired off a text. Caterina had secured all our devices over the last few days, so we didn't have to worry about that end of things, and it wasn't a risk for Nico to reach out to Carlo. It couldn't be intercepted by the Marchettis or Leones.

The actual risk would be meeting in-person.

But when it came to both Carlo and Nico, they needed to have it that way, wanting to gauge each other, read each other face-to-face over every little thing. Plus, there was certain business that shouldn't be done over the phone.

I'd take care of sorting out the precautions for the meet on Nico and Caterina's end of things and, knowing what I did about how well Carlo's men operated, I now had no doubt that he'd do the same on his end.

And that was what I was holding onto in order to look beyond my personal distaste for working with the Benzinos in the first fucking place with the bad history there.

As in tune with me as he was, Nico eyed me and said, "I can't have you there during the meet."

"I'll be fine. I've *been* fine with it every time his name has come up, haven't I?"

"Because you're taking a dangerous leaf out of my book and compartmentalizing it all."

"Nico—"

"It's not the only reason I can't have you there. I need you on something else."

I cocked an eyebrow.

His gaze darted to Julian, before he told me, "I want you to move on the location that Dante and Matteo gave Caterina."

"To take out Angelo?"

"Yes. But the operation will also involve eradicating Shawn Price and his entire base of operations. We can't risk Santino and my father gaining more power or more dangerous allies to back them." He eyed Caterina. "So long as you've confirmed the intel beyond a shadow of a doubt?"

"I have," she said. "Matteo and Dante were correct. The information is solid. The location they gave us of a string of warehouses two hundred miles outside the city function as Price's home base. I've since tapped into the security there and confirmed Angelo's presence."

I looked over at Julian, who was standing there staring into space, while now clutching his cane in a death grip. "Sunshine, are you okay?"

He blinked and looked out at the three of us. "Yeah, sure. All good."

"You understand that you can't be a part of the operation, yes?" Nico put to him. "You're not field-ready."

In more ways than one there.

"Yeah, of course. That's fine," he answered all too easily. He flinched when he saw our reactions and added, "So long as you get the bastard and put him the fuck down, I can make peace with not being an active part of the takedown."

"He will be put down," Nico assured him.

A growl left me as I said, "There will be no fucking mercy. I guarantee you that."

"I know there won't be."

"*Principessa,*" Nico spoke, reaching out and stroking Caterina's arm. "We need to discuss what we called you about on the way home."

"You mean, Marco and Santino wanting to use Camlann Corporation as their front for their despicable activities? Yeah, that's not happening. Not under any circumstances."

"I agree, but I'm concerned about what they might do to force that upon you."

"We'll keep our ears to the ground."

"We need more than that."

She pulled from his touch and folded her arms across her chest. "I know what you're getting at. You want me to join you in taking power. To rework our strategy not just to destroy, but to go about it in another way that ensures Leone assets and business ventures will remain intact so that the empire can become mine, instead of us merely burying it."

"Along those lines, yes."

"I don't want the Leone Family to be my legacy, Nico."

"I understand that wasn't how you saw things going or—"

She threw her hands up in the air, cutting him off, as she yelled, "Do you really understand? I mean, yes, when I was younger, I wanted it, I thought I'd become his heir. But when he cut me out, it shifted everything. Irreparably. And I'm glad that it did, because I've worked my ass off to build my own empire, something I'm still doing—or trying to do with all this other shit going on and not being able to be there physically running things. *That's* already killing me as it is. And now you're actually asking me to reconsider everything, upturn my plans and become the Boss of the Leone Family? To have that toxicity taint what I've been building?"

Goddamn.

"Caterina—"

"*No,*" she ground out at him. "I won't allow this. Not for Dante and Matteo. Not for the big picture of the mission. Not even for the three of you. I can't. A line needs to be drawn somewhere. And this is it for me. We can win out without *me* taking power."

"And how does that play out in your mind?" Nico asked.

"Simple. We decimate all the power players in the Leone Family, destroy all illegitimate aspects of their business, and incorporate the rest into the Marchetti Syndicate under *you*. That way, you'd already be on the road to steering things toward a much more above board approach. Maybe just keep the coke operations during the transition or share them with Carlo Benzino. The rest isn't necessary. The Marchetti Syndicate can succeed *and* prosper as a legitimate empire."

"Simple? No. It's much easier said than done," Nico told her. "It would require completely reworking long-established processes and approaches that have been deeply ingrained into the Syndicate."

"Change has to begin somewhere, and it often comes right along with unsettling and upturning what came before," she argued.

"Why this insistent need to legitimize? You've crossed lines before. Recently, even."

"Those actions were a result of forced circumstances. Of survival. The only way I could thrive while my fucking father—and now yours—is still standing tall and commanding so much power. *I'm* talking about when that's done, when they're finally fucking gone. I'm talking about our futures, our legacy, too."

"Legacy? That's the second time you've used that word tonight. Why *that* specific word? Is it something Dante and Matteo said that you might have neglected to report to me and Milo?"

"No, I—I've just been thinking a lot about it the last few days while things have been in a calm-before-another-storm state."

Julian stepped up to her and draped his free arm around her. "She's always been ambitious. This is just obviously another facet of that."

I frowned. Something was... off.

She'd texted us earlier that everything had been fine with the doctor and the tests that had been run, so it couldn't be that. Maybe having Dante and Matteo show up here had triggered her then.

"You know the amazing feast I prepared is going to be ruined all too quickly if we don't start digging in, right?" Julian interjected.

Nico snapped out of his deep staring at Caterina and swung his head toward the food.

I wasn't above it either. Neither of us had eaten all day. While Nico had been known to skip breakfast before, that really wasn't my thing, and I was definitely feeling the hunger pangs from it now.

Nico rubbed the stubble on his chin that was a lot more pronounced than usual with everything that had been going on. "You're right, let's eat. I've reached out to Carlo to arrange a meeting so we can formulate a plan to counter the proposed attacks. We'll finalize that after dinner and also strategize the operation against Shawn Price." He reached out to Caterina and took her hand, softening as he said, "Right now, though, the four of us will just take a beat, be together, all right?"

"With all this happening, we can't just—" Caterina started.

"Can't just what?" Nico cut in. "Take some time for the four of us? To be together? To have a brief reprieve from it all? Things are about to get a fuck of a lot worse, so moments like these should be taken where they can."

"They remind us what we're really fighting for," I added.

"They sure as shit do," Julian affirmed.

With her still hesitating, Nico explained, "This is what it's like to be a part of a team. The burden falls on all of us. It's spread between the four of us. It's not all on a single person's shoulders, as you were always used to. We share the load, Caterina."

The corner of her mouth turned up at his words.

And then she looked out at all three of us in turn, smiling as she said, "Okay, yeah, that would be nice."

With that, we all settled at the table, Julian taking a seat beside Caterina on the one side, then me opposite him on the other, leaving Nico next to me and opposite Caterina.

"Dig in," Julian said. "Take whatever you want. There's also seconds and a whole wealth of desserts on the counter." He picked up a plate with two egg white omelets on it and set it down in front of Caterina beside her empty plate that needed to be filled. "Had this made especially for you."

She beamed at him as she pushed one omelet onto her plate with a fork. "Much appreciated, cutie."

"He even had a bowl of berries prepared," Nico said, gesturing at the massive thing over on his end of the table and then pushing it toward her.

"That's really sweet. Thank you."

I slid a glass of freshly squeezed orange juice into her orbit.

She grinned out at us. "You do know I can feed myself, yes?" As she was in the process of saying that, she almost subconsciously lifted a plate of chocolate pancakes in front of Julian.

Pancakes with dinner? Yeah, that was him.

"You were saying?" Nico teased, as he drew attention to what she'd done.

It had her chuckling and the rest of us joining in.

"I guess we are a team, huh?" she mused.

"Sure are," I said.

Julian laid his hand on hers for a moment and told her rather intensely, "This is how it will always be. Us taking care of you, and vice versa. Taking care of each other. You won't ever be alone again. Trust us where that's concerned."

Nico and I exchanged a look. Had his need to emphasize all of that to her come about from the kidnapping and what he'd suffered through?

It was hard to tell.

And before I could analyze it further, the subject shifted as Caterina told Nico with a whole lot of curiosity, "All our years *warring* and checking into the other and I still don't know what you like to spend your time doing outside of Marchetti business and, of course, hanging with your boys." She smirked. "Well, my boys now too."

"Something you don't know about me? I like it," he teased, as he scooped some risotto onto his plate.

"Nico," she pushed. "I mean, Julian's got his social media hobby and his adrenaline-junkie thing, Milo has his fantasy figurines. What's your thing? What would you be doing if there wasn't all this three families bullshit going on?"

He smirked. "You, *principessa.*"

She rolled her eyes. "I'm being serious."

"So am I," he said, wiggling his eyebrows at her suggestively, which had the most innocent little giggle escaping her.

Julian and I grinned at each other.

"That Ducati you saw in the garage when we were heading out for our ride is Nico's," Julian told Caterina.

She raised an eyebrow. "Really?"

"You thought it was mine?" Julian asked her.

"Yeah. I know Milo is all about his Harley. Although he rides for the freedom and peace of it, not the adrenaline or thrill like you do."

"Precisely," I said, impressed that she'd read that so well. "By the way, that also goes for the hot tub in the backyard."

"He sneaks in there when all is quiet and everyone's gone to sleep," Julian told her. "It's kind of like a meditative experience for him. Fucked in there a couple of times, too."

"Just a couple?" Caterina queried.

Nico glared between me and Julian. "They tend to prefer the shower when they do go there here. Namely, *my* fucking shower."

"It's a porn shower, N."

"That was once, and I apologized profusely, Nico," I cut in.

"It was actually twice," Julian informed me. "Remember the time I did that thing with the shower nozzle that—"

"Not while we're eating," Nico cut in.

Goddammit, I *did* remember that. *Holy hell.* I must've blocked it out with how pissed Nico had been about it when he'd found out. "Was that when Nico walked in to see——"

"Stop," Nico grunted.

Julian burst out laughing. "It was, yeah, big boy."

Caterina wrapped her arm around Julian and squeezed him to her, then planted a kiss on his cheek. "Little troublemaker."

I chuckled. He certainly could be sometimes.

I watched him beaming out at her, and it was incredible to see.

I just hoped it was all real.

That he wasn't shoving down all the rest and fooling himself into thinking that it would stay there, and that he'd be able to actually operate that way for long.

The way he was discussing sex so easily and so soon after what had happened concerned me.

"Yeah, the Ducati is mine," Nico spoke. "I don't get to ride it as much as I would like."

"Marchetti business?" Caterina asked. "Or something else?"

"Mostly Marchetti business. I was focused on earning for the Family."

"Big time," I cut in. "Being the top earner consistently isn't easy. Especially not when so many things can go wrong with the types of businesses we're running."

"All the more reason to go legitimate," she said.

Nico paused on taking another bite of his risotto. "Can we not? We agreed to take a beat."

"All right," she muttered. "It's not going away, though."

"Yes, you've made that abundantly clear."

She glared at him for a moment. Then I saw Julian slide his hand under the table and give hers a squeeze. It had her drawing in a calming breath, then focusing back on the other conversational track. "Is the other reason to do with you being worried about feeding into your reckless side? That part that links too closely to your *feral* state?"

Nico nodded, his eyes lighting up at her understanding. "Uh huh," he said, between chewing his food.

As I continued piling my plate high, Julian spoke, "It's one of the things I'm most looking forward to doing when I'm fully healed. Riding again. We should all do it together."

"I've never ridden a motorcycle before. You know, except for that night on the back of yours," Caterina said.

"I'll teach you," I told her. "Don't even think about letting Julian do that."

"Hey!" he cried. "I'm a fantastic teacher."

"Not with that. Stunting comes way down the road, Sunshine. Not right up front."

He winked at Caterina.

"What was that for?" Nico asked.

"There might've been a tiny bit of stunting from our sexy woman that night."

Caterina smiled proudly. "I guess I have a knack for it."

"*Or* it brings out your reckless side, too," Nico countered.

"Perhaps," she admitted, with a glint in her eye. "Do you think you'll get back to riding once all this is over?"

He smiled. "I think I'll be able to enjoy a lot of things. We all will."

"And what about our living arrangements then?" she asked.

The question had all of us stilling.

"What do *you* want them to be?" Nico put to her.

She looked down at her plate. "I guess I have some thinking to do where that's concerned."

"I guess you do." Nico leaned forward in his seat. "But just so we're clear, the choice is in your hands."

"What? I thought we'd be butting heads over this majorly, that you'd be insisting—"

"As much as I would be overjoyed if you chose to remain here in the Manor, albeit without the separate rooms situation we're all currently operating under, it needs to be your decision. You've been through a lifetime of suffering from others trying to control you and infringe upon your freedoms." He gestured at me and Julian in turn. "None of us will allow that to befall you again. You're safe with us, Caterina. Free."

"I know," she said, smiling out at us. "I know I am."

"With that in mind, we should also start the process of getting divorced."

All of us stilled to stare at Nico putting words out there we'd never thought we'd hear.

It had taken him years to have Caterina here with him. And she was even bound to him through their marriage too. For him to give that up, it was a hell of a thing.

Off our looks, he eyed Caterina and said, "I told you when the marriage was first put on the table, I didn't want it like that with you. I wanted it to be on our terms, especially yours. It's also creating an imbalance between the four of us, with you and me being married and Milo and Julian on the outside of that."

"Thank fuck," Julian spoke. "I thought me and Milo would have to be all over you to push this issue, Nico. I figured we'd really have to bring the pressure to convince you to get it annulled, or whatever needs to be done in this strange forced-marriage situation."

Caterina looked between Julian and me. "The two of you really kept your disapproval and upset about this situation on the down low."

I lifted a shoulder. "There was nothing to be done about it at the time, so there was no point airing our thoughts about it and only serving to further antagonize an already sensitive issue for you. We know how hard it's been on the both of you, particularly you, Caterina. But now, with Nico already taking a stand against things via Leo outside the hospital that night, and other things ramping up in that respect too, it *can* be dealt with. That's all that matters."

She smiled at me and Julian. "Thank you for doing that." She eyed Nico. "I'll get the paperwork started for us then."

"Perfect," Nico said. "When this is done, when this war is won, I don't want anything of *them* tainting *us*. We need to be free of it completely."

I reached for the champagne in the ice bucket and went about filling four glasses. When I was done, I cried, "*Facciamo un brindisi!*"

Julian pushed Caterina's orange juice in front of her instead.

Off my look, he told me, "She's not a fan of champagne."

"That's me and wine, Sunshine."

He eyed Caterina. "I thought you were the same there. Right?"

"It's bad luck to toast without alcohol," Nico reminded him.

"It's fine," Caterina assured Julian. "It just requires a sip."

"You don't like champagne?" Nico queried. "I thought that was wine, that this was the exception?"

"I guess I'm not a major fan, it depends," she answered.

"Huh, that's another small thing I didn't know about you. I thought I had it all covered."

"I'm full of surprises."

Julian chuckled and nudged her. "You certainly are. Keep us on our toes, don't you?"

I ignored all the chatter and raised my glass. "*A noi!*"

They joined me, the four of us clinking glasses and making the toast.

To us!

That was what mattered through all of this.

It was everything.

20

~Julian~

Doing business in the dead of night.

That was certainly the mob way.

Or at least what I had experienced from being in the thick of it with Nico and Milo over the many long years of our friendship.

And even when this was done, things like this would still occur with Nico now intent on taking power over the Marchetti Syndicate.

Unless he could turn things completely legitimate.

Although Cat wanted that, it definitely would be a tall order to achieve in reality.

But it could technically be done.

I'd been looking into the entire thing over the last few hours since we'd wrapped up dinner, and there were ways to accomplish that. But Nico would require both mine and Cat's assistance. And it would also take time.

Given that Cat, herself, was used to operating in the dark and delving deep into illegality too, seemingly without having much of a problem with it so long as the ends justified the means, I figured that this turnabout for her had something to do with the pregnancy. It was shifting things for her. More so, it'd had her realizing that things needed to shift. It wouldn't be a leap to assume that she believed legitimizing all operations and Marchetti businesses was the key to making damn sure the baby would be brought into a safe life devoid of the darkness and brutality that existed now.

Sure, us bringing down Marco and Santino would achieve that to a massive degree, but if the Marchetti Syndicate, even under new leadership in Nico, continued to be entrenched in illegal operations, it would still invite that darkness and danger.

I shoved a hand through my hair as I stood outside Nico's office, listening in to the meeting that was taking place with him, Milo, and twenty of his soldiers.

They were strategizing the assault against Shawn Price, slated to take place twenty-four hours before Marco Marchetti planned to launch those strikes against the Benzinos.

Nico was intending to upset those plans of Marco's with this mission.

We also weren't going to cover up our involvement in it.

There was no holding back now.

We were going all in.

And I was honestly here for it.

Even Milo, who was usually more cautious and all about protection and defense, was on board with us escalating things and throwing ourselves into the thick of it.

I wanted this shit done with more than I ever had before.

It wasn't just about the Angelo of it all either.

No. What Cat had confessed to me had shifted things for me, too.

This pregnancy changed things.

There was an innocent to protect now, a baby that couldn't be brought into a war zone.

A baby that deserved better than what we'd had, that deserved everything.

I listened into the details that Nico and the guys were discussing, taking note of everything pertinent, such as the precise times for their coordinated three-pronged assault against three warehouses owned by Price, all in the same area, all of which Angelo had been moving between, according to the more in-depth investigation that Cat had been doing. She didn't trust human intelligence alone, which was what we'd gotten from Dante and Matteo. Actually, she didn't trust people as a rule. Outside of the three of us, anyway. Well, and Joseph Stover, who was also caught up in this shitshow. The fact that he'd basically thrust himself into it when he was in a position to simply disappear into the shadows, all to protect Cat, was a hell of a thing.

I stepped away once I'd gotten the information that I'd needed from the meeting.

Although they were letting me in on things more so now after I'd made it known that I couldn't take the whole walking-on-eggshells routine, Milo had drawn the line at this. At me having to listen to every little detail involved in their planned takedown of Angelo and that new Marche-tti-Leone partner, Shawn Price. They thought I was asleep, anyway.

I was about to get to that as I made my way down the corridor until I heard thuds coming from inside the home gym. Usually, you could expect Milo to be in there working out hard like a fucking machine, but given that he was in Nico's office attending that meeting, it clearly could only be one other person.

I pushed open the door and peered inside to see Cat there pounding on a heavy bag. She was clad in a turquoise sports bra with matching tiny shorts, her wavy hair pulled back into a tight ponytail, the latter of which was swinging wildly from side-to-side with her fearsome movements and each ruthless punch slamming into the bag.

Sweat was dripping down her face and her body, her beautiful features twisted with determination and what looked like a whole lot of pain and frustration.

"Hey," I spoke, shutting the door behind me and walking further into the room.

She stilled, stopping mid-punch, and swung to face me.

Her eyes went straight to my right hand and the fact that I wasn't clutching my cane and that I didn't have it with me at all.

It was my first time trying to move around without it and it was going well. A little straining, sure, but a lot better than I'd imagined it being.

"Hey," she returned, panting, and trying to catch her breath. "I thought you were sleeping," she said, as she headed over to a bench in the far corner and snatched up a towel, starting to dab her sweat-drenched skin as she walked to me.

"Just taking a walkabout."

"Restless?"

"A little. There's a lot on my mind." I eyed her pointedly. "Isn't there?"

She dabbed at her face, then blew out a breath. "I'm sorry I didn't tell them yet."

"Why didn't you? I set that feast up to provide the

perfect opportunity of togetherness so it could be put out there."

"I know. I just… I need more time to wrap my own mind around it before I bring anyone else in on it."

"Especially the likes of Milo and Nico, with their intense protectiveness and cautiousness, right?"

"They're factors, yes."

"Well, I can tell you that the cautious approach is out the window for both of them after the kidnappings happened."

"That might not be the case when it comes to this, though."

"You're worried they'll bench you?"

"Worse. I'm worried they'll try, and what I'll be forced to do in order to counter that. I'm needed on this and I also have to be a part of it. Bringing those assholes down has been years upon years in the making. I won't sit it out."

"Like I told you earlier, Cat, we can always find a way. And I'll be there in your corner to make sure that it doesn't end up with you being benched. I promise you that."

"I appreciate that. Thank you, Julian." She pulled her hair tie out and shook out her wavy hair. "But, beyond that issue, what if I… what if I can't actually do this?"

"Do this?"

"What if it's just not in me to be a mother?"

Oh.

"And what if it's a mistake to bring an innocent baby into this life?"

"It won't be like this by the time the baby is born. You're only a few weeks along right now, in the very early stages. We have a lot of time to end this and make things safe and far less complicated and nightmarish."

"That's true."

I stepped up to her and slid my hands down to her

hips, holding her to me. "As for you worrying about not being mother material, there's not really any such thing. Every mother is different. Every mother-child relationship is different. In a world where you learned the harsh way not to trust anyone, not to lead with your emotions or even to allow yourself to feel them most of the time, you managed to trust *us*, you opened yourself up to the three of us, and you've cared for us and protected us like we have with you." I smiled. "You've loved us. That's what a child needs. To feel loved and safe, for their parents to do what's in their best interests. The rest will come with time and experience. You can't learn everything all at once where that's concerned."

She threw her arms around me and held me tightly to her.

Burying her face in my chest, she murmured, "Thank you. *Thank* you."

"Of course," I said, nuzzling against her.

After a few moments, she lifted her head to gaze up at me. "You knew exactly what I needed to hear, huh?"

"Well, I've become as attuned to you as I've learned to be with Nico and Milo. And I know that you spent so long on your own being a survivor, cut off from everyone. But now you've managed to become a part of a team. You're thriving in a relationship with all three of us and you have a great deal of love and care to go around. You can do this. And if that's what you want, if you want this baby, we'll all be there with you every step of the way. We'll raise this child together, the way we do everything, Cat. As a family."

I hadn't wanted to put any pressure on her, especially not at this dicey stage, but I couldn't think of anything more perfect than bringing a child into our foursome, of expanding our family like this.

I'd never had a family I could count on, or one that had deserved the title in the first place. Beyond that awfulness and trauma of my father, there'd also been my mother. She'd stood by him every step of the way, no matter what he'd done to me. He'd never touched her. No, he'd reserved all of that for me. And she'd allowed it to play out, never doing a thing to stop it. She'd been too concerned with maintaining her quality of life as his socialite wife. Nothing had trumped that for her. Hell, she'd barely even raised me. She'd employed nannies for that. That life had ended for her, though, once that investigation into my father's fucked-up business practices and decisions had concluded shortly after his *untimely death*, and she'd lost everything. Her standing and most of her money, too. She'd used what had been left to disappear and retire to a remote location hundreds of miles away. That was the way that she'd stay as far as I was concerned. She was nothing to me. Nothing but a distasteful memory.

But through all of that, I'd found that familial unit with Milo and Nico. Cat had come along, and now there was the possibility of this baby. For me, it really was the bright spark through all the rest.

"As a family," she murmured. Her face lit up as she looked at me. "I can picture that."

"And?"

"And it's a really beautiful picture."

"I feel the same," I admitted.

She eased from me and sucked in a steadying breath. "I'll tell them once Nico and I meet with Carlo and the Price/Angelo operation is completed. Not while we're in the thick of it."

"If you don't, *I'll* have to, Cat," I warned her. "If not, this becomes a full-blown secret, and a heavy one at that.

There's a difference between giving you time to process, versus keeping it quiet over a longer term."

"I know," she agreed. "I'm sorry I put you in this position."

"It's okay, I get it. You needed to get it off your chest."

She smiled and took my hand. "Let's get some sleep."

"Good idea."

As I let her lead me out of the gym and down the corridor, she observed, "You seem to be doing well moving along without your cane."

"Yeah, definitely getting there."

I had to. I had to keep pushing it as much as I could.

As we reached the living room that they'd all decked out specially for me, I found myself pulling up short at the doorway.

"What's wrong?" Cat asked me right away.

"I just… I've been having a little trouble falling asleep."

"I'll read you a bedtime story."

"What?"

She lifted a shoulder. "It'll be good practice."

"You're gonna soothe me like a baby?" I said, chuckling.

"I wouldn't put it like that. I'm just going to help you fall asleep." She gave my hand a squeeze. "Come on."

"All right, it's worth a try."

And she thought she wasn't cut out to be a mother.

Complete bullshit there.

Caterina Leone was cut out to be anything she desired to be.

She was a force of nature.

She always found a way through.

And this would be no different.

Excitement bloomed at the thought of it all.

I couldn't wait until she announced it to Nico and

Milo, so we could get into talking about every single aspect of it.

This was something to be celebrated to the fullest.

"I'm pregnant."

Those words were going to change everything for us.

In the best ways imaginable.

I couldn't fucking wait for it all.

21

~Nico~

"Why do you keep staring at your phone?"

I jolted and looked up from it to see Caterina eyeing me with a whole lot of concern.

"What?"

"You were doing it before we left the Manor, then when we stopped for you to have that smoke break on the way here where you paced up and down, claiming that your stressed state was just a result of heading to this meeting with Carlo Benzino, and now you've pulled your phone out three times and stared at something on the screen in the last twenty minutes since we've been here awaiting Carlo's arrival.

"I don't like keeping secrets from the three of you. It leaves us misinformed and risks causing distrust, and a whole lot of things that aren't conducive to a strong family dynamic."

Something flickered in her eyes, and then she looked away. "I know," she murmured.

"What is it?"

"Nothing. I'm just concerned about this, why you're

being cagey, and why you seem so distracted ahead of a meeting where we need our full focus."

"Fuck." She was right. I needed to be at the top of my game. I couldn't have anything interfering with that.

I needed to get this shit off my chest. I had to tell her. Now.

Even though I couldn't tell the person who it impacted the most, I could at least take some of the edge off by telling Caterina.

"Late last night, Carlo sent me this."

I spun my phone and showed her the text that had come in.

She moved in close and frowned, reading it over.

Carlo: Here's that intel I promised you. Sorry for the delay. I wanted to give you the necessary time to deal with the complications of the Angelo Simone situation before forwarding this. And to give you all the necessary time to stabilize as this will challenge that. I trust that you will handle it appropriately. Ensure you do, Nico. A great deal hangs in the balance. You must proceed carefully. That necessary show of force to push back the Leones and Marchettis notwithstanding—that was a smart move.

"What intel?"

I took my phone back and opened the attachments that had come along with it. "Here."

She looked through it all, her eyes widening as she did, as she connected the dots and put together what I had.

The very thing that had kept me awake most of the night.

And the thing that had made it a hell of a struggle to even look Milo in the eye before we'd left, and before I'd sent him out to finalize the last stages of prepping for the upcoming operation within a couple of days.

Evidence that had been kept buried for years at the

request of the three families alliance, so as not to rock the boat.

Particularly for the Marchettis.

Fuck, no, particularly for my father.

It was yet another attempt to control me and keep me in line.

They'd known well that if I'd discovered this back then, things wouldn't have progressed as they had, certainly not when it came to the power structure within the Marchetti Syndicate.

I'd been wrong about my father becoming unhinged due to losing my mother.

Seeing this now, it was clear that had occurred before she'd even fallen sick for those couple of years.

It had started during the war between the three families years ago.

It had shifted something in him.

And Leo had taken full advantage of that to infect my father with his reckless and heavy-handed approach to every fucking thing. His ruthless and risky way of doing everything.

"DNA evidence," Caterina mused to herself, as she scanned everything available. "Even transcripts of verified phone calls between Marco and Leo back then. The latter caught on surveillance that Carlo had sent to himself before it was destroyed when the house was blown to smithereens. Obviously, to wipe evidence of the kills."

"Or so they thought. Carlo had been so suspicious of it all, that he'd sent in his own forensics team to check it out before anybody else got in there, before the Marchettis wiped everything—the soldiers under my father's command."

"According to this, Carlo even still has the gun in his possession that was used that night at the house."

I grimaced at the mention of the house again.

Because that *house* had been Milo's family home.

That *gun* had been used to murder his father, Enzo, and his mother, Rosa.

I scrubbed my hand over my face. "It's here clear as day. The evidence is undeniable. Leo Marchetti murdered Milo's parents."

"Yeah," she murmured, handing my phone back to me. "This is… it's horrific. *Shit.*"

"Milo wanted answers desperately back then, but my father instituted a cover up, telling us both that it had been a mistake during the war, that the Benzinos were to blame, that the Bardi house being blown up had been accidental collateral damage."

"When, in fact, Leo had stormed into the house and murdered them both with a bullet to the brain, and the explosion was just to hide that fact."

"Leo wanted the position of Underboss so badly that he orchestrated it. And my father wasn't innocent in it like I'd always thought. The way he portrays himself… that deal with Malcolm Lynch… I'd believed that to be an anomaly. Until he allied with Santino, I thought I could get him back on track if I could just remove Leo's influence over him, but… it was all bullshit from the beginning."

"It's why it's a good thing that you escalated, that when the marriage directive came down from on high, you chose to fight against the entire system instead of trying to save it."

"I know, I just… Milo's parents died so Leo could take power that he never would have gotten with Enzo Bardi still alive. He was the Underboss you fucking dreamed of. The guy believed hardcore in honor and loyalty. In *family*. And they ripped somebody like that from this world for *this*."

"They didn't want any opposition to the rash, dangerous, and insane approach they wanted to take with the Syndicate. They got rid of Enzo and they tried to leash you."

"Milo's going to be heartsick over this. Even after he lost his parents, he still stayed loyal to the Marchetti Syndicate. For *me*. And yet my father had done this? It's... all these years he's given up so much of himself for a system that's been broken longer than we even realized, for a system that was rotten to the fucking core." I looked out at her, so stricken by it, too. "It wasn't until you came into our lives that it shifted things, that I decided to fight it. You were the catalyst."

"The straw that broke the camel's back?"

"Essentially. But I should've done it sooner."

"You weren't in a position to do it sooner, Nico. And we didn't have all the information then. Besides, we were under the impression that keeping our heads down was better for all of us, rather than fighting back and starting our own war that risked all our lives."

"But it wasn't," I seethed.

"And we're remedying that now. With every move we make, we are. This very meeting today with Carlo Benzino, in fact." She reached out and stroked my bicep. "Keep your eye on the prize and everything will fall into place. We'll take those fuckers down. We *will* win out. You can't let this brutal revelation knock you off track. What happened can't be undone. All we can do is control what we do now."

I stepped into her and brushed my lips over hers. "Thank you."

I slid my hands down to her hips and breathed her in, taking in that familiar sweet scent from her, and the leather of her turquoise jacket.

It was a strain not to take it further than a brief kiss.

With everything going on, especially Julian's situation at the Manor, I'd kept my hands off her for days on end.

I wasn't sure how much longer I could keep to that, though.

I'd had to remove my hand from her thigh during the drive because just that touch had threatened to get me too worked up.

I fucking wanted her. I needed her. And I knew the boys were feeling it too.

Julian had started talking about sex like he used to, he'd stopped using the cane, and he seemed to be coming back to himself.

Seemed to. He had another appointment with his therapist right now, so I'd see how that had been once we got back to the Manor, and we'd take it from there.

As for now, I needed to be focused.

So I eased from Caterina and stepped back.

Fortunately, as I did, my attention was redirected from her to the sound of a car approaching.

We watched as Carlo's striking Ferrari in Blu Scozia rounded the corner into the lot of the abandoned apartment building a few miles outside the city.

It came to a stop a couple of stops over from mine, then Carlo climbed out in a royal blue pinstripe suit.

The passenger door opened, and he was joined by somebody I hadn't laid eyes on since the last three families meeting months ago.

Remo Caruso, the Underboss of the Benzino Family.

He was in his mid-forties, sporting that maroon bomber jacket that was basically like a second skin to him. Just like the black beanie that always covered his head, come rain or shine. The jacket barely served to contain his bulk and toned muscle, the guy my height. As he closed the door, I caught sight of a holstered Sig strapped to his black jeans. He adjusted his matching t-shirt and hid the piece beneath it.

As Carlo strolled toward us with Remo at his back, swinging his head every which way and scanning the immediate vicinity carefully, he gestured at the apartment building just behind him. "I'm looking at turning this entire thing into a housing complex and building some retail space down the road. For newcomers to the city. Housing prices are cheaper outside here, but the commute's fair. For young professionals, maybe." He looked at Caterina. "Maybe I could pick your brain about it sometime?"

She smiled pleasantly. "We'll set up a call when you're ready."

She looked surprised too, given that, aside from my father's comment at the wedding, this was the first person amongst the three families who'd actually shown respect to her for her business acumen, even asking for her advice. Actually seeing her worth.

Of course, though, Carlo Benzino made it his business to understand his audience, and all those whom he dealt with.

Then again, he could have just as easily blown past that and gotten straight down to business. He already knew we were willing to ally with him. That led me to believe that his comments to her were actually genuine, more than a necessary manipulation.

"Excellent," he said, settling before us and shoving his hands into his suit jacket pocket.

"Nico," Remo greeted me agreeably.

"Long time," I responded.

He smiled, then his gaze flicked to Caterina. "Congratulations on snagging the Young Entrepreneur of the Year

Award. Carlo and I were saying that it was about time. You should've won it last year, honestly."

I knew well that it was exactly what she'd thought too. During my *stalking*, I'd overheard her saying as much to her architect, Nova Henderson.

"Thank you. I just wish the timing of receiving it had been more desirable."

"Santino's vindictiveness knows no bounds, I'm afraid," Carlo commented.

"Especially toward his own daughter," Remo basically spat in disgust.

"Well, that's one of the things we've allied to combat," I cut in, before it fired Caterina up—in a detrimental way. Especially when cooler heads needed to prevail for this meeting. And her father was definitely one of her triggers for her *monstrous* side.

"It certainly is," Carlo agreed. "Thank you, both for the information regarding Marco's proposed attacks *and* for letting us in on the Shawn Price situation concerning Santino and Angelo. Should you require additional resources for the latter, you need only ask."

"The operation is set, thank you."

"Then we'll discuss other urgent matters."

Remo told us, "Thanks to your intel, we're well-prepared to stave off Marco's attacks."

"We need to use this as an opportunity to do more than that," I spoke. "With our assault on Santino's and Marco's joint business venture the day before, we'll already have them reeling."

"And Marco has already taken a hit from his deal with Lynch collapsing," Caterina pointed out.

"Exactly. This is our chance to strike."

"You do this and there won't be any question as to where you truly stand," Carlo warned. "They will all see this as much more than you merely responding *emotionally* to what Angelo did to those you hold dear. This will be a definitive stand. You will be classed unequivocally as their enemy. All four of you will, those soldiers who follow you as well. There will be no going back."

"We're all aware of the stakes and what this will bring about."

Carlo's lip curled. "Well then, let us prepare for war."

Yes, fucking let's.

22

~Caterina~

"Do you have a ton of data on Benzino operations, too?"

I looked up from where I'd been focusing on my laptop screen that was settled on my lap as I sat on an old wooden table in the living room of the rundown apartment building to see Remo eyeing me curiously. And my screen more so.

"Yes," I responded flatly.

After agreeing to the overall plan to use our own strikes to hold off Marco's intended attacks against the Benzinos, we'd convened into the abandoned apartment building as an extra privacy precaution.

It was more paranoia from Carlo and Nico than actually anything necessary, because the whole time we were here I had alerts set up to warn of any approach within several hundred yards of us, and I was tapped into every form of surveillance in and around this area. I was also flagging the license plates of any vehicles passing on by on roads close to us and feeding them into my software, which would then warn me if any of them were owned by Marchetti or Leone members, or even their associates.

Yeah, I had it covered.

But I also understood that paranoia was bound to be running rampant with the weight of things and the extreme measures that we were about to take.

This wouldn't just be pushing back against the Marchettis and Leones, it would be outright war. And for Nico, especially, it would be seen as treason and a massive betrayal. Those demons had brought it on themselves, no doubt, and they were driving the families into deeper and deeper depths of depravity and dishonor, ruining them essentially. On Nico's end, his soldiers might be loyal to him, and we had Dante and Matteo too, but Marco and Santino still held a great deal of power and influence.

So, yeah, he was right to be a little paranoid.

And if it made him and Carlo feel better and more secure by venturing inside here out of sight, so be it.

"That's a lot of power you hold in your hands—or at your fingertips," Remo went on.

I drew my concentration away from what I was doing —sifting through all the intel that Nico and I had combined a little ways back on both families—and looked out at him.

It wasn't worry that I saw from him, just intrigue and him looking mighty impressed.

"Sure is," I said, offering him a wink.

He chuckled. "We'd heard rumors, but we couldn't substantiate them. This is good. Really fucking good."

"I'd say so," Carlo spoke, him and Nico coming back to us after they'd been discussing Nico's confirmation that he would take power over the Marchetti Syndicate like Carlo had put to him at their last *meeting.* "I'm concerned, however, about what Nico's just told me concerning *you* not wishing to take your rightful place as Boss of the Leone Family."

"Do you really think they'd accept a woman, anyway?"

Expecting him to be like the others I'd been surrounded by all my life, I was more than a little surprised when he answered, "Yes. You're qualified. You have a well-established reputation throughout the City of Tolhurst. And you exude strength. All those qualities make for a competent leader."

"Santino has only discounted you out of fear," Remo added. "That you'd one day supplant him."

"That is true," Nico said.

Yes, he'd told me that was what my mom had revealed to him.

"I walked away from it years ago. I'm only neck deep in it now because I was forced back in. I'll help end this nightmare, but when it's done, I want no direct part of it. I won't take the reins."

"You are the most optimal candidate to take on the mantle," Carlo told me. "As I understand it, even Dante Rivera, the technical Underboss of the Leone Family, believes that to be the case."

"There doesn't need to be any candidate."

He arched an eyebrow.

"We destroy all the illegitimate aspects of the Leone Family business, then divvy up the remaining aspects, namely Leone Realty, between you and Nico."

"You want to wipe out the entire Leone Family altogether," Carlo realized.

"It's rotten to the core. With the exception of Dante, Matteo and the four soldiers they have on their side, the poison that Santino and Angelo have infected it with has spread everywhere. There's nothing to save. It's different for the Marchettis. So many are loyal to Nico. There are also good men in Cassio, too. I've been determining the true loyalties of those under Cassio's leadership, and most of them will follow Nico as well. The issue lies with the other Capo, Gio, whose soldiers are loyal to Leo. And Marco by extension. But when we draw this line very soon, there's a lot more to be saved. That's not so for the Leones. It needs to go. It needs to be fucking eradicated."

"Well, it would be easier to manage an alliance just between two families," Remo said.

"There's also a significant difference between launching a coup and realigning the power structure of an organization like the Leone Family, to completely eradicating it," Carlo warned.

"If anyone took power from my father, aside from Angelo, who he's all but tapped as a backup for the role over Dante, there would forever be dissent in the ranks. It's the way he's set things up to reinforce his position. There would be an internal war raging, the organization would be impossible to lead with constant pushback and concerns of disloyalty and mutiny at every turn," I pushed. "Sure, I could take Dante and Matteo up on their offer to help me take power, but keeping it would be near impossible. Not to mention, the damage that Santino has already done to its reputation through the human trafficking deals he's been striking all over the place. And if you think *that* hasn't made it onto the Feds' radar, you're dreaming. I have confirmation that they're launching an investigation as we speak. It will take time, yes, but they'll succeed in the end. *If* we don't cut the poison that the Leone Family is out of our lives now while we still can."

I saw Nico flipping his Zippo on and off as he took my words in.

He was trying to sublimate his frustrations.

He didn't like it.

I knew that some part of him had bought into the romanticized notion of us, as the two heirs to powerful mafia families, taking our supposed *rightful* places and leading alongside one another.

It just didn't work for *me*.

It never would.

Maybe I'd entertained the possibility before, but with the recent revelation about my pregnancy, it had made it clearer than ever that it could never be, that it could never fucking work.

Not for our family.

If I told Nico that right now, though, the real reason behind my intensity where this was concerned, he'd be sidetracked from doing what else needed to be done. He would likely stand in the way of what *I* needed to do as well.

No, I couldn't risk it until things were already in place.

Not to mention, everything I'd just outlined about the issues involved in it were cold, hard facts.

"You make a fair point," Carlo spoke. "However, in order to wipe the Leone Family off the map, we're talking about some high-level destruction, a massacre in essence too. Then it risks being us who are put in the crosshairs of the Feds."

"Mass murder isn't the only option. There's also exile for the members wherein we monitor them in an ongoing manner to ensure they settle and don't pose a threat. If they do, we take them out then, when they're scattered far beyond the city in remote areas. As for the influence that the Leone Family holds over politicians, city officials, and those in the high echelons of the financial world, we *break* that influence. Pay off some and push them into retirement, and threaten others with amassed evidence of their illicit activities, forcing them to step down from their positions of power that assist the Leones."

"I assume that *amassed evidence* already exists in the

wealth of data you've collected on their operations?" Carlo asked.

"It does. I can deploy it at a moment's notice. The same with the payoffs."

"Leone Realty is infected by corruption too, isn't that so?" Remo spoke.

"A large portion of it, yes."

"Then we don't attempt to save it either," Carlo said. "It falls along with the rest."

"You're on board with this approach, then?" I asked.

"It certainly presents additional complications, but I do agree with the issues you've raised. While the effort it will take to actually eradicate the Leone organization entirely doesn't fill me with joy, the outcome will be worth it. A world without the Leone Family will make things a great deal easier and much more manageable." He eyed Nico. "Where do you stand?"

Nico's gaze went to me. "Deploy what you have now. Break the hold that Santino has over those who give him undue influence. We'll start there."

"And then?" I pushed.

"Then we'll bring it all crashing down, *principessa.*"

I smiled out at him. "Thank you."

He came to me and slid his hand into my hair. "You've gone long enough being the victim of other people's twisted decisions. Let this mark the end of that."

I stroked his arm, his beautiful vow to me rolling through me.

"Ah, young love, it is the sweetest," Carlo commented, grinning at us.

Surprising the both of us, Remo went to him and wrapped his arm around him. "Excuse me, not just *young* love."

Nico started and eyed Carlo in confusion. "I thought you were—"

"A man whore?" Remo finished for him. "Went through women in the droves? No, that was just the image projected to outsiders." He gazed at Carlo. "To protect me."

"To protect what we share," Carlo corrected him. He looked between Nico and me. "Those snakes of the Marchettis and Leones would never hesitate to use what we love against us. Best not to give them ammunition."

"It's too late for that," Nico muttered, referencing our situation.

"Yes, what Angelo did has already outed a great deal where that's concerned. It's virtually made it public fodder who you love, Nico. The four of you."

"That's why extreme measures are called for now," I said. "To counter that, to counter all of it. No more living in fear, or having so much of ourselves closeted in so many ways."

We all took a heady moment to absorb that.

And then Carlo eased from Remo, likely so he could focus, as he told us, "With this alteration, shifting to eradicating the Leones entirely, in mind, this is how I believe we should proceed. Nico, ensure your assault on Shawn Price and his joint disgusting business venture that Marco and Santino have a stake in happens the night before their planned attacks against me. It will undercut them and shake them. The night of their proposed attacks, I will have my men intercept two of the scheduled incoming deliveries to the Flower Market to draw Gio's attention there, wherein my men will ambush him and his soldiers. They won't get near the businesses under my protection. They turn or they die."

"Agreed," Nico said. "What of your meth lab?"

"Let Cassio stay in the good graces of Marco by allowing him to carry out his mission and burn the place to cinders. We could use that, make him our inside man as a backup should we need it down the road of this campaign." He lifted a shoulder. "I'm done with that racket, anyway. It's become a fucking headache, and the payoff is no longer worth it. Besides, while a whole unit of Marchetti soldiers is focused on that futile mission, we can use the distraction to move Marchetti drugs and weapons out from under their noses, off Marchetti Syndicate territory. We'll secure it for us and thereby weaken them, resulting in Marco being unable to serve his partners and live up to his contractual obligations."

"Ruining his reputation."

"And calling his ability as Boss into question," Remo spoke.

"What of the Leones?" I asked.

"First we break Marco," Nico told me.

Carlo nodded. "It's easier to do with Nico having the inside track as Capo and via his trusted allies in the likes of Cassio."

"I have evidence of illicit activities taking place at Leone and Marchetti strip clubs. The same goes for their gambling dens, where they do a great deal of their money laundering. I can tip off the law and have them raided," I told them.

"I have contacts and assets in the Tolhurst Police Department who can assist with that," Remo spoke. "We'll work together on it."

"Perfect."

Nico and Carlo exchanged a nod, and then Nico told me, "Go for it. I'll have Julian shut down the backroom gambling he's been forced to allow at *Nocturne*, too."

"I won't let him be connected to it when we leak this intel," I assured him.

"Best to be safe."

"And you also want his business connections to the Marchettis severed before all of this goes down."

"Exactly. All of it, actually, as well as them skimming profits from his club."

"While you're focused on physical assaults, concentrating on the Marchettis, it doesn't mean we can't also strike at the Leones—just in a different way," I pointed out. "I can weaken Santino financially and the Leone Family organization as a whole," I told them.

"You're already going to break the hold he has over certain powerful individuals."

"I can do this as well."

"What's your strategy?"

"Move some money around. Redirect it. That sort of thing."

"Drain his accounts?"

"Strategically. I know where his power lies in that respect."

The corner of his mouth turned up, both at my words and the sly look in my eye that he knew all too well. "Good."

"I'd also publicize the two of you filing for divorce," Carlo advised.

Remo nodded. "The more destabilization to the two families, the better."

This strategy was certainly geared toward that.

It would pile on the pressure, have them reeling, and turn them desperate too.

Desperate people were prone to make severe mistakes.

And we'd be right there to ensure those ruled in our

favor and we used that to our advantage in the most optimal ways.

Well, in the most devastating ways.

It was nothing short of what they all deserved.

"I'll set Julian on that. No one can get the word out like he can," Nico said.

I smiled to myself, despite the stakes and the complications that abounded, strategies within strategies, and all the rest, hope sprung.

For the first time ever, I could really see the end to it all.

That light that had been so long denied us.

A world where we weren't ruled by others.

A world where the wicked would no longer reign.

Where we'd be *free*.

23

~Emilio~

We'd walked into a shitshow.

Caterina's intel had warned us of something big taking place down by our three warehouse targets of the sickening operation we were to demolish tonight.

She'd flagged the movement of Wharton Transportation Services trucks, a dozen of them headed into the area, as we'd been on our way. She'd delved deeper than the surface level as she always did and determined there had been two guys to each truck, which put us at a disadvantage numbers-wise right off the bat with that being twenty-four to our twenty-two—me, Tony, and twenty of Nico's soldiers. That wouldn't have been a big deal if it hadn't been for the two dozen we'd already identified at the warehouses to begin with.

Or the fact that last night, they'd moved their *product*—hostages, really—into said warehouses that we'd been slated to burn to the fucking ground.

They'd brought in over two hundred of them, their total *supply* from all over, that they were now going to ship out to numerous buyers in a rush via those dozen trucks they'd brought in.

It was a panicked move and clearly a desperate one to save their business, knowing that their HQ was going to be hit.

They'd fucking known we were coming!

Nico was back in Tolhurst sorting out the details for the multi-pronged attacks tomorrow night along with Caterina, while Julian was taking the brief calm-before-the-storm to attend to Carver Group in person, now that he was doing better physically.

I'd reported in the unprecedented issue of the hostages being here during our takedown, and Nico had given me the option to hold back and wait for him to send reinforcements. But that would have taken hours. I'd cited that we'd likely lose the hostages to these fuckers, to which Caterina had told me we could track them down and rescue them after the fact.

But that would have strapped our resources even more so, while we needed all we had for tomorrow night and what would hit us beyond that. This mission was supposed to be a reeling blow to Santino and Marco to throw them off tomorrow.

Plus, and something that had hit me deeply, was the fact that I could liberate the hostages here and now, this very night, and spare them any further pain and abuse. If we delayed the op, it would prolong their suffering, and the thought of them being shipped off and *sold* to some sickos and even being in their presence for a limited time made me sick to my stomach.

Julian had only been in Angelo's clutches for days and look at the damage that had been done.

No, I couldn't stand the thought of it.

Nor the thought of that sick bastard slipping through our fingers again.

I'd insisted that it had to be now, that I'd handle it.

Giving me that option was just Nico and Caterina worrying about me. They didn't want me hurt. Thank fuck Julian didn't know about this and he was currently out of the Manor attending to Carver Group business down at his flagship Opulent Grand hotel tonight. He wouldn't stand for it.

But this was bigger than that.

It didn't mean it was gonna be easy, though.

Especially now we were in the thick of it.

When we'd first arrived, we'd caught sight of Shawn Price himself directing his men to drag the hostages toward the trucks. He'd been frantic, clearly panicking, and also irate.

How the fuck had they known to expect an attack?

All of our soldiers were solid and loyal to the core. We'd made sure of that beyond a shadow of a doubt.

It was something to figure out after the fact.

That was made clear to me as I hauled another opponent over my shoulder and dropped him hard on the asphalt, only to be tackled by two more who slammed me into one of the transport trucks. One of the eight whose drivers and front seat passengers we'd killed with sniper shots when we'd first arrived to thin the herd. We'd also put every single one of the trucks out of commission, blowing out the tires, and thereby preventing the assholes from being able to send the hostages out of here to their buyers.

At that point, all hell had broken loose with Shawn directing his guys to move the hostages into the warehouses.

The fuck we were gonna let that happen.

So we'd run into the fray.

I had five soldiers laying down cover while several were leading the hostages away from the fight and into the lot a few blocks away behind an empty apartment building where we'd parked our vehicles when we'd arrived. Nico had reached out to one of Julian's contacts and the guy was sending a team to take the hostages to safety. The rest of the soldiers were with me, including Tony Amato.

As I ripped one of my attackers off me by his fucking hoodie, and smashed his face into the side of the truck, wherein he dropped like a rag doll, Tony was there, shooting another running at me. A bullet ripped through his throat and he collapsed, spurting up his own blood. I blocked a hit from the other guy still trying to hold me, wrenched his arm until he screamed and a satisfying crack sounded, then I jerked him down to me as I slammed my knee up, shattering his nose and knocking him out cold in the process.

Tony was there in the next second, putting a bullet in his chest, along with the other one I'd put out of commission moments ago.

"You're not going for the kill," he commented.

"We haven't laid eyes on Angelo yet."

"You want to leave some alive for interrogation on that fucker's whereabouts if we don't find him cowering inside one of those three warehouses over there?" he asked, gesturing at the buildings a few feet away.

"Yeah," I grunted. I couldn't let him get away again.

"Our snipers are watching the warehouses, Emilio. There's been no movement. Nobody's gone in or out. If he's here, we'll get him."

"If he's here. These fuckers knew we were coming. As we were heading up here, they fucking knew."

"You've ordered no kill shots against Shawn Price, so

we'll use him to find that fucker if he's already slipped away. Leaving any of the rest alive is too messy, though. Nico won't like it."

"No," I agreed. "He wouldn't."

And normally, neither would I.

I swung my head to see Price still bogged down under cover of one of the now out of commission trucks, four of his guys flanking him and protecting him. The guy was at least fifty, decked out in a cheap brown suit that barely fit, his curly gray hair all wild and in his face.

My earpiece buzzed, and I tapped it, opening a transmission from one of our soldiers.

"All hostages clear."

"Copy that. Stay with them. The contact will be here in ten."

"Got it."

"Time to take this up a notch," I told Tony.

His eyes gleamed with excitement, the kind that Julian got at the prospect of going all out and being able to revel in the dangerous thrill of it all.

We both jerked back as shots rang out near us, and we flattened our backs against the side of the truck.

I scanned the area, noting that our snipers were busy covering some of our soldiers forty feet away who were in the throes of a brutal fight with a dozen of Price's guys who'd strategically convened over there during the battle to attack en masse.

I shot a look back around the corner just before another shot rang out to force me back and reported what I'd seen to Tony. "Six moving in."

He readied his weapon. "I've only got two shots left. You?"

"One."

I eyed the fallen guys near us, but they'd already been out when they'd set upon us. It was why they'd engaged us hand-to-hand and come at us in a rush.

I saw several of our guys notice our predicament, running toward us, firing off shots, but they couldn't bend fucking bullets around the corner of the truck and actually hit those coming for us.

I signaled them to head over to Price and his bodyguards instead.

Despite their hesitation to leave us as somewhat sitting ducks, they followed my orders and redirected their attention over there, managing to take out a couple of the bodyguards.

We were getting closer to Price now.

So close.

Suddenly, the warehouse door flew open, and I caught sight of an RPG a moment before the person holding it came into focus.

My heart stopped in my chest.

"Julian," I choked.

What the hell was he doing here?

How had he gotten inside the warehouse?

What the—

"Get down!" he yelled over to me and Tony.

There wasn't much else we could do when he took aim right where those fuckers were about to close in on us.

We bolted forward and dove onto the ground several feet away a second before he fired the fucking thing and it shot through the air with a sharp whistle, then blasted into the guys and blew them all to hell, taking a chunk of the truck that we'd been against mere moments ago with it, a ball of fire exploding high into the air as screams and a deafening thunder rang out.

"Holy shit," Tony breathed, pushing onto his knees as I hurried to my feet as well.

A deathly still silence filled the area as I stared over the distance at Julian, trying to make sense of what was happening, how he was here, all of it.

But he wasn't done.

He'd dropped the RPG and was reaching into his pockets.

In the next second, I caught sight of grenades, just before he started tossing them near Price's position, strategically forcing him and his remaining bodyguards from their point of cover.

He pushed from the warehouse and stalked toward them as my guys had jumped back out of range of the crazed grenade blasts.

I saw Julian stagger a moment later. He was still recovering, not at his best, and wielding that RPG and then throwing those grenades had obviously taken a lot out of him.

All of it caused a hell of a distraction, though, and then he was screaming and diving at Price. He tackled him away from his bodyguards and my guys had to move in frantically to take his security out before they did that to Julian.

"Where is he?" I heard him screaming, as he smashed his fist into Price's face, then wailed on him with unadulterated fury. "Where the fuck is Angelo? Tell me, motherfucker! Tell me!"

I bolted forward only to be pulled up short abruptly as a violent thunder reverberated all around us as a series of consecutive explosions erupted from all three warehouses, windows blowing out with glass spraying out everywhere, debris flying every which way and more fire shooting up toward the sky as the structures were fucking decimated.

I watched as a figure clad in heavy duty black tactical gear with a balaclava covering their face emerged from behind the farthest warehouse, a sniper rifle in hand. He fired off a series of rapid-fire shots at all the remain hostiles.

Julian rolled off Price at the shock of it and a second later, a bullet drove into Price's skull, killing him in an instant, just like our remaining targets.

Instinctively, I took aim with my gun, all my soldiers in the vicinity doing the same.

The mystery guy held up his free hand in a gesture of surrender and even lowered his gun.

"I come in peace, *Alleati!*" he called over to us.

I started. His pronunciation left a lot to be desired, but I managed to make out his attempt at referring to us as *allies*.

What the fuck was happening tonight?

Every part of this mission was going off the fucking rails!

At a time when things needed to be going off without a hitch.

I mean, shit!

"Who the fuck are you?" I called over.

"A friend of Caterina's."

I signaled my soldiers to hold fire, and I started over there, closing the distance between us.

As I did, Julian staggered over too. "You killed our best lead to finding Angelo!"

"Your presence is what alerted Angelo and Price to an incoming attack."

"Shut the fuck up. You don't know what you're talking about!"

Goddammit. Julian was out of his mind right now—in so many ways.

"Stop," I grunted, grasping his arm when I was close enough as the mystery guy continued his approach. "Stover?" I asked.

"Correct."

When he reached us, he pulled something from one of the pockets of his tactical vest and I studied the small metallic square device.

"Be still," he warned Julian. "This won't hurt and I won't touch you either."

I released Julian, and he stood there staring at Stover with a whole lot of confusion as he ran the device the length of him, from bottom to top. It started beeping when it reached his neck. Stover walked around behind him, his eyes narrowing as the beeping became rapid and shrill, a red light starting to flash as he reached the back of his neck, just under his hair.

"Sunshine, hold still," I said, lifting up some short tufts of his hair to see a small two-inch scar there from what appeared to be an incision.

"He's been tagged," Stover told me. "That's how they knew you were coming. He was ahead of you, already here more than a couple of hours before you, scouting the area."

There was only one explanation for it. "Angelo did this," I ground out.

"No," Julian said. "You guys checked me for any bugs or tracking shit before I entered the Manor after I was discharged from the hospital. Your tech would've picked it up."

"This runs on a special, unique frequency. Only this device can detect it," Stover explained. "It's tech created by Knightsridge Engineering. As is this device I hold in my hand."

"How did you know?" I asked him.

"I keep an eye on everything concerning Caterina. During the time that Julian was in Angelo's captivity, there was a break-in at one of Knightsridge Engineering's storage facilities by somebody matching Angelo's description. Although, it wasn't reported to the police, due to the nature of the covert tech that's developed there, Roman Knight reached out to me, concerned it could impact Caterina *and her loves,* as he put it. I wasn't certain that Angelo actually had the brains to use it, but when the connection between him and Shawn Price was made apparent, the likelihood increased. These guys chip the women they traffic. Not with this kind of tech, but they have people on staff who are able to perform these minor surgical procedures efficiently. One of those was with Angelo at the location where Julian was being held."

"Why didn't you take that fucker out? Too busy trying to rig the warehouses that you couldn't spare the second it would have taken to end his miserable life?" Julian bit at him.

"That wasn't my mission. Tearing down this operation was. Not to mention, Angelo has vital intel on the Leone Family, current and future plans and strategies."

"You're saying he's an asset to you?" Julian growled.

"If you weren't so emotionally involved, you'd be able to see it too. All of you."

I took a dangerous step forward at his accusation. *Emotionally involved?* After what Angelo had done to those we loved, how could we not be?

Stover held up his hand while opening his tactical jacket with the other, then pulling out a silver flash drive. He held it out to me. "Give this to Caterina."

"What is it?"

"A gift."

What the—

"I need to sanitize the area before the authorities are alerted. We don't want your involvement being discovered. Well, not by the law. But Santino and Marco are another story. I realize you want *them* to know of this."

"Why are you doing this?" I asked.

"For Caterina," he answered simply.

"Why step in now?"

"Because it's time."

"Cryptic bullshit," Julian ground out, pulling from us and throwing his hands in the air.

He started going off then, yelling out into the night, my soldiers looking on as he lost his shit and started wailing on one of the transport trucks, smashing his fists into it over and over.

I rushed over to him and snagged him in a bear hold, pulling him from it, and stopping him from damn near crushing his knuckles to shit in the process.

"Take a breath," I breathed in his ear. "It's all right. It's all gonna be okay, Sunshine."

"No!" he yelled. "He's in the wind! Again! He… he tagged me like an animal! Like his fucking pet!"

"We'll take care of it. We'll take care of it all. I swear to you."

He screamed out into the night, an absolutely awful pained scream that tore right through me.

And then he slumped in my hold and I eased him down as he sank to his knees, burying his face in his hands and sobbing.

I crouched down beside him and looked out to see Stover pulling his phone out and calling for a *swift sanitization*.

As I held Julian and he sank into me, shaking with his upset, my earpiece buzzed.

I tapped it and my soldier taking point on the hostages sounded down the line.

"Julian's contact is here with a team to move the hostages and get them to safety."

"Good. See to it, then meet us back at the lot. We're moving out."

I swung my head toward Tony, who was looking on in shock at the state of Julian.

"We're done here," I told him. "Have the team move out. I'll be along shortly."

"You're sure?" he asked, clearly concerned.

"Yeah, I've got him. Head home, I'll follow."

He nodded and then guided the rest of the soldiers away.

Stover finished on the phone and turned to me. "Tell Caterina that I'll see her soon."

"I'm gonna need more than that."

"Not yet."

Without another word, he strode away, examining the scene and the many dead bodies, and he appeared to be making notes on his phone as he went, zoned out and ultra focused.

Jeez, the guy was intense. An oddball too, no doubt.

And I couldn't determine whether I was pissed that he'd intervened in my mission, or if I was grateful.

I couldn't determine a lot of things right now, all the while Julian was in this broken state.

Coming up here, especially when he definitely wasn't field-ready… the risks had been off the charts. His desperation to get to Angelo was another level, beyond what I'd already perceived from him, beyond what me, Nico, or Caterina had even realized.

This was bad.

So fucking bad on too many levels.

And all I could do as he continued to break down in my arms was hold him to me.

It's not enough.

Nowhere near enough.

24

~Nico~

"I need to be involved in the hunt for him!" Julian yelled.

Yet again.

It had been virtually non-stop since he and Milo had walked back into the house.

I'd even heard him in the car as Milo had driven him back, Julian arguing the whole time as Milo had reported everything that had happened earlier tonight.

I'd taken some time to debrief with Tony and those of my soldiers who had been on mission tonight after they'd had their injuries seen to by my on-call doctor. Fortunately, all of them had been mild, especially considering what they'd walked into with all the surprises tonight that hadn't been a part of the original plan. Fortunately, being able to pivot when things didn't go to plan was something Milo and I had learned well over our years involved in this fucked-up life.

A fucked-up life I'd have to continue on with now that I'd committed to taking power over the Marchetti Syndicate. Unless I could overhaul things and take the organization completely legitimate like Caterina had made abundantly clear that she wanted.

My soldiers had been unsettled and morale had clearly taken a hit despite the fact that the mission had technically been a success. Because of them witnessing Julian breaking down. It wasn't an easy thing to bear in the least. Fortunately, I'd managed to raise their spirits with commendations of how well they'd handled things tonight, bonuses I'd wired to their accounts for them and their families— with the help of Caterina moving money around within Santino's accounts—and by laying out how things would play out once we were through this fight, to keep them focused on the endgame and the light and relief it would bring to us all.

But while I'd managed to keep my soldiers on track, Julian was another case entirely.

For one, he wasn't a soldier of mine.

Nor did he possess that sort of mindset. Not close to Milo's either.

Julian didn't just fall in line because I commanded it, or because he recognized the sense in doing so, or implicitly trusted in me to the same depth that Milo did because we'd worked together under high pressure circumstances for so long. No, there was more of a disconnect there when it came to Julian. He questioned more; he pushed back more.

And, unfortunately, that was one of the worst things right now when he both needed to be reeled in *and* to recognize that it was the case.

"Can you avoid talking so animatedly for a few more moments?" Milo beseeched him as he stood before Julian, who was sitting up at the island as Milo tried to dress his battered knuckles. Self-inflicted fucking injuries.

Julian glared at him, then shot another fierce and challenging look my way as I leaned against the kitchen door, my arms folded across my chest as I regarded and studied him closely. "Well? Are you gonna answer me or just stand there with that disapproving look blazing my way?"

"The fact you showed up there without authorization is what led to the *hunting* part of the mission being unsuccessful."

Milo swung his head my way, his espresso eyes wide with disbelief.

He'd wanted me to sugarcoat it. That much had been clear from the careful and dancing-around-the-severity-of-it way he'd reported everything to me on their drive back. Of course, I could read between the lines when it came to him.

"What he did tonight was beyond dangerous. It can't be brushed aside as a mere mistake or a miscalculation," I told Milo.

He blew out a breath and looked away, focusing back on wrapping the knuckles of Julian's right hand, the left he'd already taken care of.

The doctor hadn't been able to even approach Julian to take care of it, because Milo had blocked his path and insisted on tending to him personally.

He'd clearly jumped to the conclusion that Julian's breakdown in the field would automatically mean him reverting back to being unable to be touched and he'd assumed that it would be easier for Julian to stomach it from him than somebody mostly unfamiliar in my doctor —he'd only been treated by him a couple of times over the years.

But that didn't seem to be the case as I'd watched Julian tonight. He hadn't shown any signs of being touch averse again.

Of course, it was possible that he was masking it.

Just like he'd obviously been masking his rage and

obsessive need to exact vengeance on Angelo, something he'd played so well, he'd even managed to keep it off *my* radar.

"That wasn't my fault!" Julian basically screamed back at me. "Stover could've taken him out, but he didn't. He wanted him for fucking interrogation! Like we even need that! It was absolute bullshit!"

"It wasn't Stover's job to put Angelo down. It was our mission. The fact that you headed up there caused a shit-storm of complications that Milo and my men had to improvise to overcome on the fly."

"I didn't know about the tracker surgically inserted into my fucking body, did I?"

"That's beside the point. You went around us, Julian. The mission was dangerous enough as it was when we'd strategized everything down to the smallest detail. Yet, your interference screwed all that to hell. We're fucking lucky that no one died tonight, that only a few of them walked away with only mild injuries."

"I intervened with that RPG and saved—"

"With an RPG! A fucking rocket-propelled grenade! Exactly my point. The insanity of it all, J!"

Milo finished with his hand and in the very next moment, Julian smashed his bandaged fist down on the kitchen table, rattling Milo's glass of brandy and Julian's own bottle of expensive vodka. "Nothing less than absolutely anything it takes should be used to take that mother-fucker out!"

"Not putting your life on the line. Not fucking up our overall mission. Which is what you nearly did tonight by running off half-cocked and behind our fucking backs!" I finally pushed off the wall. In a way, I'd been using it to ground me and to keep me at bay, while my rage at the entire situation was barely checked. I didn't want to have to come down on him so hard, especially after the breakdown he'd had earlier, but with him continuing to push back, I had little choice. I needed to make him see reason. He fucking had to.

If he couldn't, then he'd become a very real problem.

Worse. A threat to what we were trying to do here.

It was all on the line as it was and this... fractures within our foursome, within our core unit... they couldn't be right now. They just fucking couldn't.

"You left me no choice with doing it without me! I told you, I need to be there. *I* need to be the one to put him down, Nico!"

"You proved tonight that you're not field-ready in *any* sense. You can't be a part of the mission."

"*But* we can bring him to Julian when we apprehend him," Milo offered up. "Let him end the sick fuck's miserable life."

Normally, yes, it would be considered obvious justice by doing it that way, having the wronged in Julian finish the one who'd done him such despicable wrong.

But this was a dicey situation, especially because of Julian's history.

Milo's judgment was compromised when it came to this.

I walked to Julian and stood before him.

He was seething, clenching his fists at his sides, which really wasn't doing his damaged knuckles any favors, but he clearly couldn't check it. At the same time, he was looking up at me with a whole lot of need sparking through that rage.

"Killing your father wasn't a magical cure-all. In fact, it further complicated matters, if you remember."

"Of course I remember," he snapped. "In vivid fucking detail."

"Then you understand what I'm concerned about here."

"Yeah, you think it will push me over the edge, that I'm too fragile to handle it, and when I make the kill, all the trauma of what was done to me by Angelo will breach the proverbial floodgates and overwhelm the fuck out of me, because you believe I'm holding it all at bay, kidding myself into thinking that killing him will take it away like some kind of magic."

"And?" I pushed.

"*And* this isn't the same. That was my father. Very fucking different. Things ran too deep there, obviously." He shoved his bandaged hand through his hair. "Angelo succeeded in making me his *little bitch*, as he kept referring to it. I can't live with that. I can't have him out there, our last interaction being him dominating me, having power over me. And the only way to counter that is to end him, Nico."

"You don't feel like you can properly start the healing process until that's achieved?" Milo asked.

"Exactly," Julian confirmed.

Fuck.

"You stopped trying too quickly," I told Julian.

"What?"

"Doctor Williams told me that you didn't discuss anything about the kidnapping during your last session. She mentioned that you were solely focused on excitement about the future."

"Excitement, right. Isn't that supposed to be a good thing?"

"It was an avoidance strategy and you know it. You're not participating properly."

"And you're able to determine what *participating properly* involves when it comes to a therapy session?" He scoffed.

"You can barely feel your own guilt, you're the last person to be lecturing me about—"

"This isn't helping," Milo interjected. "And you're being so defensive that you're actually on the attack. Against Nico, Julian. Come on. *Please.*"

"If anything, *he's* attacking me!"

"He's airing his concerns. Very real concerns, Sunshine."

Julian threw his hands in the air. "Of course you're taking his side. When don't you, huh? No matter what, right?"

"You know that's not the case. Not when it comes to the way things operate between the four of us. I've been in your corner many times. Caterina's too."

"When push comes to shove, though—"

"This is about *you.* Your actions," I cut in. "You're trying to redirect to—"

"To what, Nico? To convince you guys that I should get the justice I deserve?"

I slammed my fist down on the countertop. "You'll get justice! That isn't in question! Your methods *are!* Fucking recognize that! We're in the fight of our lives. The chances of us all making it out of things alive and in one fucking piece is slim as it is without *this*, without you going rogue! Do you understand that? Do you fucking understand what's gonna happen the moment what we did earlier gets back to my father, to Caterina's? Something that will only be compounded by our assaults slated for tomorrow night? It's treason! It's an epic fucking betrayal! This isn't just rebelling. Taking this stand, taking them on, coming for everything they have… there's no going back from this. And if we don't tread very fucking carefully with every move we make, we won't survive the coming onslaught."

A shadow fell over the door in my peripheral vision and I turned to see Caterina walking in.

"He's saying that he needs you, Julian," she said in a soft, calm voice that was the direct opposite to what had been firing back and forth between Julian and I over the last few minutes.

It was such a striking oppositional force to it, that it actually managed to cut through it in a very powerful way, sedating my worked up state and soothing Julian's desperation noticeably too.

He actually softened, stepped back from me and started drawing in slow, deep breaths in a clear effort to recenter himself.

"We all need you." She added rather pointedly. "*I* need you."

There was a melancholic air to her words and her very demeanor that I sensed wasn't only about Julian and the whole situation there.

But before I could get a word out, she reported stoically to us all, "I connected with one of Roman Knight's colleagues concerning the tracking chip. It wasn't made to be a long-term thing, meaning that it will disintegrate within a few weeks without any harm being caused. It's also safe to be removed with a simple procedure. We could easily do it here and get it out now."

"*Or* we could use it to our advantage against Angelo," Julian proposed.

"After what we just heatedly discussed—putting it mildly—I won't let you come face-to-face with your tormentor until we have him incapacitated and utterly at your mercy," I said.

"Will it still be in working order if it's removed?" Milo asked her astutely.

She nodded. "As long as it's removed carefully. So we can use it as bait without putting Julian in his crosshairs."

"All right," Julian agreed.

Relief rolled through me.

That was something, at least.

A big *something* for him right now, I had to admit.

"As for the flash drive that Joe handed over, I've decrypted it."

Frowning and tensing at the same time at the unsettled look in her eyes—and all over her, in fact—I stepped forward and asked, "What was on it?"

"Intel. Concerning you and me, Nico."

I cocked an eyebrow.

"Our marriage."

"How so?"

"Remember that stand-in priest that married us because the other one had fallen ill and all of that?"

"Of course."

"It was all a setup. Joe poisoned the guy who was to marry us and his colleagues. I guess he drew the line at actually killing men of God —well, what they were supposed to be, considering their affiliations with my father—because they all survived, albeit some ended up in the hospital for a few days. He did all of that so he could put *his* guy there that day."

"Hold up," Julian said. "You're telling us that Stover was actually able to infiltrate a mafia wedding, plant one of his own guys there and make everyone believe he was an actual priest who they all would have vetted to hell and back, and have no one none the wiser?"

She nodded. "Not even me."

"Why?" Milo asked. "To make sure you weren't really married in the eyes of God, or something, at least?"

"He's not religious, so no. That wouldn't have even

crossed his mind. It was so he had somebody in a position to do what came next." She shook out her hair and revealed, "Somebody skilled enough to basically switch out our marriage documentation—the license, all of that, right under everyone's noses, without any of us noticing."

I scrubbed my hand over my roughened jaw. "You're saying—"

"I'm saying that our marriage wasn't just bullshit to us, it is legally, too. Joe ensured it and he actually went to great *and* dangerous lengths to make it so. We never signed a real marriage license that day. Our marriage isn't legal, Nico."

"I don't... no... that... it can't—"

"All the proof of it is on that flash drive. You can see it for yourself anytime you want."

I looked back and forth from her to Milo and Julian, trying to get a handle on one hell of a revelation from her.

"Why didn't he clue you in?" Milo asked. "He knows you. He would've realized how much you reviled being forced into that, pulled back into the family. Knowing Stover was doing that would have taken some major weight off for you."

"From what I can determine, he wanted me here with the three of you. *Safe* here. If the marriage hadn't appeared to go ahead, that wouldn't have happened."

"He wanted a force at your back," Milo realized aloud.

"That means he somehow knew that you were safe with us all along," I pointed out.

"It does, yes. It didn't come from me. And it couldn't have come from my mom either, because she didn't even know until after the ceremony, after we'd signed. By the way, that awful contract? That was also taken that night and destroyed by Joe's guy."

"Fuck me," I breathed. "Why wouldn't he tell you any of this? Especially about that twisted contract?"

"Because we're all fucking puppets to him, aren't we?" she burst out with, that stoic and calm façade being breached now with it all obviously compounding for her. "Just like the rest of them. Yes, this was in my best interests, but the *way* he went about it, the underhandedness of it, him determining when and what we were made aware of regarding *our* own lives… it's still manipulation of the highest level." She shoved her hand through her beautiful hair. "And I'm sick of it. I'm sick of it all. Especially all the secrecy."

Julian tensed noticeably as she stepped forward.

I even saw him give her an attempted covert nod of encouragement.

It hit me then.

She must've told him.

About the intel I had for Milo that I hadn't wanted to reveal until after tomorrow's assaults, so it wouldn't impact his focus. We were on extremely dangerous ground right now, and what Julian had done tonight had already been enough of a risk.

I really didn't want to entertain more.

But Caterina's words, about the puppet mastery, the secrets being kept that impacted other people's lives… it hit me beyond the rational, beyond the mission.

And I couldn't let her reveal it.

It had to be me.

I owed Milo that much. Hell, I owed him a fuck of a lot.

"You're right," I said, coming up on her side.

She eyed me in confusion. "About the secrets?"

I nodded.

"Right, so, in the name of that—"

I stroked her arm. "No. It has to be me."

"What are you—"

"Carlo handed me information that concerns you, Milo."

The room fell silent, and I pushed from Caterina and walked to Milo, pulling my phone out as I went.

"Me?" Milo asked, as I stopped in front of him.

"It's about your parents." I grimaced as his face fell. "Specifically, the night of their murder."

"That's what he wouldn't let me lip read that night? He was offering you intel about that?"

"Yes. With everything that happened that night, then our search for Julian, it put it on the back burner, but a few days ago, he sent it through."

"He knows what happened, who was really responsible?"

"He's known for a while. Under the terms of the alliance, he had to keep it buried."

"Which he's obviously no longer bound by," Julian commented.

"It's more than that, though, isn't it?" Milo put to me.

"Yes."

"He offered it up now to reinforce that he's with us. That means it can't have been collateral damage caused by the Benzinos."

"Correct."

His eyes darted between me and Caterina. "So their murders were either Leone or Marchetti kills."

Honestly, it would be easier if it had been the former.

But there was nothing fucking easy about the world we currently found ourselves in.

It was always a whole lot more brutal than that.

I pulled up the intel on my phone and handed it to him.

He hesitated for a moment, clearly overcome, but then

he took it and started poring over it, scanning and taking in everything rapidly.

I saw the moment he realized what it all meant, who it pointed to without a shadow of a doubt.

His eyes darkened in a way that was very uncharacteristic of Emilio Bardi.

A growl escaped him.

And then his gaze snapped to mine, grief and rage swirling.

"*Leo*," he ground out. "Leo murdered my parents."

I heard a choked sound from Julian.

But before I could get a word out, before any of us could, Milo tossed my phone back to me, then strode out of the room.

Fuck.

25

~Caterina~

I stared at the tracking chip I'd cleaned after extracting it from Julian a couple of hours ago. It had been a very easy procedure to remove it and it hadn't left him with any damage. It would heal within a few days completely, and it hadn't even required stitches.

But that had been the least of it.

The fact that he'd been chipped at all was what had done the most damage.

The indignity of it, being treated like a thing rather than a person through having that done to him, it had served to intensify what Julian had already been suffering through as a result of Angelo's other heinous actions.

But while it was despicable, it had also unwittingly revealed a very exploitable weakness in Angelo.

It had highlighted that his goal *hadn't* only been to make Julian his *little bitch*, punish him and dominate him. It had become more than that. Whether that had occurred during Julian's captivity, or whether the seeds had been planted beforehand, wasn't clear. But what was clear was the fact that Angelo was so obsessed with him that he hadn't been able to stand losing track of him, so he'd gone to extreme lengths. He was emotionally invested.

And that was definitely a weakness we could exploit.

One we could use to draw him out more than even the chip itself and get Julian the justice and closure that he truly needed, that desperate need which had been driven home to all of us tonight in a very painful way.

I secured the chip in a lockbox I'd had brought over from my apartment, then sank onto the foot of the bed.

I'd almost told Nico and Milo about my pregnancy earlier.

At first, I'd had it in my mind to wait for the perfect time to come around, but after having that talk with Julian, he'd made it clear that it needed to be a lot sooner. So I'd planned to do it after the attacks tomorrow, thinking that would have been a compromise on the whole *perfect time* thing.

There was no such thing, though.

Especially not for us, not until this was all over.

The mission tonight going haywire had just served to highlight how things could go off the rails despite the best laid plans and strategies guiding the way.

Plus, there was no definitive date etched on the proverbial calendar for when this war would be over, because there were unknowns involved. Reactions to our actions tonight and tomorrow night couldn't be determined precisely and they'd all have a knock-on effect upon one another.

We hoped we could end this swiftly, but the truth was we couldn't be certain of that.

And keeping this secret too much longer... it would become poison.

To us all.

That was the last thing I wanted.

But what had really settled it for me where confessing this secret was concerned had been walking in on the guys going at each other in the kitchen, seeing them strained with each other like that, on rocky ground. It had brought it slamming home to me how much I needed us to be together right now, how much I needed *them,* and, most of all, *us.*

I'd admired their comradery, their deep friendship and the familial bond between them all from the outset as soon as I'd borne witness to it, but being a part of it now was a whole other level. The idea of losing that, of it fracturing, I couldn't stand it.

And I wouldn't have it. *I* certainly didn't want to become a factor for risking that.

Yes, I was concerned about being benched once they knew, but I'd also been able to recognize that it was driven in a large part by my trust issues that my father and his demeaning and misogynistic treatment of me were at the root of.

The guys didn't deserve to have that put upon them.

They'd done so much to earn my trust, I had to be able to do the same in return.

And I'd been about to *until* Nico had mistaken what I'd intended as referencing Carlo's intel that he'd been temporarily holding back from Milo.

Once he'd put that revelation out there, the opportunity to reveal the pregnancy in that moment had gone to hell.

Milo had been devastated.

After he'd walked out, we'd all gone after him and he'd locked his door and told us he needed time alone.

Since then, Nico had been corresponding with his soldiers and Carlo, double and triple checking that everything was in place for tomorrow. He'd also put feelers out to find out what the reaction to Shawn Price's operations being destroyed had been from the Marchettis and the Leones, but nothing had been determined yet.

That was actually more concerning than if there had been something.

So was the fact that there'd been no activity from either Marco or Santino's phones since the first couple of days that I'd infiltrated them when we'd been searching for Julian. Given how often they used them, like an extension of themselves, with everything they had to deal with on a day-to-day basis, the only realistic explanation was that they'd ditched them and had acquired new ones, which obviously also meant they'd somehow discovered that they'd been infiltrated. I was no amateur when it came to that, so the four of us had reasoned that it had to have been Angelo who'd tipped them off. He must have put the pieces together when I'd shown up to extract Julian, when he'd seen what I'd been capable of. He must have also tried to access the surveillance footage at that godforsaken house that I'd corrupted beyond functionality.

If he didn't know it was me who was capable of that, he definitely would have suspected it was one of the four of us.

While I'd warned Nico about it during our drive to meet with Carlo that day, he'd reframed it as something positive, as both a deterrent to them now they were aware of the damage we could do even from afar, and also as another stand against them.

I believed some part of him thought that Marco would question his recent unhinged actions, including allying with my father, through seeing how much his own son was opposing him.

I understood it. I'd thought the same thing about my father until the point of no return a few years ago. I'd thought he could be saved, that he could turn back from the bad path he'd been headed down. But that hadn't happened in the least.

Whether it would for Marco remained to be seen.

My phone buzzed, cutting through my concerned thoughts, and I snatched it up from my nightstand to see a text from Julian.

Julian: What do you think?

I frowned, wondering what he was getting at until another message came in—a screenshot.

I jolted as I opened it to see what he'd just posted on his IG.

Nico had asked him to spread word about the truth of our marriage.

Well, what we'd thought had been a marriage until tonight.

I gritted my teeth and forced myself to swallow that down and the issues with Joe that had arisen as a result, and I focused on what I was seeing on my screen now.

My best bud, Nico, and his new bride? Forced arranged marriage, guys. Sickening, right? They tried to silence us, but you're getting the truth right here and now. She's ours. Our woman, our love, our everything. Loved and adored. FU Santino. You too, Marco. #ourgirl #nowandalways

As if the caption wasn't bold enough, the accompanying photo really drove it home.

Julian took a lot of selfies and shots of this and that, being an IG fanatic. But he didn't post any that he'd taken of the four of us together. I hadn't even seen him take this one, and the reason was made clear as I stared at the image of him grinning salaciously at the camera as me, Nico, and Milo were asleep, the four of us all wrapped up in one another in Nico's bed. Although we were covered by a blanket, it was obvious we were naked beneath and my hair screamed just-fucked, too.

Holy. Shit.

I texted him back.

Caterina: You certainly went above and beyond.

Julian: Did you expect anything less, darlin'?

Caterina: You openly challenged Santino and Marco.

Julian: I'm already a target.

Caterina: Not like this.

Julian: It needed to be done.

Caterina: Where are you?

Julian: In the pool. Come join me.

Caterina: I don't have a bathing suit here.

Julian: I know.

I rolled my eyes.

Caterina: Coming to talk to you.

Julian: Sure. We'll call it that. Get Nico and Milo on your way. They're in Milo's room.

Caterina: I thought Milo wanted to be left alone.

Julian: You know Nico's persistence better than most.

I certainly did.

Caterina: I'm not sure they'll be in the mood for a dip in the pool. And I thought you were sleeping.

Julian: Change of plans. We all could do with some levity. You know, fun?

Fun? Right now? With everything that had happened tonight? Was he serious?

Before I could respond, he sent another text, being as astute as he always was. Unnervingly so sometimes.

Julian: More than ever, Cat.

Julian: "Right now, though, the four of us will just take a beat, be together." Nico's words. Remember them?

Now, who was being the persistent one?

Caterina: On my way.

Julian: *heart emoji*

I smiled to myself in spite of it all, then locked my phone and left it on the nightstand before heading out of my bedroom.

I made my way along the corridor, then down the stairs, heading over to Milo's wing.

If we did decide to make us all living here together a permanent thing, we'd have to fix the room arrangements. I didn't like how they currently were so far apart, the separate rooms.

Muffled voices reached me as I neared Milo's room.

"I don't blame you in the least, Nico. I know if you'd been aware, things would have played out differently. Very differently."

"They would have. I never fucking would have had you pledging your loyalty to the people who were responsible for taking your parents from you. It makes me sick knowing this twisted truth, knowing all this time that—"

"It's all right."

"What?"

"I'm not gonna fly off the handle, or pull a Julian."

"I thought—"

"That's why I came in here, to process it all. And so we're clear, I pledged my loyalty to you."

"I know, you did. I know."

"I do need your help with this, though."

"I'm here. Name it, what can I do?"

"I want you to teach me how to properly compartmentalize this."

"You know how dangerous that can be."

"Just while we're in the midst of war. I won't let it impact me, or you, or any of us. So long as I know you'll leave Leo to me when the time comes."

"He's yours. I swear it to you. And, yes, I'll teach you how to compartmentalize it. Just temporarily, though. Understood?"

"Understood, brother."

"Okay."

"Hey, thanks for telling me tonight. I figured you'd hold off on it until all of this was over. Or at least until the attacks tomorrow and the corresponding blowback were beyond us. You must've been worried that it would fuck things up, especially if I lost it."

"I was. But you've been willing to work with Carlo when you thought all these years that Benzino collateral damage had been responsible. Besides, seeing Julian tonight, then Caterina talking about the hurt and shock she's feeling because of Stover's secretive actions, it brought it to the forefront. Secrets are poison, especially to our foursome."

I jerked back from the door, grimacing at that.

Shit.

It took me several moments to get a hold of myself and actually step back up to the door and knock. Not like me at all. This whole thing, everything that was happening… I felt like it was undercutting who I was, who I'd worked so hard to be over the last few years.

Only two things made it better, grounded me to who I was. The first was when I unleashed that dangerous, monstrous part of myself. But the second was my men. And if the first was in play, it was a risk to them. Or it had become a risk, anyway. Last time, I'd hurt Nico. And even when unleashing had been sexual and not combat-related, it had left him with marks that had taken days to heal.

I couldn't… I couldn't do that anymore. I couldn't see any of them hurt, especially not at my hands.

They'd all been through enough as it was.

And when tomorrow night's assault took place, that was only going to become a whole lot worse.

"Come in," Milo's voice called out.

I sucked in a steadying breath and opened the door to find Milo and Nico sitting on the foot of his bed, facing one another. Nico's back was to the door, and he turned as

I entered, beaming out at me in his usual loving way. Milo gave me what Julian called his *teddy bear* eyes.

Guilt slashed through me.

More so than it had already been doing as it was.

"Everything all right?" Nico asked, obviously noticing some uncomfortableness coming off me.

I cleared my throat and told them, "Julian wants us out by the pool. He said we need some levity and *fun.*"

"Fun," Nico mused.

"A foreign concept right now, yes?" I tried to joke, partially succeeding—I hoped.

"Maybe it shouldn't be," Nico said.

But Milo was frowning and then he asked, "Julian said that?"

"Texted it, but yes."

"Things like this were how he's always blown off steam in the past," Nico told him. "He's clearly trying to get back to that, especially after what happened tonight."

"Trying to, yeah. But whether he's actually ready is a whole other thing."

"There's only one way to know," I pointed out.

Milo nodded and rose to his feet. "Then we go slow *and* carefully."

"Of course," Nico agreed.

I nodded. "Definitely." And I wasn't going to bring out that dangerous side of me, either. For Julian and for them as well.

"We'll get changed and meet you out there," Nico told me. He smiled and added, "*Amore mio.*"

I winked at him. "Right back at you."

As I turned and headed out, I heard their voices carrying.

"So it's like that, is it? With everything that's been happening, I

guess I didn't pick up on it. But you've obviously declared your undying love for her and vice versa."

"Correct."

"Well, that certainly explains why you weren't so upset about the marriage falsity."

"It might have something to do with it. There's also the fact that once it sinks in, it'll make her feel better."

"Freer?"

"And more in control again, knowing she's not bound by it. And for me, it gets Marco and Santino's taint off of it, of our relationship, of all of us. It's better for our foursome."

"I agree."

I smiled to myself.

Yeah, it hadn't sunk in yet.

It had been complicated by what Joe had done, how he'd gone about the entire thing.

It wasn't like him to do something like that either, the manipulation, the extremely underhanded covert approach and basically moving us around like chess pieces on his fucking board.

At least, he'd never done it with *me* before.

Something had changed, and it concerned me as to what that was.

26

~Caterina~

I stepped out into the backyard, pulling my leather jacket closed, expecting it to be freezing, only to be pleasantly surprised when welcoming heat enveloped me.

Aside from the tour that Julian had given me when I'd first moved in here, I realized I hadn't actually been outside to the backyard, or even merely the patio once since I'd been here. I'd been so focused on other things. Finding Julian, our mission, operating Camlann Corporation remotely, that I hadn't really entertained time for anything else. Aside from bonding with the guys.

Splashing caught my attention, and I looked out toward the pool. It was a color-changing rectangular swimming pool that even had a Jacuzzi at one end and a little waterfall on the other, the whole thing surrounded by beautiful gray brick.

I took in Julian swimming back and forth in the currently purple colored water.

As soon as I started to approach, he noticed and swam to the closest end to me, folding his arms on the edge and smiling out at me. "Come on in, darlin'."

I peered down into the pool and grinned. "You're naked."

"I didn't want you to feel awkward about being without a bathing suit."

I chuckled. "Sure that's the reason."

"Come on," he said, reaching out and stroking my calf. "Strip and show me that stunning body of yours. It's been too long."

I shrugged off my jacket and tossed it on a deck chair behind me.

"That's it." He winked. "I wouldn't say no to a little show."

"Shut the hell up," I said, laughing and pulling off my Vivier pumps. Not trusting him to keep the splashing down, I walked right over to the chair where I'd tossed my jacket and nestled them on it carefully.

He whistled. "Damn, if only that skirt was a little shorter."

I spun back to him to find his eyes lit with humor.

He was just egging me on, trying to bring the fun.

Trying to loosen me up.

"You're good, I'll give you that."

"Well, I've gotten to know you, Cat. I see you struggling to let go and just be in the moment. Not surprising, considering everything."

I smiled and unzipped my embellished gold and black bustier top, sliding it away and baring my breasts.

His eyes hooded at the sight.

The intensity ramped up there as I shimmied out of my skirt.

As I reached for my panties, he rose up out of the water and hooked his fingers in the sides, then drew them down slowly, his hot gaze holding mine captive.

I'd only just kicked them off when he grasped my thighs and dragged his tongue through my folds.

A squeal escaped me and he chuckled, then snagged me around the hips and hauled me into the pool, water splashing all around us.

"You're a menace," I choked, brushing my hair and water out of my face.

"Compliment taken, darlin'," he said, grasping my arms and floating us back against the edge of the pool.

All humor evaporated as he breathed me in, then slid his hand over my belly, stroking softly, reverently. "I saw you. You were going to tell them tonight."

"I was. I'm sorry, but with Milo finding out that his parents—"

"It's okay. I get it." He looked me over studiously, the sexual edge gone for the moment as he asked, full of concern, "How are you feeling? I haven't heard you throwing up or anything."

"No. Just ravenous now."

Off his look, I added, "For food."

He gave me a withering stare. "Really, huh? *Just* for food?"

Shit. "No. Honestly, not just for food."

"I know. It's one of the reasons I insisted on this tonight."

"You... how?"

"I've been keeping an eye on you." He leaned in and kissed my cheek in such a tender way that it sent a radiating warmth through me. He murmured happily as I turned my head and nuzzled against him. "You're carrying our baby, that's everything, and I'm here for whatever you need."

"That means a lot," I breathed, and looped my arms around his neck, holding him to me.

"You can do this. There's no doubt in my mind."

"Thank you."

"I want you to know that Nico and Milo will be the same. They'll be the most supportive you can imagine. They'll be overjoyed, Cat. This absolutely won't be a bad thing to them, so if that's also a concern you've been feeling, I can promise you that it's unfounded."

"I love how you are, how you can make even the worst things seem that much lighter, you know that?"

"It might have become apparent to me," he said, smiling down at me. He stroked my hair with one hand. "*I* love how you've been with me, supporting me after what happened and actually helping to bring me back in on everything when it was being kept from me."

"Well, I know what it's like to be forced onto the sidelines. I mean, in this case, it was coming from a good place, but I understand that feeling all too well, the helplessness, the nastiness of being cast aside and discounted. I didn't want that for you."

"Even though I really didn't help matters earlier when I tried to go after that asshole on my own, huh?"

"I understand why you did it. We all do."

He winced. "But it was reckless as shit."

"Yeah," I said, nodding. "It was. But we'll find another way. Like you keep telling me, yes? We can always find a way through."

"But it needs to be together."

"Yeah, it does."

He stared at me in awe.

"What?" I asked, with amusement.

"Just that you were so worried at first about not being able to work as a team and now look at you. Also, the fact that you'd never really been in a relationship and you jumped right into this with three of us, and you're doing so well with it… it's impressive."

"You're giving me too much credit. I'm just finding my way through as I go."

"Nah, it's more than that. You've changed everything for us." He stroked my belly again. "And there's about to be even more of that with this little baby. Things were straining between the three of us before you came along and now? Now they're more solid than they've ever been. Yes, even with the argument that you witnessed tonight." He smiled. "You were that special element that we'd been missing all along. And now you're here, I can't imagine it being any other way. I love you being here with us. I love our foursome dynamic. And I love *you.*"

He certainly had a way with beautiful words and declarations. More than that with him was his endearing sincerity. Behind the image he put on to the world, he was such a loving and caring sweetheart of a man. It had become clear as I'd gotten to know him, that beneath all the rest, all that he wanted was to feel loved and safe. And he really put his heart out on his sleeve where that was concerned. It was so amazing and courageous that what had happened to him recently, and even years ago with his father, hadn't managed to take that away from him. He fought so hard for it too, to be this incredible person before me.

"I love you too," I confessed, right there with him. I brushed my lips over his. "How you've been with me, especially since I told you about the pregnancy… I'll never forget it… thank you."

"You're mine, you're ours. It could never be any other way."

"Shit, you and your beautiful words," I uttered a moment before I tugged him down to me and crushed my lips to his.

It wasn't overwhelming or insanely animalistic as I was used to it being with the guys, something both Nico and I brought to the table a hell of a lot whenever the four of us came together. No, this time it was different, maybe because I had that part of me locked down, or maybe because of the intimacy of the moment between us, but it was easy and enveloping, and intensely sensual.

It had me sinking against the side of the pool, grasping his hip and pulling him tighter to me, while running my fingers all over his upper body, his collarbone, his shoulders, his nipple hoops, and down over his deliciously hard and toned abs, the heat from his skin burning into mine.

He groaned into my mouth, his tongue curling around mine, tasting me, savoring me, just like I was doing with him.

He shifted his weight and I let out a needy sound as I felt his hard dick against my thigh.

"Getting started without us?" Milo's voice came, cutting through the moment.

We broke from the kiss and I turned my head to see Milo standing there completely naked, all that ink and that mammoth muscular form of his on display in all its glory. He was stroking his already hard cock as he looked at us through hooded eyes.

"You took too long," Julian told him, his gaze running all over him, even as he started to rub his cock against my thigh more determinedly, trying to draw my attention back to the moment, not wanting to let it slip away. "Get in here," he told Milo, his strained voice betraying his escalating need. "Fucking now."

"Mmm, I love it when you get like this," Milo rumbled, slipping into the pool and wading toward us.

He was just a little way out when Nico's voice thundered through the house, jolting all of us.

"*Are you fucking kidding me? 'FU Santino'? And Marco too? Julian!*"

I winced at Julian. "He's seen your IG post."

"What post?" Milo asked.

"I thought he was with you in your room?" Julian asked. "He'd left his phone in the kitchen."

"He went to get us some towels. I guess he stopped off in the kitchen to check his messages. With the strikes taking place tomorrow, he's on edge about everything being in place." He eyed Julian worriedly. "So, what was the post?"

"Who fucking cares?" he said, palming my breasts and smirking devilishly at me, before leaning in to suck at my nipples.

"*I care,*" Nico's voice sounded a second before Julian's head was jerked back.

I swung my head to see Nico crouched on the outside of the pool, fisting his hand in Julian's blond hair.

Shit. He'd completely blindsided me. I'd been caught up in our conversation then what Julian had been doing to me.

I looked to see he'd brought some of his fancy black bath towels out and dropped them on the table.

I drank in the sight of him completely naked and his cock raging hard as he crouched there grasping Julian's hair and basically snarling at him.

"Ouch," Julian said, grinning up at him. "Someone's on edge."

"It's your fucking post. On top of what you already fucking did."

"Nah, it's because you're desperate for a good fuck."

With a grunt, Nico released his hair. "You disrespected and challenged Santino and my father in one fucking shot with that post. And the photo—motherfucker, J!"

"You told me to get the word out about the marriage, and I did."

"Not like that."

"Please, drama and shading spreads faster than anything else. People love that shit."

"You made yourself a target."

"I'm already a target due to my association with you. And the fact that I've now untangled my business from the Marchetti Syndicate."

"This is different."

"Cat said the same thing."

"Because she gets it. The complexities of our world and—"

"It's done, Nico," Milo said.

"Pull the post," Nico demanded of Julian.

I cut in, "Even if he does pull it, with his number of followers, it would have spread by now. It's too late."

"It was too late the moment I posted it."

Nico scrubbed his hand over his face. "J, you're killing me."

"And you're killing the mood."

He gestured at me.

And then Nico's eyes were all over me, his gaze heating at the sight of my naked breasts, then dipping below the water, drinking in every inch of me. It had me shifting restlessly, my whole body heating.

He looked away, then grunted at Julian, before slipping into the pool right beside him. "I swear to fuck, this isn't over and—"

Julian grasped his cock, stilling him from the surprise of it. "I know, N. But for now, let's just be together. All hell's gonna break loose in a whole other way tomorrow night. So we need this time right now."

I expected Nico to bat Julian's hand away.

But, instead, he sank against the side of the pool and murmured, "All right."

"There," Julian spoke in a soothing tone, flicking his thumb over Nico's crown and drawing a long groan from him. "Just let it all go."

He gathered the pre-cum with his free hand that was already leaking from Nico, showing just how much he needed this, and then he reached out and spread it over my lips. I opened and slicked my tongue over it, tasting it while Nico's smoldering gaze held mine.

"More," Milo rumbled, coming up behind me and stroking my hair while he grabbed my hip, then jerked me back right against his cock as he started sliding it up and down the crack of my ass.

"Yes," I breathed.

As I pushed back against him, he released my hip, then brought his fingers around and started dragging them through my pussy. I spread my legs almost involuntarily, wanting more, needing more so badly.

"Mmm," Milo groaned as he felt my slickness. "So ready for us to devour you, beauty."

That groan deepened when he watched Julian give *more*, like he'd asked, as he released Nico and waded behind Milo, then slicked his tongue all over his muscular back, treating him to erotic licks as he reached over and stroked my hair, while dipping his hand to Milo's ass and fingering the crack of his ass, teasing up and down and making Milo grind his cock harder against me. "Yeah, Sunshine," he implored.

Nico was suddenly there in front of me.

He pulled me from Milo and spun me around, binding his arm across my chest and holding me to him as he told Milo. "Take her cunt."

I threw my head back against his shoulder as I watched Nico spread me open with his fingers, inviting Milo in.

"Damn, yes, that's it," Milo murmured to himself, his eyes glazed with need.

Nico tapped directly on my clit as he held me open, exposed and vulnerable, the added element of the water sending another slew of sensations through me. He picked up his pace, tapping rapidly with one finger over and over until he drove me right to the edge and had me writhing in his hold and panting.

I was moments away from tasting bliss when he pulled his hand away and released me.

At my whimper he told me, "Not yet. Let Milo feel your sweet cunt squeezing the fuck out of him when you come all over him."

A growl escaped Milo, and then he was hauling me up.

I instinctively wrapped my thighs around him just a second before he thrust deep inside me, making me cry out into the night, the sound echoing all around us.

I fisted my hands in his hair and jerked him to me, thrusting my tongue into his mouth as he powered up inside me with sexy grunts. I lost myself to it, to savoring him and the feel of him stretching me open and driving *so* deep, hitting so many nerve endings that had my thighs fucking shaking from the intensity.

All of that was ramped up as I felt pressure at my asshole.

"Ready?" I heard Nico asking Julian.

"Christ, yes."

A moment later, Milo and I broke our kiss as Nico eased into my ass at the same time as Julian eased into Milo's.

It wasn't rough and power-fucking right off the bat.

No, this time it was slow and easy, and so fucking erotic

as they both rocked back and forth, easing out, that pushing in deeper, making us feel every delectable moment of their dicks sinking into us.

"Ungh," Milo grunted, his eyes rolling back in his head as he ground his hips back and forth, his cock driving deeper into me. He reached back and slapped his free hand to Julian's hip, holding him to him and grinding with his thrusts and Nico's at the same time.

"Feel Nico grazing your cock too?" Julian teased him.

"Damn... yeah," Milo breathed.

Nico stroked my hair and slicked his talented tongue over my throat. "Such a sweet ass. Our filthy little princess loves having her ass filled. Don't you, baby?"

"Yes," I gasped.

"She loves being filled by us all fucking over," Julian said. He reached around Milo as he continued rocking and teased my clit with light, stimulating brushes of his fingers. "Loves being played with and worshipped by us all."

I dropped my head back against Nico's shoulder as pleasure permeated every part of me, sinking into the three of them and the heady eroticism of it all. "God," I breathed.

Nico took to playing with my pussy as Julian started teasing Milo's balls. It had him picking up his pace and growling as he drove into me harder and faster.

At the same time, Nico and Julian stabbed deeper, becoming merciless and the whole thing overwhelming me to the point of no return as I screamed and exploded all over Milo.

"Ungh... fuck, Caterina. The way you grip me. Ah, Julian... *goddammit*," Milo cried, beside himself as the torment became too much for him too and I felt his hot cum spill deep inside me.

As it set me off again and I came all over Milo's cock,

he pulled out and grabbed my hips and used his impressive strength to shove me up and down Nico's cock rapid-fire.

"Fuck *me*," Nico snarled, as Milo basically fucked his cock with my own ass.

He raked his nails all over my breasts, losing his shit, before he jerked and came all over my back.

"Jesus," Julian exclaimed, and then he abruptly pulled out, shoved Milo around, and came all over his face. "Yes... *fucking* yes!" he shouted, fisting Milo's hair and holding him to him for a long, intense moment.

He kissed him and licked the cum off his face, before swimming to me, and licking Nico's off my back too.

And then he wrapped me up in his arms, a moment before Nico and Milo were there too, the four of us all over one another, reveling in it. In each other.

Together.

In moments like this, it truly felt like the rest of the world didn't exist.

That it couldn't touch us.

But, unfortunately, it was just wishful thinking.

Moments like this were all we currently had.

And they were everything.

27

~Emilio~

This was nice.

Normal.

Cozy.

We were all sprawled out on Julian's bed in the living room *suite* that Nico had set up, in our bathrobes watching that *Merlin* show that Caterina liked. I got the appeal with her love of the myth of King Arthur, and it was certainly entertaining, although I was more of a high fantasy fan myself.

Nico was sitting up against the headboard with his arm wrapped around Caterina, who was munching on some of Julian's Maltesers now he'd had his fill. He was sprawled out in the middle of the bed, his head in her lap as she stroked his hair. And I was nestled against her other side, playing with her hair with one hand while snacking on some toffee popcorn with Caterina, deciding to lean into the whole *letting it all go* theme of tonight and actually breaking from what Julian called my *bodybuilder diet*.

"Why are so many of these things only aimed at a younger audience?" Nico mused. "There's a lot that can be done at a more mature level. A lot more of the darker aspects that could be explored."

"And the fun and dirty aspects," Julian added.

Because, of course.

I studied him as he was oblivious and focused on the show.

He'd handled what had gone down in the pool really well.

Easily, it had seemed.

It shouldn't be possible with what he'd been through.

I mean, of course I wanted him to be okay, and I'd been so fucking happy seeing him not only being able to get physical, but to be reveling in it like he had earlier, bringing his dominating edge to the table and taking the lead like he usually did. Well, usually, it was a tossup between him and Nico, often the two of them together and feeding off each other.

But I was concerned that it wasn't real.

Worse, that he'd convinced himself that he was fine and able to handle fucking so soon after what had happened, when he actually couldn't.

He'd basically begged us to back off and let him do things his way, claiming that the alternative had actually been hurting him.

So we'd agreed to it.

And we'd planned to see how it played out and take it from there.

But then he'd broken down outside the warehouses.

Then he'd been in a rage.

And *then* it had all slipped away like it had never been, and he'd been on solid ground again, even pushing for us to get it on in the pool.

It was… it was a clusterfuck.

I understood if that was just how he felt at the

moment, that it couldn't be helped, and he was swinging from one thing to the other, his emotions going haywire.

But it worried me that he was pushing himself too hard to *not* be impacted in other ways, that it was the root of his emotions going from one extreme to the other, rather than it being the result of him actually working through what he'd suffered through.

But bringing it up clearly wasn't helping. He'd only reacted really fucking badly so far.

And right now, in this specific moment, he seemed to be content, so mentioning it would only fuck all over that.

The thing with Julian was that he could hide the truth better than anybody I'd ever known. A big part of that was because he had the ability to read others so well. He knew what we'd each pick up on and he could work with it too fucking well.

"I'm thinking about selling *Nocturne*," he announced suddenly. "Or maybe just demolishing it altogether."

What the—

"Why?" Nico asked. "We've severed Marchetti influence. You're free of it now."

"Yeah, I know, and I appreciate you helping me with that, but I just don't think it's appropriate anymore."

Caterina shifted and choked a little on a Malteser she was munching on.

All that fucking had clearly worked up an appetite for her, because she'd gone through half of the bag already and two-thirds of the popcorn bowl we were sharing.

"Appropriate?" I asked. "Since when has that been an issue for you?"

Was this about what had happened? Was he finally acknowledging it again, about to start processing it?

That hope was quickly snuffed out when he told us, "It's an issue now, I guess. I just feel like a change. A shift in my brand. *Nocturne* doesn't fit with where I want to take things."

"Take things in what direction, exactly?" Nico asked. "A wholesome approach? You?"

Julian turned on Caterina's lap to look out at us. "Yeah, why not?"

"You don't need to do that, Julian," Caterina told him.

"I think I do, darlin'."

"No. It's really okay."

"What's okay? What's going on?" I pushed.

"Caterina told us that you wanted to be exclusive. Is that what this is about?" Nico asked.

Julian and Caterina exchanged a look.

And then he looked away and settled back down to his previous position. "Yeah. That's what it's about."

"You've been *exclusive* since the four of us got together," Nico reminded him. "Are you concerned it's too much temptation to keep *Nocturne?*"

"Exactly."

"That's bullshit," I said. "All of us can see that you're fully committed to our foursome. Committed in a way I've never seen from you before."

Caterina cursed and pulled from all of us, then got off the bed, handing the Maltesers back to Julian—or what was left of them. "He is committed. He's been amazing. All of you have. It's *me.*"

She started pacing then and tugging at the belt of her robe nervously too.

"Cat, it's okay. I promise," Julian told her, sitting up and moving to the edge of the bed.

"What's okay?" Nico asked, his rapidly mounting concern mirroring mine.

"It's all my fault. I'm sorry," Caterina told us, looking so out of sorts, it had my gut twisting. "So much has been going on and the timing is atrocious. I just… and after Milo finding out about Leo earlier, I thought it best to wait. Again. But waiting is just prolonging it. It's keeping a secret, a massive secret that impacts your lives too. I should've… I should've told you sooner. I'm sorry, I just—"

"Caterina," Nico spoke, jumping off the bed and going to her. "Take a breath," he said, reaching out and taking her hand, giving it a comforting squeeze. "Just tell us what's going on."

"I'm fine," I assured her, getting off the bed too and joining them. "I'm processing it and I'll handle it. Don't worry about that, all right? And certainly don't let it put you off telling us whatever this is that's clearly eating you up inside. I don't want that. None of us do."

Caterina's gaze flicked to Julian, and he gave her an encouraging nod, making it clear beyond a shadow a doubt that he already knew what this *secret* of hers was.

I could see Nico straining not to bombard her with questions, to push it along. He even had to drop his hand from hers, so he could clench both down by his sides in order to hold himself back. He really had come a long way with her, from obsession to actual love, being able to recognize and do what was best for *her* above all.

I watched with bated breath as she shifted her weight uncomfortably, then pressed her hand to her stomach and looked between me and Nico.

"I'm pregnant."

I choked as the words hung there heavily.

Nico took an unsteady step back and scrubbed his hand over his face.

He was usually the best at taking in information and processing it rapidly, then taking action.

But this wasn't just information.

This was… something else entirely.

"A baby," I uttered.

"That's what pregnancy entails, the special little gift at the end," Julian spoke, pushing off the bed with a bit of a struggle.

Yeah, he'd overdone it tonight. Another example of him trying to move along at light speed with everything. *Goddammit, Sunshine.*

He winced to himself, then tried to fake it, like he could simply shake off the ache he was obviously feeling. "Take those damn painkillers in the nightstand there," I told him.

"I'm all good."

The hell he was.

I gritted my teeth and looked away, focusing back on Caterina.

As she looked out at us, nervously awaiting our reactions, she was more emotional and unsettled than I'd ever seen from her before.

As much as I didn't want her feeling that way, I was glad that she was putting it out there now, trusting in us, connecting with us, even when it was difficult.

The fact she'd actually told Nico and me right *before* the strikes tomorrow was a big deal, too. It must have crossed her mind that we'd try to pull her from the front lines of it all the moment she put the revelation out there. Yet, here she was, trusting us again.

"Legacy," Nico rasped, at last. "That's what you meant before."

"Yeah," she responded uneasily.

Julian wrapped his arm around her. "Just give them a moment. I promise you it will be okay," he said quietly, doing his best to comfort her.

I frowned. She thought we wouldn't be happy about it? No, that wasn't it at all.

And it wasn't why Nico was struggling to absorb the

news. I knew him better than anyone, and because I did, I understood what was at the root of his shock where this came into play.

He reacted badly enough when one of us was hurt, but with a baby in the picture—our baby—it would be another fucking level where that protective intensity was concerned.

And then there was his *feral* side and where that was all rooted, connected to his intense compartmentalization of the guilt for all the fucked-up things he'd done both as Capo for the Marchetti Syndicate and from losing control too. Caterina had accepted that about him. More than that, she got off on it, she loved it. But with a baby, that just wouldn't fly anymore. He was clearly worried it would change things, change *them*, and also whether he could actually keep it in check when the time came, when the baby arrived and we became fathers.

It was a lot to absorb.

I saw him reach into the pocket of his robe where he'd put his lighter and smoke, but he stopped himself at the last second. She was pregnant, no smoking around her.

On my end, I was also coming at it from a protective angle, trying to figure out how to react when the inevitable would soon follow and she asked how this news would impact her contribution to this war.

Majorly, if I had anything to do with it.

Nico would be with me.

But I needed to get a grip and focus on the immediate and taking all this concern and upset away for her.

I stepped up to her and stroked the fluffy arms of her robe. "This is a little miracle."

"Yeah?" she asked with a tentative smile.

It was so strange seeing her this way. So… unsure.

No, it was more than that.

It was stark vulnerability.

"Definitely. No question about it."

"Told you," Julian said, grinning at her and stepping back so I could wrap her up in my arms. "You're taking the *teddy bear* eyes thing to a whole other level wrapping her up while you're wearing that fluffy robe," he teased.

"Teddy bear eyes," I said, giving him a withering look. "I love them, big boy."

"I know you do."

Caterina chuckled into my chest.

When I eased back, Nico was standing right there in front of the three of us, his gaze focused intensely on Caterina.

Emotion swam in his eyes.

"This is everything," he spoke, his voice choked up as he uttered the words.

He stunned all of us then as he suddenly dropped to his knees and wrapped his arms around her waist, pressing his ear to her belly. "Thank you."

Wow.

Caterina smiled and slid her hands into his hair. "You're happy?"

He lifted his head and beamed up at her. "Beyond merely happy. This is incredible. Are you happy? How do you feel? Now we know what was going on with the exhaustion and vomiting. And why you've been so hungry lately. Fuck, if I hadn't had my mind focused on the upcoming strikes, I would've fucking noticed. I'm so sorry. What do you need? We should make an appointment for an ultrasound and—"

"Whoa," Julian said, holding up his hand. "Excitement noted, N. But take it easy, yeah?"

Nico sucked in a breath and rose to his feet, telling a stunned Caterina, "I'm sorry." He stroked her arms. "What can I do?"

"Nothing," she said. "Now this weight is off, now you know and your reactions were better than I ever imagined, everything is good." She smiled out at all of us. "It's perfect."

It would be if we weren't in the middle of war.

"Nico, I'll get one of our safehouses ready for her. We can—"

"No," he ground out.

"No?"

"She's not being pushed off onto the sidelines."

"I wouldn't put it that way. She's pregnant. Carrying our baby. With everything coming, we can't just—"

"She's a part of this. An integral part. And that's where she'll stay."

What was happening?

He shifted the subject in the next second, asking her, "So, are you happy about this, *principessa?*"

"I am, yeah. Nervous, though."

"Of course, it's gonna be a big change, a lot to prepare for." He smiled wildly. "But it's also going to be absolutely amazing."

"Expanding our family," Julian mused, looking all starry-eyed in that sweet way of his.

That rare giggle escaped Caterina, and that was it for all of us. We crowded her, wrapping ourselves around her.

A baby.

We were having a baby.

28

~Julian~

"Good little bitch."

"You'll never survive this. I promise you that."

"Aww, don't worry, you'll enjoy it. I want you to. I want you to hate that you enjoy it."

My eyes snapped open, and I went to bolt up in bed, only to find myself weighed down by Caterina sleeping fully on me.

I frowned. That wasn't how I'd remembered things being last night.

Milo had been on one edge of the bed right beside me, his leg flung over me and his arm grasping Cat. Then Nico had been on the other edge of the bed spooning her. I mean, yeah, during the night, things could have shifted a little, but not by this much.

The night light that Nico had brought in for me was on as usual, the soothing blue glow providing enough illumination for me to take in the rest of the scene I'd woken up to.

Milo hadn't just shifted. He wasn't here at all.

Neither was Nico.

What the hell was going on?

After Cat had told them about the pregnancy, it had come up just how horny she'd been recently, and we'd all given her what she'd needed and fucked each other's brains out. Over and over and fucking over. We'd basically crawled into bed.

Thankfully, they'd been so exhausted that they hadn't woken up as I'd startled awake a couple of hours ago from the first nightmare.

I'd been worried about it happening, something I'd kept to myself because I didn't want a fucking intervention, or them—especially Milo—pushing me to face things head-on. That was the last thing I needed right now.

The only fucking thing I needed was to put Angelo in the ground.

That was all.

That would do it.

It *would*.

And I was determined to make it so through sheer force of will.

I didn't want it dragging on and becoming all I thought about, my whole fucking focus.

I had things to do. Carver Group needed my attention, we needed to prepare for the baby, to figure a hell of a lot out where that was concerned, *and* we needed to bring down the two families and settle everything there so our baby wasn't brought into a war zone.

I looked out at Cat, sleeping so soundly.

The urge to stay in her warmth was strong, but I was too restless after that nightmare to be able to do that. I needed to clear my mind, or I'd just go right back to the fucking thing.

And now I was also worried about where the hell Nico and Milo had fucked off to.

Jesus.

So, I carefully extricated myself, snatched my boxers off the floor, then headed on out of the room.

I intended to head into the kitchen to snack on some comfort foods—something chocolaty, of course—before beginning my search for Milo and Nico, but I'd only gotten a few steps down the corridor when I heard Nico's voice in the distance. I frowned when I picked up on the noticeable urgency in his tone.

I made my way down the corridor toward the sound until I reached his office.

The door was halfway open.

I was about to walk on in when another voice pulled me up short. Milo's.

"The risk is too great, Nico."

"It's too great if we don't let her remain here as a part of it all."

"I don't think—"

"This is about her choices, her power. I won't fuck all over that by sidelining her now."

"What we're about to do will escalate the danger a thousand times over. The baby—"

"If we do this, send her out to a safehouse, and hide her away, it will be over. It will ruin everything."

"Nico—"

"We. Will. Lose. Her."

I pushed the door open the rest of the way and walked on in.

Nico was behind his desk at his laptop and he jolted as he saw me, slapping his hand to his heart. "Fuck, J."

Milo spun around where he was standing opposite Nico's desk in just a pair of boxers and one of his sexy tanks. "Lose the creeping, Sunshine. Goddammit."

I ignored all the preamble and told Milo, "Nico's right. We will lose her if you ramp up the overprotectiveness."

"It's not being *over*protective. It's necessarily protective. She's carrying our child and we're going to war."

"I get it, all right? But Cat's not just anyone. She's highly skilled. She's beyond capable. And she's a vital asset in this war too, so there's also an argument from that side of things. We need her, Milo."

He grimaced and pulled at his spiky hair. "I... just... after everything we'd gone through, all the dark and dirty shit... this child is a gift from on high. I can't stand the idea of... it just... it needs to be protected at all costs."

"Not at the cost of *her*, Milo," Nico ground out. "It took me so long to earn her trust, then for her to trust all three of us. And a great deal of that was built on the fact that we don't try to exert control over her, that she's free to make her own choices, and that we recognize her power and strength. You saw what happened when I almost fucked that up to an extent when I met with Levi that night. This would be far beyond that. Shipping her off to a safehouse and essentially locking her up like a fragile thing, it's an insult and demeaning beyond belief, especially to someone as forthright and as full of fire like Caterina Leone."

"You know, it's one of the reasons she didn't tell the two of you right away?"

They both eyed me.

"She said that?" Milo asked, taken aback.

"I read it from her and she admitted it was a concern, yeah."

"Fuck," Nico said, scrubbing his hand over his jaw. "See what I mean?"

"Goddammit." Milo dug his fingers into the edge of the desk and sucked in a breath. "Well, she's not on the front lines of these strikes later tonight, so that's something. At least she won't be in the field."

"You realize she was pregnant during the crash?" I pointed out. "Also, when she massacred those assholes in that garage *and* when she came to rescue me?"

"Yeah, and it was unbelievably lucky that the baby wasn't hurt during the crash, let alone all the rest. I mean, fuck, that kind of thing runs out."

"I'm not doing it," Nico insisted. "So you need to get on board and find a way to make peace with it." He rose from behind his desk and walked to him, his tone softening as he asked, "Do you think this reaction from you has some roots in what I revealed to you about Leo being responsible for your parents' deaths? That it could be bringing up some issues there?"

"Maybe," Milo admitted.

"It makes sense," I said, walking to him and stroking his arm. "That happened during the last war and your mom was an innocent."

"But Caterina's not," Nico told him. "She's one of us. She's a warrior. Santino is terrified of her, for fuck's sake. That's how much of a force to be reckoned with that she truly is."

I nodded, brushing my fingers over Milo's cheek. "It's not the same as what happened to your mom."

His eyes met mine and my gut twisted at the stark emotion swimming in his striking espresso pools.

"It's *not* the same," he murmured. "I just…"

"You love her," I spoke.

"Yeah," he admitted, his eyes brightening as he put that out there.

"I love you too."

We all spun to see Cat standing there, leaning against the doorframe, and beaming at Milo.

She was wearing one of my white tees, and she looked sexy as fuck in it. Cute too at the same time somehow.

"I can't wait until you start showing," Nico randomly blurted out in completely uncharacteristic fashion.

The surprise of it had all of us bursting out laughing.

He was *so* into this pregnancy, even more than I'd already predicted him being.

Milo burst from us, strode across the room, and wrapped her up in his arms. "I *do*, you know? I love you *so* much."

"I know," she murmured happily into his chest. "I feel it from you."

When he pulled back enough where she could actually breathe properly from his overwhelming bear hug, he told her, "I don't know how much you heard of that, but I need you to know that I just want you and the baby safe. I'm sorry that I—"

"It's all right. I understand the impulse. And it's coming from a good place."

"But we also can't let fear control us," Nico spoke. "Especially not when it comes to this."

Cat nodded. "If we'd allowed that to be the case beforehand, we never would have gotten to this point of challenging the families. Of fighting for our freedom from all of this insanity. We need to focus on seeing this through." She eyed Milo intensely. "And *that's* how we protect our child."

"Absolutely," Nico agreed.

"Okay," Milo said, easing back from her, but not before planting a soft and sweet kiss on her cheek. "Okay, yeah, I hear you. All of you."

Nico sighed with a whole lot of relief.

I wasn't surprised.

We all needed to be on the same page more than ever with what was about to go down later tonight.

It was bad enough that I'd strained that by acting alone

—*going rogue*, as Nico called it—in my desperate bid to take down Angelo myself.

But I'd fucking failed, and I wasn't gonna let that be the case again. And I wasn't gonna hurt our foursome by going off half-cocked again either. We'd do it together. Nico had promised me justice and I would trust in that. I had to. For the good of us all.

Once these strikes were done, the time for that would come.

"Did our voices carry all the way to the living room and wake you up?" Nico asked Cat.

"No. One of my alerts woke me up."

Nico frowned. "I would've seen it as I was going over the tactical plans for the strikes," he said, gesturing at his open laptop on his desk.

"It's not concerning that. I've been trying to determine why the hell Joe interfered with the Shawn Price takedown. I know you told me to put it on the back burner, because you thought I was juggling enough as it was with manipulating the upcoming raids of Marchetti and Leone gambling dens and strip clubs, leaking amassed evidence to key influential figures backing Santino to break those connections, and also infiltrating and rerouting funds across Leone Family accounts."

"Jeez, he was obviously right about you juggling a lot," I said.

"I know, but Joe's involvement had been nagging at me. So I've been looking into it while working on the rest. I managed to identify all the buyers and partners connected to Shawn Price's trafficking business. I put tabs on them, monitoring their activity, and the alert basically signaled me that they've gone dark. All of them. They're dead."

"What?" Milo uttered.

"It's Joe," she explained. "He's killed them all, wiped out all connections to Price and that operation."

"To ensure it couldn't be revived even with the Price and Wharton aspect annihilated?" I asked.

"That sort of business does make him sick to his stomach, but he's also not a benevolent guardian angel operating out of the goodness of his own heart," Cat said. "There's got to be more to it."

"And you think whatever it is has something to do with us?" Nico asked.

"Something that can impact us, yes. There's something I'm missing, a connection I can't make. I've reached out to him in our usual covert way, but he's not responding."

"Too busy on his murder missions," I grunted.

"We'll deal with it after the strikes. We'll all pull together to figure out what's going on," Nico said, shutting down his laptop and walking to her. He pressed his hand to her belly. "Right now, however, you need to get some rest. This little baby needs taking care of, Caterina."

"And we're making another doctor's appointment too," Milo said.

"All right," she conceded. "Yes, to both those things. But first, I need to eat something really bad." She looked out at me, pouting her lips.

"Yes, you can finish off my Maltesers," I told her.

"You need something much more substantial than that," Milo spoke.

"I will. In the morning. Just a snack for now."

Milo eyed Nico for support.

"Let her have her snack. It's clearly some sort of craving."

"Fine," Milo said. "Just for tonight."

I chuckled and then the four of us headed on out of Nico's office.

29

~Caterina~

"Raids are underway as we speak. Thirteen consecutive takedowns of Marchetti and Leone strip clubs and gambling dens," I reported down the line to Nico, communicating with him via our COMMs as I sat up at the kitchen island in the Manor with my laptop.

It turned out that Remo had been playing down his *police contacts*. His asset had actually been the Assistant District Attorney, Clive Wilkins. That was a hell of a lot of power and it had been why the raids had been able to be organized so incredibly quickly.

I took another bite from the food Milo had made for me before he'd left. A frittata with feta and red peppers—a whole lot of protein and calcium, according to him. He'd also filled a massive bowl of my favored berries, so I was moving between them both.

I switched between the feeds I was watching of everything that was happening tonight with the multiple strikes and moves we were making, focusing on the surveillance footage by the Benzino's chief meth lab.

"Cassio and his soldiers have arrived at the lab," I reported next.

When there was still no response from Nico, I connected with Milo.

He was currently with Nico down by the warehouses on Nico's territory, transporting their illicit goods off-territory.

"Status?" I spoke.

"All good," Milo responded, sending relief through me. "On schedule. No interference thanks to the families being distracted by the raids and the Marchettis trying to carry out their attacks against Benzino business interests. Nico's in the thick of organizing everything, making one of his morale-boosting speeches too."

Oh, good, that was the only reason he wasn't answering.

My earpiece buzzed. "Keep me posted," I told Milo.

"Will do, beauty."

I answered the incoming contact, and Julian's voice came down the line.

"I tell you something, darlin', these fuckers are shit-scared after that evidence you collected against them. It didn't take much to get them to remove their support from the Leone Family. They were tripping over themselves to sign on the proverbial dotted line."

Julian was with a unit of Nico's soldiers down in the financial district wherein we'd set up a meeting with various power players who my father had in his pocket.

"Did Victoria Munsen show up?"

"No. You were right about her thinking she's untouchable. Foolish, considering you already sent her to jail once."

She wasn't the only one who'd been stubborn. The politicians and city officials that Julian was dealing with right now had more to lose, their positions complicated, and with people to answer to, to be accountable to. But the stockbrokers involved, as well as some high-flying hedge fund managers, had required some hefty bribes that had eclipsed Santino's compensation, in order to break their connection to the Leone Family.

Victoria would require more than that.

"We'll see to her soon enough. This is already a win, though, even without her." She'd be about the only person left who Santino had in his pocket by the time we were done.

"Perfect. Just finishing up, then I'm gonna swing by *Luster* and your lounges for you. I know you've been concerned that you haven't been able to be there in person."

"That would be amazing. Thank you, Julian."

"It's a far cry from a few months back where you couldn't even entertain the notion of my help, huh?"

I chuckled. "Times have certainly changed."

"And they'll change more. I want us to get down to working on our expansion plans once the scales tip in our favor with this war after tonight. The hit it'll be for the Leones and Marchettis should give us some calm as they're forced to fall back and retreat with their tails between their legs."

"Here's hoping."

I was cycling between feeds as I spoke with him and I picked up on the two delivery trucks carrying the coke shipments for the Flower Market—Gio's territory— crossing the border into the city.

"Gotta go, shipments are here."

"Love you."

"Love you too."

I tapped my earpiece, then snatched up my phone,

putting it on speakerphone mode the moment Carlo picked up.

"Caterina, what's the word?"

"The shipments have passed over the northeast border."

"Right on schedule. We're moving in. Is Nico done at the warehouses?"

"He's on schedule, too. He'll meet you at the apartment."

"Roger."

We disconnected, and I made an attempt to connect with Nico again via my earpiece.

"Sorry about that earlier," his voice came down the line.

"No worries. The shipments have crossed the border. Carlo needs you at the apartment." The *apartment* was the abandoned building outside the city that we'd met Carlo and Remo at before. It was where Carlo and his soldiers were going to transport Gio and his men to. He needed Nico there as future Boss of the Marchetti Syndicate to make a play for turning them.

"On my way."

"Great," I said, shoveling another bite of frittata into my mouth.

"I'm glad you're eating."

"You can hear it?"

"I can hear you chewing, yes. I was worried the stress of tonight with all the craziness would lead to you forgoing the meal Milo made for you."

"Nope. Got to take care of our baby, right?"

"Absolutely."

"Besides, everything is on schedule and progressing nicely. Thanks to your in-depth strategizing with Carlo."

"Actually, thanks to all the work you did with intel-gathering and setting yourself up as our base ops for tonight."

I smiled. "A team effort. As usual, these days."

He chuckled. "I'm loving it, *principessa*. I'll keep you posted."

We disconnected, and I cycled between feeds, keeping an eye on everything. I winced as I caught sight of Carlo's lab, now on fire. Well, he'd been willing to sacrifice it to function as a distraction so we could accomplish a lot more tonight. Nico had given Cassio a heads-up, so he knew what was really going on.

I was tapped into a couple of cameras belonging to businesses that Marco had been slated to target tonight, and I watched as Giovanni Guerra arrived with his soldiers outside one of them, but then received a call and suddenly gestured for his men to turn back around. *Good*. He'd gotten word that his shipments had been intercepted. Word that we'd had Cassio *leak* to him. As we'd planned, it put the kibosh on the attacks as Giovanni rushed off to deal with that instead.

Everything was going precisely to plan.

I blew out a breath and sank back for a moment, munching on some berries.

It was the first relaxing breath that I'd allowed myself since the guys had headed out.

Not being in the field with them was difficult to reconcile, but I knew it wasn't them pulling some overprotective move. They needed me here monitoring everything.

Besides, truth be told, I'd actually been feeling uneasy about going into combat now that I knew I was pregnant. The idea of it made me feel guilty, because it wasn't just about me anymore. And ever since I'd overheard the guys talking about making sure they weren't too overprotective with me, and Milo had mentioned how lucky I'd been that

I hadn't lost the baby during the motorcycle crash, it had really stayed with me. I *had* been lucky. So fucking lucky. The idea of pushing that didn't sit well with me at all.

There was also my concern about my *monstrous* side. It had grown so strong lately that controlling it had been difficult, and I'd noticed it worsening every time I let it out. Now I was having this baby, I had to rethink that; I had to rethink a lot of things.

Maybe they were just things that I needed a little time to adjust to, because not being in combat this one time was all it was—one time. We were at war. That definitely wouldn't last. And I had to be okay with it. It wasn't just for the good of the mission; I had to do everything it took to fight for a better life for our child.

My phone buzzed on the island and I snatched it up, expecting it to be Julian, likely sending me a photo of some sort to add some levity to the night.

Instead, my breath caught in my throat when I saw it was actually the farthest thing from Julian.

Blocked Number: How's my pretty cock slut? He's definitely still obsessed with me, frantically trying to track me down, pretending it's all for revenge when he's really craving me. Not to worry, he'll be able to get his fill soon enough.

Angelo.

Caterina: Stay the hell away from him.

Blocked Number: No can do. And you, traitorous cunt, you've signed your death certificate. Your daddy knows what you did. He's gonna force you to return what you stole and then he'll do what he should have done a long time ago and bury you. Wish I could be there in person to see it, but I'll settle for spitting on your grave. Wondering how I was able to contact you? Let's just say I have some new friends. Better than the ones your boyfriends murdered. They were just a stepping stone to these guys. Bye, Caterina. I should warn you, it's gonna be painful. Santino promised me it would be. Can't wait until it breaks your boyfriends into pieces.

I choked and pushed off the stool.

I was just about to tap my earpiece to report this to the guys when a screen opened on my laptop with a flashing image of a black shattered circle that looked a whole lot like an eclipse with red and green light breaking through.

What the—

No.

It wasn't possible.

Somebody had breached my network.

It shouldn't—no.

I rapidly disconnected from the internet.

Fuck.

I needed to put a poison pill into the system to—

Movement in my peripheral vision over by the patio doors caught my attention a second before one of the doors shattered as something was lobbed through it.

I darted back from the island a second before it erupted and thick, heavy smoke filled the area, making me choke.

It filled the room in moments until it was near impossible to see a fucking thing.

I managed to lunge at my laptop and shut everything down with a single emergency command, just a second before a hand wrapped around my throat and yanked me back.

I landed on my hands and knees on the tiled floor, and a boot smashed into the side of my head in the next second, ripping my earpiece off. Another one came, driving right into my face then, the force of it knocking me onto my back.

I tasted blood on my lips, and the monster in me sparked to life.

The very fucking thing I was trying to tamper down.

That was made all the more difficult when I strained through the smoke to see three guys decked out in heavy tactical gear with gas masks strapped to their faces crowding me and moving in.

Son of a bitch.

"Santino wants a word with you," one of them spoke.

He's gonna force you to return what you stole and then he'll do what he should have done a long time ago and bury you.

"He can go to hell," I spat back.

One of them snapped their fingers, and another strode out through the shattered patio door, then reappeared, dragging two of our security guards, their skulls now blown to shit.

Oh my God.

"You want to suffer the same fate?"

I swallowed and looked away from Nico's poor soldiers, then glared up at the asshole talking to me. "He's gonna kill me either way the moment you take me to him. But not before. He can't recover those funds without me. No matter how good your hackers are, it won't make a difference." Not with the way I'd hidden the money. "That's why I'm not already dead, isn't it?"

In the next second, they moved in.

I thrust my boot into the closest one's face, blowing him back. *See how you like it.*

It gave me just enough room to rear back and spring to my feet.

I'd barely landed stably when I had to dodge out of the way of an incoming punch. I snagged the guy's wrist, then shoved my knee into it, hearing a grunt and a crack simultaneously as it went limp in my hold, then I used it to haul him into the other two, forcing them back.

Unfortunately, it didn't last long, and they recovered far too quickly, lunging at me.

I vaulted over the island just in time to avoid them making contact.

I went for the knife block on the counter.

I shot out my hand, just a couple of inches from snatching up a blade, when an arm wrapped around my neck, wrenching me back.

Another kicked at the back of my legs, ripping them out from under me and forcing me onto my knees, while the guy with his arm around my neck applied dizzying pressure.

"No," I rasped, slamming my elbow back.

But then my arms were yanked behind me and held hostage.

I twisted on the ground and went to ram my head back into the guy trying to choke me out, but my head was grabbed in a painful grip, forcing me to be still.

The room was spinning within moments.

I could barely breathe.

And then everything went black.

30

~Emilio~

Tonight had gone exactly to plan.

Everything had run smoothly without a single hitch.

It was unheard of.

There was always some aspect that went off the rails when you were dealing with so many people and different moving parts. Especially in our world.

But in this case, it had gone swimmingly.

We'd accomplished what we'd set out to do.

All the product and the weaponry had been moved to secure storage facilities off Nico's territory, Julian worked his charms and devious business skills along with Caterina's blackmail to severe over a dozen of the most influential people from Santino, our distraction of commandeering the coke shipments of Gio's had succeeded in stopping the attacks on Benzino businesses *and* leading them into an ambush where Carlo and his soldiers had been waiting, the raids had taken down all Leone and Marchetti gambling dens and strip clubs in one shot.

Now there was just seeing if we could salvage some of Gio's soldiers as our own and turn them in our favor.

I swung my leg over my Harley in the lot beside the two Ferraris of Nico and Carlo, having come to the abandoned apartment building, now that I'd completed my own part of the mission, to give Nico a hand.

He didn't want to go *feral* in front of Carlo, so I was there to bring the intimidation factor.

My phone started ringing when I was halfway to the building. I pulled it out and looked to see Julian calling.

I stopped and swiped it open. "Still at *Luster?*" I asked.

"Yes. Listen, I can't get a hold of Cat. There's an issue at the club. A minor one that I can fix, but I don't want to make a decision for her. I need her go-ahead."

"What do you mean that you can't get a hold of her? She's running *base ops* tonight, as Nico calls it."

"Well, have you managed to connect with her?"

"Not for a little while. I've been on my Harley for the last twenty minutes, and before that I was finishing up—"

"Whatever. I don't need a play-by-play," he snapped, very unlike him.

He was worried. Really fucking worried.

And now, so was I.

"Hold on," I said. "I'll connect into the Manor security system. Give me a few seconds."

"Okay. Hurry."

Hurry. Of course I fucking would.

I pulled up the app and went to connect.

But nothing happened.

"That's not—what's going on?"

"What? What is it?" Julian pushed. "Milo?"

"The system's down. I can't access it at all."

"Jesus Christ."

"When did you last try to contact her?"

"Four minutes ago. How about Nico? Aren't you with him now?"

"I'm outside the apartment building. I was about to approach when you called."

"Well, maybe there's a simple explanation, because he'd be freaking out if he couldn't get a hold of her, anyway."

"He's radio silent right now while he's in there working Gio and his soldiers. It requires full focus and for him to slip into a certain mindset of—"

"I don't want your torturer tips, thanks."

"Right, fuck, sorry." I grimaced as the reason burned into me. "I'm just… I'm worried about Caterina."

"Me too. It's okay, forget it. Shit, Milo. Should I head back to the house?"

"No. If security is down, outside of a power outage, it's very likely been compromised. It might not be safe."

"What about the soldiers that Nico had watching the place? What the fuck were they even there for? I mean, I even called all four of them and they didn't pick up either."

"I'm gonna track her ring."

"Yeah, good. Good. Despite the whole revealed fake marriage thing, she's still wearing it because it's from all three of us."

I smiled as I remembered her saying that. "She wanted a piece of us with her at all times."

"She did."

I accessed the tracker, but a chill rolled down my spine when I found it offline, too.

"I can't track her with the ring," I told him, hating the words as I spoke them.

"Why?"

"It's offline."

"So somebody turned it off? Took it from her? They know?"

I swallowed hard. "It seems that way."

"Milo."

"Stay where you are right next to Nico's soldiers until you hear from me."

"What are you gonna do?"

"Connect with Nico and I'll call you back. Just stay where you are. Promise me. No crazy shit. Please. I can't… not again with you too, okay?"

"I promise. I'll stay here. But call me as soon as you can."

"I will."

I hung up, then rushed toward the rundown apartment building.

There were two of Carlo's soldiers guarding the door, but they each gave me a chin lift and stepped aside when they saw me.

I pushed on through the door and into the foyer.

Piercing screams gave away where Nico was, and I followed the sounds down the ground floor corridor and around the corner to a room at the back.

I shoved open the door and took in some sort of storage room, musty boxes and a couple of old appliances in disrepair filling the space.

Most notably, though, were the fifty-odd soldiers spread throughout the room.

Some were on their sides sprawled across the floor, their ankles and wrists zip-tied. Others were tied to beams. Some bound to metal chairs. And then there were a dozen standing in the corner near where I'd entered, not bound and looking unharmed.

Nico was looming over Gio who was tied to a chair, his

face a map of swelling, cuts, and deep bruising. A couple of his knuckles were shattered as well.

Nico had shed his leather jacket, and he stood there with the sleeves of his dress shirt rolled up to his elbows, blood staining the formerly unblemished sleek white material.

"Suck my dick," Gio grunted at him.

Nico sneered.

"You really aren't helping yourself," Carlo commented, his arms folded across his chest as he looked on to the side of them.

Nico pulled a knife from the holster at the back of his pants and spun it around in his hand in a casually threatening way.

This was actually nothing for him. I could see by the limited damage that had been done to the guys *and* the way he was handling Giovanni, that he was holding back majorly.

He didn't want to unleash that *feral* side of him.

I'd thought it was because he didn't want Carlo to see it, so that it didn't inspire any sort of distrust in their newly formed alliance—and what seemed to be a burgeoning friendship too, apparently. But the struggle I could see from him, how much he was actually holding back, suggested that it was more than that. Besides, thinking about it now, I recalled that Carlo had actually witnessed Nico unleashing like that a couple of times before, anyway.

Was it actually about the baby, like I'd suspected before?

Or maybe something to do with him taking power? Did he want to bury that part of himself so he could lead without having that unstable side of him coming along for the ride?

Goddammit, my mind was wandering.

It got like this when I was panicking.

And when that panic had intense emotional roots.

Just like when Julian had been missing.

"Milo?"

I blinked and looked out to see Nico had registered my presence. He strode from Gio and up to me. "What's wrong? What's happened?" he asked.

It had to be all over me.

I pulled him off to the side.

"It's Caterina. We can't get a hold of her. The security system at Charon Manor is offline. As is her ring. Physical security is unreachable as well."

I'd barely gotten the last few words out when he pulled his phone out and dialed right away.

"Rocco, head up to Charon Manor now. Take a team with you. Milo and I will meet you there. There may have been a breach. Report back immediately."

He spun then and rushed back to Carlo, telling him, "I have a situation. I need to leave right now."

"What's happened?"

"Caterina is missing."

"Home invasion?"

"It's looking like it."

Gio snickered. "Thought you had it in the bag. Thought it would be this easy."

Nico growled and wrapped his hand around Gio's throat. "Nothing has been easy since motherfuckers like you rose to positions of power in the families. It's destroyed everything. Now you'll all fall. Even if I have to rip your lives away to make it so."

Gio went to bite back, but Nico released his throat, then drove his knife through his carotid artery, shocking us all from the sudden brutality of it.

Nico snarled and thrust his boot into the chair, Gio

tumbling back and crashing to the ground on the chair on his back, spluttering and choking on his own blood as he rapidly slipped away.

With that, Nico snatched up his jacket then bolted out of the room, with me following in his wake.

Everything had gone so smoothly and to plan tonight.

And now all hell was about to break loose.

31

~Caterina~

I jolted awake in a panic, adrenaline flooding my system.

The first thing I noticed was that I wasn't free to move around.

I was bound to a chair.

Not for the first fucking time.

There had been several kidnapping attempts on me during my childhood just because of who my father was, yet none of them had succeeded. Mostly because Dante had been such a competent guard. But now, in the space of a few weeks, it had happened twice.

And at the hands of my own family.

Well, my own family by name only, because they certainly weren't anything else to me now.

I felt behind me, determining that it was a pair of cuffs that bound me. Yet again.

Definitely Santino's work.

He'd taught that to Angelo and the rest of his soldiers. It was a part of their protocol when they took hostages. Or when they tortured someone. Always with the cuffs, never rope or zip ties.

Fortunately, that was an asset to me.

As I instinctively prepared to dislocate my thumbs to escape them, I pulled up short while I scanned my surroundings too.

This place.

This *room.*

This tiny fucking room.

The lone lightbulb in the center of the ceiling that had such a creepy and kind of sickening shade of muted yellow light emanating from it. And the chill and the damp, the kind that went right through your bones.

No wonder I was shuddering.

It wasn't just adrenaline because I'd woken up bound after being beaten and stolen away from the Manor.

My jacket had been taken, so my arms were bare in my strappy black tank. Thankfully, I'd been wearing pants instead of a skirt or a dress, so at least my legs weren't suffering from exposure to the freezing damp as much as my arms were.

Another involuntary shudder took me over as I stared out at the room.

I couldn't believe he'd done this.

My father was really heading right into the psychological torment of it all.

This was the cold room in the Leone Estate. A place in which I'd spent far too much of my childhood.

When my mom had gone back to work after I'd turned four, my father had agreed to work from home running his despicable empire so I wouldn't be raised solely by nannies.

Little had she known that it would have been a much better option for me.

It wasn't her fault. She hadn't realized how sadistic Santino Leone was capable of being to his own blood. At least not back then.

He'd started by locking me in this room whenever I'd had a tantrum until I shut up and stopped making a sound. That had evolved to shoving me in here whenever I'd shown any emotion or any sort of reaction that he hadn't approved of. I'd be in here for hours in this tiny, damp and cold space until I'd begun to feel the walls closing in on me and started screaming to be let out. That had only led to him keeping me locked in here longer. So many times I'd screamed until my voice was hoarse.

It was how my claustrophobia had been born. Something I'd managed to combat over the years and learn to deal with—or bury too at times. Yet, he was clearly trying to awaken that in me.

Trying to unnerve me and get under my skin.

Trying to break me.

That would just be the beginning, no doubt.

His words to me that day in his office when he'd forced me to sign that sickening contract played on my mind.

"You're sentencing your own daughter to a life of abuse, degradation, and humiliation?"

"I warned you that there would be a price to pay for severing ties with the Family."

He'd been almost gleeful about handing down that punishment to me.

Going by Angelo's message, he now knew that I'd struck at him, so it would be a whole lot worse.

Basically, he wouldn't let me leave here alive.

And it wouldn't be a quick kill either. He'd want me to suffer.

I gritted my teeth, forcing myself past the panic that being in this room was inducing, focusing on what needed to be done instead.

"This little baby needs taking care of, Caterina."

"This child is a gift."

"You're carrying our baby and that's everything."

The guys' words ran through my mind.

I'd never been in a dangerous or life-threatening situation where I'd had to worry about somebody else before until that night I'd woken up kidnapped in that garage. I'd had my men to worry about, how they'd be if the worst had befallen me, if I hadn't been able to make it out of that shitshow. That had definitely raised the stakes for me.

But this... knowing an innocent little thing was counting on me... it was so far beyond even that.

It had a deeply protective intensity rushing to the surface that had a powerful triggering effect on that twisted side of me.

A growl escaped me and I dislocated my thumbs with a grunt, using the pain as fuel as I slipped my hands through the cuffs.

The fear of being in this place and all the crippling sensations it tried to evoke were buried beneath the ire that surged white-hot through my veins.

I brought my hands in front of me, then snapped my thumbs back into place with a snarl.

But that animalistic sound wasn't in response to the biting pain.

It was the thought of what I was going to do to my captors.

What I was prepared to do to protect my child and to spare my men from the pain and grief of losing us both.

Just how far I was prepared to take it.

And as the door opened, and I clasped my hands behind my back as a figure came into view, I knew beyond a shadow of a doubt that there was no fucking limit whatsoever.

That slicked back blond hair filled my vision and then *he* stood in the doorway with his tan wool coat. A nasty grin spread over his face as he took in the sight of me seemingly bound to the chair and shuddering.

That shuddering was far from being fear now and it was barely even a result of the cold either.

It was a massive influx of adrenaline and rage, an extremely powerful cocktail that he was going to become a victim of all too soon.

Wipe that cocky grin off his face, the sadistic bastard.

As he stepped forward, the door was thrown open all the way and two of the guys from earlier who'd attacked me and obviously brought me here too came into view. They were down to just beige t-shirts and black pants now. Both their faces were expressionless as they stood there with their arms folded across their broad chests and stared at me.

"Putting me in this room was such a pedestrian tactic, Father."

"It's just the beginning." He approached my chair. "Did you really think you could come at *me?*"

"You knew I could. It's what's had you so incredibly terrified this entire time."

He sneered. "Foolish girl. You're nothing but a fucking traitor."

"Hmm, I believe your little pet uses the phrase *traitorous cunt.*"

His eyes narrowed. "Your obstinance isn't doing you any favors."

"What does it matter? You brought me here to kill me."

"You've left me no choice where that's concerned. You've challenged me, you've hurt the Family."

I scoffed. "*Family?* That's a despicable claim coming from the likes of you."

He slapped me across the face, making me hiss as his rings cut into my skin and blood sprayed.

He did it again and again until my cheeks were burning and I was clenching my fists behind my back.

Not yet. Not yet. Hold. Fucking hold.

His lip curled in satisfaction when he stepped back and took me in, obviously happy with the bruising and cuts I could feel marring my skin.

I spat out a mouthful of blood right at his feet, some of it spraying on his shoes.

He hissed and stepped back, and I smiled through bloodied teeth, ignoring the pain as it stretched my split lip from his assault.

"Where's my money, Caterina? And keep in mind, how you answer that question will determine just how agonizing these last hours of your life are."

"It's gone."

"Playing this game really won't help you."

"It's not a game. Far from it. That's something you lost sight of long ago, isn't it? When you descended into utter madness and lost all respect for human life, for your own family, your own men. When you became nothing but a shell. So desperate to hide your failings and your weakness and inability to continue leading the Leone Family that you went to extreme and disgusting lengths. Now it's all unravelling. You feel it, don't you? Let me tell you, it won't stop. None of it will. We'll make sure of it."

"After tonight, your little resistance will be broken. It's come to my attention that not only was your marriage a ruse and that Nico Marchetti never abused you or degraded you like he was ordered to, but that you're involved with him, the Bardi boy and that showman, Carver. I'm aware of just how much they care for you. And that was foolish for any of you to allow that sentiment to exist between you, because now it will be used against you."

"You're going to use me to shatter them? Another pedestrian tactic."

He frowned at my seemingly unaffected reaction. "Your life is ending tonight, Caterina. Nico and his accomplices will be destroyed by that alone. I won't have to lift another finger to eliminate the threat they're intent on posing to me and Marco." He pulled something from his coat pocket and then I was looking at my engagement ring. "If you think they're coming to save you, they aren't. My new associates here registered a signal coming off this thing, so they've disabled it. You're all alone."

Alone? No, I wasn't. Far from it. Those days were gone now.

I even had this little baby here with me right now.

When I didn't respond, my father tossed the ring on the floor and stared at me expectantly.

"Oh, you're wondering why I'm not bursting into tears and begging for my life?"

"Yes," he hissed, not liking that one bit.

"Simple. You don't scare me."

"We'll see about that when you're barely lucid from the torture my associates here are going to subject you to and all you can do is lie there in a hole in the ground as you watch me fill it with dirt and bury you alive."

"Wow, that's a hell of a picture you just painted." I eyed him steadily and deadpanned, "I'm shaking with utter terror. Can you see it?"

He grunted and stepped back, then barked at the two guys, "Do it. Get the information out of her and don't hold a thing back. She just needs to be breathing when I bury her at the bottom of the construction site, nothing else." He went to leave, then pulled up short and burst forward and grasped my throat, making me gag at the brutal grip. "These two are schooled in the art of torture and a whole lot else. Military trained. Unfortunately, certain predilections of theirs led to them not being appreciated. I promised them plenty of opportunities to delve into that, and you're their first *present*."

He released me roughly, and I choked, sucking in a couple of desperate breaths. "You're despicable. To do this to your own daughter. Just know that you won't survive it."

He laughed nastily. "Such hubris. Foolish little girl."

With that, he left the room and kicked the door shut behind him.

The two guys moved in.

Lefty's lip curled up nastily, and he made a show of undoing his belt and pulling down his fly.

So that was how it was going to be with him then.

Righty decided to start off with a different tactic, pulling a tactical knife and drawing closer, making a spectacle of spinning it around.

I eyed Lefty with the shaved head. "I'm gonna rip *your* throat out." I looked to Righty with the eyebrow ring. "And I'm gonna slice *your* dick off."

Righty laughed. "You're not gonna be doing much of anything except gagging with my cock rammed down your throat while Reese here cuts into your pretty body."

"Then when you're vomiting all over yourself, we'll break your knuckles, one of your kneecaps, then grab the pliers and move on to your teeth," *Reese* added. He thumbed the other guy. "Tom's got a real talent for it, knows how to cause the most pain possible. Let's see if you're telling us what the Boss wants to hear by then, huh?"

"Wow, that's some vivid imagery."

"Here's some more," *Tom* said, pulling a spider gag

from his pocket. "Don't want you trying to bite my dick, do I? Besides, this will help me to get nice and deep."

He stepped right up to me, so eager to get down to it.

"Where's the third guy?" I asked.

He frowned for a moment, then some sort of realization played on his face. "Oh, right, Santino mentioned you were used to being triple-teamed."

It was actually strategic. I needed to know if their other team member was on the premises. They'd caught me by surprise before, at a time when I'd been wanting to hold back the dark and twisted part of myself, when I'd been struggling with it. But even though I was willing to unleash now, the fact that they were *military trained*, as Santino had put it, would still pose a challenge. I'd always had a one-up in combat because *I'd* been military trained by Joe, but coming up against those with a similar skill set ripped that advantage away.

"Sorry," Reese said, drawing closer—exactly where I needed him. "He's busy taking care of something else far away from here."

"That's a shame, because I'd rather make a deal with all three of you at once. I don't like to repeat myself."

"Deal?" Tom scoffed.

"You're here to extract intel from me on how to access Leone Family funds that I've confiscated. You do realize that means that I have the power to compensate you far beyond what Santino currently has on hand?"

The two of them eyed one another.

Then Reese stepped forward ever closer. *Just a little more.* "It's not just about the money for us." He gazed at his knife in a twisted, lustful way. "The work we do, it gets us off, sweetheart. There's nothing else like it."

"We're not just mercenaries for hire."

Interesting information. Keep it coming. "Santino is restricted on what he can offer you where that's concerned. This, with me, is more of a one-off. There are better places and individuals who you can work for to get that rush you need." That sick, demented rush.

Another look passed between them. *Hmm.*

They needed him for something.

Protection, maybe? Was he a buffer of some sort for them?

Why would a group like this who clearly knew their shit need that, though?

It hit me as soon as I asked myself the question.

They were being hunted by somebody like them, on their level.

Only one name came to mind that linked to all of this.

Joseph Stover.

This was the connection that I'd been unable to make before.

Because it had been buried, it was so covert that there'd been no electronic trail for me to follow.

"Last chance to give up the intel," Tom warned, bringing the spider gag closer, then trailing the metal over my lips, giving me a taste of it.

"Hmm… I'm not recalling anything," I said, glaring up at them.

"Turn her head a little," Reese spoke as he stepped right where I needed him, just to my right.

As Tom went to do as he'd asked and prepared to grab my head to attach the awful gag, I made my move.

I shot out my right hand from around the chair, snagged Reese's knife-wielding wrist, then yanked hard and drove my knee up at the same time, successfully dislodging the blade from his grip.

In the next split second, I spun it in my hand, then

drove it between his legs, slicing into his dick and wrenching it down until he was shrieking like a banshee.

"Holy—" Tom started, but didn't get much further as I slammed my left fist into the spider gag, sending it clattering across the floor, thankfully out of his reach and away from me. *Fucking thing.*

I worked with the shock of it all to twist off the chair just in time as he threw his fist.

He missed me and before he could move in for another blow, I snatched up the chair and swung it into him, clocking him across the side.

He was too well-trained to go down that easily, though, and he took hold of it and tossed it at the door, the impact blowing it open wide.

Then he came at me.

I deflected another hit and blocked an attempted kick with my shin, then I managed to get in a swipe with the knife to his cheek.

He hissed, but still kept coming, and we met blow for blow.

His hits were like cement-block forces, but fortunately I was trained well on how to absorb something that fucking intense and brutal.

Not that it wasn't going to leave a hell of a lot of bruises in its wake.

But then I hesitated as he went for my stomach and instead of taking the blow and absorbing it so I could land another strategic shot that would actually break the standoff and knock him back, I twisted out of the way, my need to protect my baby taking me over.

He slammed his hand into my chest and I blew back against the wall with jarring force.

He was there in the next second, ripping me around

and grinding my face into the rough concrete, scraping my skin like a fucking bitch of a thing.

His other hand grabbed my wrist so I couldn't wield the knife.

And then he released my head, only to wrap his arm around my throat in a clear attempt to choke me out, just like what had happened before.

No fucking way.

I slammed my head back as a fake out and it worked, making him jerk back just enough that his superior weight shifted and I was able to use the opportunity to wrench at his ankle and yank it out from under him.

He was good, I'd give him that, because he didn't actually go down, but it did destabilize him *and* weaken his grip around my throat.

It was all enough for me to twist sharply to the side and rip myself out of his hold.

I smashed my fist into the underside of his jaw, then his throat, following it up with a brutal knee to his gut. The rapid-fire combo had him stumbling back.

It gave me enough room to leap up into a flying kick and gain a lot of power to drive into his gut.

As he doubled over, I was there, yanking on his hair and forcing him down, then bringing my knife-wielding hand up and plunging the blade deep into his throat.

A push kick sent him crashing into a heap beside his screaming accomplice, while all *he* could do was gurgle and splutter as blood poured from the fatal wound I'd inflicted.

"Just like I promised," I spat, before wiping the blood on my pants, then striding from the room and out into the basement of the Leone Estate.

As I bolted up the steps, I heard the rumble of footsteps nearing the door at the top.

Adrenaline was thrumming through me like live wires.

And not just that.

I tasted my own blood on my lips, but I could smell my enemies' all over the place too, their screams infusing me, calling to my monstrous side and fueling it like nothing else.

It was most definitely taking the lead now.

Hell, it was salivating at the prospect of dealing out more brutality.

Blood wouldn't just spill, it would flow.

That was the dangerous thing about it. It wasn't always rational.

My ideal focus should be on escaping.

But it wouldn't let me accept that.

I couldn't just disappear into the night.

Not while that fire raged within me to the point of painful, scalding intensity.

Not while *he* still drew breath.

The opportunity was here, and I wouldn't allow it to slip away.

I wouldn't be safe until he was buried.

My baby wouldn't be safe.

My men wouldn't be safe.

I had to fucking end this.

I had to fucking end *him*.

All bets were off.

I'd just reached the top of the stairs when the door flew open to reveal two of my father's home security trying to barrel down to see what the fuck had happened to elicit *male* screams of agony, rather than those that they'd been expecting of mine.

I rapidly took in the situation and registered the single Glock each one of them had holstered at either hip.

I yanked one free from the guy on the left, spun it and cocked it, then fired off two headshots before either of them could make so much as a move, blood spraying all over my face.

As they dropped hard in quick succession, I stepped on them and walked out onto the ground floor.

In my heightened state of animalistic intensity, I registered the slightest movements easily, pinpointing a guard trying to creep up on me from the right at the end of the corridor that led to one of the living rooms. And to the left, a flash of a tan coat rushing away in the direction of my father's office also caught my attention.

I fired off a shot at the guard, that sent him jumping behind a column to the nearest cover.

It was the couple of seconds I needed in order to lob my blade down the corridor.

I watched as it embedded in my father's upper back, making him cry out, stumbling and crashing into the wall before he made it any further.

Motion from my right caught my attention as the guard tried to take aim at me with his piece.

I fired off a shot before he could, my bullet driving through his chest. He fell against the column and crumpled to a heap on the floor.

That wasn't the end of it, though.

Half a dozen more guards rushed into the area.

I ducked and rolled and cleared the open area, making it on to the corridor that my father was stumbling down. Bullets bit into the wall just as I'd cleared it.

I sprinted down the corridor as my father opened his office door and threw himself inside.

I was there before he could lock it, kicking the door open and blowing him back.

As he fell against his desk and ripped the knife out, I slammed the door shut and locked it, just seconds before thumping started at the door, his security trying to save his worthless ass.

As soon as I spun back, he was there, lunging at me with the knife.

I dodged the attempt, then delivered a roundhouse kick that sent him crashing into the ugly beige couch.

I stormed over there, blood roaring in my ears, the thrill of the kill heating my veins.

The thrill of killing *him* at long last, unlike anything I'd ever felt before.

Even the sounds of his soldiers trying to break down the door faded into the background compared to the immediate overwhelming need of him meeting his demise.

At *my* hands.

I couldn't think straight.

I was so deep in my animalistic state, that the prey was all that mattered.

It wanted blood.

It wanted pain.

It wanted his fucking life.

Nothing else would suffice.

Nothing else would sate it.

He pushed off the couch and came at me with the knife, but I snagged it before he could bring it down, spun into him and brought my arm down with such brutal force that it had him screaming as a definitive crack sounded *and* managed to dislodge his grip.

I yanked the blade free, then snagged his arm and used his weight to haul him around into his desk, face-first.

"What the hell is this?" he rasped.

I drove my elbow into his back, keeping him down. "This is yet another example of you not knowing your own daughter!" I roared, wrenching on his hair, then using the hold to slam his face down onto the desk. "You sentenced me to a life of degradation and abuse! You set me up to be fucking raped! Repeatedly!" I smashed his face into the expensive wood again. "All because you were so afraid I'd supplant you!" I yanked him around, then drove the blade into his chest, just shy of his heart, making him choke, his eyes shooting wide. "All because you couldn't admit to your own loss of power, your fucking inability to lead the Family! That you'd lost it long ago! I don't want it! I don't want any part of this fucking madness!" I twisted the knife, then yanked it out, making him scream, the sound beyond satisfying. "But I *will* destroy it! I'll tear it all down like it never existed. And that will be your legacy. Fucking *nothing!*"

In my mind's eye, I heard the door cracking, security coming closer to breaking it down.

I didn't care.

The only screams I wanted were his.

"Caterina…" he rasped. "I'm… I'm… sorry."

I snarled, enraged that he'd think me so foolish as to believe his half-assed apology at this late stage of things, after what he'd just left me to face in that basement. After *everything* he'd done!

"Lies. All fucking lies!"

I spun the knife in front of his face and his eyes shot wider than ever, true terror emanating from him.

"Everything you've done to me, no matter how hard you tried to break me, you failed. You fucking failed! Do you hear me? Do you?"

"Yes… I… please."

I scoffed. "There's no mercy for demons like you. You're too fucking far gone."

The door flew open.

A warning sparked in my brain.

Rushed footsteps came at me.

I blocked it out, then growled in my father's face, a second before I brought the blade down again, this time driving it deep into his throat.

Hands grabbed at me roughly and I fired off a bullet, blood and brain matter spraying all over me, because the shot had been so close range.

The grip fell away, and I fired wildly behind me, keeping the rest of them back.

There was no rationality for me right now.

Nothing but *needing* to watch my prey, my despicable father, die right before me.

I needed to see the light go out of his eyes.

I needed to see him fucking *dead!*

Finally, it happened. And the last thing he focused on was me, knowing that I'd stolen his life away, that I'd fucking ended him, that he'd failed to do the same to me, that through everything he'd done *I'd* won.

I spun back to face what amounted to four of his security personnel now. I'd apparently dropped two with my wild firing.

They were stunned, taking in the sight of their Boss, the almighty Santino Leone, now dead to the world.

I yanked my blade from him and spun it in my hand, eyeing the fools who'd pledged their loyalty to a madman.

And then I stepped forward with a snarl.

It's not over yet.

32

~Nico~

I tore into the courtyard of the Leone Estate, Milo just behind me on his Harley and Julian ripping in too in his Porsche.

I'd barely come to a complete stop before I bolted out of the car, rushing over to Dante and Matteo, feeling the boys just at my back.

"Shots fired," Dante was speaking calmly into his cell phone. "Yes. Proceed cautiously. Search for the hostage."

He might have been managing to put forth a calm and controlled front on the phone to the few soldiers he still had in his pocket who were infiltrating the mansion as we spoke, but it was obvious from just glancing at him that he was anything but. He was tapping his foot frantically and shoving his free hand through his hair.

Meanwhile, even the usually stoic Matteo was showing a visible reaction, dragging on a smoke, his eyes darting every which way as he tried futilely to make out what was happening inside.

Shortly after I'd arrived home with Milo and discovered there had definitely been a home invasion that had both taken out four of my soldiers *and* led to Caterina being taken, we'd put out feelers, beginning our search for her, only to have Dante Rivera contact me. He'd obtained intel from one of his insiders that Santino had sent hired guns to retrieve Caterina and brought her here to determine where she'd hidden his funds.

To determine through torture.

As if that hadn't been bad enough, he'd also discovered that a kill order had been given.

The screeching of tires caught my attention just as I reached Dante, and I watched as Rocco arrived with my soldiers. They were piled into two unmarked black vans and as soon as they made it into the courtyard, he and twenty of them rushed on out, pulling automatic weapons, decked out to the hilt.

I'd been able to deploy and have them ready so quickly without my father's resources at my back because of Caterina. We'd used that storage facility that she'd taken us to and kitted them out that way.

We'd been under the impression that we'd be taking on a fucking army of security personnel and several Leone soldiers.

But as I took in the scene, including what I'd heard Dante report to his men, things clearly weren't as we'd been expecting.

First off, no one had come out to give us one hell of a violent greeting, even though I, now a known enemy, was right on their Boss's turf.

"What's the status?" I demanded of Dante.

He and Matteo spun toward me.

Dante informed me, "There was an SOS call placed from the mansion by one of Santino's security guards twenty minutes ago, but to bring in reinforcements, protocol dictates that the Boss has to verify it. That verification never came."

"He's not living here at the moment because the place is still under restoration after the Lone Gunners attack on your wedding day," Matteo added in. "But he came here with a few soldiers and two unknowns—mercenaries, we think. It's possible the mercenaries turned on him, hence the SOS call. Maybe Caterina got to them? Do you think that's possible?"

Did I think that was possible? "Of course."

"She has control of Leone Family funds," Julian told them.

"She's technically got more power than him, especially if the guys are mercenaries like you believe," Milo said.

I didn't like this, all these assumptions.

We needed more concrete intel.

"Put me through to your guys doing recon," I ordered Dante. "I want a location on Caterina *now.*"

"Jesus," Julian uttered, tugging at his hair, really fucking distressed for her.

I was right there with him on that. All three of us were.

But I had to fight through it and focus. Too much was at stake.

And right now, I needed information before I sent my soldiers into a potential massacre situation. Especially if Caterina had managed to turn the mercenaries, and they were now protecting her, sending in the cavalry could be assumed to be Leone reinforcements and they could end up gunned down as a result.

"Hold up," Dante said, just as he was about to pass me his phone, and contact came in from his team. He took the call and listened, frowning, and looking shell-shocked by whatever was being reported. "No, don't engage. Stand by for further instructions." He eyed me and reported, "Caterina's no longer in danger. But she's not… approachable."

Not approachable? *Oh, fuck.*

I exchanged a look with Milo and Julian, the two of them understanding what he was getting at.

"Stay here. Watch for incoming," I told Rocco and my soldiers. "And call in a cleanup crew."

"Got it," Rocco said, pulling out his phone, then having them stand guard while he called it in.

"Come," I told the boys, and the three of us headed off into the mansion.

We stepped around the boarded up front bay window that was still under construction, and the scaffolding near the entrance doors, then pushed inside.

The moment we did, familiar snarls and shrieks inundated us, echoing through the otherwise deathly quiet house.

Deathly was definitely the word for it.

Because as we took in our surroundings, a carpet of dropped bodies lined our way.

First, one downed from a shot to the skull between the foyer and the main space where we'd had our wedding ceremony, then several more actually in that space itself, much more bloodied, speaking to a brutal battle having taken place.

I caught sight of Dante's men and they gestured down a corridor to our right.

The screams grew louder. Thuds and sounds of a whole lot of destruction, too.

"Santino's office," Milo spoke.

We burst down there and in through the open door.

And the sight inside even had *me* pulling up short.

More blood.

More damage.

More fucking death.

There were four bodies sprawled out through the room and one hidden over on the other side of the desk.

And there Caterina was, bloodied, her hair matted, her emerald eyes wild, smashing her hands into the shelves of Santino's cabinet and sending everything crashing to the floor, destroying everything.

The couch was already torn apart, shredded by a knife, it looked like.

His desktop computer was crushed to shit, a bullet even embedded in the screen. Chairs were overturned, paintings off the walls and sliced to pieces too.

Milo eyed the fallen four. "His security," he confirmed.

"Check behind the desk," I said, as I went to approach Caterina, holding up my hand and keeping Julian back. With what was going on with him, I didn't want him interacting up close with her while she was *this* far gone in her animalistic state.

"Fuck," Milo uttered as he rounded the desk, pulling my attention from Caterina losing it all over the cabinet. "It's him. It's Santino."

"What?" I bolted over there and took in the sight of the notorious Boss of the Leone Family stabbed to death, drenched in his own blood.

"Christ, she killed him," Julian gasped, coming up behind me and taking it in for himself.

Milo eyed me with a whole lot of worry. "This wasn't supposed to happen yet. It's too early. This means that—"

"Later," I said, holding up my hand.

I pushed away and walked to Caterina.

I brushed her arm, and she jolted, then spun toward me aggressively.

But then she pulled up short, her wild eyes managing to meet mine.

"Nico?" she uttered, through harsh breaths.

"Yes, it's me. Milo and Julian too. We're here."

She pulled at her hair and started shaking her head, then went to blow past me, and I was very aware of the knife in her hand as she zoned in on one of the dead guys right near us. Even though they were all dead, she clearly wanted to do more damage.

"Do you think it's a boy or a girl?" I called out quickly, while blocking her path.

She stilled again and blinked up at me. "What?"

I couldn't stop her or bring her back from this physically.

Not when she was this far gone. It would take some intense restraining and force, something I couldn't stand to use with her at the best of times. Last time in that garage had been bad enough. But now that she was pregnant, it was a whole other level. The thought of it made me sick to my stomach.

But there was something else that sometimes worked for me when I was in one of my *feral* states similar to this.

And that was being jolted out of it by a strong emotional trigger.

I was hoping that our child would be that for her, even at the early stage of things.

"Our baby, Caterina. Do you think it's a boy or a girl?"

She blinked again, but her hand holding the knife was still clenching it tightly.

"It's gotta be a boy, or Nico's gonna lose his shit and be the most overprotective dad known to man and beast alike," Julian commented, forcing a light tone that I could tell he really didn't feel right now.

It worked and Caterina swung her head toward him,

frowning, stumped by that intruding into her current monstrous state.

"I…" she murmured, blinking rapidly.

"No, it has to be a girl. A mini-Caterina would be incredible," Milo spoke.

I watched carefully as she took a step back and pinched the bridge of her nose. "I… he was going to take her away, going to kill me tonight," she uttered, her voice cracking, emotion beginning to break through.

Her?

I wanted to revel in the moment of that.

But of course I couldn't, because we never could with anything in our world.

It was always tainted, always fucking poisoned by something or someone.

Always taken from us.

Fuck.

The three of us exchanged a look, and I saw the rage I was struggling to keep buried for now reflected back at me.

I forced an even, calm tone that she needed so badly right now as I said, "I know. But he didn't. You stopped him. Our baby is safe and well. You're both well."

"It's okay," Julian added, coming near now with Milo joining us, until the three of us were essentially all standing before her.

"We're here now, we're here," Milo uttered, his voice cracking with emotion.

It had come far too close.

And it made me fucking sick.

The knife she was holding clattered to the floor, and she collapsed into the three of us.

"I had to," she cried. "I had to end it… end him."

As we held her to us, I looked over at her father's corpse.

In one shot, our strategic approach had been ripped to shreds.

And we were in really dangerous fucking territory now.

Santino Leone was dead.

Now all bets were off.

33

~Emilio~

"All right, yes. Thanks, Carlo," Nico spoke into his cell as he smoked out on the patio just beyond the shattered fucking doors.

We had people coming within the next hour to fix them up and clear the debris from the kitchen. That was the good thing about how we operated. We could call in people in the dead of night. The bad part was obviously the fact that things like this actually happened.

Aside from Caterina's infiltration a while back during her war with Nico, the Manor had only been breached once before. And that had been by fucking Leo Marchetti when he'd blindsided us, pulled rank on our soldiers and had them stand down while he'd then sent in several of his own to beat us down for an infraction Nico had committed wherein he'd challenged the bastard at a high-level meeting between the three families and embarrassed him, which he'd taken as a major demonstration of disrespect. The manipulative fucker had even managed to get Marco's blessing for the *harsh lesson* he'd delivered to Nico that night. It had put him in the hospital for three fucking days and it was also how he'd gotten those scars on his lower back and his right thigh—goddamn stab wounds from that night.

Things were different now.

For one, Nico's soldiers were now loyal only to him personally. They couldn't be swayed or ordered by Leo or Marco anymore. They were *his* force.

And the Manor had also been reinforced since those days too. Not just with surveillance and alerts, but wherein a breach would trigger a lockdown involving armored fucking ballistic shutters. We even had weapons hidden externally and able to fire automatically on a single command at those attempting an incoming assault, or when lockdown protocol had been triggered.

The fact that these assholes tonight who'd come for Caterina hadn't triggered the system at all was something else entirely. To say they were skilled to be able to evade it *and* our soldiers that we'd had stationed around the property didn't even cover it.

I walked out onto the patio as Nico finished his call with Carlo and he turned at my approach.

"What happened with Gio's soldiers?"

"They all pledged their loyalty to me."

"What? How? You had to take off."

"Apparently, me rushing off like that and dropping everything in a bid to protect our pregnant woman was received very positively. With me going against my father, Leo and Marco themselves had started to frame it as me having no respect for family and being a power hungry fuck, basically. My response to somebody I loved being in danger disproved the bullshit they'd been spouting, and with some further proof of said bullshit presented to them by Carlo, the truth came out. Why I'm really doing this, that I want to bring back the honor and loyalty of it all that has been lost along the way under Marco's reign."

"Wow, that's a hell of a thing."

"Not just that, but after the success of tonight's assaults, including the raids, *and* now news that Santino Leone is dead, Cassio's soldiers have also pledged their loyalty to me."

"You're saying that——"

"I'm *saying* that I now unofficially control the Marchetti Syndicate by numbers alone."

"Damn, that's incredible," I breathed. "We're almost there."

"So now we have Marco sign everything over to you under the threat of death?" Julian spoke, strolling out onto the patio. "Give you Marchetti Holdings?"

Before Nico could get a word out, Caterina emerged from around the side of the house carrying a laptop in hand as she walked toward us in just her bathrobe. "It's more complicated than that, unfortunately."

What was happening?

"I thought you were asleep?" Julian asked her. "The doctor gave you something to help you doze off after… you know?"

She lifted a shoulder, her focus on her laptop. "Yeah, I didn't take it."

"She told you that it was fine for the baby."

"I'm aware. I didn't want it. I can't sleep right now. There's too much to do."

"Or because of the massacre?" I asked carefully. Well, as carefully as something like that could actually be put to her, considering.

She looked out at each of us in turn. "I don't regret that. I don't feel guilty. I'm fine."

Nico frowned. "You felt a whole lot of guilt before after the garage takedown."

"Well, that was my mistake, wasn't it?"

362

Goddammit, this wasn't good. The three of us exchanged a look.

Unfortunately, she caught sight of it. "Calm yourselves. It's not a big deal."

"Not a big deal?" Nico bit back, unable to contain the edge in his tone.

"Do you deny that my father needed to die?"

"Well, I—"

"Eventually, but not yet, because of the power vacuum," Julian said. He grimaced as soon as he'd put the words out there. "I'm sorry, darlin'. I just—"

"I get it. You're worried that Angelo might return to fill the position," Caterina said. "Especially as Dante told me that he doesn't want it, that he won't take it, that he and Matteo just want this done and then they want out."

"They told you that when?" I asked. They weren't supposed to tell her anything triggering whatsoever, not until more time had passed between this night wherein she'd murdered her own father and his security team.

"Just after the doctor had checked me and the baby out and the two of them came to make sure I was okay." She held up her left hand. "And to give me my ring back. It was taken off me when they registered a signal coming off it, something that shouldn't have been possible. That's how good these ghosts are."

"So they used that opportunity to do more than that and try to coerce you into taking power?" Julian bit out, as disgusted as we were. Talk about giving them an inch and them taking a mile in return.

"Regardless, I'm going to make damn sure that Angelo doesn't have the opportunity to take control of anything. I *will* take power. Temporarily. Until we dismantle things. Turning Marco's soldiers to follow you is very different from trying to bring Leone soldiers under the Marchetti empire. It just doesn't compute. They won't trade one family for another. It's just… it's not done. Our plan was to dismantle the Leone Family anyway, and that's what we'll do. With me murdering Santino, though, the timeframe has obviously altered. And because it's my fault, I need to be the one to fix it. So this is me doing that. I'll take power with Matteo and Dante assisting me. They're actually meeting with Leone soldiers now to prepare them, so it's all in progress."

"This was the last thing you wanted, Caterina," Nico said.

"Nico, murdering eight or nine people is a whole lot different from massacring every single Leone soldier and—what—blowing up every business under its stead, including Leone Realty, which would be the only quick way to do things because of what I did tonight. It would be like firing off hundreds of flare guns to the Feds and basically begging them to arrest us all and strip everything away from us."

"You're being hyperbolic."

"Am I? This is the only way to handle this situation. Safely and without incriminating all of us."

As we stared out at her, she put her laptop down on one of the patio tables and took a seat, while typing away rapidly. "We also have another problem. Those mercenaries weren't actually mercenaries. They weren't just working for the highest bidder in Santino and doing his dirty work because of money."

"What?" Nico said, striding over to her, with us following suit.

"I know because I was in a position to offer them a lot more than what the bastard could at the time. It wasn't just for the thrill of it either. No, he was shielding them from something. And I think it was Joe. *This* was the missing connection I couldn't make before as to why Joe intervened in the Shawn Price takedown, why he was truly there." She pulled her phone from her robe pocket and accessed a text, then slid it to the center of the tabletop so we could all see. "There's also this that I received from this sicko tonight."

I frowned as I read it over Nico's shoulder.

It was just parts of a text, a lot of it blacked out. All that was available to read was:

Wondering how I was able to contact you? Let's just say I have some new friends. Better than the ones your boyfriends murdered. They were just a stepping stone to these guys.

"Why is it all blacked out?" Julian asked.

Not looking directly at him, Caterina said, "Oh, just personal insults against me that I knew would rile you guys up."

"He wrote something about me, didn't he?" Julian said.

"It doesn't matter. He won't be a problem much longer." She gestured to her laptop and told us, "I've put a poison pill in the system. When they hacked in, they would've realized just how valuable the information I have on here is, so they'll very likely try again. And when they do, it'll destroy whatever little they were able to take *and* enable me to get a foothold into their system by extension. At that point, we'll be able to put all the pieces together."

"Pieces you believe will lead to Angelo?" Nico uttered.

"Yes. He called them his *new friends.* Given how good these guys are, they're why he's been able to stay hidden so well and evade even the likes of me. They're on another level. But if I can track them and break his link to them in the process, all that goes away." She looked out at Nico. "Given that Santino and Marco were allied at the time, it stands to reason that Marco may be working with them, too. They were somehow connected to the Shawn Price operation, but they are ghosts so I couldn't pick up on it. There was no trail."

"What of Stover?" I asked her.

"Still crickets. He must be deep in this right now."

"Or he's been compromised," Nico put to her.

"No," she said, shaking her head. "These guys are good, but he's beyond them."

"Okay, what if they don't hack back in and that plan doesn't work?" Julian asked.

"I'm still trying to do it, regardless." She gritted her teeth, clearly hating to admit, "Although I might need help."

"It's hard to come by somebody else of your skill set," Nico reminded her. "The level you're at—huh, I see. You mean *him.*"

"I do, yes."

"Caterina, bringing a reckless element into an already volatile situation isn't exactly ideal."

"Reckless element? Who are you talking about?" Julian asked.

Nico folded his arms across his chest. "Levi Knight."

Off his tone, Caterina frowned out at him. "I thought you were on better terms with him now, after our call?"

"This isn't about that. It's about the rogue shit he's known for."

"Something you're aware has been tampered down in him lately."

"Something I also thought had been tampered down in *you* until tonight happened."

Oh shit.

She stilled.

And then she shot to her feet and blasted him, "I'm sorry, should I have sat there and let those bastards torture me, then bury me in one of Santino's construction sites, as was his stated plan before I turned the tables?"

"You could have responded with a little less fucking force than a massacre!" he bit back, finally blowing up about it after containing it for the last few hours since we'd arrived home, wherein she'd showered, changed, been checked by the doctor, and calmed completely.

"He didn't just threaten *me* this time! He was going to break all of you! He would have killed our child too!"

Nico started at her revelation.

That was what the extra trigger had been, which had made her take it as far as she had.

"We would have found a way through. Together! Fucking together!" Nico smashed his boot into one of the patio chairs, sending it crashing through the broken patio doors and into the kitchen. "First Julian risked compromising our overarching mission and now you with this! I mean, fuck! You want this? You all want to be free, I need you to fucking work *with* me, not against me!"

"Nico, I already apologized for what happened," Julian said. "And I fell in line tonight too, even when I was freaking about Caterina being missing."

Nico was too worked up now he'd finally let it out to pay that much mind and he went on, "Do you think Milo doesn't want to rage at Leo for what he did? Years and he hasn't had proper justice! But here he is working *with* me instead of tearing down to the Marchetti mansion and executing a fucking massacre all to get to one fucking person! I promised him his justice, and he knows he'll get it! *When* the time is right! And do you think *I* don't want to burn the whole world down for what happened to you tonight, Caterina? What Julian suffered through? And what was taken from Milo? Of course I fucking do, but I've had to leash myself lately *all* so we can do this!"

There it was.

Where some of this was rooted.

He *hadn't* been able to unleash for a long fucking time.

He'd had to keep his *feral* side checked.

First, because of the rational and systematic approach needed to carry out our overarching mission, then because he'd now be taking power, and also because of the baby.

And now, it had all clearly come to a head, with Caterina being taken tonight *and* then the mission being fucked up because of Santino's untimely murder pushing it over the edge for him.

He'd taken a lot on the chin and Nico Marchetti could handle a lot.

But everyone had their limits in the end, even him.

His phone rang in his hand, cutting into the fiery intensity he'd been letting loose a little. He grunted, then sucked in a calming breath and turned from us as he took the call.

"Rocco, yeah, what's the word on them? They're what? You're certain? When? No. Leave it until you hear from me. I'll pick up the trail on my end, then we'll send out scouts." He hung up, then told us, "My father is MIA."

"What? You mean running scared with news of Santino's murder?" Julian asked.

"We don't know at this juncture. But those Rocco and I have doing recon have reported that Leo is at the Marchetti home gathering forces."

"Leo is Boss?" I ground out.

"It hasn't been officially stated," Nico responded.

"Come on," I said. "Like it was never officially stated that you weren't considered Capo by them anymore? That's how they are. Ambiguous with their intentions. They do that to unnerve everyone. They wait and then they pounce on those who've fallen out of their favor."

"You think that's what Leo is doing now with gathering forces and all that?" Julian asked worriedly.

"Yes," I stated simply, eyeing Nico.

"What forces?" Caterina asked. "You've taken control of the majority of the soldiers across the board. All that's left is Marco and Leo's personal forces, which amounts to maybe a hundred, yes?"

"The same fuckers who broke into our home tonight and took you away," Nico revealed. "You were right, they are connected to the Marchettis too. It was a joint venture."

"They'll come for us," Caterina said.

"They'll try," Nico ground out.

"What does that mean?" I asked.

"It means," he said, pulling out another smoke from his leather jacket and firing it up. "I need to take power *now*."

"To do that so quickly, we'll have to take Marco's stronghold. The mansion, Nico," I pointed out. "The plan was to weaken them first. While tonight achieved a lot in that respect, it's not enough. Not without a fucking bloodbath."

He dragged hard on his smoke. "I'm aware."

"N, I can manipulate the narrative a hell of a lot better than anyone, but as good as I am, I can't rework a full-on massacre involving hundreds," Julian warned him. "Even if you win out, you'll put yourself on the Feds' radar. Or worse."

"Then we keep Milo's hands clean and he takes power in my stead while I'm—"

"While you're rotting away in jail?" I burst out with. "No way in hell is that happening."

"If it will accomplish the mission and end this shitshow, I'll pay that price."

"The fuck you will," Caterina told him, absolutely not having it.

"Agreed," Julian said, right there with us.

"We end this and we'll all be safe. It will be over. No more looking over our shoulders. No more putting your empires that you've worked so hard to build on the back burner, Caterina and Julian. And Milo, no more waiting on justice or feeling trapped. You'll be free."

"That doesn't work without *you*," I told him.

"It doesn't need to. You don't need to pay any price," Caterina announced, closing her laptop and rising to her feet as she pulled out her phone. "I'll make arrangements to meet Levi off territory tonight. We'll find these fuckers' stronghold and cut them off at the knees. After all this effort and fight that it's taken to turn the tables and have so many pledging their loyalty to you, we're certainly not going to allow *this* turn of events to fuck all over that accomplishment. We'll stop it before it starts."

"Leaving now and—" Nico started.

"You mean in the dead of night before shit really hits the fan as word fully spreads that Santino is dead?" Caterina challenged.

"Fine," Nico agreed easily. Too easily.

I reasoned that he was all too eager to have her out of harm's way.

He wouldn't bench her, but this was her decision, so he'd found a loophole. After what she'd done tonight, I didn't doubt that he was likely second-guessing his firm stance on the whole thing. For her to go off like that, to that extreme extent, it meant there were cracks there for her, something obviously extremely worrying.

"I'm coming with you," Nico announced.

"You're needed here," I countered.

"I'll get her down there, then when I'm sure she's

settled and safe, I'll head back." He eyed Caterina. "The drive there will give us some time to talk and analyze what happened tonight."

He was definitely the best person to have that out with her. He could help her better than anyone where that monstrous side of hers was concerned.

When Julian moved to protest, Nico told him, "I need you here monitoring Caterina's businesses and ensuring all is well with Carver Group. Resume work on the expansion from your end. It will be great to have that in place when all this is over." Something to look forward to essentially *and* something to focus him and help to ground both him and Caterina. Damn, Nico was good.

"Yeah, all right," Julian agreed.

Nico looked to me. "After the team is done here tonight with the repairs, bring Rocco here and work on ramping up security. He's one of the best where that's concerned. I want motion sensors that aren't connected to the main system, that can operate independently, so what occurred tonight with those fuckers evading detection can't happen again."

"You've got it. I'll see to it," I assured him.

"An early-warning system too," he added.

Yeah, tonight had freaked all of us out.

And the fact that we were about to be away from each other really didn't sit well, especially in light of that.

We stared out at each other as the weight of it descended upon us.

34

~Nico~

She was unusually quiet.

As we traveled down the back roads toward the college town of Stonewell where Levi was currently located, I looked out at Caterina staring down at the ravine over by the passenger side, zoning out it seemed.

I reached out and grasped her hand and she squeezed it affectionately, then finally turned her head toward me.

She looked fucking exhausted, and not just because of the late hour.

Before I could get a word into the talk I'd wanted to have with her once I'd given her some time to decompress in the car after the emotional goodbye with Milo and Julian, she asked me suddenly, "Does being able to kill without remorse make me a true monster?"

I jolted at the question and what it also meant to me, how it fucking cut at me more than I liked to admit.

The fact that I actually did think about that more than anyone was aware.

"Not in this case. Not when it comes to your father."

"No?" she asked, so worried about it.

"After what he did to you, all the abuse, every fucking thing, he didn't qualify as human anyway. *He* was the true monster. The world is undoubtedly better off without him in it."

She slipped her hand from mine. "But you don't... feel it, do you? So you can't really know that. You're just saying it to make me feel better, aren't you?"

"When have I ever done that? We're always challenging each other."

"No. You have. You do that for me."

I looked away and dug my fingertips into the steering wheel as I forced my next words out. "I *do* actually feel it."

"What?"

"Remorse. Guilt."

"You do?"

I nodded. "There are times when I let it back in, when the strain becomes too much and I don't have much of a choice." I looked at her again, finding her staring at me with a whole lot of intrigue. "But with the things *I've* done, they haven't just been to protect myself or due to Marchetti Syndicate orders. I... over the years, it became a part of who I am and I grew to... like it. To get off on it, in fact. There's no forgiveness for that, is there? So, you see, it's different for you. You're not me, thankfully. And once this war is done, you won't find yourself in a position like that again."

"I like it too. The power of it."

"But the acts to achieve that are just a means to that end, yes?"

She thought for a moment. "Yeah, I guess that's a good way to put it."

"Then it's different. I like the actual bloodletting."

"Well, everybody has their passions, Nico."

"Hilarious."

She chuckled. "I thought we could do with some *levity*, as Julian is fond of calling it."

I reached out and stroked her hair. "I love you. You know that?"

"I do. I love you too."

"My *principessa.*" I slid my hand down to her belly. "And I'm going to love this little baby just as much."

"Knowing that's possible, that you *can* actually love like that, it sounds like there's hope for you being redeemed after all, huh?" She ran her fingers over my jaw. "And, just so you know, you already are to me. I love you just the way you are. And so will our child. You don't need to change a thing."

How had this turned into her giving me a pep talk?

I was supposed to be counseling her on the issues involved in unleashing like she had.

This woman... the way she could impact me... I'd never known anything like it.

I smiled to myself.

She was so fucking perfect for us.

Headlights in my rearview mirror drew my attention.

They'd come out of nowhere.

I hadn't seen them seconds ago.

There'd been no through road that they could have come from either.

That meant they'd either been parked or... lying in wait.

Adrenaline sparked, and I picked up speed.

The vehicle behind did too.

Then it turned on its high beams, preventing me from making them out and fucking blinding me for a good few seconds.

"What the hell?" Caterina exclaimed, twisting in her seat, only to look away and rub her eyes a moment later.

The car jolted as the fucker behind us rammed into it.

I pulled my gun and cocked it, while keeping the car steady.

But then they came up on my side.

I swung my head to see a black RAM truck with tinted windows.

Just as I went to roll down mine to fire off a shot, they beat me to it.

And then I was looking at that piece of shit, Angelo Simone.

"You killed him!" he screamed across to us. He looked past me at Caterina. "That fucking cunt killed him!"

Fuck.

I fired off a shot, but at this speed and trying to keep the car steady, it only winged him.

"You don't get to live while he's fucking gone!" he roared, rolling up his window, then dropping back behind us just as a car zoomed down, headed straight for him, horn blaring deafeningly out into the night.

Not moments later, he rammed me again.

I looked over at Caterina, my gaze dropping to her stomach, as she pulled her own gun, then went to fire.

No. This whole thing was too fucking dangerous.

I couldn't risk it.

Couldn't risk her.

Couldn't risk our child.

"I'm gonna pull over," I told her. "It's gonna be a rough ride. Hold on tight. We'll take him on solid ground."

"Okay," she uttered, readying herself.

The word was barely out there when Angelo came up on my side again and veered into the car, jolting it.

I shot a look over at Caterina's side, seeing the drop of the ravine below, mostly blanketed in darkness.

He kept coming then, slamming into us again and again.

We hit a rough patch of ground as he forced the car over to the edge and my wheels screeched in protest, fighting to find traction.

I just needed a second to regain it.

But he didn't give us that.

He smashed into us again, and the car lurched.

And then it was too late.

There was no stopping it.

Caterina screamed and grabbed my hand as we hurtled over the edge, tumbling down into the ravine, everything a violent blur as the car flipped and careened down the hundred foot drop, jostling us violently from all angles.

The last thing I was aware of was my head smacking into the window.

Lights out.

To be continued in THEY MAKE MONSTERS

Next Book in the Series

THEY MAKE MONSTERS
COVETED KINGDOM, Book 3

Brutality is our legacy.
Pain is our lifeblood.
But family is everything.

Or it's supposed to be.

They've violated that time and again.
To our enemies, power is all.
They'll strike down their own blood to secure it.
They'll bury us all.

At least they'll try.

The chains have been broken now.
We'll cut down anyone who stands in the way.
They made us monsters.
And now they'll fall by their creations.

Coveted Kingdom Series

WHERE THE WICKED REIGN
VICIOUS LITTLE PRINCESS
THEY MAKE MONSTERS

Connected Series

VICIOUS THINGS & COVETED KINGDOM

VICIOUS THINGS
Brianna, Levi, Colton, Mason
THEY BREAK BEAUTY
WHEN KINGS FALL

COVETED KINGDOM
Caterina, Nico, Emilio, Julian
WHERE THE WICKED REIGN
VICIOUS LITTLE PRINCESS
THEY MAKE MONSTERS

WALKING WITH MONSTERS & TWISTED TORMENT

WALKING WITH MONSTERS
Aurora, Asher, Killian, Jonah
LOCK UP THE DARKNESS
SCARS RUN DEEP
BURN IT DOWN

TWISTED TORMENT
Skylar, Bastian, Caleb, Caspian

WRECK ME
HATE ME
CRAVE ME

———

IMMORTAL PASSIONS & IMMORTAL FLAME

IMMORTAL PASSIONS
Mia, Jaxon, Ryker, Lucian
IMMORTAL BURDEN
REIGN OF THE BEAST
FALLEN ANGEL
OUT OF ASHES

IMMORTAL FLAME
Ariana, Kai, Vorzyr, Nyx
HARBINGER
LEGACY
MANTLE

Leia King ARC Team

Leia is looking for passionate fans to join her ARC Team!

CHECK IT OUT

Leia King Library

WALKING WITH MONSTERS
LOCK UP THE DARKNESS
SCARS RUN DEEP
BURN IT DOWN

TWISTED TORMENT
WRECK ME
HATE ME
CRAVE ME

VICIOUS THINGS
THEY BREAK BEAUTY
WHEN KINGS FALL

ELECTI ACADEMY
WICKED HEIRS
CURSED HEIRS
FALLEN HEIRS

COVETED KINGDOM
WHERE THE WICKED REIGN
VICIOUS LITTLE PRINCESS
THEY MAKE MONSTERS

IMMORTAL PASSIONS

Leia
KING

About the Author

Where Damaged Heroes and Badass Heroines Collide.

Leia writes edgy and emotional stories across multiple genres. She enjoys crafting flawed heroes with a dark side and strong women who hold their own.

WEBSITE
INSTAGRAM
PINTEREST

Printed in Dunstable, United Kingdom